Hunter's Amazon Adventure

B. J. O'Neill

PublishAmerica
Baltimore

ISBN: 1-4137-9034-8
PUBLISHED BY PUBLISHAMERICA, LLLP
www.publishamerica.com
Baltimore

Printed in the United States of America

To my dearest husband, Bob
…in loving memory.

Acknowledgments

The Amazon: Past, Present, and Future. Alain Gheerbrand
Amazon Journey. Dennis Werner
Welcome of Tears: The Tapirap'e Indians of Central Brazil. Charles Wagley
The Evolution of Horticultural Systems in Native South America. Johannes Wilbert
The Cloud Forest: A Chronicle of the South American Wilderness. Peter Matthiessen
Exploration of the Valley of the Amazon. William Lewis Herndon
The Sea and the Jungle. H. M. Tomlinson
Journey to the Far Amazon. Alain Gheerbrandt
Amazon Journey. Jacques Cousteau & Mose Richards
The Rivers Amazon. Alex Shoumatoff
The Shaman's Apprentice. Dr. Mark Plotkin
National Geographic: Every one I could find that had mentioned South America.
McDonnell Douglas: Literature on their Md Explorer
Scott Tuck: Pilot and advisor on helicopters
Robert O'Neill: Advisor on welding and dams.
Tim and Dan O'Neill: Advisors on guns and finders of mistakes.
Sean O'Neill: Advisor on autos and crashes
Dr. Brian Stainken: Who really was stung by a stingray in South America and really was cured by a native holding his foot in the smoke over a burning ant hill!
Sharon Stainken, Kathleen Hooven, and Shelly Loftin: For their help on the computer.

Characters

Tom Murphy—retired engineer in St. Louis.

Letty Murphy—his wife.

Jerry and Maueeen Allen—their son-in-law and daughter.

Jim Murphy—their son in St. Louis.

Gordon William Hunter (GWH)—head of Hunter's Amazon Jungle Adventures.

Gordon(Bud) Hunter Jr—his son, raised in St. Louis.

Nat—GWH's Peruvian friend and assistant.

Ryti—Nat's native wife, educated by missionaries.

Don and Ellen Mason—jungle cruise winners from Manchester, New Hampshire.

Lois Wadleigh Chastain—Lincoln High School's teacher of English and Art, and winner from Boston, Massachusetts.

Nora Jane Smythe—her friend and guest on the cruise.

Dr. Dennis and Mrs.Carla Evans—winners from Florida.

Ginger Evans—their daughter.

Fenton Cranshaw—owner of Tip Top Jungle Cruises in Manaus.

Orem Tharp—native friend of Fenton Cranshaw, missionary raised, sent to New York for further education.

Ralph Wayne—bought Murphy's Weldment from Tom Murphy.

Lester Thomas—customer of Murphy's Weldment in South Dakota.

Glen Gleason—employee of new company, Wayne's Weldment

Native Community

Kanchinapio—old chief, head of a "lost tribe" in the Amazon jungle.

Maeuma—son of the old chief.

Panteri—the old chief's cousin.

Wanapio—elder whose son has a deformed foot.

Kamanar'e—son of Wanapio.

Uanica—shaman, or witch doctor.

Ne'I—elder native.

Bokra—elder native.

Negrenhre—Maeuma's stepmother.

Mikant'u—Orem's sister in Manaus.

Anawani—her husband.

Bep—handyman on the *Cacador* (Hunter's boat).

Ke'kra—in charge of the base camp.

Teptykti—daughter of Wanapio, sister of Kamanar'e.

Chapter One

Tom awoke with a start. He had dozed off in a lounge chair by the fire. The television running softly in the background didn't disturb him, but the sudden crash of the wind-driven door against the doorstop sent the adrenaline surging through him.

"What...what...that you, Letty, what are you doing?"

"I just went out to get the mail, the wind is so strong it blew the door out of my hand. My, it's getting cold out there, and the snow is really coming down now."

"Why didn't you tell me that the mail was here? I'd have gone out to get it. Letty, you must let me help you with things like that. Now that I'm retired, I want to make things easier for you."

There was an earnest look on his rounded face. Thick gray eyebrows arched over sincere, milk chocolate brown eyes. His thinning hair that matched the eyebrows was in need of a trim.

"You were having such a nice nap I didn't want to disturb you, anyway, I wanted to blow the cobwebs out of my head." She hung her red parka in the hall closet and hung the plaid scarf she had on her head on top of it.

"Was there any good mail?" He pulled his red sweater closer around the beginning of a little potbelly. Cold air from the open door made it necessary. They both were comfortably clad in jeans.

"Nothing much, a few bills, charity pleas, two catalogs, and a letter for me saying I just may have won five million dollars if I enter right away, by Friday. It says here."

"Going to send it in?"

"You know I will."

"That is just a waste of postage, those…"

"I know, but somebody has to win, it's just like putting coins in a slot machine. For the price of a stamp I could get something wonderful."

Letty handed him all the mail except the sweepstakes envelope. She took it to her old roll-top desk in the far corner of the den. Pushing the little pile of clutter to one side, she slit the flap of the colorful envelope and removed the contents. It said, *$5,000,000.00 is yours, Letty Murphy, if you are the lucky winner! It's the chance of a lifetime,* was the promise. She scanned the list of prizes: houses, boats, vacations…this one was to cruise the Amazon. *A fantastic jungle cruise down the Amazon, guided by HUNTER'S AMAZON JUNGLE ADVENTURES, noted Amazon cruising company for twenty-five years. All expenses paid! Three lucky couples will get a chance to go and an expert guide will make it an unforgettable journey, if you are among the fortunate winners.*

Tom was flipping through the mail, nothing earthshaking. He glanced at Letty staring out at the ever-thickening snowfall.

His heart warmed a little as he looked at the light making a halo of her white hair. He laughed to himself at the thought. *I've loved her through brown, auburn, yellow, and now white hair. None of them made any difference.*

"What are you thinking about?" he asked.

"My Uncle Alfred."

"Why him?"

"Because, he was always going on safaris in Africa or treks through the rain forests of South America."

"What brought that on?"

"One of the prizes is a cruise down the Amazon."

"Letty, there is no way in Hell that you are going to win a cruise down the Amazon. They send out millions of letters every day. Did you ever know anyone that won one of those sweepstakes?"

"No, but people really do win, don't they? I've seen them on TV. I don't think I could win the five million, one of the beautiful houses, a luxurious yacht, or even one of the expensive cars, but maybe I could win the last one on the list of prizes, the Amazon jungle cruise."

Tom shot her an amused unbelieving look.

"It could happen," she said as she made a little face at him when she saw the expression on his face.

"The odds are enormous. They even have to print the chances of winning in that small print—so small that you can hardly read it."

"I know, but it's fun to think that maybe…"

"Would you really want to give up this house for a larger one?"

"No, I like this house. I don't want a larger one."

"What about a large yacht?"

"No. I really wouldn't know what to do with one here in St. Louis, I would feel silly on Alton Lake in a huge boat, and it would need a crew and everything."

"What about a big expensive car?"

"No, our old station wagon is perfect for us. You can't pack those new cars with as much as we can get in the wagon."

"The only thing left is the cruise down the Amazon, do you want to do that?"

"Yes! You can bet I would, that would be great!"

"You never mentioned it before. It has to be full of huge insects and other disgusting critters, and the climate either drowns you or roasts you."

"We were too busy before—raising the family, school activities, then paying for all of that college. We didn't have a chance to even think of it. I used to listen to Uncle Alfred regale the family with his tales of adventure when I was a child. Do you know, he even met Frank Buck once?"

"The famous game hunter?"

"Yes, he stayed in his camp overnight once when their groups came together in Africa. Uncle Alfred's guide was a friend of Buck's. Uncle Alfred was so interesting, I'm sorry you never did get a chance to meet him before he died."

"He sounds like quite a guy."

"I think we have some of his things up in the attic. Things that Dad had after Uncle Alfred died. He didn't want to throw those things away, so he just kept them in his attic. When Dad died and I had to do something with his things. I didn't want to throw Uncle Alfred's things away either, so, as a result, I have piles of both their belongings in the attic."

"I haven't been up there in ages, what else is up there?"

"All the books and household things the kids brought back from college. They stowed their things away till they 'need' them. Now they don't seem to want any of it, but I dare not throw any of it away in case they do. Remember the search for Maureen's yearbook last year when she came home for her high school reunion?"

"I remember some kind of rumpus about it."

"That is one of the reasons that it's such a mess up there. We turned things upside down till we found it, and I never did get up there to straighten things out."

"What do you hear from her and Jerry?"

"They are fine. His business is expanding, I hope he isn't extending himself too much."

"Don't worry about Jerry, that boy has a good head for business. He'd have to have, or he wouldn't be where he is today at his age. Are Maureen and the kids okay?"

"They're fine, the whole family went skiing over the weekend, they had a great time."

"It beats me the way those little kids get around the slopes the way they do. It's a wonder they don't break their necks."

Letty had been filling the sweepstakes papers exactly as specified. She sealed and stamped the envelope with a flourish, winking at Tom as she did. "HUNTER'S AMAZON JUNGLE ADVENTURE, here we come!" She rose from her chair, walked to the window to watch the snow swirling down. "It looks like one of those little village scenes in glass that have snow storms when you shake them."

Tom was clicking through all the TV stations without stopping long enough to see much of anything that was on them. He finally settled on a news program that was playing a segment they had already seen. He picked up his current spy novel and pushed back his lounge chair to a comfortable position.

"I think I'll go up to the attic and see if I can find Uncle Alfred's things."

There was no reply from Tom. He was deep in his book about some spy's daring-do. She went upstairs—bringing an armful of things that had been placed on the stairs to be brought up the next time anyone went upstairs. She distributed them where they belonged.

Letty began to reminisce about the last time she saw Uncle Alfred. *What a sweetie, and so much fun. He always had a funny way of putting things and never talked down to me. I think he took a trip down the Amazon River in South America. Sometime in the middle seventies, I believe*

She paused at the attic stairs, then went over to the linen closet and picked an old torn pillow case from the rag bag to use as a dust cloth and went on up the stairs. She opened the attic door and quickly closed it.

"Burr! It's cold up here!" she said aloud. She went back down the attic stairs. In her bedroom, she picked out her heaviest sweater, hesitated, then put on a light blue wool turtleneck first, then the heavy navy blue sweater and buttoned all the buttons—only then did she return to the attic.

What a mess! she thought as she surveyed the jumble in front of her when she turned on the light. *That darned Jim, he didn't help things much when he was looking for something to use as a costume last Halloween.* She threaded her way amid the boxes. There was old furniture and other miscellany, too good to throw away, or *might come in handy some day. I am the packrat, not Tom,* she mused. *I guess it is because I was brought up during the Depression. Nothing in our house was thrown away that could possibly be of some use. Talk about recycling!* She remembered saving "silver paper" in a big ball for Sister Mary Agnes. The nun was so happy when the children turned them in so she could redeem them for a little money. *I wonder what she'd think of the rolls of aluminum wrap they have today? Lord, rest her soul.*

Letty had made her way to one side of the attic banked with bookshelves. She was busy scanning the titles, and then she picked up a slim maroon volume.

"Aha," she said softly to herself, "here it is!"

She took the cloth from her waistband and dusted it off. There was a metal case with Alfred Cook printed on the name tag lying flat on the bottom shelf. Letty dusted it too and gathered her treasures and made her way to the door. As she turned off the light, she shivered.

It's too cold up here, she muttered as she turned out the light, pulled the door closed and went downstairs to the den.

"Tom, I found Uncle Alfred's things in the attic. We really must straighten that place someday, it's a sight!"

"I know how to get it clean. I'll call Goodwill or the Salvation Army and they'll take it all away and your worries will be over."

Letty placed the things on a footstool by the fireplace. Made a moue at Tom. It was an old argument, no that's too strong a word, more of a kidding, wrangle about her never throwing anything away. "Never mind, I'll tend to it someday when the kids are here and they can decide what they want."

She held her hands out to the fire, then turned around and warmed her backside. She was average in height and weight, neither fat nor thin, tall nor short. About a size twelve. She usually wore slacks around the house with a blouse and sweater in the winter. Letty was fond of scarves and had a rainbow of solid colored ones and many printed ones. Today she was dressed in blue. Blue slacks, a blue blouse, the blue pullover sweater and a gold and a blue scarf she had bought in Paris on their trip to Europe the year before.

"Cold up there?" asked Tom. "Why don't you make some tea or hot chocolate? That'll warm you."

"That's a good idea, I'll make some hot chocolate, want some?"

"Sure do, I'll come in the kitchen with you."

Letty picked up the book and the case and they went into the kitchen.

"Look through Uncle Alfred's case while I fix the cocoa, will you, hon?"

Tom flipped the fasteners and opened the case. He began to place items on the table. A Swiss army knife caught his attention. He began to spread open all the things it contained. It was a large one. "I'll bet this is the largest Swiss army knife they ever made. It has everything! Besides the usual knife blades, that mine has, it has a saw, pliers, can-opener and, a hole puncher, a phillips screwdriver, and that's not all. There is a plastic ruler and at the end is a tiny compass and even a tiny magnifying glass! This is really something, and here is a fish scaler!"

"Uncle Alfred always said, 'you have to have the right equipment if you want to do the job right'"

"Well he certainly crammed a lot of stuff into this case. He has a small hammer and a box of assorted nails, a first-aid kit, a measuring tape, and a larger compass. Here's a small fishing kit, and this is a collapsible fishing rod, only a foot long. Look here, Letty, it fits in the lid along the edge. I'll be darn, this is quite a thing he has here, come look at all this stuff."

Letty poured the hot chocolate in the mugs, popped a marshmallow in each cup and went over to the table. She looked at the array of things that were lying on it. The lid was made so things could be held in it securely. The only thing in it now was the collapsible fishing rod. There was a collapsible cup, a set of silverware inside an arrangement of metal dishes. One could turn into a frying pan when the bracket that held it together was taken off and screwed onto it to form the handle. There was also a flat round metal mesh disk with small fold-down legs.

"I wonder what that is for?" said Letty as she blew on the cocoa to cool it a bit. While it cooled, she took some homemade oatmeal cookies from the cookie jar and split them with Tom.

"I think it is to set in a fire so you don't have to hold the pan." Tom informed her. He took out a little metal bucket, where a myriad of small things was stored. After checking its contents, he put everything back into it the way it had been and replaced its lid.

Letty picked up the first-aid kit and opened it. There was some old dried-up adhesive tape, a few yellowed bandages and some metal instruments. There were two clamps, a probe, a scalpel and even a dental set. The instruments were tiny, but functional.

"It looks like Uncle Alfred was ready for anything. Look, the back of this first-aid kit can be used as a mirror. Isn't that clever?" As she was returning things to the kit a small object fell from between the yellowed bandages.

"Look at this, I wonder where he found this?" she said, handing it to Tom.

He turned the intricately carved wooden disk, about the size of a quarter, over repeatedly, studying it carefully. "It looks like some native doodad," he said, giving it back to her.

"It has a place here for a chain, a cord, or a thong of some kind. It's lovely, I could put it on my gold chain. With the right outfit it would be very chic. How would it look with my jungle print blouse and my khaki divided skirt?"

"It would be just the thing to wear when you are cruising down the Amazon," Tom said with a twinkle in his eyes. Then he sobered.

"Seriously, would you really like to go on a trip to South America, actually go on a jungle cruise?"

"Of course I would, wouldn't you?"

"I didn't ever think about it much. I'm not much for hunting."

"They don't kill the animals anymore, they aren't allowed to. Though I guess there are poachers and people like that, but mostly they just observe the animals and take pictures of them."

"Can't you do that at the zoo?" he asked, kidding her.

"Of course you could, silly, but it wouldn't be the same. It would be like watching a game on TV. You see it, but the atmosphere, the excitement, the smells…"

"I'll bet there are some very pungent smells," he said, smiling.

"You know what I mean. We aren't getting any younger, we ought to do it while we still have our 'parts' and 'smarts," she said, raising her right eyebrow as she was apt to do when she said something in earnest.

"Well, I would rather not be in a wheelchair someday wishing I had done some exciting things when I could have and didn't," he said.

"I surely wish I could win that sweepstakes," she mused as she ran her hand through her short curly white hair.

"Letty, if you want to go on a jungle cruise, we'll go. We don't have to wait for some impossible dream to come true. We'll do it now!" he said, rising to his feet.

"Let's call the travel agency right now before you change your mind," she said joyfully, going over to him and hugging him.

"Right," he said, going over to the telephone, taking the directory from inside the table and beginning to thumb through its pages.

While Tom was looking for their travel agent, Letty picked up the maroon book and was soon lost in Uncle Alfred's journal.

"We are going! I've ordered the tickets on our American Express Card and we leave in four months," Tom said with a satisfied smile on his face.

"I can't believe it!" squealed Letty, jumping out of her chair. "But why that long?"

"The rainy season is over then."

"Whoopee!" She grasped Tom by both hands and they twirled around, laughing. "Do you think we ought to wait and see if we win the Sweepstakes?" Letty joked.

"No siree, I don't," laughed Tom.

"Lets go upstairs and see what we have that we can take with us. I guess we'll have to buy some clothes and things."

"Now let's not go emptying all the closets and drawers. We must only take the essentials—it's better to travel light. We don't want to be bogged down with too many suitcases, do we? Besides, we have four whole months," said Tom as they went up the stairs.

"No, I guess one bag for each. The one's with the wheels and Uncle Alfred's case, of course. Oh, and I'll take my large shoulder bag. I can get by with that. What will you carry?"

"I can get all I'll wear in one bag and probably have room for some of your things if you need it. Do you want to take the camcorder? It's rather bulky with all the batteries, the charger and tapes."

"It would be a shame not to take it though, what if..." She stopped.

"What if what?"

"I was only thinking about the new, smaller camcorders that are available now. They are much better than our old one, easier to use, with color screens and much lighter too, and you can put the pictures into the computer."

"I really don't want to be a two-camcorder family." He made a face.

"Well, we could give it to one of the kids, Jim doesn't have one and I know he would like to have the fun of owning one"

"Why not? Since I'm going to be the last of the big-time spenders."

The next day was beautiful. The sun was shining, dazzling on the untrammeled snow. The trouble was that the snowplow had not been by yet and there was no way they could get into town. They stayed snug in bed, had a lovely amorous morning, and didn't get up till about eleven.

Letty got out of bed, stretched a little, and went downstairs to put the coffee on. She looked out the window, squinting against the too bright light reflected from the snow. She went back up the stairs and headed for the tub.

Water, hot and deep, with scented bubbles is the only civilized way to bathe according to Letty. She eased herself down into the steaming water until she submerged her shoulders.

"Mmmmmmmm," she sighed as she lolled back with eyes closed. Letty was thoroughly relaxed.

"Need me to scrub your back?" Tom stuck his head in the door and leered.

"Not now." She smiled. "The coffee's just about ready, I'll be down in a minute."

She finished her bathroom chores, dressed in warm slacks, blouse and sweater. This time she was in shades of lavender. She checked herself in the mirror, then went downstairs.

"We certainly are getting a slow start today. I didn't fall asleep for hours. My mind wouldn't let me. It was just spinning with all the things we have to do before we can even think of leaving."

"You've got that right," said Tom. He was in his robe and slippers, his hair tousled, warming his hands on his coffee mug.

It had "ALL'S WELL THAT ENDS WELDED" printed on one side and "MURPHY'S WELDMENT CO," on the other.

"I was thinking about our passports, do you remember if they have expired? I know we'll have to get shots, I just don't know what kind."

"Wait a minute, what shots? I'm not going to get any shots. You can forget that!" he said vehemently as he went to the sink and put his cup on the counter.

"Don't get so excited, maybe we won't even need shots. Why don't you get dressed and I'll fix us a great brunch? Cheese omelet and some Canadian bacon. I'll even make biscuits. I'll have it all ready by the time you get showered and shaved."

"That's a deal," he said, and he went up the back stairs.

Letty busied herself with the meal preparation. Her mind was whirling with things she wanted to do that day. She stopped a minute to look out the window. No snowplow in sight. *Well, there is a lot we can do right here before we can go anywhere*

After they ate their brunch, Tom went on a hunt for their passports. Letty went upstairs to her closet and started laying different outfits on the hurriedly made bed. *The divided khaki skirt for sure, and the jungle print blouse. I can wear that carved thing of Uncle Alfred's on my gold chain with it. My navy blue slack suit, my red three-piece suit, my white...no, it will get too dirty and it has to be dry-cleaned. I wonder if I should take any good dresses? I could take my wild printed gauze skirt. It's supposed to have that wrinkled look. Any one of my solid colored blouses would go with those wild colors, and with a matching belt I can go anywhere. I'd better take my dressy lavender three-piece suit too. I'll take my zebra necklace and earrings and my zebra print blouse, to go with slacks. Now, with a few t-shirts, shorts and unders I'll be set. Shoes! Which shoes? Mmmm, my white walking sneaks? They are very comfortable; I can walk all day in them. Black sandals too. I wonder if I'll need boots? I don't have any that would be suitable for warm weather. Mine are snow type boots, too heavy.*

"I found the passports. They were in one of my desk drawers, way in the back. The expiration date isn't until next year in November. On Jim's birthday too, which will be easy to remember."

Tom was looking at the passports as he entered the room. He looked up, startled by the kaleidoscopic collection filling the top of the bed. "What's all this? I thought we were going to pack light."

"It's hard to decide, I am going to pack lightly. I'm trying to color coordinate the things I bring. I can wear black and blue and red things together…but then I don't usually wear black and navy together, I'll ditch the blue one. If I had a lightweight, gray, glenn-plaid suit with a tiny red line in it, every thing would go together wouldn't it? The khaki skirt will go with red. I won't have to wear a jacket much, will I?"

"It's too complicated for me, but I'd be surprised if you had to wear a jacket very often. I think it's pretty hot all the time, though sometimes it might get a little chilly in the evening when the sun goes down."

The bedside phone, ringing, interrupted them.

Letty answered. "Hello, hi there, Jim, are you snowed in?"

"No, I left after the snowplow went by and it wasn't too bad, the sun is starting to melt it already. How are you two, do you need anything from the store? I could bring some stuff on my way home tonight."

"Thanks, honey, but we have everything we need. It's sweet of you to think of us, but we're just fine."

"What's new? Anything shaking?"

"I guess there is, we are leaving for South America in four months!"

"Wow! What brought that on?"

"Oh, the traveling bug bit us, I guess. That and the cold weather. We want to go some place warm and have an adventure."

"South America ought to qualify on both counts, it ought to be fun. I wish I could go with you. I was calling to say that I am going out of town myself. I'm going to Houston on business. I'll be gone about six months or so. The company is starting a new office there and I have to get things started right."

"There is no chance of you being transferred, is there?" Letty asked as she motioned for Tom to come to the phone.

"I don't think so, that's why I want to take my time and hire somebody responsible and innovative so I won't have to go down there too often," Jim answered.

"Just a minute, Jim, I know Dad will want to talk to you about it."

Letty handed the phone to Tom and then began hanging those clothes that were scattered all over the bed back in the closet. While Tom was discussing business with Jim, her mind was going over all the things that had to be done to get ready.

The plants! I thought I would have Jim here to water my houseplants while we are gone. I'll have to ask Jane to bring the mail in and water the plants…no that is too much to ask. I'll stop the mail and bring the plants over to her house, then it won't be too much bother. I'll bring her something nice from South America. Good, that's settled

"Okay, son, I'm sure you'll handle things in Houston just fine. You have the right idea about the better man you hire, the fewer problems for the home office, and the least likely you'll get transferred. I surely would hate to have you leave St. Louis. It's bad enough having Maureen and her family on the West Coast. We don't get to see them nearly enough. It's tough having grandchildren so far away. They grow so fast and we miss so much of their growing up," Tom said, winding down the conversation.

"I'll do my best, Dad, but give me time. I'm not even married yet, so no grandchildren from me in sight. I know you will have a great time. I will be talking to you a lot of times before you leave. I promise I'll call you often and when we all return we can trade adventure stories, okay?"

"Yes Jim, take care now and good luck."

"Thanks, Dad, you too, watch out for Mom, don't let the natives get her."

"I won't, but someone better look out for the natives—she's deadly with a camcorder in her hand. Bye now, Jim. Oh, Jim, that reminds me. We'll be buying a smaller video camera for the trip, would you like to have our old one?"

"Wow! I guess so. For free—take it, I always say. I'll come by and pick it up before I leave. Thanks, Dad, I'll have fun with it."

"Bye, Jim."

"Bye, Dad."

Tom looked up to see Letty standing there with their personal phonebook in her hand waiting to use the phone.

"I'm going to call Dr. Benson to see if we need shots to go to South America and make an appointment for us if we need them."

"Letty, I really don't..." Tom began.

"Tom, don't be a baby. If we must have them, we must have them, and that's the end of it!" She shook her head as she dialed the number.

Tom went out of the room and down to the den just in time to see the snowplow at the end of the block. He grabbed his jacket hanging by the door in the utility room. He went through the house to stand on the front porch and waited for the plow to reach the driveway.

"How much to clean the driveway off?" he yelled to the driver.

"Not much." The driver of the snowplow smiled and began to push the snow aside.

It only took a few minutes and the plow had cleared a wide path in the driveway so they could get the car out. Tom gave the driver a liberal tip, a jaunty wave, and returned to the house.

"Bad news," Letty said, coming down the stairs. "Dr. Benson said we need shots. We go next week, okay?"

"Okay, I guess we have to do it," he said. "Some good news though, look out the front window."

She went to the window. "Great! Free at last, free at last." She laughed. "Let's go shopping."

They hurried into their warm coats. Then they went into the garage, got into the car and slowly backed out of the driveway. Tom headed into town—carefully avoiding slick looking spots.

"How about trying that army outlet store first?" said Tom.

"Okay, but I would like to go to the mall too"

"We can do that. You know we have plenty of time to get this stuff, we don't have to do it all in one day."

"I know, but what else do we have to do today? It will be fun."

As prearranged, when they entered the store, Tom headed for the men's shirts and pants and Letty went to the shoe department. There were some jungle boots like the Army used in Vietnam. They were protective, yet light and airy. She had trouble finding boots that fit. Since it was mostly self-service, she had to look awhile before she found a pair small enough. She put them in her basket, along with some boots in Tom's size. She added a package of khaki socks—one size fits all, four to a package. Two each ought to be enough. Finished in the shoe department, she wandered over to the men's pants department looking for Tom.

He wasn't in sight. There was a handsome young man sorting through the pants. His bright red hair attracted her attention. Apricot colored freckles dusted his nose like cinnamon on cheesecake. He wore ill-fitting tortoise shell frame glasses. They kept sliding down his nose, requiring him to push them up constantly, resulting in two red spots on either side of his nose.

"Excuse me, did you see a man in a red jacket around here?"

"Yes, he went into the dressing room to try on some stuff." He was pawing through a pile of khaki trousers with a puzzled look on his face.

"What size are you looking for?"

"That's just it, I really don't know. You see, my mother died recently and she used to buy all my clothes. I didn't pay attention to sizes and things like that."

"Oh, I'm so sorry." Letty said, her maternal instinct shifting into high gear. "Maybe I can help. You are about the size of my son. Here, take this one in the dressing room and try it on. Wait a minute, take the next size too, one of them is bound to fit. Are you going to get a khaki shirt also?"

"Yes, I'm going to South American along the Amazon River, and I need a whole wardrobe. I'm going there to live with my father now. The things I wore at college won't do at all."

"My goodness!" Letty gasped. "What a coincidence! My husband and I are leaving in about four months for South America too."

"It sure is, what part?"

"Bel'em and Amazonas first. We are going on a jungle cruise, and we start from there as soon as the rainy season is over."

"That is what I'm waiting for, too. That is the area where my dad lives—most of the time, anyway. I'll go and see which size fits, bye and thanks." He went to the dressing room with the two pairs of khaki pants over his arm.

Tom came out of the dressing room a few minutes later and spying Letty came over to her. "Did you find some boots?"

"Yes, and some socks. I think these will fit you, but you better try them on." She took his boots out of the cart and handed them to him.

"Let's see, these look like just the thing." He looked inside at the size, "They'll fit. I'll get three pairs of these pants and three of those short sleeved shirts that match." He walked to the stack of shirts.

"Don't you think one of those webbing belts with the sliding buckle would go well with the pants, they're the same color?" She pointed to a belt display farther down the aisle.

"Just the thing," he said, picking one off the table. "You ready to go?"

"Yes, let's go check out."

As they went toward the checkout counter, they passed some khaki jackets with four big pockets that buttoned down.

"Look, Tom, isn't that a perfect match for my skirt?"

"Well, I guess you'd better put it in the cart then. How about that backpack across the aisle? No bag to carry and your hands would be free."

"Great, let's go."

Back in the car with their purchases in hand, they headed for the mall.

Tom waited in the lounging area as he always did when Letty was shopping. He hated to go from shop to shop, trailing after her. This way he could be comfortable and people watch. Before they hit on this arrangement, he was always losing her. He would say, "Someday I'm going to lose you in some department store and never see you again!"

Later Letty came walking toward him, no packages in her hand, a bad sign.

"I haven't found the gray suit I've set my heart on. Are you tired waiting? Do you want to get a book? There's a book store down that way a bit."

"Maybe I will go on over and pick up one. I'll pick up some that you like too and then we can trade, okay?"

"That will be fine, a mystery or a spy story, huh?"

"Right, then I'll meet you back here. Take your time. We'll go to the food court later, then we won't have to cook a big dinner. We'll just grab a sandwich or something."

"Sounds good to me, soup and sandwich it is." She turned and was off on her quest again.

After quite awhile, Letty came to where Tom was deep in his new book. This time when Tom looked up she had a plastic covered something on a hanger slung over her shoulder. A tired, but happy look on her face.

"Whew! I am exhausted, let's not go to the food court, let's go to a hamburger drive-thru and go straight home."

"Okay with me," Tom said, closing his book. "I thought I had lost you for sure, this time."

"I finally found just what I wanted, but it took a lot of searching."

It was dark by the time they reached their house. The dusk to dawn porch lights were shining a bright welcome across the snow. They ate the burgers and fries along with some other snacks and some hot tea to warm them. After they cleaned the debris left from their fast food meal, they went into the den.

Tom took his new book out of the bag and settled into his lounge chair.

"I think I'm going right to bed, hon. That running around all day wore me out." Letty took their purchases from the couch where they had dropped them when they came in from the garage.

"I don't doubt it a bit. You must have walked miles in that mall."

"You'll turn out the lights and lock up before you come upstairs later?"

"Yes, I want to read awhile. This is starting out to be a good book."

She gave him a little kiss as she passed by, her arms very full. "I need a rain-check tonight," she grinned.

"I'll see you in the morning about that." He gave her a pat on the bottom as she passed by.

Chapter Two

It was the rainy season, with all that it implies. Wind and rain, sometimes slow and steady, and sometimes so wild and violent men and animals could only hunker down and endure the tumultuous assault.

Occasionally, a man would grab a spear and run out of the hut. He would toss it as far as he could at the dark clouds, then run back, frightened at his audacity, daring to tempt the gods.

In another hut in the compound there were two men. One was young and ill. He was Maeuma, the son of Kanchinapio, who was the head of the tribe. The temperature was excessive, the atmosphere muggy. It was difficult for a normal person to breathe. For the gasping young man on the primitive bed of moss covered with animal skins, it was life threatening.

Uanica, the only other person in the room, was worried. Not only for the suffering man on the bed, but for himself as well. He had done all he could think of to stop the labored wheeze that was sapping the strength of this important person. He had chanted every chant, pleaded with every god, he even sacrificed a monkey with the holy Great Dagger. It had been handed down through many generations.

An uneasy thought came into his mind. Perhaps the monkey was not really important enough to ease the hunger of the Great Dagger. Still, it is the animal most like a man. The suggestion of human sacrifice would not be welcome. Things were not the same today as they were in the past; but the people in the tribe still expected him to handle everything that happened so that nothing upset their lives. Yet, they tied his hands and wouldn't let him bring out the full magic power of the Great Dagger.

It must be done!

He leaned the skull mounted on a staff against the wall of the hut. The noise it made when shaken was caused by some small bones placed inside. There were intricately carved wooden pieces that were fitted tightly into its natural orifices. Inside were placed the bones of the right index fingers of past rulers.

The purpose was to call down the Spirits of the Great Ones to point the tribe in the right direction and to aid the people in their needs of today. There was a special pattern to the movements that made the rattle sound. There were special chants and special feathers and different ornaments placed on the staff that held the skull for their various needs. Even the markings on his face and body and the headdress changed when the reason changed for his petition.

He was Uanica, shaman, witchdoctor, wizard of the tribe — and he was disturbed.

If Maeuma should die, he certainly would lose his position, if not his life. Add to that, he really did love the boy.

He had protected him often from his father's wrath. He had tried to teach him to excel in hunting and to win over his cousins in the wrestling contests and playing atalieah, a type of soccer; but it was not to be so. He couldn't run fast or long. His accuracy with bow and spear was poor and his precision with the blowpipe was worse because he couldn't obtain the distance required when he would try it. What was worse, it would set him coughing, thus scaring away the targeted game so the others couldn't hit anything either.

Uanica would try to comfort him after these humbling occurrences and the displeasure and embarrassment of the Chief, his father. Uanica began to teach him the secrets of being the tribe's Shaman. Along with Kamanar'e, who was born with a deformed foot. One thing he taught them was how to make the ceremonial masks.

Maeuma was bright and learned quickly, and the bond between he and Uanica became strong. The three of them would go out together in the forest. Uanica taught them the ways of making traps for small animals, finding turtles and their eggs and other things the tribe enjoyed eating.

Uanica also told him to leave earlier on hunting days. In doing so he could run farther into the forest and get closer to the animals before the noise of the others hunting frightened the game into flight. That helped Maeuma quite a bit.

Maeuma, alone, would go with him to collect healing herbs and learned other things Uanica used to conquer the evil spirits causing his people to become ill. Uanica was preparing Maeuma to be able to take over his position when the time came for him to step down.

It was not inevitable that Maeuma become Chief on the death of Kanchinapio. Panteri, a much younger cousin to Kanchinapio, coveted that position. It was he who made fun of Maeuma, and pointed out his inadequacies at every chance. But not in front of Kanchinapio.

Maeuma's mother, Mikant'u, died of a snakebite when Maeuma was three. A Fer de Lance bit her as she was gathering firewood in the forest. Ngrenhre raised him; Kanchinapio's other wife, who was barren. She was not mean to Maeuma, but there was no love there either. She saw that he was fed and cared for physically, but that was about all. Maeuma's life was not joyous.

Uanica had seen this and spoke to Kanchinapico about it. Uanica told him how quickly Maeuma learned things. Maeuma had heart, he was wise, he would be a good ruler, and others

30

could hunt and play games. The Tribe needed a wise and caring leader, and since he was learning the secrets of Uanica, he was that much more valuable as a ruler.

Uanica bent over Maeuma's bed and wiped the perspiration off his face because of the heat in the airless hut. He went to the door of the hut where Kamanar'e was looking out at the storm. The violence was over, but now, there still was a steady rain.

Kanchinapio listened and began to let Maeuma sit at council meetings and asked his opinions and, when he could, he acted on his suggestions. Maeuma learned more every day. This impressed the members of the council. All except Panteri, who wanted to take over as Chief on the death of Kanchinapio who was showing the effects of his age.

This was not usual, a cousin being Chief, but it had happened. However, it had only happened when there was no heir, or the son was too young. It might be difficult to arrange, but since Maeuma was sick so often it could happen.

The tribesmen were starting to leave the huts to cool off in the natural shower. This hut was a low rectangle with holes made like windows along the length. The end sections had no doors, but were protected by roof overhangs that protected the openings from rain. It also shielded the sunshine in the morning and the evening and helped to take advantage of every available breeze

"Kamanar'e, Maeuma needs to be fanned while I go see Kanchinapio." Uanica spoke in their language, a mixture of the different tribes that had come together to survive. Uanica handed Kamanar'e a fan of woven leaves and went out the door. Kamanar'e limped to Maeuma and started to wave the fan across his body. Maeuma stirred, then sat up.

"Kamanar'e! I thought Uanica was here. It seems cooler, I can breathe easier."

"He went to see your father, he will return soon. The storm has cooled the air. Would you like a sip of Uanica's brew?"

"I am thirsty, though that drink is not pleasant, I will take it and it might help me" He sat up.

A pretty brown head peeked around the door. When she saw Uanica wasn't there she slipped in quickly and knelt at Maeuma's bed platform.

"Maeuma!"

She had startled him when she came rushing in.

"Teptykti!" He grasped her hand. "What are you doing here?"

"If Uanica finds you here, he will tell the Elders and then you will be in very big trouble. It isn't right for you to be in this room and you know it!" Kamanar'e remonstrated.

"Even if my own brother is here with me?"

"If our father, Wanapio, knew he would tell you yes."

"Teptykti, you must go."

"I am a little better, but very tired, I must rest."

"I will leave, sleep well, Maeuma." She gave him an impish smile. "I had to come to see if you are better. Dream sweet dreams of me," and she slipped through the door.

"I am sorry that she bothered you, Maeuma. She is a bothersome girl."

"It is no bother, Kamanar'e, she stays in my mind very much." He reclined and soon he was dreaming and very likely Teptykti was in them in some capacity.

When Uanica left the hut, he went out to talk to the old Chief Kanchinapio and his retinue. They were assembled in an open area under a roof made of grasses and leaves.

Their worried looks turned hopeful when they saw Uanica, his face and body painted, and on his head the ancient feathered headdress. It had seen better days. Its donors had long since sung their last sweet songs. The meticulously applied colors on his face and body were being smeared by the rain and from his perspiration while he was in the hut.

He sat on the mat next to the Chief, and dashed the old man's hopes when he told them that there wasn't much change. His only son was still in danger.

The five other men in the assembly murmured among themselves while giving the newcomer uneasy and harsh looks.

The old Chief, however, was oblivious to this discord, of which Uanica was only too aware. Kanchinapio's only thought was of his son, who, with his blessing, was already beginning to take on some of the business of ruling the tribe.

Uanica was right, he told himself. *His son Maeuma was wise and ruled well. The people respected his judgment and only occasionally were uneasy when this mysterious devil captured his air.*

The old Chief's duties were as that of a figurehead at tribal meetings now. Maeuma always deferred to his father, as he should, but it was the son who made the decisions more and more, and with Kanchinapio's consent, carried them out. It was a good arrangement, but how long could they go on like this?

The problem was a serious one to those assembled under the rain sodden roof. The humidity had lowered some, but was still high.

The men discussed the dilemma, but couldn't come to any conclusion.

Maeuma had fallen into an exhausted sleep when Uanica returned to find Kamamar'e, though tired, still employing the fan to its best advantage. Uanica dismissed the grateful boy, who rubbed his cramped arm and using his distinctive gait left the hut.

Maeuma's breathing was easier, but still a bit labored. Thankful for the improvement of his charge, Uanica wiped the invalid's face again and sat by his side, ever on guard against the breath-stealing devil.

Maeuma mumbled something in his sleep. Uanica couldn't understand what it was, it sounded slurred, "tepi" or something like that.

Kamanar'e went to report to the assembled dignitaries the slight improvement in Maeuma's condition.

"You see, there was no need to sacrifice one of our people to feed the hunger of the Great Dagger!" Kanchinapio was greatly relieved. Uanica's magic was still enough to satisfy that hunger. The spirits of the Old Ones were still protecting them.

"This time the monkey was enough," said Panteri, Kanchinapio's greedy cousin. "But we must decide now what we must do if the breath-stealing devil visits again."

"I will not kill one of our people! What would you do if it were you chosen as the sacrificed one?"

"We wouldn't offer a young or important one. We would choose one that is old or sick or deformed."

"You do not have one of those in your house, so you are not qualified to judge," Kanchinapio said. "What do you say of this action?" He pointed to Wanapio, father of Kamanar'e, who was born with a deformed foot.

"I would never agree to that," he said, "My son might be considered as one to be sacrificed because of his imperfection. He is very wise and manages to get around—he even hunts well enough to bring in food for the family. He has even been to the edge of the Far Forest and watched the 'Others' in their carriers that run on the wide paths. Kamanar'e has even watched them when they walk into the Far Forest and stop and eat and sleep. He is very brave and can move a boat far and fast in spite of his affliction"

"We should not sacrifice one of our people. Our tribe is not growing, our numbers are lessening now and we need every soul." Ne'i, another of the elders said.

"Yes," said Bokra, another elder. "It seems that we should sacrifice only a perfect human to the Great Dagger. Imperfection would be an insult and bring anger instead of satisfaction. It is clear to me that we must capture one of the 'Others,' in good condition, to appease the hunger of the Great Dagger."

Murmurs of uneasy surprise greeted this last statement.

"That would be a very serious thing to do. It might cause a war that would destroy us." Kanchinapio shook his head. "We have been peaceful and have not been hostile to any tribe. We live in security and seclusion because the Old Ones were wise enough to disappear deep into this forest. Long ago, when the Strangers came to take the juice from the trees, they enslaved and killed our ancestors. The 'Others' are not aware that any of our tribe is still alive."

Bokra arose from his mat and stood in front of Kanchinapio.

"We could satisfy the Great Dagger, then bring the body to be eaten by the fish who eat everything. There would be no body found and there would be no war."

When no one answered, he went on to say, "It is something that must be done or else we must choose another to rule after you join the Old Ones. Later, Kanchinapio, when you become one of the Spirits and your finger bones are added to the music of the skull."

Kanchinapio was disturbed by this turn in the proceedings. He was not afraid to die, but he wanted his line, Maeuma, to be the one the future chiefs came from. Panteri would be very happy if it could be his line that would produce the future chiefs. Any one of the men assembled there could make the demand that he or his son be the next ruler. A dispute over the next ruler would be a disaster for the tribe and for Kanchinapio himself.

"We must think on this serious task. I will seclude myself till tomorrow at this time. Then we will meet and decide what we will do." He took up his Staff of Office and went into his own hut.

The rest of the men dispersed. Their concern was etched on their faces—they had much to think about.

Teptykti was with the other women. They were preparing Manioc. They peeled and grated the manioc roots and put the result in a tub. Then they put it in a press. It was four poles stuck in the ground with sides of crossed sticks and lined with banana leaves. A large sturdy pole was used as a lever to squeeze the mash to drain out the poisonous prussic acid in the manioc water. The residue in the water is tapioca. The pulp is then toasted on a grill, six feet in diameter on a clay oven. It takes two people full time to keep the fire going and stirring the manioc. It was a hot and tiring job.

Teptykti was very tired when she went to her sleeping place. She fell asleep right away, curled up lying on her side. She didn't move all night. A scorpion had crawled into her bed. It was seeking warmth from the coolness of the rainy night. It snuggled next to the middle of her back. In the morning when she awoke and turned over on her back she rolled over on the scorpion, whose last act before dying was to sting her hard.

"OOWWOUEEE!" she howled, awakening everyone nearby. She couldn't reach the stinger, she was dizzy, there were violent muscle spasms, and she fell to the floor.

When Uanica arrived with his medicine pouch, she was wheezing. He gave her some of the same liquid that Maeuma had taken. He had some other things in the pouch for her. He did some dancing around and did some shaking of the pole topped by the scull. He didn't have time to paint his face and put on the headdress. Something worked and the wheezing gradually subsided. There was a numbness that lasted a few days.

Then she was up and about and it was Maeuma who inquired about her health.

Chapter Three

To say Ellen Mason was a golf widow wouldn't be too far off the mark. Don would play golf in sunny weather and the other kind: too cold, too hot, too wet, too everything! Oh, he was good at it, you had to give him that. He was also good at the card games in the clubhouse afterward too. His winnings were substantial. The heavy gold jewelry on his neck, wrists and fingers attested to that.

A perfect day for Don was, on a non work day, a full day of golf. Coming in under par, of course. Cards from about three to six, winning of course, then home to his beautiful house, where there was a delicious home-cooked dinner and a loving, beautiful wife to enjoy it with him. Then a little TV, the late news, and so to bed, with a sweet bit of loving to top it off.

On a workday, starting with a shower, (with towels on a warming towel bar) then, stepping into a terry robe, he steps into the bedroom where all his clothes are laid out. There is a GQ type suit, a perfect fit, hung on a wooden valet. The shoes are placed on the shelf below. The watch and wallet are on the tray. Socks, shirt and belt, matched or blended splendidly with the suit; all these clothes plus underwear, are laid out, on the bed. There is a nice breakfast, of coffee, orange juice, with bacon and eggs, or cereal and fruit, or pancakes or bagels and lox before going to the office. Working at his office until noon. Then a quick bite at the Country Club before his eighteen holes of golf with his buddies, and so on as before.

In winter he would substitute hunting or ice fishing for golf, only the clothes and equipment would change. The card games were the same wherever he and his buddies were.

He could get away with leaving the office every day at noon because he was the boss. He was intelligent enough to have hired excellent managers for each department of "The Emporium" that had been the Mason family for generations. It was well known in Manchester, the Queen City of New Hampshire, as a store that gave good value for the dollar and stood behind its merchandise. It survived against the onslaught of the different discount companies that came to town to cut it down to size. The sober New Englanders were loyal to the store that had given them good service for generations, was a good source of employment and generous to community charities.

All he had to do was meet with the department heads each morning. He listened how their plans for the day, the month, the year, were progressing. Agree or disagree and things would go on from there, almost automatically.

He was good looking, with a sportsman's body. He had dark hair with blue eyes. When people learned his true age of forty-eight, they were surprised, in spite of the few strands of gray hair beginning to be seen at his temples and a few laugh lines starting to show near his eyes.

He was always in a good mood, and why not? He was king of this castle. He always gave her a big kiss and a hug, maybe a sly pinch on the bottom before he drove off in his blue Dodge Viper. Handsome and happy, it was a perfect life.

That was not the perfect day for Ellen. She would get up about an hour before Don, bathe and dress before he came downstairs. Her day started in the kitchen, breakfasts for two in the breakfast nook. Locating the misplaced items that Don needed for his office or the golf course took some time. She always laid out the clothes of the days while he was in the shower. They discussed his attire at breakfast. If he were to play golf after the office, she would pack the things he would need in his sports bag. His golf clubs were always in the car.

After Don left she would straighten the house, twice a week she had a maid that came in and did the heavy cleaning and the laundry. Ellen liked to go to the market because she really did like to cook and she always bought the finest produce and meats. Her collection of cookbooks was a gourmet's delight. Her table settings were splendid and ingenious. She often won blue ribbons in her garden club's flower shows in the Table Settings category. Her Roses had won a time or two also.

Afternoons were tedious. What to do till time to get dinner? They didn't eat until at least seven, sometimes later. She had friends, but usually they had to be home by 2:30 to be there when the children came home from school.

They had lost their only child to leukemia at age three and she never conceived again. They were both hit hard, but went on with their lives, submerging their feelings and not talking about it, ever.

To pass the time she belonged to a monthly Bridge group, watched the soaps, knitted some, read some, and took in a matinee now and then. She even tried volunteering at the hospital near them.

Her job was pushing a cart full of candy, cosmetics, books and other things the patients might want, but she really didn't like being around sick people that much. She salved her conscience by writing a substantial check to their various fund drives.

Her world revolved around the comings and goings and wishes of Don Mason. If anyone took the time to ask her, she probably would have said she was happy. She had everything she wanted. If she saw a dress she liked, she could buy it on the spot, including all the accessories it needed. What could she possibly want? She bought all Don's clothes at The Emporium.

She loved being at the store shopping for Don. That is why he always was so well turned out.

She wanted Don to notice her! To talk to her, and ask her opinion about the Mason's Department Store. She had many ideas about improving its operation. She had even asked Don if she could go to work there.

Ellen had a flair for decorating and would do well in the furniture or drapery departments. The kitchen equipment department would really benefit from her expertise. When she mentioned it to him, he thought it was a great joke at first, then when she convinced him she was serious, he was shocked.

What would his friends think of him if his wife worked in the store? It was impossible!' he thought. He told her to think of something else to do.

"Go knit something!" was his advice to her.

When she mentioned it again, his reply was, "What would you like to do there, cutie?" he said, determined not to lose his temper.

"I would like to be put in charge of one of the departments."

"Now who do you want me to fire so you can do that?" he answered facetiously, still trying not to get mad.

"No one, I would just direct the current head of the department."

"So you know all about running a department!" he said sarcastically.

"No, I don't, that is why I wouldn't ask you to fire the current manager. I could help by bringing in new merchandising ideas, new projects, and new methods. We could work together to improve sales. That is the whole point isn't it, to improve sales?"

"We are doing just fine. You aren't hurting for anything, are you?"

"Yes, I'm hurting for something to fill up my time that is worthwhile, I know I have a flair for decoration—people have told me so. I know I would do well in the furniture or fabric departments. The kitchen equipment department could really benefit from my ideas for expansion."

"What a joke! Are you kidding me? I can just see you telling all my managers who have been doing a good job for years how to do their jobs."

"I said I would work with them. I am not joking—some of the departments have fallen behind the times. They are getting, er, ah, fusty."

"FUSTY!" he yelled, shocked. "I will put up my store against anyone's"

"Okay, it isn't fusty." She made the mistake of giggling at his reddening face and bulging blood vessels in his neck.

"Do you think this is funny?"

"No, I don't, but I would really like to work in…"

"What would our friends think of me if you worked in the store?"

"Who cares, it would be our own business?"

"They would think the business was going down the tubes and I have to bring my wife in to help out."

"Hogwash!"

"This is impossible!" he said as he stomped off, very agitated. She had swallowed her reply in the interest of harmony. She hated to fight

The days would have gone on like that forever if only that gaudy sweepstakes letter hadn't come to her attention. It was one day when the long expanse of the empty afternoon loomed before her. She read the whole thing. She even sent for a few novelties she came across in the catalog. She sent it off, then promptly forgot all about it.

Later, when the trinkets arrived, she thought about the contest for a few seconds, then shrugged it off as impossible and forgot it again.

One morning, in April, Don had his breakfast and was in the shower. As usual, she had placed his attire for the day on his bed. She was returning to the kitchen to clean the breakfast mess when the doorbell jangled, and jangled again. Someone was in a hurry.

She answered and there were the contest people, laughing and congratulating her, taking her picture and pouring into the front hall. Someone handed her a bouquet of flowers, and all of them wanted to hear what she had to say. There were balloons everywhere!

By the time she recovered enough from the shock of the moment to say anything intelligible, Don came to the head of the stairs, his hair dripping, half dressed, astounded at the commotion and demanding to know what the Hell was going on!

When it finally got through to him that Ellen had won an Amazon Jungle Cruise he was amazed. Ellen was too, and delightedly answered all the things the contest people asked her. She happily posed for their pictures. Ellen had a youngness about her. Although she was forty, she didn't look it. She was pretty, with a good figure and a sweet shy smile that dimpled her cheeks. She had tawny, honey-colored hair. Astonishingly, it matched her eyes exactly so that one's own eyes were drawn to hers unerringly. She wore her hair in a short fluff.

Ellen made a good subject to interview, and her surprised look and thrilled excitement was very appealing.

Don, on the other hand, looked a little foolish, and felt even more so. He was used to being in command of every situation. Now he didn't quite know how to handle this, this, melee of people milling around in his front hall.

"Well, what do you make of that?" he said, when they finally cleared out.

"Oh, Don, wasn't that wonderful? I am so excited about the trip. Won't we have a fantastic time? What incredible luck!" She was glowing.

"Wait a minute, When is that trip?"

"The first part of June"

"That is when we have the Annual Charity Golf Scramble at the country club. Roy and I already signed up for it weeks ago. I can't possibly leave town then."

Ellen turned and faced him, head on. A strange look came over her face. It was a wild stormy look, which he had never seen before. There was an almost tigerish look in those big honey-brown eyes. Her mouth opened and a formidable sound he never heard before came out of it. And it was LOUD!

"EOUGHOW," (or something like that) she roared.

That certainly got his attention. Arms akimbo, she thrust her head forward and upward to get as close to eye to eye as she could and bellowed, "Don't you dare even think about ruining this trip!" she thundered. "Think of all the times that I have submerged my plans to do what you wanted me to do. I have entertained your business friends, ROYALLY. Only to sit alone while you play golf. I always sit and listen to the boring accounts of games past, gone over, hole by hole. And TV! Do you know that watching golf on TV is like watching paint dry to me?

"Just think of all I do for you, how I smooth the bumps in your path. I make life easier for you every day and what do you do for me? Just a little wham-bam-thank-you-ma'am before you turn over and go to sleep. You never talk to me as an adult, or let me know what you are thinking or doing at the store. You never go anywhere with just me. I'm just a convenience, a convenience, DO YOU HEAR?"

A fleck of spittle landed on his chin. He didn't dare wipe it off. *She has lost her mind,* he thought. *I'll have to call Doc Haley to give her a sedative.*

When Ellen had finally run out of steam, she said, "ARRAOUGH!" raised both her hands in a plea to Heaven. Don thought she was going to hit him and he ducked. He felt foolish after he did.

She turned and ran out the door, grabbing her purse as she left. He stood there, open-mouthed, as he heard her car, uncharacteristically, roar down the driveway. Don slowly went back upstairs to finish dressing. When he came downstairs, he noticed the unusual mess in the kitchen. He put the perishables in the refrigerator and the dirty dishes in the dishwasher. He sponged off the counter and stood there staring out the window, unconsciously listening to the rumble and swish of the dishwasher doing its thing.

He went out to the car and drove to the office. He forgot the sports bag with his change of clothing for the afternoon's golf game. It was still upstairs where Ellen always left it. As he was driving, he mulled over what had just happened. He was stunned. He had never seen Ellen like that. *He really loved her, he thought she knew that. They never fought. Well, that time she wanted to work in the store, for God's sake, what an idea! They did have a few words then, but when he reasoned with her she soon came around. And as for taking her anywhere, every year the club has that golfing trip to Biloxi. I always take her there. They have things planned for the women who don't golf.*

He was late and all the department heads were waiting for him in the meeting room.

"Sorry about the delay, let's get started."

His mind retained the morning's developments and he kept dwelling on them.

When each manager in turn reported his activities, he was only vaguely aware of what was said. When they left, he went into his office, shuffled a few papers around and called his home. He got the answering machine. He hung up without leaving a message.

I wonder where she went? he pondered. *What could be the matter with her?*

Ellen's sigh was long and sad. She was sitting in the mall, people watching. *This ought to be a happy day,* she mused. *Don has ruined it for me. Well, I'm not going to let him do it! I am going by myself if he won't go.* Tears formed again and spilled over down her cheeks. She didn't know how long she sat there, but after awhile she gathered herself together and went to the movie in the mall.

It was one of those noisy movies about half-dressed wild teenagers and their noisy music,; along with bad language and bad acting. She couldn't keep her mind on the story. She replayed the events of this bittersweet day over and over in her mind.

Coming out of the movie she went by the food court. She was starved—she ordered a slice of pizza and a coke.

She wanted to go home, but she wasn't ready, so she went back into another movie.

This one was about kickboxers with a lot of fighting, wild auto chases and cursing. If they had removed every sentence with an obscenity in it, it would have been a silent movie.

Then when that movie was over, she drove home. She couldn't have told anyone what either one was about if anyone had asked. No one did.

Don didn't go golfing or card playing. Instead he visited every department. He talked to the sales people. He inspected everything. He even stooped and picked a piece of crushed paper off the floor and deposited in the trash bin behind the counter. He straightened, smoothed and rearranged stock as he passed through each department. He was satisfied with what he saw.

Dad would be proud to see everything just as it was when he was running the store.

He went back to his office. He looked out the window. He had a nice view of the Meramec River. He watched the water flow by for awhile.

He picked up the phone and called Roy on his cell phone. "Hey Roy."

"Don! Where the Hell are you?"

"I'm still at the office. I won't be able to join you today. Something came up, but I'll see you tomorrow."

"Too bad, anything serious?"

"Nothing I can't handle," was the macho reply. "I just wanted to give you a heads up."

"Okay, see you tomorrow."

When it was time, he went home for lunch. It was quiet without Ellen there. He never went home to an empty house. It was really quiet. *Maybe that is what is the matter with Ellen. Maybe I should get her a dog, or a cat. I know a parrot would be just the thing. They make a lot of noise and you can talk to them and teach them how to talk. That is just the thing to get her. I'll do that when she calms down.*

He fixed himself a peanut-butter sandwich and a glass of milk. He tried to get something on TV to watch while he ate. Soaps, game shows and shows with odd people telling their intimate secrets. He turned to a news station. After a while it started repeating itself. He turned it off and went back to the office.

He looked at some reports by the department heads, ones that he had already talked about that morning. Nothing new there. He called one of his buddies and learned the details of the golf game he had missed. By that time he decided he had put in enough time for that day and could go home. He wondered if Ellen would be there. He hesitated. *Should he call? What would he say?* He couldn't make up his mind so he just went home.

He entered the still quiet house, went to the bar and made himself a drink. He sat there sniffing and sipping the brandy, missing Ellen. He put on a CD of their favorite songs. It grew dark, but he didn't turn on the light. Some of the light shone in the window from the dusk-to-dawn light in the yard.

He heard her car in the driveway.

She dreaded facing Don. He was sitting in the living room when she came in. She came in and sat beside him on the couch. He didn't say anything—he didn't know what to say.

Ellen finally said, "Do you want something to eat?" She knew that she didn't want to eat.

"No, I got a burger and ate it in the car on the way home."

She got up and made her way into the kitchen. "Thanks for loading the dishwasher," she said as she came back into the living room.

"No problem, ah, Ellen…"

"Huh?"

"Are you feeling all right now?"

"Yes, I've calmed down a bit, but I haven't changed my mind. I am going on my trip whether you go or not."

"I see."

"Are you going to go with me?"

"Do you want me to?"

"Of course!"

"I'll have to tell Roy to get someone else as a partner for the Scramble."

"Big Deal!" she scoffed. "There are plenty of fellows that would be glad to scramble with Roy. "I'm sure you will find someone," she said coldly. "There is certainly plenty of time."

"I'll get on the phone and see what I can come up with."

Of course he had no trouble at all finding a partner for Roy.

Things were a bit frosty for a while. However, when they went to the store for their wardrobes for the trip they got into the spirit of the whole thing. They even ended laughing together on the way home. Their bit of sweet loving was lots more than wham-bam, and things between them was much better than before.

He really did love Ellen. He was shocked at the things she had said, and eventually realized they were accurate. He was frightened at the thought of losing her.

As the time to leave came closer, even Don was looking forward to the day they were to leave Manchester. As a surprise for Ellen he made plans to leave a day earlier for their plane connection out of New York.

He booked an expensive hotel room, tickets for the theater, reservations for a late supper afterwards at the latest hotspot where the celebrities are apt to be. He really did love Ellen, he just forgot to show it often enough. He realized that he had had a close call—one that could have had serious repercussions. Things would be different from now on, he assured himself.

I am going to make this a second honeymoon, he said to himself.

This is going to be like another honeymoon, Ellen said to herself.

They fell asleep snuggled together. Life for them really was going to be a lot different from now on.

Chapter Four

Lois unlocked the front door, balancing her purse, a briefcase and a handful of mail she had just brought in from the mailbox. She shut the door with a swivel motion of her hip. She dumped everything on the hall table just in time to keep it all from landing on the floor. It was 3:30 p.m. on a sunny Friday in February.

"Thank God it's Friday!" she said aloud. Lois had acquired the habit of talking aloud when alone after her husband had died five years ago. She picked up the mail, went into the den, switched on the TV, flopped into her comfortable lounger and kicked off her shoes. She tuned out the obnoxious commercial that was screaming at her about the advantages of a certain car. She began to sort through the mail. No personal letters, a catalog, three assorted bills for her and a sweepstakes letter.

A movie started, one she had seen years before with Geoffrey. She ignored the usual tug at her heart when something happened to cause her to miss him and went to the hall and picked up her briefcase.

Lois went back to the den and sat at her desk and began to copy the grades from a stack of papers into her class records' notebook. When she finished this simple chore, she was free for the weekend. Her mind could even keep up in a general way with the progress of the movie. When she finished, she put the school things away, then went to the kitchen for some milk and cookies to eat while she settled down to give the movie her entire attention.

Lois Wadleigh Castain, English teacher, age fifty-five, had lost her husband five years before. It was a sudden heart attack. He was a CPA, age fifty-five, seemingly in perfect health, but the stress of the busy tax season had overwhelmed him and he had died at his desk. Since he was so expert in money matters, he had planned their finances so that through insurance and money market programs, she was comfortable financially

Instead of buying a house in the suburbs, as most of their friends had, Geoffery had convinced Lois that their purchase of a four-family apartment was the better financial choice. They found the perfect place. The units were roomy, almost soundproof, bright and up to date with built-in appliances. It was on a large lot and each unit had its own space, enough for a small storage area and a car in the large four-car garage. The entrance to it was from one of the few remaining alleys in the city. The high school was only a few blocks away and two bus lines intersected at the nearest corner.

She was the only child of a professor of botany, her father, and an author of children's stories, her mother. She was quite naturally steeped in the world of books and plants.

Lois had come along late in her parent's marriage when they had just about given up ever having the child they wanted so badly. She was very much wanted and loved. She was nurtured as an exotic, precious plant by her father and taught the womanly arts of cooking, decorating, housekeeping and style and grooming by her mother. She was a well-behaved child and her parents enjoyed taking her on vacations. They instilled in her a love of travel. She had a sympathetic interest in the habits and mores of peoples of all nations.

They were a quiet family and each always had a current book going, and as she grew older they would pass a favorite book on, one to another.

There was not much of a surprise when she chose Academia for her career. When her parents died within a year of one another, she retreated into her world of books and art. All she did for a while was teach her English Literature and Art Appreciation classes.

She met Geoffery at the Art Museum when they were standing in line to see an important showing of Monet's paintings. Both admired the Impressionist's school and there were many other things they had in common. She was thirty and he was thirty-three when they married. She always felt a little cheated that they never were able to celebrate their twenty-fifth anniversary.

She was softly pretty, not flashy. Her ash-blond hair fell in waves and didn't require much attention, just a haircut occasionally to keep it at its medium length. Her blue-gray eyes reflected her mood and she wasn't very successful hiding her feelings. As for telling a lie, forget it! She found out early in life that she had to be truthful.

Lois became adept at being creative in her response to uncomfortable questions and social situations that required an expressed opinion where the truth would be hurtful.

She was of average height, five-foot four about, and not really plump, but not slim either. Since she would rather sit and read than be active in sports, she was not as svelte as she could be.

Geoffrey and Lois had landscaped their property with the help of her father and they had something blooming almost the year round. She almost always had fresh flowers in the house. The back yard of the apartment was larger than most. There was a bar-b-que area for the tenants, with a picnic table in a screened-in gazebo. They had planted a grapevine there and it had produced a significant amount of luscious grapes last year. She enjoyed making them into jelly and even a few grape pies.

When Lois and Geoffery found that they were destined to be childless, and since his work kept him away from home frequently, she decided to go back to work. The high school was ideal because it was so handy. Geoffrey would drop her off at the school on his way to the office. Most of the time she would walk home, or if the weather was bad she would hop on the bus which stopped practically in front of her door.

After Geoffrey's death she kept his old Oldsmobile that was his pride and joy. It was eleven years old and was still running. She used it for shopping, going to church on Sundays and other small trips. Lois followed rigidly the routine maintenance schedule Geoffery had set up the year he bought the car. She kept the same mechanic Geoffery had always used. He was an old boyhood friend of Geoffrey's who knew the car and took good care of it for her.

Her best friend was Nora Smythe and she lived in the apartment above her. She was a widow too, and she also taught at Lincoln High School. She was tall, with a wiry, sinewy athlete's body. Nora was raised in New England, Connecticut, to be exact. Nora was the middle child with four brothers, two older and two younger. She spent her childhood trying to keep up with them. It was only natural that she majored in Physical Ed. Her brothers were all deep into the Boy Scouts, and one even became an Eagle Scout. Nora, of course, was a Girl Scout. She still went camping as a counselor once in awhile. She was an expert gymnast and could have been of Olympic quality if her family had the money for the extensive, and expensive, training and coaching it would have taken to raise her to competitive standards. As it was, they all had to work while going to college. It took some of the children longer to get through college, consequently. Then, there were the student loans to pay off.

They were a boisterous, competitive, joking family. The father was a carpenter/contractor and the boys always had a job as helpers when they needed it. Only one stayed in the family business. One was a computer whiz and left for Silicon Valley.

One married the daughter of the local hardware dealer and went into that business with his father-in-law. The youngest wanted to be an actor and went to New York. After a few years of small parts in off, off, Broadway shows and some summer stock, he got a few TV commercials now and then. He recently had found a significant role in a soap opera. He married an actress who had a role in another soap opera on the same network, and things were going along well.

Nora had married her college sweetheart, Joe. He was also a Phys. Ed. major. They were perfect for one another. They enjoyed all sports together. Sailing was their favorite. Skiing, both kinds, was next. But camping, climbing and then rappelling down was enjoyed often and, of course canoeing and white-water rafting was indulged in occasionally. The family members all had their favorite football, baseball, and basketball and hockey teams, and at times the pandemonium at the Super Bowl or the World Series, or even a single game, was colossal.

He fit right in with her family, as an only child he missed the camaraderie that abounded in that family.

Alec, the youngest, took Joe aside at his first family dinner and told him, "The best seat at a large family dinner is at one of the ends, or else you'll be passing things all through the dinner."

Joe had felt he was really accepted when Alex had given him that bit of advice.

The first five years they were married, they were gym teachers at different high schools. They were so busy that they didn't get started having the family they had planned, but they were going to, soon, maybe next year. It wasn't soon enough. Joe was killed on Spring Break by an avalanche while skiing at Copper Mountain in Colorado. Nora narrowly missed being carried away by the slide. It was only because she had stopped to apply some lip balm on her chapped lips that she survived.

Since she grew up with the family code that stressed that "Only sissies cry," "Buck Up," and "No pain no gain," she didn't allow herself to mourn. She plunged into her Girl Scout work with a dedication to her charges that helped replace the children she never had. Nora was fun and the girls loved her.

Nora knew Joe was from a wealthy family. He had lost his parents in an auto accident when he was seventeen and was raised by his paternal grandparents. He stayed with them mostly in the summer and during holidays because they lived near where he went to a Prep boarding school in Connecticut.

His grandparents died while he was in college and he was left with a sizeable trust fund, a large house in Wilton, Connecticut and a summer/winter lodge in Vermont. Now it was Nora's, and she was quite well off, financially.

After some years passed, and all her Girl Scouts had outgrown her, she quit her job and traveled. She bought an Air-Stream trailer and in two years she went to every state that she could drive to, including Alaska. She grew tired of her traveling life, no roots, only casual acquaintances, and no real friends, so she put the trailer in storage and went looking for a job.

She was forty-five now and it was harder to get a position. She was accepted as gym teacher and coach of the girl's teams at Lincoln High School just outside of Boston.

She met Lois when she answered her ad about an empty apartment near the school. When they found out that they would both teach at Lincoln there was no question about the apartment. They began walking to school together on nice days, but they each took her own car on bad days. Nora often had to stay after school, or had to attend some kind of game, depending on the season. When vacation or holiday time came around, they would take a trip, or go off to the lodge in Vermont. They made wonderful traveling companions.

They didn't go everywhere together—each was free to do the things she enjoyed. Sports activities for Nora and museums and sightseeing for Lois. Of course they did these things together sometimes, but they were free not to, and neither was ever put out about it.

In winter in Vermont, for example, Nora would invite friends for skiing. Lois hated the cold weather. Skiing scared her to death and she was awful at it. She would bring a load of books she wanted to read and she always had a hot delicious meal for the skiers when they came home. She had a big pot of cocoa on the stove at all times then. The skiers would do the dishes so she wouldn't feel like the maid, they said.

The only difficulty was that Lois didn't have the financial freedom that Nora did. She was comfortable, but she was raised not to squander money and Geoffrey believed in a budget and sticking to it. She had just finished a childrens book that did have a moderate success. She had enough from that to be able to go to Hawaii like Nora wanted to and then some.

When not vacationing together, their lives went in different directions. Due to their disparate interests, "Stay-at-home" Lois had her books and her garden, also her writing and sketching. "Off-and-running" Nora had many friends and was often busy with her weekend sports. She walked for every cause and worked for many charities. She belonged to a bicycle club, a skiing group and she still went camping with the Girl Scouts occasionally, and she was a sort of stand-by with them.

Occasionally, Lois would join her with the Girl Scouts. Lois would help them with their cooking and sewing badges. She really was of value with their botany projects from the things she had learned from her father.

Nora's idea of cooking was a quick TV dinner and a salad. Lois would have her in for a meal, especially when she herself wanted to cook something that was too much for one. Other times she would bring her a casserole or a dessert.

Lois kept busy with her friends. She belonged to the Shakespeare Club at the university. She enjoyed volunteer work at the zoo and belonged to the Friends of the Art Museum.

Sometimes when there was something Nora and Lois both wanted to see on TV they would watch together. Lois never watched games on TV. There were days when they only spent their brief journey to school together in the morning. Lately Lois tried to get a few hours working on her little stories after school and in the evening. Sometimes she even sold one.

When either one of them came home, they would give the "shave and a hair cut" rhythm on the other's doorbell in the front lobby. The other didn't necessarily answer, but it was their way of saying, "I'm home."

Things went on like this. One year they toured Europe in the summer. The next year they cruised the Greek Islands and the next year they drove the Air-Stream down to Mexico, which wasn't the best thing they ever did! Lots of car trouble, it was very hot, and both got the "Tourista." Not something to look back on fondly, but they survived and even laughed at the experience after awhile. Nora sold the Air-Stream when they returned a week late and without seeing half the things they had planned to see.

It was then that Lois saw the letter for the sweepstakes, and almost without thinking, sent it in. She told Nora about it, and being Nora and so Gung Ho, she set about and entered it a dozen times.

They were elated when the team of Sweepstakes People greeted Lois one morning just before they left for school. She had won the Jungle Cruise for two down the Amazon! Nora was a bit chagrined that her dozen entries lost out to Lois' one, but not for long.

Their lives were full and happy as they waited for the rainy season to end.

That is except once. A boy named Drew, who was in Lois' English Lit. class and hated it was the reason. He couldn't draw a straight line in Lois' art class either. Mainly because he just gave up and wouldn't try. Lois gave him a poor grade because he didn't hand in all his assignments and the ones he did hand in were slapdash. Disgruntled, he made a remark about the two of them to another boy. He was implying an unnatural relationship.

It happened one morning, bright and sunny, so they walked. There was a small patch of uneven sidewalk and Lois tripped on it. Nora quickly reacted and prevented her fall by clasping her around the waist. The boy spoke his filthy remark in a loud, shrill voice. Those near enough to hear gasped and stared. Nora and Lois were appalled! The odious moment unnerved them and they hurried into the school.

They could not let it go by, and after an unpleasant meeting with the parents, the boy and the principal, the boy apologized. He explained that he was angry because he was doing badly in Lois' classes. He was disciplined, his parents were embarrassed, and the principal was annoyed. In time it was forgotten. But after that they were aware of what others might think. It did make them think twice about friendly pats and any other previously unconscious gestures that friends make to one another. It was too bad.

Chapter Five

The phone was ringing, the dog was barking to get in out of the storm and the smoke alarm was screaming. The toaster had gotten stuck and black smoke was pouring out. Ginger flipped the lever of the toaster up. It took a few times to unstick the black mess within. She heard the answering machine take over the phone call as she opened the door to let Sparky in and the smoke out. She opened the kitchen window, the doors to the basement and the garage and turned on the overhead fan. The wind was blowing some rain in on the kitchen floor, but it was also dispersing enough smoke to hush the wail of the smoke detector.

"Whew! What a smell!" she said as she closed the door to the back deck. She walked to the garage door, reached in and took the sponge mop from its hook and mopped Sparky's muddy tracks and the rain spots from the floor in front of the door. She looked out at the palm trees doing a wild dance with the wind.

A rainy day at the beach, she thought, *Dismal*. She put the mop away and started some new toast, watching it carefully.

Dr. Dennis Evans came downstairs in a hurry. A young looking fifty, with all his hair and no potbelly in sight, he was the picture of a successful young doctor.

"Hi, Gingy. What's that awful smell? What was that excessive din?"

"The toaster stuck and made a mess, then the smoke alarm went berserk. This batch turned out okay, you want it?"

"If you don't mind, I'm in a rush this morning. We are having special Saturday rounds today, visiting VIPs." He smeared the toast with a low fat yogurt butter substitute. Then he sprinkled a mix of cinnamon and sugar-substitute over that. Keeping that potbelly away required some discipline. He helped himself to some coffee in the pot and sat at the table.

"Who was on the phone?"

"I don't know. I let the machine take over. I was a little busy at the time. Sparky needed to get in, the smoke needed to get out and the rain soaked the floor," she said as she handed him a glass of orange juice.

"Looks good now, though." He took a big gulp.

"Mom's having Bridge Club this afternoon, so I thought I should repair the damage."

"Where's Mom?"

"At the store getting some last minute stuff for the party."

"Oh, after I'm finished at the hospital I was supposed to play tennis, but it looks like the storm will take care of that. What are you going to do now that your beach plans are over?"

"I don't know, maybe go to the mall and hang out. A little later I'll call Brianna and see what she wants to do."

Dennis went over to the answering machine and played back its message.

"Hi, Ginger, it's Brianna, looks like the beach is out. You want to go to the mall or the movies, or what? Call me, Bye."

"Two great minds...call Brianna when you get a chance, okay?"

He wiped his hands on a dishtowel and went to the garage door. "Bye, sweetie, tell Mom I'll be home early. We can all go out to dinner tonight, okay?"

"Great." She threw him a kiss. "See ya."

Virginia Lee Evans had never been called anything but Ginger. She never used her middle name either. "Ginger Lee" was too bizarre. Dennis and Carla had thought their darling daughter would never grow any hair. Carla would tape a tiny ribbon to her pate so people would stop calling her "he." Finally after about three months the brown fuzz fell out and delightful reddish blond fuzz replaced it and grew slowly and steadily into stunning ringlets. Dennis started calling her Ginger, and that was the name they entered her into school under. She was a beautiful child then and a beautiful teenager now. Her long hair was a stunning strawberry blond and her jade green eyes were attention getting.

Her skin had a golden glow, and surprisingly, for her age, without a blemish. She was seventeen and a high school senior, but she wouldn't be seventeen too much longer. Her eighteenth birthday was next week.

Ginger had straightened the kitchen and was in the den talking to Brianna on the phone when Carla came in from the garage.

"Ginger, Ginger, I need help with the groceries."

"Just a minute, Bree. Okay, Mom, just a minute. Got to go, Bree. I'll meet you on that bench near the bookstore around noon, okay? Bye."

"It doesn't look like the storm is going to let up, but that won't stop my bunch. They would brave any weather for an afternoon of Bridge." Carla was unloading her purchases on the counter. Ginger brought two grocery bags out of the garage.

"I thought you were all ready for the party? I saw the tables all set up in the lanai, the place looks great. Do you want me to go out and rescue some flowers from the storm?"

"Oh, honey, would you? See what you can salvage and put them in the containers on the tables."

Ginger, in a raincoat and scarf, went outside armed with a shears and carrying a basket. She began to fill it with the wind-blown flowers.

Carla was busy in the kitchen doing all the last minute things a party like this required. She was a svelte forty-two-year-old "matron," but was not a bit matronly. Her reddish brown hair was cut short. She liked tennis and swimming at the country club and kept busy with a few charity groups. She never missed daily Mass if she could help it. She was sure, when she finally became pregnant after eight years of marriage; it was because of her many prayers and novenas at daily Mass. So she never lost the habit—it became part of her day.

When Carla was almost finished, Ginger came in with the flowers all-awry in the basket. They worked together, each on her own chore, and talked about this and that till they were finished. They had a good relationship without the angst occurring in many families with teenagers.

"Well, it's all ready. I'm going upstairs to get beautified."

"I guess I can still have the car, huh?"

"Yes, I know you'll be careful. The roads will probably be slick. When are you planning to be home?"

"Your guests will leave about four, won't they?"

"Yes, maybe even earlier if the storm hangs around."

"I'll be home around then. Dad ought to be home by then and we can decide where we want to go to dinner."

"Good, he mentioned Anthony's last night. See you then—thanks for the help, honey."

Later, after the successful card party, Ginger, had returned from the mall and was upstairs changing for dinner. Dennis came into the den where Carla was sitting in the lounger with her feet up watching TV. When he came in carrying the mail, she turned it off with the remote. He bent over and kissed her on the top of her head.

"Hi, Sweetie, what's in the mail? I was too busy to get it this afternoon."

"Check it out," he said. He dumped the assorted clutter in her lap and took off his coat. Dennis threw it on the back of a chair and sat on the arm of the lounger beside her. He had a busy day and was grateful to be able to sit.

"The storm's over at last," he said while loosening his tie. "How was your party?"

"Great, we all had a lovely time." Carla was separating the mail, junk in one pile, bills in another and a single personal letter from her mother. She opened her letter and avidly read it through. Dennis took the junk mail pile and sifted through it.

"How's your mother?"

"She is just fine. She is busy entering her genealogy data into her new computer. She is going to take some classes to help her learn the intricacies of the personal computer. Mother says computers are just like kids, they don't do what you say and they talk back!"

"She's got that right. It took quite awhile for me to get the hang of it, but it surely is worthwhile when you do master it."

"Not much in the mail, do you want to look through it?"

"No, let's get ready and go to dinner, where are we going?"

"Do you have any preferences?"

"How about Italian?" she said. "I could eat something substantial after that light party fare. Everyone is on a diet and I had to serve accordingly. How about you?"

"I didn't eat any lunch at all. After rounds, Dr. Wells wanted me to see one of his patients at his hospital across town. When I finished over there, it was too late to eat then, so I came on home."

"You must be starved, I'll hurry Ginger and we'll leave right away. I guess we'll go to Anthony's, it has good food and is nearby. Okay?"

"Okay!"

At this point Ginger came downstairs—the scent of Oscar De La Renta floated down with her.

"Mmmmmm," Dennis said, "I always did like that fragrance, that's why I bought it for your mother's birthday present last month."

Ginger blushed. "I didn't think she'd care. Do you care, Mom?"

"No, I don't care, if you use it sparingly."

"What's in the mail, anything interesting?" Ginger said, pawing through the junk mail that was left. Dennis had removed the bills and had neglected throwing the rest in the trash.

"It's all yours, Gingy." That was a throwback from her childhood, the junk mail was always, "Her Mail," but only after her parents had discarded it. She brought it with her to read in the car.

On the way home, stuffed with the heavy meal, Ginger saw the sweepstakes envelope on the seat beside her.

"Did you see the sweepstakes for $5,000,000.00?"

"I ignored it," said Carla.

"Humph!" Dennis gave his opinion.

"Do you care if I send it in, Dad? It's addressed to you."

"You'll waste a stamp, but it is all right with me if you want to."

"I'll give it a try." She put the envelope into her purse.

Later, when the sweepstakes crew came knocking on the door they were so surprised, every one of them. Not even Ginger had an inkling they would win.

Chapter Six

"Mr. Hunter, the phone is for you." Ryti peeked in his office door.

"Thanks, Ryti." Gordon William Hunter picked up the office phone and Ryti darted back to her desk. She rarely spoke or called attention to herself, but the office could not function without her. He had been doodling on his business stationery. GWH substituted letters in his name, making it read "Great White Hunter." That was his nickname among the other jungle guides. It suited him, like FDR, JFK, and LBJ. And everyone in the business knew whom it meant.

"Hello."

"Hello, Bud, is that you?"

"Hi, Dad, how are you?"

"Fine, are you all set?"

"I bought my ticket today. I leave for Miami as soon as the rainy season is over, in about a month. I have about a three-hour layover and then on to Bel'em. I'll meet you and the boat there. I'll call you from the airport in Miami to touch base then, okay?"

"Right, did you get your immunizations?"

"I have an appointment this week. I bought some new clothes too. I'm ready."

"That's great, Bud. I'm looking forward to our being together. I'll teach you to be as good a jungle guide as GWH!"

"I don't know about that, Dad. You'd better not plan on that. I'm not like you, I don't think I can ever be as good a guide as you are. The things I am good at are different. I did rather well in college. You'd be proud of me if you knew the details."

"I know, your mother did a good job of seeing that you had a good academic education, but now I can teach you the things a real man knows…"

"Dad, I think I already am a 'real man.'" The tone of his voice chilled.

"Now, Bud, don't get your nickers in a twist. I didn't mean to step on your toes. You get your feelings hurt as easily as your mother did."

"I just want to start out with certain things understood. I am a college graduate, I have letters in Tennis and Swimming and I was accepted in a Master's program before Mom died. I have nothing to be ashamed of, and I particularly want you to respect that. You will have to if we are going to make a success of this new living arrangement. If not, I can start on my Master's program in the fall instead of making my home in Amazonas with you."

"I certainly do want you to do that! I'll do my best to see that we get started out on the right foot. I'll be waiting for your call from Miami, okay, Bud?"

"Okay, Dad, see you then. In the meantime I'll keep in touch."

"Bye, kid…"

"Oh, Dad?"

"Yeah?"

"I'll be glad to learn all your jungle tricks. It will be like getting my Master's in guiding from the master." He held out the olive branch.

"It's a deal, see you then, bye."

GWH turned to Nat. "Oops, I almost blew that one!" GWH said aloud as he hung up the phone.

"What you done now?" Nat, his Peruvian secretary\companion\assistant guide\ and best friend, entered the office in to hear his last remark. Nat had been with him for many years and was on as familiar terms with GWH as anyone. He was a legacy from a group of anthropologists and botanists, studying the flora and fauna, who hired him to guide them. He and Nat hit it off right away, so he stayed on in Manaus when the group went back to America.

He was also shy Ryti's husband. When Nat realized that he wouldn't be returning to Peru to find a wife, he went to the Missionary orphanage and chose Ryti from the graduating class. She could speak two Indian languages, Portuguese and a basic English. She learned quickly and was soon the backbone of the office, quietly seeing that everything was done efficiently and on time. She adored Nat and he was proud of her and the way she took over the operation of the office when GWH and Nat were away on business.

"I guess I hurt Bud's feelings. I hope I don't have to tiptoe around him to keep from pissing him off. I want him here, but I'll be damned if I'm going to change my ways to please him! I can't, I couldn't do it to please his mother, and I can't do it to please him. He'll have to take me, warts and all, or just forget it!"

"You lost his mother, do you want to lose him too?"

"His mother coddled him too much. He always had his nose in a book every time he would visit me. You remember what a wimpy kid he was? Couldn't do anything without wheezing, couldn't go out without his pills and inhaler. I was petrified that something would happen to him while he was with me. May would never let him come here again."

"I remember you almost drowned him when you threw him into the river trying to teach him how to swim, boss."

"Yeah, that was a mistake."

"I had to dive in and get him, he was scared to death!"

"Hell, Nat, that was the way I learned to swim. Then later May took special pride in writing to me about how well he did winning swimming awards at the country club's swim meets. I couldn't win for losing with that woman! I loved her, I truly loved her, but I couldn't live with her or she with me. She said we were oil and water, and that is just what we were. We couldn't mix, even little Buddy couldn't homogenize us. So divorce was the only answer. Buddy and I suffered through weeks every year during semester break, or Christmas, or summer vacation, whenever May decided to send him."

Nat looked at GWH earnestly. "I'd have just let him be, instead of trying to toughen him up. You got him so afraid of you, and so fearful of disappointing you that he never was comfortable with you. He'd jump if you just said his name."

"I never laid a hand on him. I tried to teach him how to do things. Nat, I really love the boy, er, ah, and I want him to love me." It was hard for this rough and tumble man to admit this, and he could do so only to Nat. He was a John Wayne sort of man. He was tough, with a tender side that he tried to hide. Tall, ruggedly handsome, with a craggy face, creases that used to be dimples were like a parenthesis around a sensitive mouth with strong white teeth. His eyes were startlingly blue, smiling out of a tanned face. His hair was brown, shot through with some gray, had a slight wave when it was allowed to grow long enough. He was somewhere between fifty-five and sixty, a little cagey about his age.

"You've got to help me, Nat. When I get too heavy-handed with him, give me some kind of sign, will you? This will probably be my last chance with him. My wish is for him to take over the business some day, though it doesn't look like it will ever happen."

"Okay, GWH, I'll give you a high sign when I think you ought to lighten up. Now to get to what I came in for. I went to the post office and there's a letter from that sweepstakes company. Maybe they have the names of the winners. There were a few bills and I gave them to Ryti. Oh, yes, there is a letter from McDonnell Douglas, probably an ad."

"Let's have that letter from Sweepstakes U.S.A."

Nat handed him the letter and GWH opened it with an unusual letter opener on his desk, a gift from one of his customers.

"That is what it is all right. Mr. Don and Mrs. Ellen Mason from Manchester, New Hampshire. Mrs. Lois W. Castain and her friend Mrs. Nora J. Smythe from Boston, and Dr. Dennis and Mrs. Evans, Carla, to be exact, from Fort Myers, Florida—these are the winners. Oh, oh, they want to bring their daughter Ginger with them and will pay for her trip themselves." He read further. "The tickets were hand delivered in a big ceremony and they will be here June first. We will have to issue a ticket for the daughter and send it off. Hmmmm, doesn't say how old the daughter is. That could be a problem if she is too young. We'll have to find that out before we send any ticket. They must be on the same flight that Bud is taking out of Miami."

"That's great! I'll have Bud get there a day early and be their greeter in Miami. He can be the firm's representative and take care of all that stuff"

"Yeah, and we can take his expenses off the income tax." Bookkeeper Nat was always thinking.

"I'll call Bud and give him their names and the other information. Nat, will you take care of the hotel reservations?"

"Yep, I did that when we got the job. I'll send off a letter to the agency. They can call the winners and tell them about the trip. They can tell them what to bring, what not to bring and mention that Bud will meet them at the airport in Miami. Okay?"

"That's fine, while you are at it, you'd better reserve a room for Bud the night before at that hotel near the airport. That would be the thirtieth of May. I'll tell him so he can change his airline tickets."

"Sure thing, boss. Oh, I forgot to tell you that Mr. Tom Murphy and his wife Letty are to be on the same cruise as the winners, our only paying customers. So you can tell Bud to look out for them in Miami also. They're coming in from St. Louis."

"Okay, that all?"

"Only that I saw Cranshaw, he was bummed because we got the sweepstakes job. He knows it's good publicity. I don't know how many letters were sent out with our name on them."

"It was a good break all right. We'll be getting bookings for a long time because of it. What else did he say?"

"Oh, he was saying that you used your influence with Lawrence at the Embassy to get the nod from the sweepstake company when they inquired, and that he didn't get a chance to bid for it."

"They wouldn't have given him the booking anyway. Everybody around here knows how he screwed that last bunch from New York. When those people arrived at that flea-bitten excuse for a hotel with no air conditioning, only those ceiling fans, and that is what was hit by you- know-what!

"It got the whole trip started out on the wrong foot, and it went down hill from there. I've always said, 'give first class service and you'll get repeat business, they will tell their friends and they will be your friends, forever.'"

"That's for sure. The Christmas cards you get from all over show how many friends you have made—that and the repeat business. Is the June first trip ready to go?"

"Yes, the boat is ready to go. I have two helicopters, ours and a rented one. We just have to load them up with the equipment. The supplies are ready to be taken to the first stop—when it stops raining, that is. Then all we have to do is set up camp. We'll get the perishables the day we leave, as usual."

"Did you read all the mail yet?"

"Not yet, but I will. I'm finished with the Sweepstakes U.S.A. letter, that can be filed."

"I gave the bills to Ryti, she is taking care of them."

"You've got a great girl there, Nat."

"I know, I know." He smiled and looked over to her desk where she was busy taking care of business.

GWH opened the letter from McDonnell Douglas. He was sitting there stunned.

"GWH, what is it?" Nat, seeing the astonished look on his face, went over to him.

"What? What is it? Will you please tell me what happened? You look shocked. Did you win the Lottery?"

"Close to it, a new helicopter! That's Bud's surprise! Wow! Now we won't have to rent one for large groups on those side trips; we'll have two! What a kid! I guess he is trying to spend that huge inheritance May left him." He handed the letter over to Nat.

"Wow! Oh, wow!" Nat whooped.

The letter told of a delivery of one of their MD Explorer helicopters in the next week. His son Gordon Hunter Junior had ordered it. An employee will assemble and test it before they sign for its acceptance.

"What a kid!"

"What brought that on?" Nat queried.

"The only thing I can think of is that my birthday is next week. Some present!" said GWH with a great big smile on his face.

The office door slammed open, startling the two men at its impact, quickly dissipating the feelings of joy, and sending Ryti into a panic. She ran into the supply closet to get away from the intruder.

A sodden Fenton Crenshaw entered, reeling. The fumes of the drinks he had been consuming at the Bola De Borracha attested to the fact that he hadn't been drinking water. He was soaked because he had left his rain gear at the Bola De Borracha, which is Portugese for Rubber Ball.

"Hello there, Fenton, what can I do for you?" GWH rose from his desk chair.

"You can stop running me down to your friend Lawrence at the Embassy. You are causing my business to fall off, and I won't stand for it!"

He staggered over to the desk, leaning on it for support, and shook his finger at GWH. His clothes were soiled and reeking, somewhere he had lost his hat and his hair was plastered to his skull. His eyes were bloodshot and he needed a shave.

GWH stepped back a step to get away from the stench. Nat prudently moved to a position where he could step in to help if needed.

"If you don't quit it, you will be one very sorry SOB. I have ways of getting back at you that you wouldn't believe!"

"Aw, Fenton, sit down before you fall down. I didn't even mention you to Lawrence. He was the one that told me of all the flack those people gave him. They came back from your last pitiful excuse for a jungle cruise angry and out for revenge. As you know, they all wanted you to give them their money back, and when you wouldn't do it they dumped it all in the Embassy's lap. You don't want to know all the names they called you and what they said about the trip."

"I know you cut me out with those sweepstakes people. I know six reservations aren't much, but the exposure would bring lots of bookings for a long time."

"That's right, Fenton, and that is why I gave those tickets to them at a rock bottom price—for the future business that it will bring. I won't make a dime on those tickets; they're at cost. Reputation means everything in this business. Appearance too. Go over to the bathroom. Get a look at yourself in that mirror over the wash bowl. You look awful and smell worse. You really need professional treatment. Have you ever thought of AA?"

Fenton ignored his invitation to look in the mirror. "Never mind about how I look or smell, I expect you to get Lawrence to put me on the preferred list of guides at the Embassy."

"No way, not the way you operate. Maybe next year if I see that you have cleaned up your act. Get off the sauce and give a good trip for the money. If you can't do that, you can forget it."

"I don't have to come to you for advice. I have a booking of a boatload going out June first. I have only one plane, but I'm going to get the camp set up in two trips and give them one Hell of a cruise."

"I'm going out that day too. Are you taking the A route or the B route?"

"Why should I tell you?"

"Because whatever route you take, I'll take the other, so we won't get in each other's way."

"You can take any damn route you want, I'll be far ahead of you, you can bank on that."

"That's the trouble with you, Fenton, you just want to hurry up things. You have to take advantage of all the natural opportunities that come along. If it's hot and there is a safe place in the river, let them get their feet wet, checking for critters first. Their enjoyment must come first, not the timetable. You must be flexible. Fenton, you must get to know your clients, their likes and especially their dislikes."

"I am a guide, that's what I do, guide! I expect you to talk to Lawrence about getting me on that list, today! If you don't then watch out, oh Great White Hunter," each word accompanied by a dirty finger thrust upon his chest. "Or else you won't be hunting anything, anymore, I'm warning you!" GWH's cheeks reddened with his suppressed anger. "I've had enough of you, Fenton, GET OUT BEFORE I SEND YOU OUT, ASS FIRST."

Fenton glared at both of them and stormed out of the door, and of course, slammed it behind him.

Ryti, hearing him leave, peeped out of the supply room door. She smiled at the two men, shrugged her shoulders and returned to her desk

"Can you believe that?" GWH exhaled a mighty breath, then went to the window clasping and unclasping his fists. He watched Fenton weave his way down the block, on the bias, back to the Bola De Borracha.

"Nat, you'd better call Dave at the Bola De Borracha. Tell him Fenton is dangerously overloaded and to water down his drinks; he'll never know the difference. I'm going home for lunch and I'll call Bud from there about the clients."

As GWH left the office, he saw Fenton stumbling down the block and enter the Bola De Borracha. The local saloon was dedicated to the era of the Rubber Boom. It was decorated with artifacts from that time, notably; a huge hunk of raw rubber that looked like it was ready to be shipped, as it was in the old days when the economy was patterned by the price of rubber.

GWH shook his head at the pathetic sight of Fenton entering the saloon. Sober, Fenton was one of the best guides in the business and he deserved a place on the select list of guides that the Embassy supplied upon request. Drinking, he did have a mean streak.

I'd be glad to recommend him if he could stop drinking, or even hold his drinks better, but that guy just has to smell the cork and he's 'round the bend. It is such a shame. He is so well educated, with a brilliant mind. But he is really heading for trouble if he keeps on the way he's going, GWH mused in his Land Rover as he drove the short distance to his home. The rain had let up but the street was still full of puddles.

When Fenton Cranshaw entered the Bola De Borracha, he sat at a table instead of at his usual place at the bar. Dave saw him enter, but avoided eye contact and turned his back so he could delay serving him. He had just hung up after Nat's call. Fenton sat with his chin cradled in his hand, elbow on the table. He was seething at the exchange he had just had with GWH. At least two snappy comebacks came to his mind that he wished he had thought of at the time. *I'd surely like to get even with that guy. He thinks he's so great, what an ego! There must be some way.* He sat there scowling and contemplating one disastrous occurrence after another, all happening to GWH. *If I do anything, everybody will suspect me. I need a stranger to help me. Someone to help me get even, without the blame falling on me. Who? Who? If only Orem Tharp was here, there's a guy with a devious mind. He could devise a*

Machiavellian plot that no one could unravel. I wonder if I still have his phone number? I'd better go home and have a look.' He struggled to his feet, and to Dave's surprise started toward the door.

"Hey! Mr. Cranshaw, here's your hat and rain coat. You left them behind this morning." Dave ran after him with the hat and plastic coat.

Fenton took them without thanks, never losing his scowl. He was able to walk home; his office was nearby with a modest apartment on the second floor. He used to have a regular house on the outskirts of town, but it went as part of his divorce settlement about five years ago.

It was just about then that his drinking began to get out of hand. He held onto the banisters as he went up the stairs to his apartment. As he opened the door, his nose was assailed by the fetid odor of the unwashed clothes he had pushed under the bed. In the kitchen, on the cluttered table of dirty dishes, there was rotting fruit in a bowl, with a halo of tiny flying insects hovering over it. At least a week's worth of trash and garbage, not quite all contained in the trash can under the overloaded sink. Old whisky bottles were scattered throughout the place, lying where they were dropped when they no longer held any more of their stupefying contents.

"Ugh!" He gagged and went inside and threw open all the windows. He winced at the assortment of insects flitting around the fruit bowl and camping out in the overflowing trash can and its environs. Despairing, he went into the bedroom and fell across the clutter on the bed and was soon snoring away.

Later, when he awoke, it was dark and he was ravenous. There was nothing fit to eat in the refrigerator. He began to remove all the spoiled leftovers and other food that was now garbage. Fenton took out the resulting mess and put it in the trash bin outside.

He went down the street. The night was muggy, but the rain had let up for the time being. He went to the nearest restaurant and had their special of the day — Amazonas' answer to corned beef and cabbage. It was corned beef all right, and the cabbage and potatoes were similar, but not the real thing that they serve in New England. It was good though, and he was hungry. There was real corn bread on the menu and he devoured it. He started to order a beer, changed his mind and ordered a large glass of soda.

The restaurant had a few customers that Fenton knew, but he didn't acknowledge them. Fenton was so malodorous, unkempt, and scowling that they were glad to be ignored. Fenton finished eating and lit a cigarette. He became aware of a conversation going on in a booth behind him. He listened without turning around.

"Did you hear about Ed's trip into the jungle?"

"I heard something about it. Didn't he watch a bunch of natives kill a monkey in a sacrificial ritual?"

"That's only part of it! The dagger that was used was unique, it had a handle that was made of a huge uncut emerald."

"How could he tell that? Wasn't he too far away?"

"He is very experienced with them. He used to be an overseer of an emerald operation in Columbia when he was younger. He has a great pair of binoculars and could see it clearly when they set it on a stone altar. The new road has made it easier to reach those groups that splintered off from the main tribes years ago."

"What tribe was it?"

"Nobody knows and Ed didn't say. He believes the natives should be left undisturbed. Ed was even sorry he mentioned it when he saw the reaction to his story."

Fenton paid his check and hurried back to his apartment. His knowledge of the various tribes was extensive. He could speak Tupi and had even mastered its glottal stops. He also knew Ge fairly well and some words in a few other tongues that he could use with sign language and get along well enough. He felt sure that he could find that tribe with a little searching. If he could get his hands on that dagger, it would answer all his financial problems.

Sober now, he was revolted at the condition of the apartment. Although the hour was late, he started to repair the resulting damage from his neglect. Only when the place was presentable did he shower and crawl into the freshly made bed. Fenton fell into such a deep sleep that he wasn't even aware of the smell of the insect-repellant laden air.

When he awoke around noon, he felt better than he had in a long time. Since there wasn't anything to eat in the house, he took the car to the market and laid in a supply of necessities, including a bottle of whiskey. His mind was racing as he put the things away.

I've got to get my hands on that dagger! Who could I get to go with me? Who can I trust to keep quiet about it?

He was mulling this over in his mind as he sprayed the whole place with the most potent bug spray he could find. The small amount of spray he had left that he had used last night wasn't near enough. He sprayed air freshener around to offset the resulting chemical stench. Satisfied that it was all he could do, he went into the kitchen and started to open the whiskey. He paused, started to open the bottle again. Fenton stared at it for a minute.

"No!" he said aloud, as he put it in the cabinet and slammed the door. *I've got to keep my mind clear to do this right,* he told himself.

He went to the telephone table and removed his personal book from the drawer, paged through the T's and punched a long series of numbers and waited.

"Hello."

"Oram, my friend, this is Fenton."

"Fenton! How are you? Where are you?"

"I'm in Manaus. I was thinking about you. Wouldn't you like a vacation from all that noise and strife that I hear New York is having?"

"Man, you know it! It would be the answer to a lot of problems"

"Anything serious?"

"I got fired. The boss caught me snatching some stuff in stock. The good news is he didn't call the cops."

"You need a break, and I have a job we can talk about. What do you say?"

"Sounds like just what I need. I've been thinking about the folks at home."

"Are you okay to leave? Do you have enough money for a ticket?"

"Yeah, I'm fine, I'll get a ticket and see you soon."

"Orem, don't let anyone know who you are coming to see, and come to the apartment after dark. And, Oram, don't speak English, you are coming back to your hometown. Do you have any of the clothes you wore here?"

"Who wore clothes?"

"You know what I mean, missionary handouts."

"None at all. When I came to America five years ago, I became an American! I went to classes to learn how to talk. The Sisters there in Manaus taught me Portuguese and some English, but I wanted to talk American. I hang out with the brothers and I am so American now you couldn't tell me from my neighbors. They have some ethnic shops here with a few things that look like it comes from home, should I pick some up?"

"Just get one outfit to travel in. Don't bring anything from the U.S.A. No luggage, no nothing!"

"What do I carry my money and passport in?"

"Get some kind of straw or cloth bag."

"Okay, but I feel like 007."

"You aren't far off, I'll explain when you get here."

Chapter Seven

Letty was busy emptying the dryer and folding the laundry. She would grab an article out of the dryer as it was still twirling, quickly close the door and deftly hang it on a hanger, or else fold it for the drawer. She hated ironing, so she did her best to avoid it by prompt and efficient emptying of the dryer.

The phone rang—she answered it in the kitchen adjoining the utility room.

"Hello."

"May I speak to Mr. Murphy, please?"

"Just a minute, I'll get him."

She set the phone on the counter and went to the back stairs. "Tom, the phone is for you."

"I'll take it in the bedroom."

Tom was propped up in bed. He had been reading the newspaper. He reached over to the phone. "Hello."

"Hi, Tom, this is Ralph Wayne."

"Well, hello there, Ralph. How are things going?"

"That's what I'm calling about. Do you remember that job in Pittstown, South Dakota, a few years back?"

"Yeah, what's the matter?"

"Some guy named Lester Thomas called and wanted to talk to you. I told him that you had sold the business to me and are now retired. He was not happy. He thinks that only you can help him with his problem machinery. Mr. Thomas wants you to go there and fix it. He also wants to expand his operation considerably and wants your advice on how to do it."

"When is all this going to happen?"

"As soon as possible."

"I'm scheduled to go on a jungle cruise. I have to leave for Bel'em on June first. It's our first trip since I retired and we are really looking forward to it."

"If you take this on, Tom, you'll make enough to take quite a few trips. Can't you postpone it?"

"Well, we have to time it between rainy seasons. I hate to disappoint Letty, let me talk to her and I'll get back to you."

"I'd like for you to leave next week, Tom. Glen Gleason is leaving on the noon flight tomorrow and, er, ah, well, we made a reservation for you too, just in case you said yes." He gave an embarrassed laugh.

"Thanks a lot! I'd really like to help you out, Ralph. Lester is one of the good guys. I'd like to help him out too, but I'll have to get back to you. I'll talk to Letty and call you right back. So long, I'll be talking to you."

"Bye, Tom, and thanks."

Tom went downstairs where Letty was putting the last load into the dryer. "That was Ralph Wayne, he wants me to help him out with some job."

"Did you tell him to go fly a kite?"

"No, it's quite important and I'd like to help him out on this. When I left the company, I told him I would help him out if he needed me instead of working two extra years as part of the buyout agreement."

"Well, I guess you should do it then. When we get back, you'll just have to do it."

"That's just it. He wants me to leave tomorrow, on the noon flight out for Pittstown, South Dakota."

"No way! Did you tell him of our plans? That we are leaving Friday?"

"Yes, but this can't be postponed, and it means a lot of future business. I'd really like to help him out. Postponing our trip won't be such a big deal, and the money I'll make will be like winning the trip on the sweepstakes, and then some."

"I can see I'm not going to win this one. It's a good thing everything is clean and ready to pack."

He reached over and gave her a big kiss. "That's one of the reasons I love you so much. You are so agreeable all the time."

"You'd better get going and tell Ralph that 'Mommy' said you can go out and play."

Tom went to the kitchen phone and punched in the number of his old company. "Wayne Weldment. How may I direct your call?"

"I'd like to speak to Mr. Wayne. This is Tom Murphy."

"Yes, Mr. Murphy. He is waiting for your call. I'll connect you."

While he waited, Tom thought of the older woman that always had answered their phone with a warm and cheery "Murphy Weldment." She had retired when he sold the business. He wondered how she was. This return to his old business wouldn't be too bad. He had enjoyed his job, and this problem was intriguing.

"Ralph Wayne here."

"Hi, Ralph, all systems go here, I can make it tomorrow."

"Great, I really appreciate this, Tom. I'm sending Letty some roses today."

"That's not necessary, Ralph. We'll just postpone our trip a bit. Tell me, what kind of trouble is old Lester in, what isn't working?"

"The new surge tower they are building is giving them trouble. They want to expand that dam they put on the Missouri

River, I guess it was about thirty years ago. They want to add another turbine and that means another surge tower, only they are having trouble making the welds hold. Lester said you were there when that dam was built and know all about welding surge towers. He won't be satisfied till you are on the site."

"What kind of trouble?"

"Some of the welds are cracking."

"What kind of equipment are they using?"

"The same type they used before, the Three O'clock Welder."

"The welds ought to hold then, that's a great machine for that job."

"That's what Lester said, and that's why he wants you out there as soon as possible. Between the two of you the problem will be solved in no time. I know you can figure out what's wrong."

"Okay then, I'll meet Glen at the airport, what time?"

"A little before noon. You know you have to fly to Kansas City, then fly to Mitchell, South Dakota, then rent a car and drive to Pittstown. If you want to you can spend the night in K.C. and go the rest of the way the next day. That way you'll get to Mitchell in daylight and you won't have to drive into Pittstown at night."

"Sounds like a good idea."

"Keep in touch."

"Yeah, yeah, so long."

Letty had followed Tom to the kitchen and was listening to his side of the conversation, which didn't tell her much. She was full of questions. "What's the story?"

"They are having trouble with the horizontal welds on a surge tower at a dam site in South Dakota."

"What is a surge tower?"

"It is a big thing that's about a hundred feet high and fifty feet in diameter made of one and a quarter inch, high strength steel."

"What does it do?"

"You know that a dam has one or more turbines, and as the water runs through a turbine it generates electricity."

"Yes, I know that."

"Well, when they want to stop the turbine for any reason, they divert the water away from the turbine into a surge tank. That way, the water bypasses the turbine without putting much pressure on it."

"You mentioned a great machine, tell me about that."

"It's a welding machine that runs like a little tractor around the rim of the tank. It has two welders in it, one on the inside the tank and the other on the outside. They communicate by telephone, while welding horizontally, and automatically."

"That sounds quite ingenious."

"It has been used for a long time. We used it when we built the original surge towers over thirty years ago."

"Well, how do you get those large pieces together so the little tractor can run around the rim?"

"Originally, there were plates of pre rolled steel, each about ten feet wide. It took about fifteen of them to make a course, or a circle about a hundred and fifty feet in circumference. Then they tack, that is, put a temporary vertical weld on it to hold the circle together. They do that to two circles, then with a huge crane; they lift the arcs making the circle rest on top of another one. Oh, I forgot to tell you that the bottom circle has flat edges and all the circles or courses after that have one flat edge and one beveled edge. The beveled edge is joined to the flat edge."

"Why is that?"

"That way it allows the welding wire in the groove to form the root of the weld. To do this it takes ten passes on each side to make the weld. That's a total of three thousand linear feet to weld each course."

"I am impressed, then what do they do?"

"Then they pick up the machine with a crane and lower it down on another course. That one has been lowered onto the first two courses which are now welded together, inside and out. They keep on doing that till it looks like a big smokestack."

"It must take a long time to get all that completed."

"It is done five to ten times faster than a man can do it by hand. It saves time and the cost of man hours."

"How do they finish the vertical welds that were only tacked?"

"You have to have a vertical welder to do that. It's a small machine that runs on a ladder. It, too, goes inside and out, oscillating the welding torch in a zigzag and vertical motion. This is a most difficult weld to do by hand and it must be done very slowly so the molten metal doesn't drip down and out of the seam. The machine goes at exactly the right speed and is easier, faster, and forms a better weld."

"Tom, you should have been a teacher. I think I really understand everything you told me. You have a big job ahead of you, that is certain."

The next day dawned bright and sunny, good flying weather.

Letty needed her sunglasses against the glare of the sun. She was driving Tom to Lambert International Airport, St. Louis' busy airport. They had enjoyed a leisurely breakfast and had ample time to repack Tom's bag.

"What are you going to do while I'm away, any special plans?"

"I thought I'd fly out to L.A. and spend the week with Maureen and Jerry and play with the kids while you are gone. Now that I'm all packed, I feel like going somewhere. There's no sense hanging around here. Do you think you'll be gone more than a couple of weeks?"

"Well, I won't know till I see what's waiting for me, of course, but it shouldn't take much more than that. I don't want to rush though, Lester and I are going to talk about doing some more business and we have to iron out the particulars. Why don't you plan to be in L.A. for two or three weeks? You might as well make the trip worthwhile."

"Okay, I'll call Maureen when I get back and see if it will be convenient for me to go out there."

"I'm sure they'd love to have you. Maybe you can give them some quality babysitting while you are there, and they probably could get in some sailing."

"That would be fun for all of us."

"Oh, by the way, would you take back those boots? When I wear them with those khaki socks, they are a bit tight. Just get a half size larger and they will be just fine."

"Okay. I thought you should have tried them on," she said in a "I told you so" tone that comes natural to most wives. "I'll cancel our trip when I go to the travel agency to get my ticket to L.A. It's a good thing you thought to buy cancellation insurance. Were you still hoping we'd win the trip?"

"No, but you'll never give up!"

"It's a good thing we have our shots already, we won't have to bother with that when we can go."

"I'm surely glad that's over. I was sore where I was injected for about a week."

"Me too, but it wasn't too bad."

They drove to the disembarking terminal, but Tom couldn't unload his bag at the gate because he didn't have his ticket yet. They had said their goodbyes at home. Tom hated to say goodbye at airports and train stations, and they never did. Even during the Korean War he would go to the station alone. Letty knew he was too softhearted and didn't like to show emotion in public, though it took her awhile and some hurt feelings before she realized this.

Before Tom got out of the car he leaned over and gave Letty a quick kiss. "Bye, hon, have a good trip and I'll see you in a few weeks."

"Okay, be careful now, and I'll be at Maureen's if you can, call." She blew him a kiss as he retrieved his bag from the back of the station wagon. Then all of her attention was taken up negotiating around taxis, shuttles, and other wives dropping their husbands off as she was doing.

————— ···•••··· —————

When she got home, she brought in the mail. There was a large envelope from the travel agency, with all the tickets. There was other information about what to wear, what to bring along and what to leave home. She would have to rethink about the packing. She put the mail on the desk and went to the phone in the den and placed a call to L.A. to Maureen and Jerry.

"Hello, you have reached the Allen residence, leave your name and number at the beep and we will get back to you soon."

"Honey, this is Mother. I'll call you back in a couple of hours. If you are still away, I'll hang up and call later. I'll be talking to you."

She went to her desk and read the things from the travel agency. One of the things that caught her eye was a caution against wearing bright colors in the jungle because they might startle the animals. Letty mused to herself, *I guess that means the red suit stays home. I'm glad I bought the glen plaid things. I'll build my outfits around it and the khaki things. I'd better call and postpone everything and get new reservations for later.* As she was reaching for the phone, it rang.

"Hello"

"Hi, Mom, you rang?"

"Yes, that was quick. I wanted to see what you're up to these days."

"I've been cleaning my head off. I even cleaned out the closets and drawers! Jerry's folks are coming to visit for about a month. They arrive tonight. The kids and I just came back from the market. I'm going to bake a ham. It can hang out in a warm oven if the plane is late. We can have leftovers for sandwiches for lunch, or ham and eggs for breakfast if anyone wants that."

"I can see you are going to use everything but the squeal."

"Where do you think I learned that?"

"From old Depression-raised me, I guess, and the things I learned from my mother who had to make do with very little. How are Jerry and the kids?"

"They are all excited about Grandma and Grandpa's arrival. We all ought to have a good time."

"I know you will, tell them hello from Tom and me. I won't keep you, honey, I know you have a lot of last minute things to do. Call me after they leave and tell me all about it."

"Okay, Mom. Bye, I love you."

"Love you, darling, bye."

She hung up the phone and walked over to the desk. Her eyes fell on the tickets. She went back to the phone and punched the number of the travel agency that was on their letterhead.

"Archway Travel Agency."

"May I speak to Kathy Lemon, please?"

"Just a moment, I'll connect you."

"Kathy Lemon here."

"Hi, Kathy, this is Letty Murphy, the tickets arrived today, but I'm afraid I have to cancel." She hesitated. "Uh, er…" Then said in a rush. "One of the tickets, Tom, was called away on business, but I've decided to go alone."

"The price quoted was for double occupancy, so your ticket will be a bit more, but we can take it out of the refund on Tom's ticket. It's a good thing that Tom took out travel insurance when he booked the trip."

"Yes, he has a good head for business."

"Did you find the information helpful that I sent along with the tickets?"

"Yes, it changed my packing a bit, but I'm ready to go."

"I just heard today that the Hunter Amazon Jungle Adventure representative will be in Miami and will be on the plane to South America with you. He is Gordon Hunter Jr., the son of the owner."

"That will be fine. I feel better already, I was a bit uncertain about making the trip without Tom."

"No problem, if you need any help just call for your 'Lemon-aide.' The overseas phone number is on the reverse side of your luggage tag and also on my card in your packet."

"Thank you so much, Kathy, for the 'Lemon-aide' we have had all these years of excellent service. Bye now, I'll call when I return."

Letty held the phone button down till she heard the dial tone then pushed a series of buttons again.

"Hello"

"Hi, Jane, this is Letty."

"Hi, I haven't talked to you in awhile, though I have seen you drive in and out a few times."

"What's new?"

"Lots! I just put Tom on the noon plane. He'll be gone a few weeks. I decided to visit Maureen and Jerry while he was gone, but Jerry's parents are arriving at their house tonight for a visit. I didn't want to intrude on their time with them. Jim is in Houston for about six months. So on the spur of the moment, since I am all alone, I'm going on a jungle cruise down the Amazon."

"A jungle cruise! Whatever made you decide to do that?"

"Tom and I were going to leave Friday. We had the tickets and everything. Then Tom had some sudden business to tend to and had to leave. I was going to cancel the tickets. Tom still thinks I did. I'll have to let him know. I did cancel Tom's ticket, but since everyone was gone I decided to go alone. I guess the devil made me do it." Her giggle was positively girlish.

"Aren't you afraid of being in the jungle alone?"

"No, I'm really not. What could happen? It's a tour with experienced guides, so it ought to be safe enough. The same tour is taken every two weeks. What I called you about are my plants. Would you let me bring them over to your house while I am away?"

"Of course, bring them over now if you want to."

"I thought I'd load them in the back of the station wagon and back up into your driveway and I can bring them in through your garage."

"Okay, when I see you coming I'll open the door."

Jane had some tea and cookies ready, and when they finished moving the last plant, they sat down and Letty filled her in on all that had happened recently. She gave her a copy of the itinerary so if there was any emergency she could be contacted

"What time do you leave for the airport tomorrow?"

"I ought to leave by 6:30 a.m., which would get me there in plenty of time. I'll order the taxi to be here at six, that way if it is late I won't get into a stew."

"I know how you are about catching planes. You have to have lots of time to spare."

"I guess I have a complex about being on time."

"Letty, you know I always get up early and I have to do some grocery shopping anyway, so let me drive you to the airport."

"Oh, that would be too much of an imposition."

"No, it won't. You can bring me something from the jungle and we'll call it even."

"I'll be glad to do that, the ride will be great. I'll be ready to load my bags at 6:25 a.m., okay?"

"I'll be there, and on time."

Letty went back home and reorganized her luggage. The mail stop card was all filled in, all she had to do was mail it. She could do that at the airport. The excitement mixed with a tiny bit of guilt made her heart seem to beat faster. *What will Tom say? I'm going off without him and he doesn't even know it yet!*

Heeding the travel agency, she took some bright things out, put some other things in, put the luggage tags on them and brought them to the front door. She hesitated about the backpack. *Will I need all of that Boy Scout stuff? I'll be on a boat for heaven's sake! Oh well, Tom has it all packed so efficiently I might as well. There is room with all of Tom's things out.*

———

Tom Murphy and Glen Gleason drove to Pittstown, South Dakota, in a cloudburst.

"Wow, I am certainly glad that we decided to stay in K.C. overnight. I would hate to be driving in this at night!" Tom peered out the windshield.

"Me too, there is the motel, at last." Glen wiped some condensation from the glass.

They registered for their rooms and settled in. Glen came into Tom's room and they put in a call to Lester Thomas.

"Les Thomas here."

"Hello there, Les, This is Tom. Glen and I just checked into the motel. I guess no one is working today, right?"

"Not out at the site. I'm doing office stuff that I never get time for in good weather."

"Have you worked on your problem with the weld?"

"Yes, I thought maybe hydrogen was getting into the weld from the rain, or even the air. I checked the argon and carbon dioxide gas mixture and it was covering the weld all right, and protecting it from everything. That wasn't it."

"What about the gear box lubricant?"

"We use a special lubricant with a high tolerance for low/high temperature. No trouble there."

"Well, I guess Glen and I will hang out here till the weather clears. Call us here at the motel when you want us to show up at the site."

Glen turned on the TV news station, and he and Tom watched for awhile until it started repeating itself.

"This is going to be boring if the weather doesn't clear up soon."

"Did you bring any books, Tom?"

"Yes, two. I'm almost finished with one. Did you bring any?"

"Yes, I brought three, and some *Field and Streams*. We can trade off when we finish them if we are cabin-bound too long. I think I'll go back to my room, call June, then read awhile. Call me when you want to go to dinner. I guess we'll eat right here in the motel, right?"

"Right, I don't want to go out in that mess for anything. How about around six for dinner?"

"That is fine with me, see you later."

When Glen left, Tom put in a call for Letty.

"Hello"

"Hi. It's Tom."

"I was hoping it would be, how was the trip?"

"It was tough driving through all the wind and the rain, but we're settled in here, waiting to be able to start working whenever the weather allows. Let me give you my number here. Though once we are at the site I might be hard to contact. Sometimes we might stay in the trailer on the site. I guess we might as well not even try to get in contact too often, unless it's an emergency, it will be too difficult, okay?"

"That will be just fine because I'll be…"

"Here's the number, 555-342-1129."

"Wait, my pen isn't working." She searched and finally found one that worked.

"Okay, I'm ready."

"555-342-1129."

"Got it. Uh, ah, Tom, I decided to…"

"Wait a minute, Letty, someone's at the door. I guess it's Glen."

It was. There he was with a big grin on his face.

"Hold on, Let, it is Glen."

"What's up, Glen?"

90

"I've got the number of a pizza place, how about a snack?"

"Great, make mine with mushrooms, onions and pepperoni with extra cheese and no anchovies."

Glen left to phone in the order in his room.

"Letty, so, are you flying out tomorrow morning?"

"Yes, but..."

"How are you getting to the airport?"

"Jane next door is going to drive me. When I brought the plants over for her to babysit, she suggested it, and it sounded excellent to me. Also, I..."

"That's fine, it will make things easier for you."

"Oh, yes, she's a doll. Uh, Tom, I didn't get to tell you. When I was talking to Maureen..."

"How is she doing? Are they ready for a visitor?"

"More than that, she..."

"Be sure to take them out to dinner and stuff like that."

"Uh..."

"Oh, I know you will, You know how to do just the right thing, I didn't even have to mention it."

"Well, have a good time, and don't worry if you don't hear from me. I'll be busy and you'll be busy, so I'll see you when I see you, okay?"

"Okay, but I've..."

"Bye, darlin', take care now, love you."

"Love you too, honey, bye."

Letty hung up the phone. "Now, why did I do that?" she said aloud. She thought, *I should have told him about my trip. I guess I was afraid he'd be upset. Oh well, I can tell him later. I'll call him from the airport in Miami.*

Chapter Eight

A gathering of the council was waiting for Maeuma, the old Chief's son. Fully recovered now, he was healthy and strong and concerned about the discussion that had taken place when he was fighting the breath-stealing devil. Maeuma had vanquished him again, but it was not good to agitate the villagers and have them question his ability to rule. He must regain their confidence. That is why he took special care with his appearance today. He wore a new feathered head ornament for the occasion. The old one had become full of dust; a few mites had taken up residence and the feathers were faded. When he was ready, he strode to the meeting place where all the Elders were assembled

When they saw him, they stopped talking and gave him all their attention. Maeuma walked over to his father, who was seated on a stone throne-like platform and made his bow of veneration. This was done by placing the right arm, bent in a right angle against the forehead, while bowing at the waist. He took his place at Kanchinapio's side. The old Chief looked over the group of somber men.

"My children, we must decide if the Great Dagger needs to be fed with human life. Or if it can be nourished with the nearest thing to our own flesh, monkey flesh."

Maeuma rose and looked at all the men who were watching him. They were trying to discern any change in him.

"Look at me—I am well. The sacrifice of the monkey was enough. There is no need to do anything more. Any deed that would call attention to our village would result in troubled times for us. We have been hidden and at peace for many years. Our wise ancestors, though of many warring tribes, made peace among the members of these different tribes for their own benefit and safety. To disturb this pattern of benefit and safety would be foolish. Let us continue to follow the path of our wise ancestors and retain our safety."

Panteri, Kanchinapio's cousin, rose to speak. "We honor you, Maeuma, but we worry about our village if something should happen to you. What if you are dominated by this breath-stealing Devil's spells after our old Chief is with the Spirits?"

"We will wait until that event occurs," said Kanchinapio. "Then you can decide what actions to take if Maeuma becomes under the spell of the breath-stealing Devil again"

"We must decide now," said his cousin Panteri.

"Yes," said Wanapio, whose son had the deformed foot, "we must have a plan. I must know that my son is not to be used as food for the Great Dagger!"

Maeuma, who had seated himself when the Elder cousin, Panteri, began to talk, jumped to his feet again.

"We must never allow that to happen!"

Kanchinapio, the old Chief, and the others murmured assent.

"The plan will be, the next time Maeuma is felled we will discuss the possibility of sacrificing one of the Others. Then, if we decide to do so, we will let the fish eat the body," said Kanchinapio.

"So be it," said Maeuma. "You have spoken, Father."

The assembly agreed to do nothing now, and accepted the plan, if it was needed, to use at some future time.

The tribe went about its usual activities in the days that followed. At this season, they spent their time hunting, tanning the hides, and turning them into bedding.

Later they occupied themselves by trapping birds for their feathers and catching monkeys for pets or food. They even made a drink from the contents of the stomachs of monkeys or macaws, mixing it with water and letting it ferment. It was a favorite. The men wove weeds and grasses into ceremonial masks. They would dance in them. Masked dancers represented the souls or the spirits of animals and fish. They were completely covered, with the masks made of buriti fibers; all that could be seen was their hands and feet. If the dancer was the spirit of a wild pig, his mask would have clusters of pig bristles stuck into the headdress. Pig hoofs made into rattles worn around the ankles completed the outfit. Bird Spirit masks had the red feathers of the red macaw on the headdress and on their bows. The masks of Up'e represent the spirits of their enemies that they have slain in battle. Another mask, in the form of a giant face, was carved from the umba'iba tree. Holes were bored into the wood for the eyes and mouth. Then they covered it with beeswax and decorated it with red macaw feathers and mother-of-pearl. They made the headdress on top of this of black hawk feathers and the red macaw.

They forbade the women to see this, but some of them would try. If they caught such a woman, they would carry her into the forest and all would rape her. Then she would have no steady man and must become a prostitute.

Preparation of food and preserving it was a constant chore for the women. The mainstay food was mandioca. It was high in starch and gave a feeling of fullness and quick energy, but the vitamin and mineral content is nonexistent. The women made mandioca flour from the plant that grows wild and in that state is poisonous. The Indians squeeze out the poisonous juice from the grated root. They toast this residue into gritty fragments, like gravel mixed with sawdust, which they sprinkle over other food, eat as a snack, or put it in their soup.

They also had fish, yams, peanuts, bananas, and Kwai soup, made with peanuts. Also, fish soup made with manioc flour and peppers. Other things are on the menu also, like insects and caterpillars. They squeeze out the insides of the caterpillars and eat only the skin. It is said to taste like rubber bands!

Chief Kanchinapio decided to have a feast like this, because the storehouse was full and their needs were met, and no one was sick or injured. He wanted to help them forget Maeuma's former problems. It was time for a celebration, so he declared a feast in the honor of Maeuma's recovery.

The revelry lasted three days. There was much dancing and drinking Kashiri. That is the fermented drink the women make by chewing and holding sweet potatoes in their mouths and returning it to the container. The result is let stand for two days. Their saliva is the fermenting agent. It becomes strongly alcoholic. Then the women add the juices of palm fruit, pineapple and sugarcane. It is a refreshing drink if one doesn't dwell on how it is made.

There were many people who excelled at story telling. The feats of valor in past wars, or on the recent hunting expeditions were retold and extolled. Historic tales about the times when the spirits of the Old Ones were with them, were recounted. The combination of drinking, dancing and merriment ended with lovemaking and not a few of the women were left with child as a result.

Some of certain tribes' descendants perform a phallic dance, in which each dancer holds a phallus made of bark attached to two cones full of seeds. This is to entice the spirits to bestow fertility to both women and the earth. The dancers are first made wildly erotic by drinking Kaopi. This is a drink that puts the person in a hypnotic trance, capable of feats of telepathy. The dancers perform an animated dance during which the bark and cones are manipulated with unmistakable meaning and the seeds are scattered in all directions. Promiscuity exists before marriage, but not after. Usually there is greater marital fidelity among them than some Christians. Polygamy exists, but is usually limited to the chief, who may have as many as twenty wives.

A chief may offer a visitor one of his wives, but a monogamous warrior would kill to protect her from others. Some believe that whites were born when an Indian woman had sex with a monkey.

They are mostly naked. They wear a few beads on neck or waist. The men wear tiny grass shields tied off on their foreskins that make their penises point skyward.

Some of the men still wear large red wooden disk stretching his perforated lower lip.

The women carry infants in a woven straw sling lying across their bodies. An unmarried girl who wishes to be let alone may wear a virginity shield. This is a triangular bit of pottery three inches across, curved to fit and sometimes is decorated with colorful designs. Then if a woman wishes to attract love she wears the vaginal bone of a freshwater porpoise.

In another tribe, an adolescent girl is kept confined for six months in a special hut until puberty is passed. She is made drunk to dull the pain, and then her relatives join in pulling every hair from her head, causing it to swell to a large size. A baldhead is a sign that she is on the marriage market.

Maeuma and Teptykti feasted and danced along with all the others. They had a wonderful time. Kamanar'e danced too for a little while, in an odd little way. The three of them were drinking Kashiri, not the stronger Kaopi. They were all a little tipsy and exhausted with all the dancing. Maeuma wanted to go into the jungle with Teptykti very much. Wanapio had asked him not to before the feast.

"Teptykti is too young and I ask you as a loving father to let her wait for one year. She loves you very much and would go willingly into the jungle with you. If you love her at all, you will wait. She is too young. The two of you can continue the feast and be with Kamanar'e and have a good time being together. Will you grant me this favor? I know it is too much to ask, but I do ask it."

Maeuma did as Wanapio asked. Teptykti was a little upset when he didn't ask her, as she was expecting him to run in the jungle with her. She kept hinting to Kamanar'e to leave them, but he had his orders from his father and didn't dare leave them alone. They had fun together dancing and eating and drinking and getting sillier and sillier as time went by and as long as the Kashiri lasted. The three of them fell asleep at last. They awoke with the rest of the partygoers with a very bad headache. Uanica was prepared though, he had gallons if a painkilling potion in the morning and ladled it out generously.

"How are you feeling, Teptykti?" Maeuma asked the next day

"My head is starting to feel better, but it really hurt this morning before I had some of Uanica's potion."

"The same thing happened to me. Uanica has been teaching me how to use herbs and other things to ease sicknesses. He didn't tell me about his potion yet. That is the next thing I want to learn."

Maeuma noticed that Teptukti was not as vivacious as usual. She seemed to be in a somber mood. Since she said she was feeling better it probably wasn't physical. He asked, "Are you all right?"

"Yes," she answered, but she still wasn't smiling as she usually was.

"You seem sad."

She turned away and hung her head.

"Please tell me why you aren't your happy self," he coaxed.

"It wouldn't be good for me to say."

"If you won't tell me what is wrong, how can I change things, or help to make things good again?"

"I thought you had warm feelings for me."

"I do, Teptykti. I have very warm feelings for you." Her back was toward him. He placed his hand on her shoulder and turned her toward him.

She still hung her head as she murmured, "Why was I not good enough to go in the jungle with you?" She raised her head and looked into his eyes. Tears were brimming in hers.

His heart melted in his breast. He drew her to him in an embrace. "I wanted to very much, but I had promised your father that I would not. You are too young and it is better that you and I wait awhile before we do that."

"You wanted to?"

"More than I ever wanted anything."

"We will wait then?"

"Yes, we will."

The usual sparkle returned to her face. Her sweet smile had returned. Everything was fine again.

Chapter Nine

There was a soft knock at the door. Fenton was dozing in his chair and a forgotten newspaper lay crumpled in his lap. He went to the door and opened it a crack. He could barely make out the figure furtively hunched beside the door.

"Who is it?"

"It's me—Oram."

"Come in quick, did anybody see you?"

"No, I hung out at the airport till dark, then took the jitney to the edge of town. I walked the back streets and alleys till I came to your house. I waited awhile to see if anyone was about. When no one came, I rang the bell."

"I knew I did the right thing when I called you." Fenton motioned for him to sit down and closed the door. "Have you had anything to eat?"

"No, and I'm starved. What's in the refrigerator?"

"Cheese, sausage, lots of stuff for a sandwich, but no beer though. I've been on the wagon."

"No kidding? I didn't think you would, or could, ever do that."

"I have to if I'm going to pull off this deal that I have in mind."

"That's why I'm here, no doubt."

They walked into the kitchen, still clean and neat from the great cleanup. Fenton now found it easier to maintain by cleaning often and not letting it go for too long and then tackling the mess.

Fenton began to fix Oram a sandwich and poured them both cold drinks made from a lemon-flavored powder.

Sitting at the kitchen table, they got down to the business at hand.

"Tell me about this great deal, Fenton."

"There is a remote tribe that is now not so remote since they built the road across the jungle. They have a ceremonial dagger with the hilt made of a giant emerald. So, if you and I can't con some obscure native out of that dagger, then we might as well give up."

"Do you think we could get away with it?"

"I know we can, but we have to keep quiet about it and do our looking under the guise of a jungle cruise. I will hire you as a helper and you can quiz the natives along the way and see what you can find out. We won't speak English at all, just Portuguese; whites and blacks will not be on their guard around us. You never know what information we can pick up that way. We can forget hiring you out to GWH. He'd find out all about you. Anyway, Nat is too shrewd.

"We'll keep our eyes open on the next trip. You can scout around to find the tribe with the emerald dagger. When you rejoin us, we will bring the customers back. Then, with money from that trip, we can return and make the grab, just you and me? Huh?"

"Right, I'll go find a place to live, maybe with my family or an old friend, and when I get things ready I'll come back."

"That sounds just about right to me."

Orem said goodbye with a grin that showed his beautiful white teeth gleaming out of his shiny, brown face. He was handsome and had broken quite a few hearts back in New York. Which is why his English was so good. He had a lot of help from his lady friend. A grade school teacher from Bel'em, educated by those same missionary Sisters.

The Sisters had found a job for her in New York while she continued her education in a school the Order ran there. She saw that he had an unusual intelligence. The missionaries who had given him his name taught him Portuguese; he was easy to teach. He had also learned many native dialects from the other Indian children in the orphanage. He was eager to learn and made himself well liked by those in charge. She was influential in getting Orem sent to a missionary high school in New York.

There he discovered another life. He graduated, then left the school and began a seamy life on the streets. Orem forgot the good things he was taught and learned from lesser models.

Then he met Lila, a young black paralegal who fell hard for his good looks and virile body. Between bouts of savage sex, Lila was determined to educate him, not only in the ways of the city but in "white" English. He used some English, but Lila said it was "black" English. He had stopped talking the missionary way and adopted the jargon of the New York streets. It was crude and the syntax unclear and he misused words, like "axe" for asks. He really knew better, but he wanted to fit in. Sometimes his friends thought he was showing off, or "talking white." He knew some people who talked "white" at work, but felt that they had to talk "black" in the neighborhood.

Lila was a good teacher and he was an apt pupil. She wanted him to learn so he could get, and hold, a good job. He was very intelligent and learned quickly. He had a fantastic memory and once told something, he never forgot it. It was a compatible union, for a while. She persuaded a friend who ran a small convenience store to hire him and it was in this store that he was caught stealing, once too often. Orem was a thief, and an astute one. He and his ladylove had a falling out because she was honest and abhorred dishonesty. He tried to reform, but it just wasn't in him so she was forced to break off with him.

It was soon after, that the phone call from Fenton brought him back to South America.

After about an hour of conversation with Fenton, Oram slipped out the door and made his way to his sister's house.

His welcome was warm, and two of his nephews shared a bed so he could have one of theirs. Oram had presents for the family. He had secreted his bag at the side of Fenton's house during their visit. Orem knew Fenton didn't want him to bring anything from the U.S.A., but he couldn't leave his treasures behind. Ballpoint pens, throwaway razors, and a small solar powered calculator made a big hit. His present for his sister was a bikini in a wild print of flowers, the colors of which never grew in any garden or jungle either, for that matter. They were glad to see him again and made him welcome. He always made them laugh and was there to help whenever it was needed.

The next evening, around happy hour at the Bola de Borracha, Fenton went in and ordered a soft drink. Dave was glad to see him stick to his vow to stay on the wagon. He joined in on the conversation between the regulars as they discussed the news of the day. After a bit of chitchatting someone mentioned GWH and the sweepstakes winners. Fenton became quiet and listened.

"I hear he's been talking to that Garson fellow that told us about the emerald handled dagger."

"Ed Garson? I thought he wasn't talking to anyone about it anymore."

"Well, he and GWH have always been very close. Ed trusts him, I guess."

"Did Ed tell him anymore about that monkey business?"

"I think he did because GWH has been buying maps and looking for natives that can speak as many of the native languages as he can find."

"That can only mean one thing, he is going to contact them." Fenton said his goodbyes to those present, paid for his drink and went down the road to Hunter's office.

Though it was past the usual quitting time, GWH and Nat were still finishing the day's paperwork. Ryti had gone for the day. She was at home fixing Nat's dinner.

GWH and Nat looked up apprehensively when they saw who had entered.

"Howdy, GWH, howdy, Nat."

"Hello, Fenton, what's the good word?" GWH asked.

"I just wanted to say I'm sorry about that argument we had awhile back. It was all my fault. The drink got the better of me, and I thought I ought to come by and mend some fences."

"That's okay, Fenton, I'm glad to see you looking better."

"How's business?"

"Okay, my son is coming with me on the jungle cruise Saturday."

"Is that right? He must be getting to be pretty near grown by now."

"Yes, he is out of college and I'm trying to get him interested in going into business with me."

"Are you thinking about retiring?" Fenton asked, hopefully.

"No! As long as I can keep going, I'll stay with the company. I enjoy what I do too much."

"I heard you were talking with Ed Carson about that tribe that sacrificed the monkey."

When Fenton said that, it was clear to GWH why he had come to see him and the reason for the big reconciliation scene.

"What Ed told me is confidential, Fenton, and I'm not at liberty to say anything about it. I gave my solemn word."

"Are you going to try to find that tribe?"

"I might after this next cruise is over. I plan to let Bud take the next one out, and I'll go on an expedition into the jungle with Ed and see what I can find."

"Would you mind if I went along?"

"I don't think that would be a good idea. We want to keep it small, just Ed and me and some natives that can speak some dialects that between us we can't understand. I am looking for someone now. If you know anyone that fits the description, send him to me."

"I might know someone at that. Nat, do you know a guy named Oram?"

Nat had been clearing papers off the desk, filing some, and tossing the rest in the wastebasket. He looked unconcerned, but he had heard every word that was spoken.

"Can't say if I do? I know of him, Mr. Cranshaw. Wasn't he taken in by the missionary Sisters with that bunch of orphans that got into trouble for stealing? I heard that someone from there took him to America some years ago with some church group. I have never met him, though."

Fenton realized he had made a mistake, he didn't want Nat to know Oram spoke English. *Oh well, it's too late now,* he told himself. "He just came into the town recently, he has been living in the U.S.A. and is visiting some of his family. I heard he speaks quite a few dialects. You ought to track him down to see how well he speaks and just what he speaks."

"I just might have Nat do that, Fenton, thanks for the tip."

"Well, now that things are all patched up, I'll be on my way. If you change your mind about that trip, let me know. So long." He gave a little half salute, half wave as he went out the door.

"Now, what do you think of that, Nat? Do you think that whole visit was a fishing expedition?"

"I think you are right about that. Do you think I ought to look up this guy visiting that family?"

"Do you think you can find them? He didn't mention the family's name."

"I don't think I'll have any trouble. A newcomer is always news."

"See what you can find out tonight. Let's get out of here, I'm starved."

———•———

That evening Nat was walking down a path that led from the unpaved road through the poorer native section. He passed a house; the family was sitting outside and laughing and talking. Nat looked over and saw a cluster of crystal-colored bubbles floating toward him. It startled him; he had never seen anything like it. He stopped, then walked over to them.

"How do you do that?"

"You dip the stick with a hole in it into the magic water and blow softly on it and the balls float out." The boy holding the wand demonstrated by blowing some bubbles his way. They all laughed.

"Where did you get that?"

"My Uncle Orem brought it to us. Many other gifts too."

"Where is he now?"

"He went into town to see his woman friend."

"You are lucky to have a good uncle, where did he get that magic water?"

"I guess he got it in 'Merica. He just came home from there."

"It's been good seeing the balls, I must go home now."

In answer the boy blew another blast of bubbles at him, then guffawed.

———•———

The next day, Nat told GWH all about his encounter.

"Hm, Fenton mentioned the name Orem. He seemed very anxious for us to hire this 'friend.' I wonder what he is trying to do? He does sound too good to be true. Nat, try to see him and find out what he's all about."

"I'll go to the marketplace this morning and see what I can see. I'll be back around noon, shall I bring some fruit and cheese and stuff for lunch?"

"Good idea, see you later. I'm going to call Ed Garson and set a date for our trip."

It was a busy morning at the market. Produce of all kinds was stacked in mounds. Flies were a problem and each vender was trying by various means to keep them off their goods.

Nat joined a few of his friends outside a café for a cold drink. It wasn't long before the subject of the new arrival was mentioned. Nat listened to their conversation.

"Did you see the new outfit Mikant'u is wearing today?"

"Strange flowers, never did see flowers like that."

"Looks good though."

"Anawanti, her man, has a new calculating device, very magical"

"Where did they get their new things?" asked Nat.

"Her cousin came back from long time in 'Merica,' and brought many presents."

"What's his name?"

"Don't know, she calls him by his child name, but he is old enough to have his new name now. He had a foreign name, but I don't know it."

The men changed their names at least three times, sometimes more. The women changed their names at least twice. Their childhood names made them ashamed. It is no wonder because they might be names like "Kai" which means monkey, or "Chiwi," which is the name of a small jungle rat. A boy lost his childhood name when he began to wear a penis band—just about the only clothing a male jungle Indian wore. Girls changed their names on the occasion of their first menstruation.

Some men changed their name when they "tie their hair," or go through the ritual of becoming a man. An adult would sometimes change his to honor a deceased kinsman.

So, it was no wonder the men didn't know Orem's current name.

These were city Indians, but they fell into the old ways when they were together. They wore regular clothes and didn't paint their faces, but the mind set is hard to change.

Nat was certain the new man was Orem. It remained to be seen what he called himself now.

———————

Nat did his shopping for their lunch and ate some of the fruit as he strolled back to the office.

GWH was on the phone when Nat returned.

"Large packages, huh? Well, how big are they? When will it be delivered to the hanger? Okay. See you soon."

Only hearing one side of the conversation Nat was puzzled. "What was that all about?"

"Bud's big surprise for my birthday. It has arrived, along with a fellow to put it together and check it out. I guess I'd better call Bud and tell him it's here. It is a wonderful gift, I don't know what to say to him."

"You just don't know how to say thank you, that's all. Just say 'It's what I have always wanted, thank you very much.' That will cover anything."

"I guess you are right about that. Toss me some of that fruit, will you, Nat? Let's take time out for lunch while you tell me what you found out about Orem, then we'll go over to the hanger and see this guy about the helicopter."

———————

When they reached the hanger, they saw a group of large containers there. GWH went in the office and met the pilot, Ken Johnson. He had ordered the containers hauled there from the port and signed all the necessary papers. GWH made arrangements to keep it in the same hanger with his old, but trusty helicopter. GWH and Nat were both checked out in helicopters, but this was very advanced, it didn't even have a tail rotor.

Ken walked them through all the particulars and details about the new helicopter.

"This is a MD Explorer." Ken pointed to the machine as he handed a large envelope GWH. "Here is a brochure from the McDonnell Douglas Helicopter Company. I just came from their Mesa Arizona plant. It is an eight place, twin-turbine that features the NOTAR rotorless tail system."

"I was wondering," said Nat. "I've heard of them, but this will be the first one I've ever seen,"

"Wow," GWH said, still in awe over the marvelous gift.

"Whew! This is some hot potato," whistled Nat, reading the brochure. "I need time before I solo in that!"

"I'm not here to give you a lengthy aerodynamics lesson. I'm here to fly with you by commercial airline to Mesa Arizona after I put her together and do a test flight. Mesa is where McDonnell's factory training school is for flying and maintaining this bird. Your son paid for the school for both of you. When do you think you could be ready to leave?"

Both GWH and Nat were flabbergasted at this news. GWH took awhile to digest this, but said with a grin. "Well, let's get started." GWH laughed.

Ken said, "Wait a minute! I've got to rest a bit. Then I have to do my thing getting this whirlybird ready for business. I'd say we can leave next week."

"That's fine with me!" said GWH. "That will give me time to tie up a few loose ends and pack some duds."

"I'll be right behind you, boss!" Nat smiled.

"We can use the time to go over the brochures and learn a little more about this sweet baby, Nat. We can watch the work that is done here and check out the way she operates in the test flight. We'll be more familiar with her before we start the school."

"How come you just can't check us out here? Why do we have to go to Arizona?"

Ken said, "Well, Nat, they have a better setup there and better teachers. That's all they do. Some police and all DEA pilots are required to take factory flight training for safety reasons, and various large corporations send their pilots there for training also. Your son just wants you guys to be safe. After all, the people who know the aircraft best can provide the best training."

"I guess we just have to be patient, huh?" GWH said.

When it was all assembled, gassed up and ready for the test flight Ken said, "There it is, I guess you want to get in, huh?"

"That sounds about right," said GWH. He looked at it, cherry red, shining in the hazy sun peeking through the misty clouds. He went over to the open door of the helicopter and climbed in. Like a child with a new toy he began to explore all the gadgets within. He opened a sliding door and discovered a peculiar red bundle secured with a nylon cord.

"Hey, Ken, what's this red thing?"

"That's a Bambi bucket, Bud paid extra for that."

"And what the Hell is a Bambi bucket?"

"It's what air support units of police and fire departments use to fight fires in the deserts and mountain areas in the States. This one is a seventy-gallon one, but some of them carry ninety gallons. All are wired with electrical connections needed to operate the buckets that can be unpacked and installed in minutes."

"Oh, yes, I saw it in the brochure, but I didn't know that is what they called it."

"How much does a thing like that weigh with a full load of water?" Nat asked.

"About 600 pounds, and it can do its job with a full load of fuel too."

"Wow! How do you like them apples?" GWH was impressed.

"But why did Bud get us one? We aren't in brush fire country around here."

"He's been reading about the burning of the rain forest and I think he may mean to do something about it."

"Oh, boy, he could get into trouble there. Some very influential characters are running those operations, somewhat ruthless too, I've heard."

"Then I suggest you caution him convincingly. These college boys get fired up about saving the environment and lose all prudence in the face of reality."

"The kid's right though, but I think I can head him off in a different direction. I'll keep him so busy he won't have time to unfold his Bambi bucket."

"Boss, we better get back. I've got things to do before we take off, and you do too."

"Okay, Nat. Come on, Ken, bring your school books. I have a place where you can bunk at my house. I can look over your papers at home. It is going to be a great adventure going to that school." He laughed. "Hunter's Aerial Adventure!"

Chapter Ten

Bud Hunter was shuffling through his notebook. He was in Miami. Arriving from St. Louis the day before, he had checked in at the airport hotel. Then he satisfied himself that all the rooms were set aside for the contest winners and the Murphy's. The fruit and wine were in all the rooms. Only fruit in the single room for Miss Evans, he still didn't know her age so he stayed on the safe side.

The Evans family was driving in from Fort Myers Beach and going directly to the hotel. He had to meet the flight from New York in an hour. The Masons from New Hampshire, Lois Chastaine and Nora Smythe from Boston all had taken the same plane out of New York. He would stand outside the arrival gate with his sign HUNTER'S AMAZON ADVENTURES in view and wait until they all found him. Things just had to go well, he didn't want to make a mistake and disappoint his father.

GWH had called Bud in St. Louis from Mesa. He told him how delighted with the helicopter and how fascinated with the school he and Nat were at. He was grateful, but very embarrassed in showing it. Bud knew that and brushed it off, very like GWH would have done himself. Things looked like they were going to work out okay between them.

"Mr. Gordon Hunter, please answer a hospitality telephone."

Fleetingly he wondered who was calling his father, recovered and sheepishly walked toward the nearest white phone. Even in college he was known as Bud Hunter, only official papers had his full name on them.

"Gordon Hunter here."

"One minute, I'll connect you"

"Mr. Hunter, this is Kathy Lemon of Archway Travels. I have been trying to locate you to tell you that Mr. Tom Murphy will not be joining you at this time. However, his wife Letty is on the flight from St. Louis. The hotel told me where to find you."

"Thank you, Ms. Lemon, I appreciate it. Do you know what happened? Why the change?"

"Mr. Murphy had to tend to some unexpected business and Mrs. Murphy decided to come alone."

"Mmmmm, that's unusual."

"Don't worry about Letty. She is a very good traveler. I have booked them on many trips and they do well, even in an occasional crisis."

"Well, thanks very much, I'll be sure to meet her and give her your greetings."

"That will be fine, I hope you all have a pleasant cruise."

"I hope so too, Goodbye and thank you."

"Goodbye."

Bud hung up and made his way to the gate where the plane from New York would soon discharge its passengers. He held his sign, "HUNTERS AMAZON ADVENTURES" so it could be seen. While he was waiting, he enjoyed the pastime of people watching. He marveled at their diversity; from the grungy, hirsute, often tattooed young people with tattered jeans and backpacks to the sleekly coifed, expensively clad business people lugging their laptop PC's so they can still carry on their commerce while in the sky. He smiled at the young families bravely corralling their young and their carry-on baggage until time to fly off, perhaps to doting grandparents.

"Hi, you must be here to meet us."

"Yes, I'm Bud Hunter, you must be Don Mason," he said, startled back to the present. "And you must be Mrs. Mason." He shook her hand and then Don's.

"So glad to meet you. You may call me Ellen," she said with a shy smile.

"Call me Don," he replied, heartily shaking Bud's hand.

"Most people call me Bud, and only my Dad can get away with calling me Buddy."

"Bud it is then, shall we go?" Don asked.

"Let's wait here for a moment, there are two more of our party on this plane."

It wasn't long before Nora and Lois, seeing the sign, joined them. After greetings and introductions were exchanged, they went to the baggage area. Bud helped them round up their bags and load them onto the hotel's shuttle.

"The shuttle will take you to the hotel, I must stay here and meet another plane coming in from St. Louis, but we are all to meet in the hotel dining room at seven-thirty. I'll see you then."

"Oh, Bud, we have a special evening planned. A play and a night on the town. Where shall we meet you tomorrow?"

"We'll all meet in the café for a continental breakfast at the hotel, Don. I'll see you then."

He left the four happily chatting and becoming acquainted.

———— ••••◆•••• ————

Bud made his way to another concourse to wait the forty-five minutes before Letty's plane was scheduled to arrive. He stopped by a vending machine and bought a candy bar. He hadn't taken time for breakfast and it was now past noon and he was beginning to feel it. As he waited, he began to worry about the lady he was to meet. He knew she was a "senior citizen" traveling alone, and he was not too thrilled about that. That meant he would probably be the one designated to shepherd her around on the trip.

He had previously decided that he would probably get the job of looking after Ginger Evans. They had not met, but she was at least near his own age.

He was alerted to the arrival of the plane from St. Louis by the squawk of the speaker above his head.

Hmm, they are early, must have had a tail wind, he mused as he picked up his sign and made his way to where the passengers would disembark. He smiled in spite of his misgivings when he was approached by the smiling, pert, vaguely familiar, little white-haired lady wearing a backpack and carrying a large purse.

"You have to be Mr. Hunter," she said as she offered her hand to him, blue-gray eyes twinkling, and wondering where she had seen him before. She could never forget that red hair and those blue, blue eyes.

"Just call me Bud, Mrs. Murphy. I'm Gordon Hunter's son and I refuse to answer to Junior."

"In that case, I am Letty and where have we met before? I know I have at least seen you somewhere. I won't fret about it, because it will come to me. Did Kathy Lemon tell you that Tom is unable to join us?"

"Yes, she found me here at the airport a little while ago and told me he had other business."

"He does, and I must find a phone right away to tell him I am here and not in California."

Bud pointed to a bank of phones along the wall and tried to figure out what that meant while she was punching in endless numbers on the phone.

"Hello, is Mr. Tom Murphy there? Oh, will you tell him that his wife called and that I'll call again this evening? Thank you very much, Goodbye."

"What now?" Letty said.

"Well, I guess now we go get the luggage."

114

They started walking the long walk toward the baggage area, each searching their memories for a glimmer of recognition. Bud noticed her backpack and how incongruous it was, and then it came to him. At the same time she realized where she had seen him.

"The Army store!" they said in unison.

"I guess you found your husband."

"Did you find out what size you wear?"

"Yes, and you were a big help. Tell me about his thinking you are in California."

They went about the chore of getting the bags and loading them on the hotel shuttle. On the drive to the hotel she filled him in. He was told why she was there alone and why Tom didn't know where she was. He couldn't understand how that could happen.

She agreed to meet the rest of the party for dinner at the appointed time, then when she reached her room she made a beeline for the telephone. No luck again. She kicked off her shoes, curled up on the bed and read her current book until time to get ready to go to dinner.

―――― ∙∙∙●∙∙∙ ――――

She finished the book. She only had a couple of chapters to go, and put it down with a smile. It was a good one and she knew Tom would like it. Letty decided to get dressed and go down to the lobby and find something to wrap it in so she could mail it to Tom at the airport tomorrow. While she was waiting for her purchase, she viewed Bud through the glass partition of the shop. She hurried out to meet him.

"Bud, wait for me."

"Hi, Letty, I see that you are early too,"

"Yes, I finished the book I was reading and I didn't want to just sit in the room."

"Is your room comfortable?"

"Oh, yes, thank you for the goodies. I just wanted to see what's going on, how about you?"

"I was just about to place a call to my Dad to tell him everything is on schedule and we're leaving tomorrow."

"I'll go up to the room and do the same thing, I have been trying to reach Tom, but have had no luck. I want to wrap a book to send to Tom also. When I finish, I will meet you in the dining room."

"Okay, see you later."

Bud went to a pay phone and soon was talking to GWH.

"Hi, Dad, How was the flight back from Arizona?"

"Be-you-tee-ful! That bird is the greatest! Nat and have taken turns testing it out. The school was exceptional. I haven't had so much fun in ages. I really must thank you, Bud. It is a wonderful gift. Nat still can't believe our good fortune. How are things going there? Do you have all your chicks under your wing?"

"Yes, I surely do, those that are going. Tom Murphy had to cancel out, but his wife is coming anyway."

"They were that retired couple, weren't they?"

"Yes?"

"Do you think the lady can handle it alone?"

"You don't know the lady, Dad, She looks like she can handle anything. Don't worry, I can look after her if she needs it."

"Okay then, Bud, see you soon."

"Good-bye, Dad." He hung up and made his way to the dining room.

He spoke to the maitre d' about the evening's arrangements, then sat at the table and waited for the group to assemble.

Letty was the first to arrive; she looked regal in an orchid colored suit. The blouse was plain and it was a setting for the ornament she retrieved from Uncle Alfred's box.

"Hello again, Letty, here sit next to me," Bud said as he pulled out the chair for her.

"That will be lovely, thank you, dear."

"Did you reach your husband?"

"No, but I will try again after dinner."

"Here are Mrs. Chastaine and Mrs. Smythe," Bud said rising to meet them.

"Lois and Nora, please," said Nora, offering her hand.

After shaking hands with the two of them, he introduced them to Letty. He was still standing when Dennis, Carla and Ginger Evans arrived. Again introductions all around and everyone agreed to be on a first name basis. There was the generalized conversation you find among friendly strangers.

Don and Ellen Mason arrived in a flurry of apologies because they weren't staying. Bud made the introductions to Dennis, Carla, Ginger and Letty.

Bud said, "Don and Ellen, we will meet here at 7:00 a.m. The shuttle to the airport leaves at 7:30." They chatted a few minutes and they left for the theater.

They were all excited about leaving tomorrow. Even Don Mason, once he knew he had to go, entered into the swing of things. He was looking forward to the play and Ellen was in Seventh Heaven.

The remaining group had a delicious dinner, sprightly conversation and friendships were beginning to blossom when they said good night and went to their rooms.

Bud made arrangements for a wake-up call for everyone, including himself. They were to meet at 7:30 a.m. at the shuttle bus for the airport. Bud had suggested that they take advantage of the continental breakfast in the coffee shop before they left.

Lois and Nora were tired and went straight to sleep with only a little conversation about their new friends. Both agreed that it was a congenial group and they ought to have a fabulous time on the cruise.

Don and Ellen Mason were in a romantic mood after they returned to the hotel. Don opened a split of champagne and turned the radio to soft music and made love to Ellen sweetly, tenderly, and with no hint of any Wham-Bam at all.

Dennis, Carla and Ginger were too excited to sleep. They had taken a long nap after they arrived and weren't a bit sleepy. They played poker, dealer's choice, with Carla and Ginger choosing outrageous wild card combinations, while Dennis stuck to five-card stud. They used paper matches for chips, each match worth a penny. It ended after a long game of "In Between" with the bet being to match the pot. Ginger had won five dollars after they all settled up thanks to her good luck with "In Between."

The next day the maid shook her head at the destroyed matchbooks in the wastebasket. She wasn't surprised though, she had seen a lot worse.

Bud took a long soak in the tub, going over in his mind the events of the day. He was happy, things were going well and it looked like they were a compatible group. He went to bed, going over the things he had to see to tomorrow for the umpteenth time. He was delighted that the "old lady" was so spry and even more so that Ginger was the way she was and not some little kid. Sleep came upon him in about five minutes.

Letty, after a soaking bubble bath, put her hair in pins. In her nightgown and snuggled in the bed she tried again to reach Tom.

"Hello," answered Tom.

"Darling! I have been trying to get you, did they tell you?"

"I just came in the door, there is a red light blinking on the phone though. How are you doing! I miss you already."

"Miss you too, darling. What kept you so late? Are you working too hard?"

"No, but we have a lot of trouble here. It's too complicated to explain over the phone. The concrete base that this whole thing sits on accidentally had a huge electric charge go through the iron bars that strengthen it. This caused them to expand, then contract, and that caused a defect in the concrete. Now it will all have to be replaced before we can even start to do the main job we came out to do. Glen is going back to St. Louis tomorrow."

"When are you going to come home?" Letty asked, not knowing what to say or do, hoping he could catch up with her in Bel'em.

"Well, hon, I told you that Les and I were going over some plans for some other work he has for the company. We thought we could get that all ironed out while we were waiting for the repairs, then I won't have to make another trip. When we are ready to go again, Glen will come out and everything will be all finished and you and I can go on a vacation."

"That will be wonderful, honey, but I didn't get to tell you about..."

"Wait a minute, hon, Glen is yelling something and knocking at the door."

He answered the door and there was Glen, his hand covered by a bloody towel.

"Tom, I really cut my hand. My razor slipped off the washstand, and like a nut I made a grab for it. I sliced all four of my fingers! I was shaving tonight so I didn't have to take the time tomorrow.

"You and that damned straight razor! Why don't you use a safety or electric like everyone else? Wait till I hang up with Letty and we'll get you stitches. Damned showoff," he muttered as he grabbed the phone.

"Letty, I've got to go, Glen needs stitches in his hand! Call me tomorrow, Ah no, call me in a few days. I'll be so busy you probably couldn't reach me. Love you, Bye."

Letty stared at the now silent phone. "This is unbelievable," she said aloud, placing the phone back in its cradle.

Chapter Eleven

The plane landed amid the roar of the engines breaking the forward momentum in reverse thrust. There was a loud squeak as the tires hit the runway, a shuddery, bumpy few seconds as it slowed to a stop. Then the passengers sprang into life again. The long, lethargic flight made them stuporous, but the noise of the landing and the excitement of the moment shook that stodgy feeling off at once.

They began to unload the overhead compartments, gathering the paraphernalia that they believed they couldn't do without for the duration of the flight. They crowded the aisles and slowly moved forward. They returned the cheery goodbyes of the perky flight attendant, who deserved an Academy Award, and made their way to the exit.

A wave of humid, sweltering air hit them broadside as they trudged down the stairs, leaving them breathless. They struggled into the airport building and gratefully inhaled the cool air-conditioned, though stale, air there. Someone had mopped up a spill with a sour mop and it still tainted the atmosphere.

Bud was as helpful as he could be in assembling their bags. He was thankful for Nat's foresight in providing them with bright red luggage tags. It simplified his task and soon his charges were chattering happily as they boarded the air-conditioned bus that Nat had chartered to take them to Bel'em's dock.

GWH and Nat had their boat, *Cacador*, which means Hunter, waiting their turn to dock. They had to stand off till the officious dock steward cleared a place for them.

The ENASA boat was there. It is the government's bimonthly line to Manaus. Also, the "Amazonas" catamaran was loading passengers for its six-day cruise to Manaus. Diesel boats, spewing oily black smoke were taking up some space, some waiting for passengers, some waiting for cargo, and some for a little of both.

Since they were unable to board the *Cacador* immediately, Bud had the driver give them a tour of Bel'em.

He took them by the Ver-O-Peso, on Avenida Castilho Franca, where there were numerous stalls piled with cooked food, fruit, flowers, meat, fish and vegetables. There were blocks of stalls selling everything imaginable: Clothing, pottery, hammocks, even crocodile teeth, dried boa constrictor heads and sea horses. They saw shell rosaries in a stall next to a stall selling weird looking charms. They were made by believers of Macumba, a version of Voodoo, and positively a cure for any problem from love to money.

When the group wanted to stop and shop Buddy reminded them that they would have almost a whole day to explore on the trip back home.

"You don't want to carry the things you'd buy around with you the whole time. Anyway, prices are high here, things are much more reasonable at the villages we will visit, and not so much mass produced."

The bus brought them to the central square called the Praca de Republica, beautifully shaded by luxuriant plants, flowers and mango trees. As they drove down the Avenue Presidente Vargas they could see people of all ages enjoying a rest in the charming gazebos placed here and there. People were talking, eating, or just strolling along. Bud pointed out the Teatro Paz on the plaza. This is a beautifully restored theater of white marble built at the turn of the century during the rubber boom. It still has concerts, ballets and touring theater troupes.

On the way back to the port Bud had the driver stop at one of the many vendors to buy vatap'a. He figured that since it was cooked shrimp made with coconut milk they wouldn't pick up any bug. Besides, he wanted some himself, it is very tasty. Since the crowd was champing at the bit to get off the bus, this was a good opportunity to let them stretch their legs and spend some time.

When they reboarded the bus, he decided to give them some history of the area.

"Does anyone know when the Amazon was discovered?"

"Francisco de Orellana discovered the Amazon in 1592," Ginger spoke out. "He was with Pizarro looking for the mythical El Dorado, a wealthy lost Indian city. He split off from that group and explored the river. He didn't find anything but fights with the Indians and starvation which caused them to eat their shoes and saddles to keep alive," she said with a self-satisfied smile and a little swagger. "I once had to make a report on him for school, we could choose a subject and, since I knew we were coming on this trip, I chose Francisco de Orellana." She grinned, proud that she could show the adults her knowledge. She reminded herself that she was an adult, since she was eighteen now.

"You did well, that is exactly right," said Bud. He looked at her flushed face and was pleased at the sight. *She was going to be the best part of this trip*, he told himself. "Since we will be spending most of our time on and around the Amazon River, I have a note here about the 'Worlds Greatest River.'" Bud took a small notebook out of his breast pocket and proceeded to read from it:

"For sheer volume no other river even comes close to it. The Amazon is 3,900 miles long. The Nile River is 232 miles longer, but not nearly as wide, so the Amazon holds seventeen times as much water." Bud looked up from the book. "Perhaps you haven't seen the Nile, I'll pick one closer to home." He returned to the notebook. "The Amazon holds fourteen times as much as the Mississippi River, known as 'Old Man River,' which is the longest river in the United States. It flows 2,348 miles from its source in northwest Minnesota, to the delta in the Gulf of Mexico. The second longest river in the United States is the Missouri, which flows over 2,315 miles." Bud looked up from his notebook. He saw that they were still interested, so he continued. "The Missouri is known for the large amount of mud in its water. Pioneers called it the 'Big Muddy,' and farmers have said it is 'too thick to drink and too thin to plow.'"

Letty said, "I'm from St. Louis and I can relate to that. It is the Missouri that makes the Mississippi so muddy. It is clear to the north, but south of St. Louis it is entirely different."

"Compare that with the Amazon. It is forty miles wide downstream and for long stretches it rolls along five miles wide. Think how wide that is!" He looked up from his notebook and arched an apricot eyebrow over a piercing blue eye in emphasis. He returned to his notebook. "There are four basic types of rivers in the Amazon Basin. White water rivers are clear, pure rivers in the slopes of the Andes Mountains. Brown water rivers slowly collect sediment. The Amazon River is a brown-water river. Blue-water rivers are tributaries to the south of the Amazon River. They flow so slowly that the sediments sink to the bottom and collect in wide sections of the river. The black water rivers are tributaries to the north of the Amazon River. They get their brown/black color from rotting vegetation in the water. The vegetation usually sinks to the bottom in swampy areas before it reaches the main rivers. The Amazon Basin is about the same size as the United States without Alaska. Twenty percent of all the fresh water on earth is in the Amazon River. Some of that water comes from melting snow high in the Andes Mountains.

"There are at least two thousand species of fish in these rivers. Many are commonly caught for food. Others are caught for the tropical fish market. The local people use a variety of methods to catch fish. Harpoons, spears, nets and traps are used. Some Indians use bows and arrows, or use a potion they make that paralyzes the fish.

"The Amazon has five hundred tributaries; of these rivers that flow into it, fifteen of them are a thousand miles long!" He looked at Ginger. "Can you imagine that?" He looked back to the notebook. "It flows across 4,000 miles of South America. The Amazon River starts at over eighteen thousand feet elevation, in the Peruvian Andes. In spite of four hundred years of exploration there are still large tracts of it that remain unknown. It is constantly changing, and some parts are still uncharted. Some call it the 'River Sea.'" He closed his notebook and replaced it in his pocket.

"But, uh, Mr. Hunter." Ginger, suddenly shy and cheeks a peachy glow, stammered, not knowing how to address him.

"Please, Ginger, remember, we all agreed to use first names. I'd like everyone to call me Bud, or I'll even hold still for Buddy, but please, not Junior. How will that be? Is everyone comfortable with that?"

Everyone agreed and Bud gave his attention to Ginger. "What did you want to say, Ginger?"

"I just remembered something else from my report."

"Tell us then, honey," said Letty.

"Well, the reason Francisco de Orellana and his followers split off from Pizarro's group was because they wanted to find the famed 'warrior women.' They were thought to live in the mythical realm Amazon, ruled by women. The river was given the name Amazon because Orellana and his men had a glimpse of what they thought were women warriors along its banks." She smiled, secretly pleased with herself. Carla and Dennis were pleased also. She was their pride and joy.

Now, the bus was back on the quay. The *Cacador* was just beginning its docking process. Bud explained that the name of the boat meant "hunter" in Portugese and that GWH thought it was appropriate.

"I think that was very clever of him," said Lois.

Bud left the bus, had a brief shouting confab with GWH and returned.

He gave orders to the bus driver to let everyone off at the Gloria Café. The bus returned to the ship to wait to unload the bags.

When everyone was settled and had ordered a little something, he explained that GWH and Nat would join them when they completed the formalities of docking.

It wasn't very long when the two came into the café. The passengers-to-be greeted the owners, who came and sat near the group.

"Hello, I have waited a long time to see all of you." He gave Bud a hearty slap on the back.

"Hi, Bud, I see you made it okay?"

"Hi, Dad. Hi, Nat." He offered his hand to both of them to shake. "Let me introduce you to these fine people. I know you are familiar with their names, now let me match them up with a face." He went around the table and introduced the group to GWH and Nat.

"How was your time at the flight school?" asked Bud.

"Bud, that was the greatest gift I ever received! The plane is wonderful, and Nat and I learned so much at the school."

"I feel like I could repair anything that could ever go wrong," said Nat. "That is, if I had the right equipment. They even taught us how to put out fires with that Bambi thing. If there ever is a forest fire nearby, we can take care of it."

While they were in the café, the bus driver and some dockhands unloaded the bags from the bus and put them in the proper rooms in the boat. The tags had all the information, so there was no problem.

The *Cacador* was a three-deck river boat with an open lounge area on the top deck. The cabins were comfortable and clean, but small. They had bunk beds and a dresser, a tiny bath, two chairs and little else. The were clean and comfortable.

GWH insisted on good food, not gourmet, but surprisingly tasty for being in the wilds of a third world country. He and Nat saw to it that cold bottled water, a variety of sodas and beer were available when anyone felt the desire for something anytime throughout the trip. Of course, the coffeepot was full and available twenty-four hours a day in the dining room. It was emptied frequently because GWH hated the acrid smell of burnt coffee.

Though not a luxury liner, the *Cacador* was a good clean ship constructed in 1983. The crew cleaned the cabins and they replaced the sheets with clean ones daily.

When the group left the Café Gloria they made their way to the *Cacador* It was dark, though early, when they boarded and were shown their assigned cabins.

Letty had more room than the rest and made use of the top bunk for her bags. She did have more luggage than the rest—she never had learned to travel light.

Before they left Bel'em Letty tried to phone Tom, no luck. She talked to her daughter's answering machine and left an innocuous message. She mailed a letter explaining everything to Tom. She had written it on the plane and had been carrying it around with her waiting for a chance to mail it.

This had gone on long enough! she thought.

She joined the others. She told Bud, who had helped with the stamps, that it was mailed at last.

They all turned in early. It had been a very long day.

GWH, Bud and Nat were awake and talking about the duties of the trip, assigning tasks and schedules. They gossiped about the passengers. They were, after all, only human. They decided that it was a vigorous group and the trip ahead ought to be pleasant.

The *Cacador* pulled away from the dock and headed upriver at dawn the next morning. This section of the Amazon basin is appropriately called the Narrows because the boat must weave through a maze of small islets, at times coming close to the jungle shore. In the daytime small fishing boats can be seen bringing their catch to the markets of Bel'em. Other boats were loaded with bananas and vegetables. The back portion of these boats had a covered area, like a hut of woven sticks. They were strong enough for a person to sit on the roof. Canoes are very common for covering short distances, others used motors.

Gradually the passengers made their way to the dining room for breakfast. GWH was at the helm, so Nat was poised at the stove in the kitchen ready for orders. Bud was there to seat them and take their orders to Nat. They had many choices, and they were all good.

While they were eating, the native couple who were the rest of the "crew" were busy cleaning the cabins. They were an interesting couple. They belonged to the Mekranoti tribe. Both were orphaned as children and were raised by the Sisters in the same orphanage that Orem was, though Orem was there later. They spoke enough English to get by, but they usually spoke Portuguese together. They had almost forgotten their Indian language. They could speak it, but as a three-year-old would speak. Bep, the husband, was tall for an Indian. He was thin, but wiry and strong. He was in his late thirties and Kamerti was in her early thirties. At least that was what they thought they were, they didn't know exactly.

They did know that they had been married fifteen years in a Catholic ceremony at the orphanage. They were unhappy that they had no children, but they loved one another and had a happy life together. Their work for GWH in the tourist season gave them money to live in Bel'em in comfort during the rainy season. They spent their time then making native trinkets to sell to the tourists.

GWH allowed them a corner of the boat to display their handiwork for the passengers, and he made sure the prices were right. They soon learned what pleased the buyers and what they thought was just junk. Sometimes they were surprised. They were happy and pleasant to be around, so everyone liked them and treated them almost like pets.

After breakfast the passengers went to the top deck. There were comfortable chairs in conversational groups with a view of the river for everyone. Occasionally an Indian's boat loaded with produce for Bel'em would be seen floating with the current. He would paddle periodically to keep the boat on course. They were still in the Narrows, so GWH would have to steer away from the islands in his path.

It was a hot day and the humidity was high. Ginger put her hair in a ponytail to get the weight of her hair off her neck. Lois had a hair clip that pulled her medium length hair in a cascade up off her neck. Letty's white hair was shorter and curly with the dampness and off her neck. She and the other two wore sleeveless blouses. Nora had cut her hair before they left in a short shingle back that made her look young and boyish, and cute. Ellen's hair, on the other hand, was lank in the steamy weather. Although she usually wore her hair in a short fluff, she had let it grow longer and the weight of it pulled out the curl. She had a cool sleeveless dress on, but she looked uncomfortable.

"Lois, what a cute hair clip, I'll bet that makes you a lot cooler with your hair off your neck like that—becoming too," Ellen said, lifting her own hair off her neck.

"I have another one that you can have, Ellen. It is a brownish tan, sort of honey-colored like your hair. You can have it, I have an assortment of colors and I can spare it."

"Lois, how sweet of you, I thank you so much."

"Let's go to my cabin and get it now."

"Fine, I'm right behind you."

They left, and as they did GWH came in. He gave them a wave/salute combination and turned to greet the others. Don and Dennis had been talking together in the front of the boat. The merchant and the doctor were getting to be friends. Each was interested in the other's occupation and enjoyed telling the other about his own.

Carla was with them and when she saw GWH arrive she went to join the others. Don and Dennis followed. Dennis wiped his tanned forehead with a damp handkerchief. Its condition showed that it wasn't the first time that day that it had been put to good use.

GWH greeted them with a wave, showing a dark-stained armpit.

"It will get better when we get out of the Narrows and can pick up some speed, the breeze will dry us off a bit. Bud will take a turn at piloting the boat next shift."

Lois and Ellen returned, with Ellen's hair looking a lot cooler up in the hair clip.

GWH gave Lois an appreciative look. He smiled at her as he said, "We try to give each one a chance to do each job. Wait till you lay a lip on the dinner I am cooking tonight. Don't eat too many sandwiches at lunch, I want everyone hungry."

"My, you are talented. You guide, fly, pilot a boat and cook too? I am impressed," Lois said earnestly, fascinated by his rugged good looks.

"Well, you better wait till you taste it first," he replied, secretly pleased at the compliment. "I've got things to do in the kitchen, see you later." He turned and went down the stairs.

Ellen and Lois returned with Ellen looking sharp in her new hairdo.

"Ellen," Don said with admiration, "you look cute and cool, honey."

"Thank you, dear, I feel much better."

Carla, whose short reddish hair gave her no problem, had not heard the previous conversation and looked puzzled, but let it pass. She said, "Ellen, Don tells us that you and he are demon Bridge players."

"Yes, fortunately, we both enjoy the game."

"We do too, shall we have a game before lunch?"

"Sounds good to me, how about it, Don?"

"Where are the cards?"

While the Bridge game was in progress, Lois was, of course, languidly reading a best seller. What else?

Nora and Letty were getting acquainted relating the different experiences they had in their travels to the same cities.

Ginger, tired of watching the Bridge game and tired of the grown-up conversation, went to talk to Bud who was piloting the boat. She thought he was darling. Hoping that he would notice her, she strolled along the deck in his direction looking out over the water, but keeping him in her peripheral vision.

He was glad to see her coming toward him. *She looks…golden,* Bud thought. *She doesn't have the kind of skin most redheads have.*

Her father's darker skin tempered it and she had a golden tan. Bud always had to put on the strongest sun block or he would blister, just one other thing that annoyed GWH while Bud was growing up. May once gave GWH holy Hell for sending Bud back with a severe sunburn.

Ginger and Bud were getting acquainted too. They exchanged information about schools, their hometowns, and their lives before now. That inane, but fascinating small talk, exciting only to those who are falling in love. Words to be analyzed in private, gone over and over in the mind, reliving each inflection of every word.

CRACK! RUMBLE, CRUMBLE, THUNK! The motor stopped and slowly the boat stopped momentarily, then slowly moved backward with the current. Bud quickly threw out the anchor and steered toward the shore. By the time an angry GWH arrived, wearing a stained dishtowel tied around his middle for an apron, Bud had pulled the boat up to the shore and made it snug. He turned to face his angry father. Trepidation showed in his face. Just the look of fear GWH remembered from his younger days. It brought him up short.

"What happened, you hit a log?"

"I...I don't know. I was too busy stopping this thing to find out."

Nat came running toward them from aft. "We hit a big submerged log and it is stuck in the propeller, boss."

"It could happen to anyone, I've hit my share of logs and so have you, Nat."

"Sure have! Don't worry about it, Bud, we can fix it. We always bring extra gear for just this sort of emergency."

The passengers were all staring at the three of them, uneasy, to say the least.

GWH took the lead. "Bud, get the scuba gear on and see if you can get the log free. Nat, you bring the spare propeller here and start making it ready to install." He suddenly realized he had the apron on and swished it off. " While they are doing that we will have our lunch in the dining room, it's just about ready."

The group dispersed and soon was eating a satisfying repast of river fish of some kind and a large fruit salad. It was delicious.

Nat and Bud were still working away after the group was finished eating. To keep the passengers away from the work going on aft, GWH told them they would take a walk through the jungle and had them get on their walking shoes.

Soon they were following him through dense underbrush, tangled vines and fallen trees. Vegetation along the banks of the

Amazon is very dense because it gets plenty of sunshine. That is why GWH needed a machete to go exploring. Farther away from the banks of the river, the canopy overhead blocked the sunshine, so there is much less vegetation. The foliage shut off the sun and it was cooler in the shade, but the humidity made them pant with the exertion. It was almost smothering and they perspired profusely.

Suddenly there was a high clear cry ending in an earsplitting shriek.

" Jesus, Mary and Joseph!" Carla cried, reaching for Dennis.

"What in the world…" said Dennis.

Ellen squealed and hung onto Don, who blanched. Letty jumped a foot.

Lois was startled, but unafraid because she knew it was the call of a howler monkey and told the stunned Ginger and Nora what it was. GWH was surprised and pleased with Lois. He thought she was pretty, but timid, and was glad she wasn't the scairdy-cat type.

Amidst the answering crescendo of the Araguato monkey's roaring clamor, he explained about the different types of monkeys.

Calm restored, they went on.

GWH was cutting a path for them with his machete. The ladies went after him with Dennis and Don bringing up the rear. Soon they came upon an anteater who reluctantly scampered away leaving his unfinished lunch of Tucondeiro ants.

GWH had them retreat a few yards and struck out in a different direction.

"Those are Tucondeiro ants, sometimes their bites can be fatal."

"They can grow to be two inches long," said Lois, again surprising GWH. *Hmmm, such a little thing to be so unafraid in this environment,* he mused. *Smart, too.*

The ants were busy running around their nest and ignored these intruders.

They went onward for awhile, sweaty and uncomfortable, when they were brought up short by a piercing scream from Ginger. She was frozen in the path looking down at a centipede at her feet, almost a foot long. It marched on into the underbrush unconscious of the fright he had caused.

"That is only a centipede," GWH said. "Don't worry about it."

"Uh, GWH, could we turn back now? I have just about had enough of going through this jungle," Ginger complained.

No one of the group objected, secretly glad Ginger had asked.

The way back was calmer and they admired flights of beautiful blue butterflies at least five or six inches wide. They stood rapt in admiration. The squawk of a parrot was heard nearby and they got a glimpse of it when he flew away. They did get a sight of the anteater that was returning to continue his interrupted meal. He was about seven feet long from tail to the tip of his nose. The anthill was about ten feet tall made of clay and as hard as cement. His four-inch razor-like claws had no trouble knocking it down. His snakelike tongue was about two feet long with a sticky substance on it that made the ants adhere to it, writhing in an attempt to get away.

"They fight by slashing or squeezing like a bear hug," said GWH.

"Let's get out of here," said Ellen.

They all agreed and trekked onto the boat, happy when it came into view.

Nat and Bud were eating their delayed lunch.

"Dad, we fixed the propeller. I'm sorry it happened, but I just didn't see it."

"It's okay, Bud, those submerged logs just seem to appear out of nowhere. Let's get going again."

Soon they were cruising up the river again. They were happy to sit on the deck with a cold drink and enjoy the breeze that the forward motion provided. The Bridge players, Don and Ellen Mason and Dennis and Carla Evans had started another rubber.

"Let's switch partners," said Carla. "Then we can concentrate on the game without worrying about who's winning money and who is losing." She said this because when she was playing for money she was in agony of suspense and played badly. When she didn't have to worry about money loss, she was a better player. She knew it was bizarre, but true. It wasn't that they needed the money, they didn't, but her maiden name wasn't McNab for nothing. She just hated to throw away anything, money especially.

"It's okay by me," said Don. "Okay with you, Ellen and Dennis?"

"It's fine with me," Ellen said. She was very pleased with the switch. She, of course, loved to be Don's partner when they won. He was an aggressive player and took chances, most of the time successfully. When they lost, it was a different story, especially, Heaven forbid, she make a poor choice of discarding! He was truculent and contentious as he pointed out her shortcomings, endlessly. With this arrangement, she could relax and enjoy playing the game. She too played better without the stress of worrying how he would react to each choice she made.

"Great, I'll cut for deal," said Dennis, smiling. He knew why Carla suggested it and couldn't care less about the money end of it. He enjoyed the game, especially with someone new. He won the deal.

Damn, Don said to himself, looking at his cards, maintaining an unconcerned air. *This is going to be hairy.*

Ellen knew Don was worried in spite of his casual attitude when she saw his hand. He was a great one for a poker face. She mentally hailed their switch again.

Don ended up the winner by adroitly playing his cards. Everyone congratulated Don on a stunning demonstration of refusing to concede defeat until everything else had been tried.

Kamerti interrupted them with a cart of cold soft drinks. They thanked her, made their choices and went on with another game. Don's exuberance set the tone and shouts, moans, jeers, laughter and good-natured teasing from that group were heard often.

Kamerti went over to the lounge area where Lois was doing some needlepoint project she had brought along while she talked with Nora and Letty. Nora and Lois were telling Letty about their school and relating some of the funny things that had happened there during the year. Letty told them about the chain of circumstances that led to her being alone on the trip and the hard time she had telling Tom where she was.

Ginger and Buddy were working on a crossword puzzle, enjoying just being together. They were sitting on a couch. Of course, working on the puzzle dictated they sit very close together. That disturbed neither.

GWH was piloting the boat and Nat was doing some kind of boat maintenance thing.

Bep and Kamerti were setting the dining room tables for dinner. Fresh exotic flowers were on the table and Kameri saw to it that each lady had one on her napkin for her hair.

This is the life, mused GWH, *The boat is running smoothly. Bud is here where he ought to be. The crew is doing what they ought to be doing and the passengers are a pleasant bunch.* His mind wandered to Lois. *She is the kind of girl I should have married. No highfalutin' society dame she! She is a down-to-earth regular woman. She is the kind of person I could be comfortable with. A sweet woman, nice looking, without all that fussing about her looks. She is astute in so many areas. Too bad this is such a short trip. I would like to know her much better.*

He steered away from a half-submerged boat, whitened by bird droppings

Well, what the Hell is there to stop me?

Now, the Narrows gave away to the Amazon's full width. Flat-topped mountains appeared in the distance. Small villages were seen in clearings at the river's side. When they were passing the small village of Monte Alrgre the natives ran out to wave at the *Cacador*.

Later GWH alerted the group to get ready to go ashore at Santar'em.

"We are coming into Santar'em and we are just halfway to Manaus. From this port you can look at the river and see the blue clear water of the Tapajos, which is fifteen miles wide at Santar'em, joining the Amazon in a parallel voyage before they merge about a mile downstream."

While the group was waiting for the boat to dock, Bud, with his ever-present notebook was giving them a short history of the port. "This is a city of over 190,000. People from South Carolina and Tennessee settled it in 1865 when they fled the Confederacy when slavery was abolished. Brazil allowed slavery only twenty-three years after they arrived, but the Southerners still prospered. They built a town that became an important trading center. Today it is a supply center for miners, prospectors, rubber tappers, Brazil nut gatherers and the jute and lumber industries."

"Are there any of the descendants of the Southerners left here?" asked Letty.

"Yes," said Bud, "several bars still fly the Confederate flag and there are some descendants who have mixed with the multiracial Brazilians and have surnames that are American, though their given names are not. They are a friendly slow-paced people and sections of the city still have colonial architecture."

When they entered the bustling port, they saw small fishing boats and dugout canoes delivering a day's catch of fish, or others were unloading produce from an interior settlement. They were jostling for room with large oceangoing cargo ships loading fruit and huge balls of crude gray rubber.

As they disembarked, they noticed wooden signs and a loudspeaker announcing the price and time of the next departure of small boats to Manaus. Their attention was attracted to vendors shouting the lowest prices of bananas and fish. They saw Kamerti and Bep bargaining for both and placing their purchases in a large basket.

Bud led them into the center of town to the Mercado Modelo, which is the open-air market. It isn't as vast as the one in Bel'em, but they enjoyed seeing the local harvest and the people socializing. It was time for lunch, and after seeing all the food on display, they were hungry.

"What would you like to have for lunch?" Bud asked. "You have choices. The Mascote is a restaurant that specializes in fresh fish, or the Churrascao, that is the best of all the barbecue places in town?"

They took a vote and the Mascote won easily. It was a good choice and they ate heartily, despite the heat and humidity.

After lunch they strolled along the eastern sea wall. It was a walkway with benches and flowering shade trees and was a good place to relax after lunch in the hottest part of the day. They enjoyed the unsophisticated, charming small-town atmosphere of Santar'em and when they returned to the boat it was with the feeling of enjoying a pleasant time in a different place.

―――――

On the last three-day stretch of river travel to Manaus they were back at their old occupations of reading, needle pointing, playing Bridge and, of course, talking and becoming friends. Some were falling in love, though they wouldn't admit it even to themselves.

The ship passed several tiny villages and they would stop fifteen to thirty minutes to stretch their legs, buy some trinkets from the natives and just explore. There was a city of around thirty thousand, more or less, but they passed it at night and all were asleep, except Nat, who was the pilot at the time.

Early in the morning the boat swung into the Rio Negro, the largest of the Amazon's tributaries, and docked ten miles beyond in Manaus. Manaus Harbor is laden with oceangoing vessels that sail up the river some thousand miles from the Atlantic, bringing food and other staples and loading Brazil nuts, black pepper, jute, rubber and lumber. In 1965 Manaus was turned into a free port with generous tax incentives and duty-free trading.

Since then it has prospered and is now thriving with hundreds of large and small shops packed with foreign merchandise. They have televisions, cameras, watches, boats, motorcycles, cars, air conditioners, clothes and everything imaginable.

When everyone was all packed again and their bags outside their cabins, Bud and Nat shepherded all eight of them to the Tropical Hotel Manaus, one of the largest and one of the most exclusive resorts in South America. It had over three-hundred and fifty air-conditioned rooms with colonial furnishings of natural wood. The grounds on the Rio Negro were beautifully landscaped with forty thousand orchid plants, a zoo, a casino, shops, tropical patios and a floating river bar. They were stunned.

"Good gracious!" said Letty.

"Wow!" Ginger exhaled.

"Well, I'll be..." Don whistled his surprise.

Dennis didn't say anything, but kept looking around with a flabbergasted look on his face, and Carla did the same.

Ellen, Nora and Lois, who were bringing up the rear, stopped and gasped when they saw the beautiful lobby.

"I had no idea they were so civilized here," said Ellen.

"This could be one of the hotels on Miami Beach!" exclaimed Carla.

Nat was standing by smiling. This was his favorite moment of the whole trip. He knew these people didn't know what to expect this far upriver, and when they were confronted with this opulence they were always surprised.

"I expected we would have to stay in a rough hut." Ginger said what the others were thinking.

"Yes," said Letty, a little sadly, thinking of Uncle Alfred's stories that had nothing like this in them. *Well, he did mention scads of orchids and animals, but not in cages.* She thought. *I sort of wanted to be in the jungle.*

"Will we get to be in the jungle?" Lois verbalized Letty's thought.

"Of course," Bud answered. "We will use this as a home base and go into the jungle daily, either walking to see the plants and animals, or in the small boats for fishing trips. Today you will get settled, have some free time exploring around the hotel. There are plenty of things to do and see around here today. Tomorrow we will have a bus here to take us to the dock. I have a fishing trip planned, then a fish fry for lunch by the river. Don't worry, you will have more than enough time to explore the jungle," Bud said with a smile. He didn't know how true that was.

The group dispersed to their different pleasures. Bud and Nat went to their office.

Letty went to her room and made a beeline for the telephone. The line to Tom's room was busy. "Well, at least he is at home," she said aloud. She dialed all the numbers it took to reach Maureen and got the answering machine for her trouble.

"Hi, Maureen, this is Mom. Everything is fine with me, just checking in. Bye, I love you"

She hung up and began to dial all the numbers it took to get back to Tom's room.

"Hello."

"Hi, Tom, it's me," she said.

"Letty, where the Hell have you been? I have been trying to find you for days. Maureen and Jim didn't have a clue and no one was ever home when I called, and I called at all hours. Where have you been?"

"Didn't you get my letter?"

"I got the book you sent, but nothing else."

"Well, I sent it last Sunday from Bel'em."

"BEL'EM," he yelled. "Where are you now?"

"Honey, now don't get excited, I'm in Manaus."

"What in the…"

"For once let me finish a sentence. If you ever did, you would have known the whole thing."

"But…"

"Listen! I found out that Maureen was having her in-laws visiting so I didn't want to intrude on their visit. So, since I was all alone, and would be for awhile, I decided to go on the trip."

"You could have let me know," he said sullenly.

"Let you know! I called you from home, from the airport in Miami, numerous times, then from Bel'em, where I finally mailed you a letter. You remember, honey, when we did talk you kept cutting me off. Once about the pizza, another time about Glen's cut hand, you would never listen to me. I really did truly, honest. Are you mad that I came here?"

"I guess not, but I was really concerned, I didn't know what happened."

"Whatever happened with Glen's hand?"

"He had to have stitches on all four of his fingers. He went home the next day, he was supposed to go home that day, but the time was taken up with getting to the hospital, getting stitched up, getting a tetanus shot and some pain medication. By that time it was too late to catch the plane for Kansas City. The next day we did that. He is still in St. Louis; things here are still at a standstill. Are you having a good time?"

"Yes, the people I am with are very congenial, I miss you though," she said wistfully.

"Now that I think about it, I am glad you are having fun instead of sitting at home alone. Now that I know you are okay it is fine with me. What have you been doing?"

"Oh, just cruising down, or rather, up the river. We ran into a log once and took a walk in the jungle and saw an anteater, some ants and a giant bug, some monkeys and butterflies while we waited for the boat to be fixed."

"Do those people seem to know what they are doing?"

"Oh, yes, it could have happened to anyone, the log was submerged and Bud couldn't see it."

"Where are you in Manaus?"

"In a beautiful hotel, the Tropical Hotel Manaus. The phone number is 092-238-5757 and I am in room 203. We are going to use it as a base and go on trips into the jungle and on rivers from here. We are all going to the casino tonight."

"The casino! What kind of a jungle place are you in? It sounds like Monte Carlo."

"Oh, it is a beautiful place, I'll wear my best dress tonight."

"Well, I'll be darned. Don't let any gigolo get you."

"He'd drop me at the first lamppost if he did."

"Don't be too sure of that."

"Well, I'm glad we finally got in contact with one another. Take good care of yourself and ask at the desk for my letter."

"I will do all of that, try to call me in a week if you can."

"Okay, I'll do that. Bye bye, honey, I love you."

"I love you too, Letty, take care. Bye."

Letty let out a big breath. "Whew, I am glad that is settled," she said aloud.

At dinner that evening, she told everyone about talking to Tom at last. They were happy for her. They knew it had been bothering her that he didn't know where she was and that she was afraid that he would be angry with her.

"Was Tom mad when you told him?" asked Don. He knew he would be plenty mad if Ellen pulled off such a stunt.

"When I got a chance to explain everything he got over it, but yes, he was mad at first. He was worried about me. Everything is fine now, he is even glad I came and looks forward to hearing all about it." Letty smiled, glad that it was resolved.

The next day they went to Alter do Chao. There they visited the "Museum of Indigenous Art."

They returned to the *Cacador* for a tasty lunch. It was mixira, a manatee meat dish for the entree and the dessert was creme de cupuacu, a delightful concoction of tropical fruit.

They waited a suitable time after lunch, then donned their bathing suits. The boat had docked on a beach in the pristine waters of the Rio Tapajos, an Amazon tributary. It was cooling and they wanted to stay a long while.

It was fine with GWH—he always wanted to keep his clients happy. Besides, he and Lois were having a splendid time swimming and playing in the river with the others.

Relaxing afterwards with a cool drink on deck, they were telling one another their life stories, GWH sympathizing with Lois at the loss of Geoffrey at such a young age and Lois understanding how he and May could never be compatible with all their different characteristics. Poor Bud, caught in the middle, had a hard time of it too.

Gradually the swimmers came on deck, happy and refreshed.

"That was delightful," said Letty, drying her white curls briskly with a towel.

Ginger and Bud came on deck laughing at a private joke. It did not go unnoticed by Dennis and Carla.

"What do you think is going on there?" Dennis whispered to Carla.

"It looks like young love, but I don't think it is anything to be concerned about. It is probably just a shipboard romance. Don't you think so?"

"He looks very serious to me."

"I think Ginger is just flattered by the attention of an older man. She has only dated high school boys up to now, those her own age and class. Bud has much more allure and sparkle for her than anyone she has known in the past. She is fascinated by him."

"I know, that is what worries me," said Dennis, toweling off and handing a towel to Carla so she could do the same.

"Don't you like Bud?"

"Yes, I like him, but I am not ready to turn over my only daughter to him. Are you?"

"Of course not, she is barely eighteen, for heaven's sake," Said Carla, beginning to be troubled too.

Nora, Don, and Ellen were seated on deck sipping a cold drink that Kamerti was offering to everyone.

They came upon the village of Boca da Valeria. It is on the agenda of the large cruise liners. The natives put on a show and give the passengers an opportunity to witness native Amazon culture.

Since the *Cacador* was not expected, the natives were not in their costumes, just shorts. Some ran to their huts to get into character for them. They did buy some of their trinkets and played their game. GWH and Bud knew them, so they put on their folkloric dances and songs for the little group. They were generous with their applause and money, but they were not fooled that they were visiting a "real" primitive village.

"What is on the agenda for tomorrow, GWH?" asked Don as they made their way back to the boat.

"I thought we might go fishing for our supper. How would you like that?"

"Great, what might we catch?"

"We could catch tucanar'eare, surubim, piraiba, pirarara and dorado . It can be found weighing up to one hundred eighty pounds."

Don was unfamiliar with most of those fish and asked, "Tell me about them, I have no idea what they look like."

"I have a book about the fish in the Amazon. It has pictures and tells all about them. I'll let you all study it tonight and you'll know what to look for tomorrow."

"I guess we will need heavy tackle to catch fish that big."

"No need to worry about that," chimed in Bud. "Dad has all the equipment you'll need."

Bud starting reminiscing about past fishing trips with GWH when he was small. GWH was pleased to hear him recount those days with such pleasure.

The next day everyone was equipped with the appropriate fishing gear and soon shouts of glee were heard when they would get a bite. Dennis and Don and Nora, not surprisingly, were doing well. Letty, Lois, Ellen and Carla did more squealing than anything. Bud helped Ginger land a piraiba, which required some very close contact. Carla and Dennis exchanged knowing glances and Dennis moved himself on the other side of Ginger.

Nat was busy cleaning the catch of the day, then cooked some for their lunch and put the rest in the freezer.

Sated, they went back to their indolent ways, talking or reading. The Bridge players were hard at it. You could tell by the laughter, groans and shouts.

Lois had taken her needlepoint to sit by GWH as he navigated the *Cacador* along the way upriver.

This was the last day; they were to reach Manaus soon. Lois would be sorry to see this trip end. She wanted to stay as near to

GWH as possible, for as long as possible. GWH was pleased that Lois had sought him out. He was pondering how to approach Lois. He didn't want to frighten her. And yet, his feelings for her were growing daily. What to do? And, more important, what not to do.

Nat broke into their thoughts.

"People, this is a sight not to be missed! It is the 'Wedding of the Waters.'"

They were about twelve miles from the port of Manaus, the Rio Solimoes and the blackish Rio Negro, both about two miles wide at this point, converging with terrific force, causing whirlpools of black and brown swirling water. These two waters flow side by side for more than five miles before mixing, because of their differing velocity and density. Eventually they become a muddy brown, or the café com leite (coffee with milk) color of the Amazon.

Soon they were busy with the landing of the *Cacador* in the capital of Amazonas, Manaus, where Colonial architecture and modern skyscrapers coexist in this remarkable city of over a million inhabitants. Turn of the century buildings, remnants of the once lucrative rubber trade, sit beside the modern high-rises indicative of present commercial operations.

While Nat and GWH were tending to the business of docking, Bud, with his trusty notebook, was educating the group about the history of Manaus. Some of them like Letty, Nora and Lois had studied some about the city, but they listened as Bud talked.

"Manaus's history is a classic story of boom-and-bust one crop economy. Rubber, made from a milky juice that flows from the Hevea Brasilensis tree, was known to the explorers accompanying Columbus, who saw Indians playing with hollow rubber balls in Haiti. In the early 1800s, with Charles Mackintosh's invention of the raincoat and the development of shoes that could withstand the snows of European winters, rubber became an important Brazilian export. But the rubber boom really began in earnest when Goodyear discovered the process of vulcanization and car and bicycle wheels could be made consistently pliable.

"Because the Amazon forest was the only place to get the rubber, foreigners flocked to the area and made enormous fortunes overnight. The residents grew fabulously rich and built a lavish jungle city that competed architecturally and culturally with major European capitals. They brought marble from Italy, tiles from Portugal, and the best china from England and constructed huge mansions in the jungle, a few of which still stand between the skyscrapers in the hilly section of the city. But the greatest remaining monument to this era is the grand, ostentatious opera house, Teatro do Amazonas (Praco Sao Sebastio)"

"I have read about the area, but I had no idea it was so modernized," said Letty.

"Nor I," said Lois

"That part about depending on one crop is true," interjected Don. "I've seen it in business time after time. That is why we run an emporium, an old-fashioned name, but one that denotes quantity of types of goods. Our old store has had that name a long time. But I keep current on all the new trends also. We are holding our own against the chains by offering quantity of choices and quality goods. You must, or the discount chains will put you under."

"Do go on, Bud, don't get Don started on business," said Ellen, giving Don a friendly shove. He ducked and smiled sheepishly, embarrassed.

"Just one more thing," said Don. "When did things start going bad for the rubber business?"

"Manaus lost its monopoly on rubber in the early 1900s, when rubber seeds were smuggled out of Brazil to Celon. The competent cultivation of these trees, lower taxes, a lack of health hazards, and better access to the shipping lanes made the Ceylonese rubber an instantaneous success and vastly curtailed the Amazon market."

"Ha! Taxes, they had trouble with them even then," said Don.

"Do you want me to finish this?" asked Bud, not wanting to bore them.

A chorus of assenting voices reassured him, so he went on reading.

"Dozens of foreign artists and architects were brought to the jungle in 1892 to create a magnificent building. Italian marble, English porcelain, French furniture, and wrought iron were imported to embellish the ornate edifice. The walls of the lobby and the ceiling were adorned with a mural of angels playing harps and another of Amazon Indians. There were mirrors here and there throughout. There was a massive dome lined with green and yellow tiles and painted in gold leaf.

"It is said to have cost ten million dollars then, today it would be much more," said Bud. "Besides that, exorbitant amounts were paid to attract world-famous performers of the day such as Pavlova and Sarah Bernhardt. Opening night was in 1896."

Bud looked up from the notebook.

"Just think, this was over a hundred years ago. Can you visualize it? Manaus society at its most resplendent, the ladies in Paris gowns and the poor men sweltering in woolen tail coats and tight collars in this heat." He returned to the book.

"The Teatro do Amazonas was remodeled in 1962 and again in 1975; it is open to the public Tuesdays through Sundays, 9:00 a.m. to 6:00 p.m." Bud closed the notebook.

"That is enough for today. We will visit the opera while we are here, perhaps tomorrow, and other interesting sights too."

"I would like to see the jungle," said Dennis.

Another chorus of agreement resounded.

"You will, the jungle literally creeps up on the city. To get an idea of the plant and animal life around us, I have planned a trip to explore the museums, botanical gardens and zoos. Then when we are deeper in the jungle and you see something you will have a better idea of what you are looking at. We will go to Salvadore Lake where there is a reserve open to the public. It is near the Rio Negro and is a perfect place to observe the ecological system of the jungle. It has an exotic variety of Amazon animals, such as tapirs, jaguars, boars, alligators, turtles, monkeys, snakes and parrots. All these can be seen from floating pavilions instead of thrashing through the insect infested jungle where you couldn't begin to see all these types, but you may be seen by them."

"That is just fine with me," said Ginger with a shiver, remembering their last walk in the jungle.

"I can set up a picnic, then a short two-mile hike through a forest trail and the boat can meet us in the Guedes River narrows. We can do that tomorrow if you would like, after our visit to the opera."

They were agreeable to this plan.

Back at the hotel they went off to their own devices. Bud made a date with Ginger to take in some of the nightlife, promising to return her at a reasonable hour. The Bridge players met in the card room, and Letty, Nora and Lois walked around the beautiful grounds after dinner.

The next day went just as Bud had planned. The next few days were spent exploring. They went to the CIGS Zoo where they saw the same animals that they saw at the Salvadore Lake reserve. They went to an Indian Museum full of authentic Indian costumes, weapons, crafts and art objects dating back from the discovery of Manaus. Bud took them through Turislandia, a twenty minute drive from downtown Manaus in the Aleixo

District that features Brazil nut trees, cocoa, rubber and guaran'a trees. They went swimming, fishing and picnicking and saw just about every sight available to be seen.

While this was going on, GWH was preparing for a trip for them into the jungle to a real native village by helicopter, a four-day trip. It was to be their last adventure before going back down to Bel'em.

Chapter Twelve

Fenton Cranshaw and Orem Tharp were finished with their latest cruise. They were replenishing and refurbishing their gear. Things would be ready for the next trip, that is, if there ever was one.

Toward the end of this last trip Fenton fell off the wagon a little. The clients were less than pleased with the result. Not enough for an official complaint, but neither Fenton nor Orem thought there would be any future bookings from this group, nor any word-of-mouth bookings either.

"Everything shipshape again, Orem?"

"As soon as I stow these boxes away, Fenton." Orem replied sullenly. He was chagrined at the way Fenton acted on their trip.

"Well, shake a leg, I'm starved. Let's go over to the Bola De Borracha as soon as we're finished here."

"Okay, I want to wash up a little first, don't you?" This was Orem's diplomatic way of letting Fenton know that he didn't look or smell good enough to go out in public.

"I guess so, I'll get cleaned up and rest a bit and you can call me when you are ready to go." Fenton said, getting the message. He did just that and was snoring loudly when Orem awakened him about two hours later. The nap was just what he needed to regain his aplomb.

The early diners were just leaving the Bola De Borracha when Fenton and Orem arrived in clean clothes and smelling of aftershave. They sat down at the table and ordered their meals. Fenton noticed Ed Garson. He was sitting at the bar talking to Dave the bartender. That reminded him of the coming trip into the jungle that Ed was to make with GWH, after his present trip was over.

"Orem, I want you to hire on with Ed Garson and GWH for that trip they are going to make into the jungle. I know that they plan to try to contact that lost tribe of Indians they were talking about before we left."

"Do you think they will hire me?"

"Tomorrow I want you to go over to GWH's office and apply for the job. If he will take you on it will be okay with Ed. No use trying to fool him as we planned, that Nat is too close to the native population around here and he is sure to spot any phony stuff that you might tell them."

"I didn't think that would fly, but I was willin' to try."

"I know, Orem, you are a good friend. I think, though if you see me making a big mistake you'd better mention it. I know I goofed on this last trip. It is just so damn hard!" he whined.

"The thing to do is just not bring any hard stuff with us!"

"The clients wouldn't stand for it, they like their drinks at the end of the day and would feel cheated without them."

"Yeah, I guess so. You'll just have to get a grip, as they say in New York"

"I know it, and I mean to do it, but when the booze is there and the clients expect me to join them, and I want to so bad, it is really hard for me to refuse."

" We've got to think of a way. Do you like gin and tonic?"

"I could drink it by the gallon!"

"I'll fix you a bottle of 'gin.' It will be water. You can make your own drink with a little tonic, a little lime juice and your own private bottle of 'gin,' I can even put some in your flask and no one will ever know, I'll see to that. The bottle and flask will stay full and you stay sober. You will have to if we are ever going to get anywhere."

"I know it, and thanks. Let's go over to the bar and talk to Ed and Dave. I'll introduce you to them so when GWH talks to Ed about you he will know who he is talking about. I want you to impress him with your knowledge of Indian languages."

"Okay, boss," Orem said with a grin.

"You can dumb up on the English, though."

"Yas'sr," he drawled, getting into character.

They walked over to the bar and greeted Ed Garson and Dave. Ed Garson had rented a room nearby while waiting for the projected jungle trip to be organized. As a result, he spent a lot of time hanging out with Dave, the amusing bartender. He ate his meals there, but carefully spaced his beers far apart.

Fenton introduced Orem and they talked awhile about local happenings. Ed conversed with Orem in a succession of Indian dialects. Orem passed the test handily; surprising Ed who was conversant in a few dialects, which even he, who was considered the local expert, didn't understand.

In reaction to his surprise Orem thought, *After all, who is the native anyway!*

"Well, goodbye to you both," Fenton said. "I have to get out there and scout up some business. I have nothing scheduled, so I have to get out there and hustle up some livelihood. Anything you can do to help Orem till I need him again will be helpful."

"Okay, Fenton. Happy to meet you, Orem, take care now," said Dave. After they left, Dave turned to Ed.

"How did Orem strike you, Ed?"

"He certainly can talk the talk," said ED, "though I thought I detected a deviousness, and a shiftiness about the eyes, but maybe I'm mistaken and too hard on him. There is really no reason to suspect anything. Perhaps I'm getting paranoid as I get older."

————— ••••◆•••• ——

The next morning, Orem went into GWH's office. Ryti was the only one there.

"Mr. Hunter in, please?" he said, fawningly, surreptitiously eyeing her beauty, not quite succeeding in pulling it off.

"He is due in tomorrow, may I be of help?" Ryti answered.

"Does that ring on your finger mean you have a man?" He gave her one of his special, never fail, "bedroom eyes" glances, speaking as one native to another.

"It does, I am married and mean to stay that way," Ryti icily replied.

Orem decided to behave, this was too important. "He sure a lucky man." His smile was not the leering one he wore before. "Would you tell Mr. Hunter dat I like speak him sometime soon, if he can see me? I be here in morning to find out when if dat okay?"

"I will tell him what you said," Ryti answered, unsmiling.

"Please, not all, just about meeting with him." This time he left with a repentant smile.

————— ••••◆•••• ——

The next day, instead of visiting the office, he followed Fenton's suggestion and called to make an appointment. He was told to be there at ten o'clock.

GWH made time for some office work while the passengers were having a sightseeing bus ride around Manaus. He sent Nat off to do the driving, while Bud did the talking.

Orem was already there when GWH arrived. Ryti introduced him to GWH and went about her business. There had been no flirting from Orem that morning, everything was strictly business.

"Orem Tharp?" GWH said with a smile and a handshake. "That is an unusual name." GWH didn't add "for a native," but the phrase hung in the air unuttered.

"It was given to me at the Mission where I was raised." He remembered his role and continued. "Ah was named after someone's kin."

"Well, what can I do for you, Orem?" said GWH, catching the slip.

"I jus off a trip with Fenton Cranshaw. Ah'm need work. Ah talk lots Native talks an a good hand on trips. Mr. Cranshaw sent me."

"Orem, I am going to be straight with you, as you haven't been with me. I know that you are trying to 'dumb down' for me. Why, is something I don't know. Usually job seekers put their best foot forward. Why don't you?"

"Aw, I knew it was a bad idea. It was Cranshaw's suggestion, he thought it would be better if you thought that I was fresh out of the jungle."

"That Fenton! He would rather be crooked than straight anytime. I really don't need anyone right now. My son just joined me and unless we expand our operation we can handle, things. Sorry, Orem, I don't like to deal with schemers either. Next time we try to do business you'd better be on the up and up and we'll get along much better. Don't get infected with Fenton's shady ways and you'll be a lot better off."

"Thanks for the advice, Mr. Hunter. I am sorry we can't do business at this time. If you ever need me, though, I would do a good job for you," he said with a handshake and then he left.

"Shifty," GWH said aloud to the empty room. He went to his desk and tackled the paperwork that had piled up while he was away.

—————

Orem went to Fenton's office and reported what had happened. "Damn!" Fenton exclaimed. "We have to change that setup."

"What do you mean?"

"I mean we have to see that they are one man short. Then they will remember you and take you along. I will trail the party and at night you can report any information you can pick up to me."

"Do you think that you can stay hidden while you keep up with us?"

"Of course, that won't be a problem, the problem will be getting rid of GWH, Bud or Nat. Who and how, that is the problem."

"I think it ought to be GWH. He is the key man. He might think he can manage with either Nat or Bud."

"Yeah, he has an ego that won't quit. Orem, you are a smart man." Fenton smiled, really meaning it, and shook his head in Orem's direction.

"I thank you, sir," Orem gave a little bow. "Now, the question is how. We don't want to kill him, do we?"

"If I could do it without getting caught I wouldn't mind much," Fenton growled emphatically. "GWH will have to be in some kind of accident. I can't think of any way to get him sick, can you, Orem?'

"Naw, maybe we can slip a snake into his bed."

"What kind? How could we manage it? No, it would be too hazardous. You might end up being bitten yourself, or nothing happening at all. It has to be something else." Fenton brooded.

"Boat gas explosion? Car accident? A fall?" Orem queried.

"He is too careful for the boat gas explosion, if we could manage that. It could end up killing him and the others on board. A fall? Where is he going to fall from? That would really be hard to manage. The car, that old Land Rover of his could have a brake failure. He always wears a safety belt I've noticed, he might get hurt, but he reasonably could survive the injuries that would follow a brake failure."

"It would easily be discovered that it wasn't an accident. They would be able to tell if it was deliberate or not. That snake bite, let's think about that again."

"Where would he be likely to have a catastrophic snake bite?" Fenton pondered.

"In the office or in the house?" Orem asked.

"In the car! Double the chance." *Snake bite leads to local's crash.* A fiendish grin was on Fenton's face as he pretended to read imaginary news headline.

"Where and how?" Orem asked.

"I guess that left turn down the hill from his house would be a good place where it could happen. He comes down that side street at a good clip, the left turn would be where trouble would be the most critical if a snake were tossed in the window at that spot."

"No way! I am not doing that! There isn't much of a shoulder on that road, the sides slope down to a ditch," reasoned Orem. "There is nowhere to stand and no place to hide."

"Yeah, but he'd be wrestling with the snake and trying to control the car at the same time. I can't see him winning that battle, one is bound to get him and the other will naturally follow." Fenton's sinister chuckle caused Orem to stare.

"We have to think of some other place. We'll do that later— after I find a snake."

A silence fell over them. Fenton, doodling at his desk, Orem was picking at a hangnail, then ended up biting it off.

"Well, now we have the 'what' and the 'how.' Next we must decide the 'who' and the 'when.'" Orem looked over at Fenton dubiously.

"You know I can't do it, I must be where I can be seen. I would be the first one suspected of foul play. As for the 'when,' the sooner the better.' Fenton brooded.

"Another thing, where do I get the snake?" Orem questioned

"You're the native, you get it. I'm sure I don't want to. If you don't want to either, hire one of your kin to catch one, or steal one. I don't care, just do it and get it over with," Fenton stormed. "Get out of here and do something."

Before dawn the next morning, Orem, equipped with a metal case the size of a man's briefcase, left for the local zoo. It wasn't a very large one. The night man left about midnight. The staff didn't arrive until around 8:00 a.m. It was a minor thing for Orem to open the locked door. He was even bold enough to turn the light on because he knew the staff would not open up early. It would be a lucky thing for it to open on time.

A chorus of animal and bird noises greeted him as he made his way to the snake cages. There was one Fer de Lance and two Bushmasters. He decided on one of the Bushmasters. They were both in one cage, one coiled asleep in a small leafless tree. The other was awake; his upper body was creeping up one side of the cage. A Bushmaster is a pit viper. The pits are holes between the eyes and nostrils that detect body heat in nearby prey or enemies. They grow to six or seven feet long and are highly poisonous. They are most active at night, and since it was getting on to 6:00 a.m., it was beginning to get sleepy. Orem opened the metal case and removed a folded piece of canvas. His heart was pounding—he could feel the blood pulsate through his body.

"God! How I hate snakes!" he said aloud, startling himself. He shuddered, took a deep breath, then unfastened the cage door, but didn't open it yet. He paused, getting his nerve up, then, moving quickly, he opened the door and threw the canvas over the moving snake. Then he clamped the metal case over the canvas. He grabbed the metal case and slammed it over the canvas, sliding it out the door of the cage and shutting the case in one swift movement. The vibration caused the other snake to fall out of the tree, confused and angry.

Orem snapped the lock shut on the metal case and sat on the floor. He let out a big gulp of air in a loud "Woossssssh!" His hands were shaking, his heart pulsating, causing his blood to race through his body.

God! How I hate snakes!

When he calmed down, he picked up the metal case, guardedly, and retraced his steps, turned out the light, locked the door and left. He went over to Fenton's house, leaving the case in the car. By that time he had regained his composure.

⸻

"Did you have any trouble getting the snake?"

"Naw, I didn't want to spend a lot of time tracking one down, so I lifted a Bushmaster from the zoo. It was quicker and easier that way," Orem said with a little shrug.

He told Fenton all about his adventure, omitting the part about how frightened he was. He was too cool for that.

"I gotta hand it to you Orem, I couldn't do it. Snakes scare the devil out of me, ugh!" Fenton shivered at the thought.

"Okay, we have the snake, now what?"

"Now, we put it in GWH's car."

"What do you mean 'we'? By the way, do you have any suggestions how I should go about it?" Orem felt as if the whole sorry plan was to be carried out by him alone.

"Well, he always parks his car behind his office. I don't think he locks it."

"Puhh!" He expelled some air. "Even if he does, I can have it unlocked in no time. That is Street Smart 101, in New York," Orem answered as he prepared to go. "I assume this is going to be worth my while, eh, Fenton?"

"Absolutely! We will split everything 60/40."

"Try 50/50, old buddy. I am a full partner, not a hired hand, since I seem to be doing all the work."

"I guess so." Fenton stuck out his hand to shake Orem's . "Okay, full partners then." He knew he couldn't do without Orem, and Orem knew too much too.

⸻

Orem went into the Bola de Borracha where he placed the metal case at his feet and ordered coffee and a roll. He wanted to give GWH plenty of time to get to the office and absorbed in his business before he tended to his own business matter.

When he felt sure GWH was in his office he made his way to the back of the building to the small parking area. The door of the car was conveniently unlocked. He opened the door, leaned over the seat and dumped the snake behind the front seat on the driver's side and slammed the door shut. The closed car was hot inside; the snake coiled itself into a tight ball and went to sleep.

GWH, Nat and Ryti were just finishing up the sprinkling of paperwork left over from the day before.

"I guess you and Ryti can have the rest of the day off. Bud is off with the clients, I think they are fishing today. I am so pleased with the way he has pitched in around here. He is always willing to guide the clients around, it takes a load off our backs and we are finally caught up with things around here."

"I guess that cute little Ginger girl doesn't have much to do with it, huh?" Ryti said, laughing. "Nat told me about how they are always together."

"Now, you mention it, I don't often see one without the other. She is a mighty pretty little lady—he can't go wrong there."

"What about the Evans'?" asked Nat. "Do you think they will object? She's a little young and that Carla hovers over her like a mother hen."

"Aw, they don't have anything to worry about. Bud and Ginger are too young for anything serious."

"He is twenty-two, how old were you when you married May?"

"Well, I was twenty-one." GWH pointed his finger at Nat, emphasizing each word with it. "I was a very mature twenty-one."

"I see, I rest my case."

"You two get out of here, I'm going home and take a nap. We are taking the clients out to dinner at a different place tonight. They have a new chef at the Amazonas Hotel, down by the docks. I have arranged for the fish that they catch to be taken there and prepared as only he can. After the clients have rested they can go there for a great dinner."

"I think they will like that, and I know if the catch is light that they will add to it, right?"

"Absolutely, go on now, have a nice afternoon off."

"So long, boss."

"Bye, Mr. GWH."

GWH locked up the office and left by the back door, checking the lock as he pulled it shut. A wave of hot air hit him and he rushed to the car, wasted no time in turning on the air conditioner. Behind his seat, the snake slept on. When GWH arrived at his house he bounced out of the car and slammed the door. The snake stirred and changed his position. He slithered under the front seat and up under the dash above the pedals. He went to sleep again.

GWH showered and shaved and slipped into bed for a nap. He set the alarm for 5:00 p.m.

Orem and Fenton had arranged to meet at the Bola de Borracha at 5:00 p.m.

"Have a drink, Orem," Fenton said, motioning to the chair beside him. "What will you have? I'm having a Shirley Temple myself," he said with a rueful laugh.

"Atta boy, that's the way to go," Orem answered, genuinely pleased. "I'll have a gin and tonic."

When Orem had his drink in front of him, he leaned toward Fenton. "Did you hear anything?"

"Not a thing."

"I hung around out of sight, and GWH got in the car and drove off. The snake was just behind the driver's seat."

"Well, we will surely hear something soon, in the meantime, let's eat."

When the alarm went off at 5:00 p.m., GWH got up, refreshed. He dressed, paying more attention, than usual to his toilet. He wanted to look nice for Lois. He even splashed on some special aftershave someone had sent him from the States last Christmas that he had never opened. He left the hall light on as usual and went out the front door. He even remembered to lock it.

He hopped into the car, fastened the seat belt and was soon driving down the street. He braked slightly at the top of the hill—the snake was awakened. Halfway down the hill, preparing to take the sharp 90-degree left turn, he hit the brakes with more force because he was gaining more momentum.

The snake was fully awake—the vibration of the car's motor had disturbed him. When GWH came to the middle of the hill and forcefully applied the brakes to slow down for the turn, the snake was dislodged from his perch and fell onto GWH's feet! In an understandable panic he removed his feet from the brake pedal to kick the snake off them. He took his eyes off the road too, and grabbed at the snake. The second he took his hands off the steering wheel was all it took for the car to become airborne.

The seat belt saved GWH's life as the car rolled over and over. The poor snake, since he was beltless, was thrown all over the car with each revolution. He survived, but barely. Dazed, he fell out of the car onto the grass when it came to rest. After a pause, he escaped into the vegetation and freedom.

———— ᴥ●ᴥ ——

When GWH became conscious he was being moved to a stretcher in preparation to being put in the ambulance.

"Watch it, you morons, that hurts!"

"Good, he is conscious now," somebody said. "What's your name?"

"Gordon Hunter."

"GWH?"

"Yeah, that's me. How come I can't open my eyes?"

"You have some injury there, please hold still."

"I can't see!" He started to sit up; he was frantically trying to remove the first-aid bandages.

"Get these damn things off my eyes, I have to see!"

The man in charge nodded to his partner and GWH was given a strong sedative into an IV tube they had inserted into his arm while he was out cold.

When he awakened again it was in the hospital room. His eyes were bandaged, his leg felt restricted, his arm had a cast and he ached all over.

"Owwwch," he moaned, and put his hands to his face.

"Don't do that, Dad! They were going to tie your other hand down, but I wouldn't let them. I promised them that I would stay with you till you were fully awake and that I wouldn't let you touch your eye bandages."

"Bud, is that you?"

"Yes."

"What time is it?"

"It's about 10:00 a.m."

"How was the dinner?"

"Fine, I guess. Nat called me at the hotel before I started to eat and I came right over. A friend of his who works in the ER division at the hospital had called Nat. What happened, Dad?"

"There was a damned snake in the car, it was on my feet! I saw it just as I was beginning that left turn on the hill down from the house and I lost control of the car. Did it bite me?"

"I don't think so. They didn't say anything about seeing a snake and that wasn't on the list of injuries."

"Hm, what was on the list?"

"Lacerations to both eyes, compound fracture of the right femur, hairline fracture of the humerus and numerous lesser lacerations and contusions. Everything is all sewn up and fixed up. You are lucky that you put your seat belt on, or that would have been all she wrote."

"My eyes, did they say if they will be okay?"

"No, we just have to wait till he finishes his rounds and gets to us. Do they hurt?"

"Well, there is a drawing, tightish feeling. No real bad pain. Kind of itchy, I want to rub them."

"Don't do that!"

"I won't. I said I wanted to, not that I would," he grouched. "When can I get out of here? Did they tell you?"

"No, it all depends on how you get along, I guess,"

"Where are our people today?"

"Nat is taking them in the forest today. Animal and bird watching, photographing when they get a chance at a good shot. He is better at pointing out flora and fauna than I am. Anyway, I wanted to be here when you woke up. Did you know that Lois has been getting photographs of animals and birds and all kinds of plants everywhere we have been?"

"Yes, she wants to catalog it all for a book she is writing. She says it's for children, but I think she should try for the adult market. Oooh, I feel like I've been beaten with sticks! Can I have some water?"

"Okay, here." He helped him to a few sips from a glass straw. "Not too much at one time. You think a lot about her, don't you, Dad?'

"You could say that." He was uncomfortable talking about this. "How about you and Ginger?" *Turn about is fair play.* "You think a lot about her too, don't you, Bud?"

"You could say that." He imitated GWH's tone. "I guess the love bug has been flitting around both of us."

"Yeah, but has it bitten them? That's the big question."

"Time will tell, Dad, time will tell."

"Time will tell about your eyes, Mr. Hunter," Dr. Webb said as he came through the door in time to hear Bud's last statement…"I know that is the first thing you are going to ask me and I am not ready to answer it yet. The bruises and lacerations will be fine shortly. I won't know till I am able to do some other tests later to see if there is other damage. The leg is something else. The lesion has to heal. We must guard against infection. Then you will need therapy too, before you are able to go home. By that time we will know about your eyes. Your arm won't be a problem. It will depend on your behavior how soon we can fix you up. If you try to hurry things, if you don't follow orders, you will be the one to suffer because of it. Also, it will prolong your healing time. Do you plan to be macho or sensible?" He really had GWH's number and just how to handle him.

"That's what it comes down to, Dad," Bud chimed in before GWH had a chance to speak.

"I guess macho is out, huh?' GWH sighed, resigned to his fate.

"I would suggest so, Mr. Hunter," Dr. Webb said, and reached over and shook his good right hand. "I will see that you are comfortable. There is a radio along with your call button to keep you amused."

"My eyes itch something awful, Doc."

"I'll order something for that, it is just the stitches pulling a little. When they are removed, it will be fine."

"I feel awfully helpless, it's hard to lose control of things."

"It's natural to feel that way, try to adjust by resting, sleeping, and allowing us to help you."

"That won't be easy."

"Give it a try, I must go now, but I will leave orders for your care. Goodbye now to you both," he said as he went out the door.

"Don't worry about things, Dad. I can run things with Nat's help. It will do me good not to depend on you for my every move. You and Nat can go over the plans and tell me what you want me to do and I will do it."

"Well, Bud, that is just about the way we'll have to do it. Send Nat over this afternoon and we'll go over it."

"Let's wait a day or so for that. I'm to take the group out and about this afternoon, and when we get back I'll bring them by. They are all very concerned about you and would like to visit."

"Oh Hell, I don't want them trooping in here, stirring everyone up..."

"I won't let them stay long, we'll have to go get ready for dinner. It is to be a bar-b-que tonight."

"Okay, I will 'see' you later. Uh, get me some soft sleepy music on the radio before you leave, will you, Bud? Oldies, if you can, Uh, my oldies, not your oldies."

"Okay, Dad." Bud fiddled with the dial awhile and came up with some "elevator music."

"Is that the 'floor' you want, Dad?"

"Yeah, funny man, get out now and let a guy get some sleep."

———— ••◦•• ————

Bud stopped by the hotel and dropped off a cassette and a book on the native birds. He was going to let the group listen to the birdcalls and match them with the birds in the book. This to make them familiar with what they will probably be seeing on their trip to Parrots Island up the Rio Negros.

When he found them on the veranda, waiting for him, they were very subdued, talking softly in groups. No loud laughing and joking as they usually did. He was glad they were all together and ready so they could leave immediately. He gave them a rundown on GWH's condition.

"Is everyone all set to go?" he asked.

"I ran through your checklist with each one." Lois smiled at him. "Cameras, binoculars, batteries, notebooks and a tape recorder with blank tapes."

"I made sure everyone is thoroughly drenched in bug repellant, can't you tell?" Don waved a can over his head for emphasis.

"I wasted my 'Oscar,'" complained Carla. "If I had known he was going to saturate us with that smelly stuff, I wouldn't have bothered!"

"You'll be glad he did when we get out there, Carla." Bud added, "That sweet smell would have lured the insects straight to you."

He hurried them along, getting them headed toward Parrots Island in the *Calcador*.

———————— ···•●·•· ————————

"Trill,trill,chirp,chirp,trill," he whistled. "What bird is that?"

He was met with blank stares.

Dennis started the tape recorder and they all listened to the calls to try to discover which one he meant.

"Okay, which one was it?" Nora asked.

"I don't know, I just wanted to see if you were paying attention." He laughed, trying to get them back in their carefree mood.

"Oh you, that wasn't fair," said Ginger as she punched his arm. She was sitting near him, as always.

"Look at the two colors in the water!" Carla interrupted. "One is brown and the other is almost black, just as we saw from the boat. It still startles me."

"Weird!" said Letty. She had read of these two rivers side by side, unmixed for miles. It was different to actually see it. "The way each color stays to itself as the river flows along. Sort of like life, isn't it?"

"Now, Letty, don't go getting philosophical on us, it all ends mixed together in the end anyway, doesn't it?"

Chapter Thirteen

Nat and Ryti were in the office. Nothing was happening; the paperwork was all done. The phone had stopped ringing. All morning long GWH's friends kept the line busy inquiring about his condition. Nat regaled those who didn't know the details with a chilling account. He also rendered a gruesome picture of GWH bedridden and blind in the hospital, making it much worse than it actually was.

Nat opened a drawer and took out his quina, a musical instrument made from a hollow tube with a blow hole at one end and other holes down the side that were covered and uncovered by Nat's slim brown fingers. He began to serenade Ryti with a haunting, melodious rendition that brought to mind his Peruvian ancestors, who, during the time of the Inca Empire, played similar music upon a similar instrument.

This tranquil time was interrupted by the jarring sound of Fenton and Orem entering the office.

"Hi, Nat, hello, Ryti," Fenton greeted them ardently.

"Good afternoon," Orem bobbed his head.

"Hello there, you two," Nat responded, putting the quina back in the drawer.

"If you'll excuse me, I am going to the post office now. I'll be back soon, Nat," said Ryti. On the way out she nodded at the two men. "Good-bye" she said as she left.

"I heard GWH is in a bad way," said Fenton, sliding his rump upon a nearby desk. Orem stayed quiet and standing.

"Yes, he'll be laid up for some time."

"You know, Orem and I would be glad to help out if you need any help finishing up with this group."

"That is very kind of you, Fenton, but you know GWH's son is here now and with Ryti in the office, Bud and I can manage. You know we have Bep and Kamerti on board the boat too. They are a great help. She can cook and clean and Bep has become a great mechanic. He can fix just about anything that goes wrong on the boat. He has been on that river all his life and he knows all its turns and tricks. We can do okay without the boss. We don't have another trip booked anyway. GWH wanted some time off to go off on a trip of his own."

"I guess you mean the one with Ed Garson," Fenton said with a scowl.

"You'll have to ask him about that," Nat answered.

"Do you think GWH will ever be as he was? I heard he was blind and crippled."

"You can't keep GWH down, he'll be just fine, given enough time to heal."

"What exactly happened, anyway? I heard he missed a left turn and turned over."

"That's what happened."

"Well, what caused him to do that?"

"A snake, a bushmaster snake, caused him to do that Fenton."

"A bushmaster! Naw, he'd be a gonner if that were true."

"That's what he said, and he knows his snakes. No wonder he lost control of the car. If he hadn't had his seat belt on he'd be dead."

"Did they find the snake?"

"No, and it's a funny thing, I saw an item in the newspaper about a bushmaster stolen from the zoo. It was a small one, not full grown yet, but just as poisonous. I thought it was strange for a bushmaster to be so close to town, they usually like their privacy. Who would steal a bushmaster? And why?"

"Somebody might want to buy it, maybe." Orem spoke up for the first time.

"Somebody crazy." Nat snorted at the thought.

"Yeah, I guess so," Orem answered.

"Well, Orem, we'd best be moving along. Can't spend the whole day jawing, we've got to scout up some work to do. Don't forget, Nat, tell GWH to get well soon and if we can help in any way just let us know."

"I'll be sure to tell him."

Fenton and Orem left. Nat let out a sigh. He couldn't figure them out. *Was that a fishing expedition, or were they really concerned about GWH?* he thought to himself, knowing the answer.

Fenton led Orem into the Bola de Borracha. He bought Orem a beer and he had his "Shirley Temple."

"Dave, what is the latest on GWH?"

"I hear he is quite banged up. Some even say he is blind, but I also heard his eyes are okay, but there are some cuts around them so he has to have them bandaged shut."

"Who told you that?"

"A guy that does lab work at the hospital was in here and he said that was the rumor going around the hospital. You know hospitals are like small towns, news gets around."

"I guess that will delay that trip he was going to take with Ed Garson," said Fenton craftily, hoping to get some information from Dave.

"You have to ask Ed about that. Here he comes now, speak of the devil. Hi, Ed, What'll you have?"

"Gin and tonic, Dave. Somebody taking my name in vain?" He said, casting a wary eye at Fenton and Orem.

"I just wondered if you were going to cancel your trip now that GWH is going to be laid up for quite awhile," explained Fenton.

"I really hate to do that, Fenton. Everything is all ready to go. I was just hanging around waiting for GWH to finish this trip. I've heard he may lose his sight, poor man."

"I guess he is in a bad way and could be out of commission for some time," said Fenton in a solemn tone. Then he added, "Look, Ed, Orem and I could be a great help to you. My calendar is open, we could leave whenever you say."

"I know, Fenton, and I do want to get going, but..." He hesitated, not wanting to hurt Fenton's feelings. He was a gentleman of the old school.

"Heard things about me, have you?"

"Frankly, yes."

"You see what I'm drinking?"

"Something tall and cool and kind of pinkish."

"They call it a Shirley Temple, made of soda and cherry juice. Isn't that right, Dave?"

"Yes, Ed, I haven't served Fenton anything but that in some time."

"Do you plan to keep on that way, Fenton?"

"I promise you, Ed, I am through with drinking."

"I will be bringing something for me to drink, will that bother you?"

"I won't let it! I tell you, Ed, that part of my life is over."

"I'm inclined to take you at your word, Fenton. Years ago you were a fine guide. It's only lately that you've gone to seed."

"What about Orem? He knows a lot of the native lingo, he showed you that."

"Yes, I was very impressed with the scope of his knowledge of the different native tongues," Ed said, warming up to the possibility of being able to go find the lost tribe at last.

"Then it is a deal then?" Fenton held out his hand.

"By golly, I'm tired of waiting, it's a deal," he said, giving the outstretched hand a vigorous shake. "Come over to my house and we will settle the financial arrangements and lay out our plans."

The three of them left the Bola de Borracha avidly chatting away about their plans for the big adventure.

———————

"Hello, GWH, Ed Garson here," Ed announced as he entered GWH's hospital room.

"Hi, Ed. Glad to 'see' you. I need someone to talk to, I'm glad you came." GWH held his hand out to be shaken. Ed obliged with a firm one.

Ed sat down in a chair at the bedside. "I have been keeping track of your condition the last few days. Dave has a pipeline to the hospital and gives out bulletins periodically."

"Is that right?"

"Yes, I think there is a lab worker that gives out the reports. You know how hospitals are like small towns. Things get around fast."

"That is what I've been hearing. What was the word for today?"

"That you have been better lately. Off the pain shots, taking only milder pain medications, and that you tend to be a bit testy when told you can't do something."

"Any idea when I can get out of here?"

"If you are a good boy and do everything they tell you to, maybe next week,"

"Hell, that's more than anyone has told me."

"Well, that is just what I heard, I can't vouch for accuracy. I came to see you to wish you well, and to see for myself how you are, but also to tell you my news."

"What is that?"

"Since you are going to be out of the picture indefinitely, I have made plans to go on the search for the lost tribe. I hate to go without you, but I want to go before another rainy season is upon us."

"I understand, Ed, and I don't blame you. Who is going with you?"

"I have just made a deal with Fenton Cranshaw and Orem Tharp."

"Those two?"

"Yes, now hear me out before you blow. I have asked around and Fenton has been behaving himself lately. He has sworn he is off the booze. He was a good guide in the past and I'd like to give him a chance. Everyone deserves a second chance, GWH."

"Yeah, I guess you are right. Who have you asked about Fenton?"

"Dave at the Bola de Borracha, I figured he ought to know."

"He would be the one to ask. What about Orem? I have an uneasy feeling about him, sometimes he doesn't ring true."

"I know what you mean, but Fenton swears by him and he is doing a great job with the supplies. He came up with some good suggestions and the prices are better than I could have gotten."

"Well, that's something."

"He knows the dialects too, some that Fenton and I don't know."

"That will be a big help. I wish you all the best, Ed. Take care of yourself, you know you aren't a spring chicken anymore."

"I'm only too aware of that, and I intend to let those guys do all the heavy work. I will take an ample supply of my pills, anti venom, and insect repellant and I will be fine."

"Go with God, my friend, I wish I was going with you. Let me know as soon as you get back."

A nurse at the door interrupted them. She was carrying a covered tray. Ed had spent some time in hospitals over the years and could tell it was an enema tray even if it was covered. He also knew the 'three day' rule from experience and knew what was in store for GWH.

"Please excuse us, sir," she said.

Ed beat a hasty retreat and was half way down the hall when he heard GWH's loud roar of dissent.

The group had returned from a tiring trip to the island. After they had cleaned themselves and had a little rest they gathered in the hotel dining room. Nat had shot a peccary that morning. He left the group in Bud's charge, returned to town and gave it to the chef to prepare for their dinner.

After their dinner, which was delicious, Bud brought them to GWH's room for a visit.

"Hi, Dad, how are you?"

"Fine, Bud, come on in." He could tell from the sound that Bud was standing by the door.

"How do you feel about more company?"

"Fine, who do you have with you?"

"I have the whole group here, I couldn't hold them back any longer."

With that they all filed in, filling the room. Each one gave him a personal greeting. GWH felt great, 'seeing' them all. He realized that he felt about them the same way they were declaring their feelings about him.

"What did you do today?"

"We had a wonderful walk through the island's forest," said Letty.

"Nat shot a peccary this morning and brought it back to the cook at the hotel," said Don

"We had it for dinner and it was delectable," said Ellen.

"We saw a poison dart frog eating at an ant hill," Dennis reported. "I guess you know that they have poison pockets in their skin. I was surprised that something the size of a thumb could be so poisonous that when put on an arrow can paralyze an animal."

"We saw a Goliath bird eating a spider too," said Carla, "It was as big as my hand. Ugh!" she said with a shudder.

"There was a whole flight of Blue Morpho butterflies," Ginger said, to say something nice to counteract Carla's shudder. "It was breathtaking the way that beautiful blue flashed on and off against the green of the forest."

"That is because their wings are only colored on top, the underside of the wing is brown," GWH said.

"I know, Bud told me that." She turned toward Bud and the smile she gave him was breathtaking itself.

"When we disturbed a group of black spider monkeys, they set up such a din!" said Nora.

"We saw so many different birds and animals and insects that I filled my notebook already. I started when we arrived, writing about them," said Lois.

"I used up all my video film already," moaned Letty.

"What I really want to do is ask if you are feeling well? Are you in much pain now?" Lois' face showed her concern.

"I am feeling much better and am looking forward to going home." GWH said it as a challenge, looking at Bud.

"I don't know about that, Dad. We still have the rest of the trip to make in the helicopter. It's the most important part of the trip. I think you would be better off here until we return. You can't take care of yourself yet."

"I can get to the bathroom now with my walking cast. What else do I need to do? I know the house thoroughly and can find my way around with this bandage on." Then, as an afterthought he said, "I'll even let you put guide ropes up to guide me."

"I don't think so, Dad. All you would need to do is fall down to undo all the surgeons did to repair your leg."

"Bud, what if I stayed here and watched over GWH?" said Lois. "I would like to get started cataloging my notes, organizing my pictures and doing some research here. I plan to put it into a book I want to write," Lois said hesitatingly. "That is if you think I can do it. If he will be safe with me, I mean."

Everyone was quiet. They looked between GWH and Lois, then at Bud to see how he was taking it. GWH was astounded. He didn't know what to think about it. He admitted to himself that he had amorous feelings toward Lois, but having her taking care of him was something else.

"I don't know about that," GWH said.

"Well, who is going to fix your meals, for one thing? Nat will be with the group and Ryti has to be at the office. Bep and Kamerti have to maintain the boat. It would be impossible for you to stay at home alone."

"I think that Lois' idea has merit," Letty interrupted, "if she wants to stay here instead of flying to the Indian camp."

"Oh, I really do," Lois turned to GWH. "Please say yes, GWH."

"I think it would be great, Lois." He reached out to the sound of her voice and she took his hand. "But what about the rest of the trip, flying to the remote Indian village in the helicopter is the best part of the whole trip."

"It wouldn't be any fun with you not there. Besides, you really need me if you admit it or not." She reddened when she realized how bold it sounded.

"Dad, it really would be a good idea to accept Lois' generous offer. She could organize all her data on that old PC that has just been sitting in the den since you did all that upgrading. You know you really want her to stay," Bud cajoled him.

"Okay, I'm sold. Ryti will only be in the office a half day, then, she can report to me on business. She can stay with us and fix the dinner and do some chores, so Lois can have some time to concentrate on her work. How does that sound?"

"Sounds good to me," said Bud. "How about you, Lois?"

"Fine, it's all settled then?"

"It looks like it is," GWH said.

"GWH, Lois will take good care of you, and when we get back we will tell you both all that happened on the trip." Don, uneasy in a sick room, had been silent up to then. "Lois, I will take your camera, if you want me to, and get the shots you may have missed by not going along. I'd use mine, only it isn't as good as yours."

"I can't find any tape for my camera and no videotape to unload it on, so I will leave it here." Letty said, "but I will take notes."

"That will be fine, Don and Letty, I appreciate that. Nora will help you, like she always helps me."

"I certainly will, I am very good at spotting hidden birds. I even saw a Paloo and pointed it out to Lois. They are about the size of a crow and their posture and coloring makes them look like part of the tree. They hold perfectly still and blend so well with the tree it is hard to see them in plain sight."

"Well, we don't want to tire you, Dad, so we'd better clear out of here and let you get some rest," Bud said, making a move toward the door.

GWH was glad that they came to visit, but he was tiring. *I guess I'm not so well as I thought I was*, he thought as he wished them goodbye and thanked them for coming.

Bud started leading the group out the door. Lois was the last in the line of the leaving visitors. She turned back and stepped to the bed, bent over and kissed GWH on the lips, turned, and rushed out.

GWH was surprised when he felt the light touch of Lois' lips on his, as light as a butterfly's touch. He breathed in the scent of her, mixed with the smell of the insect repellant and it set his heart thumping. Now, he was even more eager to go home with Lois there.

Chapter Fourteen

The next day was one of preparation. GWH was coming home. Nat and Ryti prepared the room. A hospital bed was installed and supplies were on a bedside table in readiness. All was in order.

Lois and Nora went to GWH's house to arrange Lois' things the way she wanted them. The room she was to use was across the hall from the room GWH always used. It was large and airy. There was a window air conditioner as well as a Casablanca fan with a cluster of lights below it. It hung down from the high ceiling about a yard. Keeping cool was no problem. There was a large roll-top desk, completely empty and a double bed with mosquito netting folded back left from the time when they had no air conditioning. Then the windows and French doors, the exit to the veranda, were left open with only the screens repelling the insects. The bedspread was cream-colored, crocheted in the old-fashioned pineapple pattern, a gift from GWH's mother Geneva, when he left for South America. Geneva's mother, Ruth, had given it to her when she went away to college. Ruth was proud of her handiwork and had worked her name and the date in a corner in pale yellow. The stitching was very tiny and almost invisible. She felt it would be a part of home in the stark dorm, and it was. Geneva gave it to "Gordy" for the same reason, a part of home in a distant land.

She had died three years previously, quickly, with an embolism to the brain. She had been a widow for some years and since he was an only child, they were very close. When May and Bud had left, they were closer still. They would trade visits yearly. He went home during the rainy season and she would visit him between his trips when the weather was nice.

On each side of the bed were matching bedside tables with matching lamps. Each table had a drawer. When Lois pulled them open, she found them both empty.

A fiber rug in shades of beige, ecru and tan covered most of the hardwood floor. The walls were eggshell—the room would have been a bit bland had it not been for large pictures of the flora and fauna of the rainforest. They were the only wall decorations. The dominant colors in the pictures, in golden frames, were repeated in the large flower printed valences lolling atop all the windows and French doors, spilling carelessly over the sheer cream curtains that puddled on the floor by the windows. The doors had no curtains, just the beautiful view of the back garden.

There were sets of sheets in the linen closet in the solid dominant colors in the pictures. The present sheets were white, but when the other sheets were used, the color peeked through the spaces in the bedspread and the room would look slightly different with each sheet change. Small pillows in the same bright colors were tossed about on the bed and on a chez-lounge seen through the French doors on the veranda.

The pillows had just been put out there that morning. They had been stored away during the rainy season. This was left from May's brief tenure. In fact, this was May's room, not used since she left. The bathroom was large, as was the adjoining dressing room with built-in drawers along one wall

"Lois, look at this large walk-in closet." Nora had turned on the light so she could see the space with shelves and poles for hangers. "It could be made into a grand darkroom."

"Hmmmm, water, it would be good to have water piped in," mused Lois.

"The bathroom is just on the other side of this wall," Nora remarked. She went into the bathroom and knocked on the wall. "The washbowl pipes are on this wall." She raised her voice so Lois could hear her. Lois noted the spot.

"Nora, you've got it. It would be simple to install a sink in here," Lois told her when she returned. "I'll ask GWH if I can have it done. It could easily be transformed into a great darkroom."

"I'll call Nat at the office, then he can ask GWH when he picks him up at the hospital. Since we are leaving tomorrow, it's best to get things moving right away." She went to start the process, thinking, *I think I'll get a phone extension in Lois' room.*

While Nora was on the phone, Lois walked out the French doors. She walked around the perimeter of the veranda enjoying the view of the garden and surrounding grounds. She sniffed the vase of flowers on a round teak table at the far end of the veranda, turned, and went toward the chez-lounge. As she lowered herself into the pillows and stretched, she thought, *I could stay here forever in this lovely place.*

She closed her eyes and listened to the songs of the birds and the hum of the insects in the flowers going about the business of their lives.

"Lois! Get up. We really don't have time to loll around."

Lois jumped up, startled back to reality, peace and quiet shattered. " What else needs to be done?"

"Nat said he would arrange for the plumbing work to be done right away. We are to go buy the sink and other supplies that are needed to do the job. The job will probably be done next week. He is to bring GWH home this afternoon."

"I'll be so glad to have him home, yet I am worried too, worried that I won't be able to take care of him well enough. I would hate to cause him more pain."

"You will do fine, it isn't like you to think negatively. Come on, let's go shopping for a sink. Nat gave me the directions to a place that sells the things we need. He even made arrangements for us to charge everything to GWH's account."

"I guess we can take Ryti's truck. She is getting things ready for the homecoming. I'll ask her if she needs anything."

"She and Nat have a lot to do. She, here at the house, and Nat, to get ready for the trip. Maybe this closet construction is too much to ask when they are so busy."

"No, you are kind enough to stay behind to tend to GWH, you ought to at least be able to do your own work in your spare time."

"Does GWH know all this about the closet?"

"No, not yet, but he told Nat yesterday to do anything he can to make things easy for you, so I guess that covers it. Come on now, let's get going. We'll get the car keys and a list from Ryti on the way out. We have a lot to get done in a little time."

"I guess we'd better."

" On the way back you can drop me off at the hotel, I have to pack for the trip." Nora squeezed Lois' hand.

"Okay. Isn't this exciting!" She flashed her an infectious grin.

"It sure is, I feel that we are both on the edge of a great adventure."

Nat was going over a "to do" list. "Guns," he said aloud. He walked over to a locked closet. There were some guns and ammunition on a shelf. He wanted Bud to be armed. *You never know what's going to turn up in the jungle.*

He picked a Brazilian-made Taurus .357 Magnum. It was small, with a four-inch barrel and a six shot capacity. Complete with a holster, it was unobtrusive, but easily available. GWH had trained Bud with this gun long ago and he was comfortable with it.

For himself he chose a 12-gauge Rossi single-shot shotgun, also made in Brazil. Of course they didn't plan on doing any hunting but you had to be ready for all comers. He knew that they were clean and ready. One of his chores was to keep them that way.

It is going to seem odd to be going without the boss, he reflected. They had been together a long time and were the best of friends. "Please, God, give him back his sight and his mobility," he prayed aloud in the quiet room.

Chapter Fifteen

The ambulance drove up to the front of the house. Lois ran to the door and held it open for the men to bring GWH into the house and deposit him on the hospital bed that replaced his own double bed. This was accompanied by a series of grunts and groans and a mild oath or two.

When all the people left and things settled down, Lois went into his room and requested his order for lunch.

"Now, Lois, don't come in here like a servant. Honey, I'd give anything not to have you wait on me."

"I'm not acting like a servant, I'm trying to act like a friend. One who wants to help another friend out of a bind…"

"But…" began GWH.

"Just as that friend would help me out of a bind if need be."

"You know I would do that."

"Yes, I do. Now what do you feel like eating? Ryti is waiting in the kitchen to fix anything your heart desires," she said with a smile.

"Oh, I don't care, just anything will do."

"That is not an answer."

"Oh, a toasted cheese sandwich and a glass of beer."

"Fine, that sounds good, I'll have the same. But I'll have fruit juice instead of the beer."

She went to the door and called to Ryti and gave her the lunch decision.

"Would it be okay if I eat in here with you? I can sit here at this little table by the window."

"That would be great."

"Then, after lunch, I will give you your medications and you can have a nap."

"I guess that would be best. A nap doesn't sound bad."

Bud entered with the whole group behind him and heard the last remark. "I am glad to hear you are doing what you ought to. I must say I am surprised you aren't putting up a fuss. It must be Lois' influence." He walked over to his Dad and gave him a cautious hug.

"Hi, boss, how you doin'?" Nat asked.

The others greeted him and gathered around the bed.

"I told Bud that we couldn't possibly go off on our jungle trip without saying goodbye to GWH and Lois," said Letty.

"I am glad to see all of you. I know Bud will do a good job for you. You will really enjoy your 'Amazon Adventure.' I only wish I could go with you, but I have Lois here for company, so I will enjoy being with her."

Goodbyes were said and the group made their way out to the van. Nat and Ryti took a private moment for a hug and kiss.

"I have decided to stay here while you are gone. No use going back and forth to the office. I will work out of GWH's home office. I can sleep on the daybed in there and be near to help out. There won't be much office work to be done anyway, just the monthly bills and a few things to tend to. We won't be making new plans for awhile."

"I guess so, Bud already canceled the next trip coming up. We have to see how things go with the boss."

Ryti walked out to the van with Nat and waved as they left. She went back into the kitchen and picked up the tray already prepared with the lunches on it, and brought it into the bedroom. Lois took her plate and glass and napkin off the tray and placed it on the small table, so she faced GWH. Ryti put the tray on his lap.

Lois went over to him and placed her hand on his. "This is the way we can do it. Your sandwich is in the middle of the plate, and like a clock, the glass of beer is at one o'clock, the napkin is along the left side of the plate. I'll put a towel down the front of you in case of spills, okay?"

"Fine, I can find things then."

"If you need anything, just holler. I'll be sitting at the little table by the window."

"That would be great."

"One thing I must say."

"What's that?"

"I would rather not call you GWH. It's too, I don't know, too stiff, too cold, and too hard to say."

"Well, what do you want to call me, darling?" he said with a grin.

"Of course, that, at times, but every day, I mean. What did your mother call you?"

"She called me Gordy."

"Great, it is a sweet name. May I call you Gordy, darling?"

"Gordy darling. Hmmm, of course, that, at times, but don't you think just Gordy for every day," he said, mocking her tone.

"Oh you, I mean just Gordy."

"Just Gordy, don't you think that is a little demeaning?"

"Will you stop! You know what I mean."

"Seriously, I would like my old name back. I have never been thrilled with the 'Great White Hunter' tag. It is a bit politically incorrect, isn't it? The name Gordy brings a feeling of love that I haven't had for a long time. May called me Gordon."

"Gordy it is then from now on."

"Right."

"Did anyone tell you about the darkroom we are putting into the closet?"

"Yes, Nat filled me in on the plans, and I think it is great. You'll be able to get all your work done easily with the darkroom so handy."

"I thank you so much for making it that way."

"It's the least I can do to repay you for giving up the rest of the trip for me."

"It will take me a while to do all I have to do. I have many pictures that I have taken so far and there are even a lot of flora and fauna that I can see from the verandah. If I run out of things to do, I can go seeking other things in the area. By the way, what about the snake that started all this?"

"That is the mystery, how it got in the car with me. I usually have the windows shut for the air conditioning, and I don't believe the snake was small enough to enter through any cracks. I've been stewing about that very question. Would you think me paranoid if I said I think it was put in the car deliberately?"

"Is the car, when it is all shut up, snake proof?"

"I believe it is. I didn't lock it, I never do, but it was closed up. Someone had to put it in there!"

"Did anyone tell you about the article in the paper, the day after your accident, about a stolen snake from the zoo? It was a Bushmaster."

"No, who would want to steal a poisonous snake? Come to think of it, the snake that was in there looked a bit like a Bushmaster, as I remember from the quick look I had of it. That may mean that my visitor wasn't there on his own."

"Who would do such a thing?"

"There is one guy I know that just might, and he benefitted by my injuries too!"

"Who is that?"

"His name is Fenton Cranshaw. He used to be an all right guy, but he had a bitter divorce and started to hit the bottle and he fell to pieces. He turned his hate onto me out of envy. He lost some jobs that came to me when he goofed, and he couldn't get over it. He could be the one who did it."

"It is a wonder he wasn't bitten himself."

"It sure is, and I can't see him taking it out of the zoo either."

"Maybe he had some help."

"That's got to be it! He has a native buddy that is really at home in the forest, and is an excellent hunter. His name is Oren Tharp"

"That doesn't sound so much like a native's name."

"The missionaries named him after a benefactor, I believe."

"Well, it could have happened that way. I can't think of any other way it could have happened."

"Fenton is away on a job that I was going on after this trip was over. If this had not happened to me, he wouldn't have had a chance at it. Orem is with him too."

"What do you intend doing about it?"

"Without proof, I don't think I can really do anything. I intend to let him know what I suspect though. You can bet on that!"

In his agitation he waved his arm around and knocked over his beer.

"Oops, I'll get it," said Lois. She mopped it up with her napkin. Luckily, she had placed the thick towel over his chest and lap the long way and he didn't get wet.

Bud was standing by the helicopter. It was all packed with everything they could possibly need on their four-day trip into the jungle. The group was chattering excitedly as they came out of the air-conditioned airport building into the blinding sun, in preparation for boarding.

Letty was wearing her khaki jacket and looked very uncomfortable in the heat.

Dennis said, "I hope you don't faint in this heat."

"It has all these pockets and I want to bring along some things that can help us in the jungle," she panted.

"Bud already packed all we will need, honey." Nora added.

"Well, I've brought them this far, I might as well bring them the rest of the way. Anyway, I will take off the jacket when we get into the helicopter. I'd rather wear it than carry it now."

They positioned themselves in the seats. Bud, the pilot, was the last to enter. Nat was in the copilot's seat. Behind Bud sat Ginger (naturally) and her dad, Dennis. Then Nora, Letty and Carla were seated and in the very back seats were Don and Ellen.

The takeoff went smoothly and they all relaxed to enjoy the ride. About an hour into the ride Nat brought out some soft drinks and snacks he had stowed handily under the front seat.

"I'm going to drop off some mail to Father O'Toole in a minute or two. It will save him a long boat ride to Manaus."

Nat prepared a mail pouch with the mail fastened inside. Bud buzzed a settlement of about ten huts. The inhabitants were jumping and waving, waiting for the pouch. Father O'Toole was among them. As Nat tossed the pouch, he threw candy out also and the children scampered to get some. There was also some in the pouch for Father to distribute later.

As they pulled away, all were waving, on the ground and above.

"Tell us about the priest. How long has he been way out here?" Letty inquired.

"As long as I've been coming here, I guess over ten years, I don't know exactly. He is a good friend of Dad's. He married my mother and dad. He knew Dad even before then, though. I guess I've known him all my life. He is a great guy—full of fun, but when he talks about his faith he gets very serious. He used to play a lot of basketball. I don't know if you could see him very well, but he is about six foot two. The Indians were in awe of him because of it, even afraid at first. He soon won them over with his winning ways. He has done great work with them and for them. They love him very much. He protects them from the outside world.

"Very few people know of this place. It is extremely difficult to get in and out of here. He keeps it that way. He has studied some medicine, though he is not a doctor. He has studied these tribes and their languages. He even put himself in isolation before he made contact with them in person. He was sure he was disease free because he didn't want to hurt them in any way. They really love him."

As they flew above the treetops, Bud would occasionally point out things to notice, but the trees obscured most of the things below. They were heading for a base camp from which they would take side trips into the jungle.

They hovered over the base camp. There was a landing strip long enough for a small plane to land. Surrounding it was a group of long houses, open at each end. At the far end of the strip there was a simple frame building used as the airport office. It had a place to fuel a plane and even do minor repairs.

Bud noted a small plane parked behind the building. He thought he recognized it as the one Ed Garson rented sometimes.

There were a few little cabins on the other side of the office. This is where the group was billeted, family groups together and Nora and Letty in one and Bud and Nat in another. They unloaded their things and gathered into the office.

They were pleasantly surprised to find it air-conditioned and that it had a cafeteria. It even had a TV set running. There were about five natives watching an old John Wayne movie in the area set aside for TV viewing. Quite unusual, but a benefit of the large generator installed for the electric system needed for the airport. As a result the native population was more modern than the usual ones away from the cities. Some even spoke some English words and understood even more.

"Ke'era, good to see you." Bud shook the hand of a scantily clad native standing at the door as he entered the office with the group

"Bud, you say my name better now!" There was a guttural "click" that was hard to master to his name and Bud tried hard to get it right. This was much appreciated by Ke'era.

"Finally!"

It was a matter of dignity, GWH had explained. Ke'era was in charge of the airport and was a competent mechanic as well. They depended upon him for many things and wanted to give him respect. Taking the trouble to say his name correctly increased his stature with the other natives, and also made his job of leading them in performing the necessary work around the airport much easier.

"Oh, by the way, is that ED Garson's plane parked in the back?"

"Yas, but he and his people goin' soon."

"I'd like to see him, where is he?"

"He and his people in last hut. Here they come now."

Bud looked out the window and saw their group headed toward the office. Bud told them to take their things to their cabins and he'd see them later. He then went out to meet Ed, Fenton and Orem. The chattering group dispersed to their assigned cabins.

"Hi, Ed, howdy Fenton. Orem, are you coming or going?"

"Hi, Bud, both. We came back for more supplies, now we are heading out again."

Fenton and Orem nodded a greeting and went on to tend to the Indian bearers and see their loads on the boats weren't too heavy or too loose. Doing their jobs, while Ed talked to Bud.

"Did you have any luck finding the lost tribe?"

"No sign, we are heading in another direction this time. We are going to take another stream that shoots off the main stream a few miles down. I've found bigger boats that will hold more supplies and hold more help to do the rowing."

"How are Fenton and Orem working out?"

"Fine, just fine, no problem at all."

"That's great.! Say, do you have time for a beer or soda while they are loading up?"

"I'll have a root beer with you, Bud. I want to hear all about your Dad."

They walked into the office and sat at the bar and ordered their root beers.

"You see to the boat loading and placing the rowers, Orem," Fenton said. "I am going to take a look at their new helicopter." He knew the helicopter was so much better than his old one. Envy, then anger rose up in him. Fenton went to the boat he was to ride in and helped with the loading. He was seething over the fact that they were able to get such a great new helicopter.

I wish they'd crash, he said to himself in his anger. A bag of sugar fell and split open. Fenton took it over to give it to those in the office and trade it for a new one. He stopped, changed his mind and went to where the new helicopter was. He hurriedly opened the gas tank and poured the sugar in and closed it.

It only took a few seconds. He turned and went back to the boat loading. No one saw him—he was hard put to suppress an evil grin. Orem looked at him, questions in his eyes.

"What's up, boss?"

"Nothing, are we all done here?"

"Yeah, and a good thing. Here comes the big boss."

Ed and Bud came walking over to the boat.

"Have a good trip, Fenton and Orem," Bud said. "You too, Ed. Don't try to do too much in a day, watch out for your health."

"I know I'm no spring chicken, so I'll watch my step," he replied. "Bye, have a good trip yourself." He stepped in the boat, settled himself and waved as they cast off.

————

Bud headed for his cabin and stowed his gear. It was very hot and humid. He then found the group watching TV with the natives. It was a motley bunch. The natives were clean because they loved to play in the river. They were barely clothed for the same reason. They looked healthy and happy. Their teeth, however, were in bad condition or missing. Easy to see because they smiled a lot and laughed out loud at the show.

After the TV show, Don and Ellen, Dennis, Nora and Letty, sans jacket, took a short walk into the jungle with Lois' camera. Don had taken some pictures of the natives around the TV. He thought that was so funny and wanted Lois to see it. They hadn't gone far when they came upon a Forked-tailed Wood nymph. Don took the picture. They knew that was what it was because Nora looked it up in her bird book. It was smaller and more delicate than a sparrow.

Nora read, "It goes out in the daytime, eats tiny insects and nectar from plants. It is a hummingbird, and can fly backward, forward and can hover. Its wing beats 75 times per second! They require lots of energy to maintain body heat, and eat more than they weigh every day. They live from Alaska to Argentina, 200 species in South America and only 12 species in North America." She placed a check mark by the picture in the book, as Lois always did when she finished taking a picture.

They walked along the bank of the river awhile. They didn't see anything that wasn't already checked in the book. On the way back, Don photographed the beautiful orchids, trumpet vines bromeliads and iris along the way.

There was an eardrum-shattering screech from Ellen when she came across a few rhinoceros beetles along the bank that made them all jump.

"Those bugs were as long as my fingers!" she wailed, still shaking.

"They are beetles, rhinoceros beetles. See the picture in my book?" Letty said. She had Lois' insect book. "See the horns on some, those are the males. Don't be afraid, they only eat other insects."

When they returned to camp, they joined the others at the TV area of the office. Bud and the three Evans' were playing Bridge.

The usual handful of natives were watching an "I love Lucy" rerun. How much they understood is a question, but they laughed along with the laugh track.

After dinner they sat around talking awhile, but turned in early because they were to fly on to another camp the next day.

———— ···●●··· ————

Bud dressed for the day. He put the gun and holster on, just like his Dad always did on a trip. Bud rousted the group out early. They had fruit and some sort of corn meal cakes with lots of hot coffee. It was still very humid and warm. It was plain to see Letty was uncomfortable in her jacket. She insisted on wearing it though, and its pockets were bulging.

Nat finished loading the plane and helped them board. He put the shotgun in a special holder GWH had made in the plane.

Soon it was time to get on board. Ke'era led a gaggle of waving and smiling natives to the helicopter to watch them take off. A flurry of good-byes and they were off in a dusty cloud. Each had taken their original seat. Letty slipped out of the jacket.

"Now the fun really begins." Ginger turned and smiled at those sitting in the back.

They flew in silence for awhile. It was noisy in the helicopter. Each was lost in their own thoughts. Letty was thinking of Tom, wishing he were here with her. Nora was thinking of Lois and GWH. She wondered if anything permanent would come of their attraction for one another. It would be so nice for Lois. What would it mean in her life?

She would miss her so much, all the things they did together would stop. *I mustn't interfere in any way or show how much I'll miss her. I'll plan a series of visits to each of the guys*, she thought. *A New York stay after this jungle trek will be just the thing. I'll take in a lot of plays and visit the TV studios with June and Alec. I'll keep busy, I know that.*

Don Mason was wondering how the golf scramble had gone. Ellen was thinking of how much fun she'd have telling her friends all about her exciting trip. She glanced over at Don, gave his hand a squeeze, which he returned with a wink. Their love life certainly had taken a turn for the better in spite of the humid conditions.

Dennis was thinking about some of the more seriously ill patients that he had left behind. He had left them in good hands, but he couldn't help wonder how they were faring.

Carla was worried about Ginger's infatuation with Bud. *She is so young,* she thought. *Bud is so attentive, you can tell he is smitten.* She sighed as she wondered what she could do about it. Nothing came immediately to mind at the moment. *He is a very nice young man, and handsome. That he is well off is easy to see. His future is assured, albeit a bit dangerous, the way he flits in and out of the jungle on this whirlybird. Anything could happen to him. I wouldn't want Ginger to be a young widow with a handful of kids to raise alone.* She put on a wry smile and brought herself to the present. *Stop it, you goose!* She told herself. *You have her married, a mother and a widow and she is only eighteen with her first real crush. I'm not going to let it bother me on this trip, but I will keep my eye on her.*

Bud was thinking of Ginger and Ginger was thinking of Bud and Nat was thinking of Ryti.

Bud was checking the dials and wondered why the motor was running so rough. It started spitting. "Nat, what do you think is wrong?" Bud quietly asked Nat.

"What's up?"

"What is causing this coughing and spitting?"

" Well, it ought not to. It was running fine when we left."

While they were checking the dials, it coughed again and sputtered…"We are losing altitude!"

"Oh, Oh, are we past the point of no return," he said softly, not wanting to be overheard by the rest.

"I'm afraid so," Bud answered.

They were flying over a thick carpet of green; the tops of very tall trees, very crowded together.

"Is anything wrong?" Dennis asked. "The motor sounds funny."

"What's happening?" Ginger asked.

"Is there something the matter?" Letty anxiously inquired.

Nora and Ellen leaned forward, waiting for Bud's reply.

Don couldn't wait for an answer, as Bud was trying to figure out what to tell them. "Spit it out, man, we have a right to know what is going on!"

"We are having trouble with the motor. We will have to abort. Nat, get out the Bambi and connect it." Nat scrambled to do just that. He opened the door and a blast of hot air hit them. Nat threw it out. Bud had the helicopter in a hover. The Bambi was nestled in the top of a tall tree, looking all the world like a giant bird's nest.

Bud turned to speak to Nora. "Nora, you have been telling us how you repel down mountains, Well, do you think you can shinny down this line and fasten the Bambi to those two trees at each side to steady it?"

"I am sure I can if it is necessary," she answered.

"Then each will take turns getting down to the tree," Bud said.

A chorus of "What?" "Oh no!" "Are you crazy?" and the like followed that announcement.

"We better throw out everything we can. Luggage, gas cans, maps, EVERYTHING! AND HURRY!" Nat screamed over the noise of the wind through the open door. He helped Nora with the harness and put it on her, and sent her out the door. She had a handful of bungie cords tied onto her. She had some gloves on that were in the helicopter and she slid down the line in spurts. It took awhile, but she made it and started securing the Bambi to the thickest branches and leveled it out as best she could. One side was much higher than the other.

While this was going on, Ginger leaned over Bud who was steadying the plane. "How are you going to steady the plane while you get down?" Her voice quavered. She was doing her best to keep from screaming, as Ellen was. Bud didn't answer and Ginger persisted.

Don was trying to assure Ellen that they were going to be all right, and not even convincing himself.

Letty was softly praying as she threw everything that she could lift out of the other door. Nat was busy throwing things out, Carla was crying and praying as she handed Dennis things to throw out that door too.

Nora had sent up the gloves and harness on the end of the safety rope.

"Dennis, you are next. Got to have a man to help catch down there, and it better be a doc, just in case," Bud was saying as he tended to Dennis' lines, while Dennis put on the gloves. He took off his holster and put it on Dennis.

"Ginger, you are next," he said as Dennis scooted down the line, too fast.

"Whoa!" Bud shouted to Dennis. "Take it slower, you'll tear up your hands."

Dennis had already realized he was going too fast and stopped, just swaying there on the line.

"Dennis!" screamed Carla.

"I'm okay," he muttered, slowly sliding down to the Bambi.

"When you get down there, you and Nora get off the Bambi and start climbing down the tree, but be careful. Remember, everyone should get off the Bambi and get down off the tree as fast as they can," Bud said to Ginger as he tied the line to the harness while she was putting on the gloves.

"But, Bud," she cried, "how are you going to get down?"

"I'll get down, don't worry. I'm not going to leave you alone down there." He gave her a quick kiss. "Now, GO!"

The motor was really coughing now and was getting hard to control.

"Nora, Bud said to get off the tree right away," Ginger informed her.

"Dad, you are to help each one land and then start them going down to the ground."

"I know, honey, that's what I am going to do. Now you follow Nora."

"EEEEK!" Nora was taken by surprise when she found she was on a branch that was occupied by a sloth hanging upside down. She stepped over on another branch. The sloth gave her a sleepy look, but didn't move, just hung there, staring.

"Ginger, don't be afraid, but there is an animal down here hanging on a branch, but I don't think he is dangerous. Just move over to another branch and go by him, uh, or her, or whatever." Nora continued her descent. When Ginger came near it, she recognized it as a sloth.

"Dad," she hollered, "tell each one as they come down there is a sloth hanging on a branch down here, not to worry, it won't hurt them."

"Okay, Ginger, I'll tell them."

Nat had taken over the controls while Bud was helping Ginger. The engine gave a cough and Nat adjusted some dials.

When Ginger was down and the line and gloves returned, Bud wanted to send Ellen. She was hysterical by this time. They decided to tie her to Don. She was a little thing, and send the two of them down together.

"Don, when you get down, help Ellen climb down the tree to the ground. Take it slow and easy, she will probably be much calmer by then."

When the line was returned, Bud said to Nat. "That worked so well, I'm going to send Carla and Letty together, then you go."

"No, I can't face GWH and tell him I left you to die, you go!"

"No," piped up Letty, "I can stay till the last. Just tell me what to do. I've lived a long happy life, it must be me that stays."

"We are wasting time, Carla and Letty, Go NOW!" Bud shouted, when the motor started making more coughing noises and cutting out. It didn't stop when Nat adjusted the dials.

Letty had slipped her Uncle Albert's case onto her belt, put on the jacket, then she and Carla shoved off and were going down at a good rate.

"Nat, change places with me, now. I'm the captain of this thing and I am the one who stays. The cab of this model has been reinforced. Lots of guys survived crashes in this model. You are the one who has the knowledge to get this bunch back, and you know it. And don't forget to cut the line as soon as you get down! NOW GO!"

The line returned and Nat decided not to waste time arguing, and started getting ready to go down. He tied the shotgun to his belt. It was ungainly, but manageable.

"You are just as stubborn as your Dad. The nut doesn't fall far from the tree," was his parting remark as he went over the side.

When he was sure that Nat was down and had cut the lines, Bud moved the coughing helicopter away from them and slowly descended into the trees in another area. The rotors went first, in a wild noisy tearing of tree limbs, disintegrating rotors, and other helicopter parts flying in all directions. Without the rotors the plane cab plummeted, bouncing through the limbs that slowed it somewhat. The back part broke off and went bumping off at an angle. The cab, landing with a thump, remained as a unit and made a depression in the damp jungle floor.

Though Bud was bounced around a lot and had more than a few cuts and bruises, the worst was a broken arm.

It was momentarily quiet. Even the monkeys and the birds abruptly stopped what they were doing and then all started screeching together. It was quite a din.

The group had gathered at the bottom of the tree.

"What was that furry thing hanging upside down?" asked Letty. "If I hadn't been warned that it was there, I'm afraid I would have lost my composure." She laughed shakily.

Ginger, still in shock, but remembering from her class at school said, almost by rote, "That was a sloth, they spend most of their lives hanging upside down in the trees. They even give birth hanging upside down there. Did you notice that its fur had a greenish tinge? That is algae, and you know what? There is a grub that grows into a moth there too and it only eats those algae, and that type of algae only grows in the sloth's fur. Isn't that amazing?"

"Not now, Ginger," Dennis hissed.

"Thanks for the lesson, Ginger, but let's all…" Don broke off in mid-sentence, the awful noise of the helicopter falling through the trees froze them in their tracks.

Nat led the group in the direction of the downed helicopter. Nora was hovering over Ellen and helping her along. Ellen had quieted down and was feeling somewhat calmer again, and a bit subdued and shaking.

Carla's lips were moving in hurried prayers for Bud.

Bud was trying to extricate himself from the damaged cab. He was able to do so before the group managed to thrash through the underbrush to reach him.

They had scratches on their faces and arms from going through the vegetation so quickly. Letty still had her jacket on, so she only had a scratch on one cheek.

There was a lot of hugging and nervous laughter, and much relief that they had all survived.

"Now," said Bud, "we have to go back and retrieve all the things we can find that we threw out. The first is the Bambi."

"No," Dennis said, "the first thing we must find is my medical kit. We must treat everyone's broken skin. Even the slightest cut is just asking for an infection, and I must set Bud's arm. People's health comes first." He set the arm quickly, it wasn't too bad, and the skin was unbroken. Then he cut the sleeves off Letty's jacket. He made a sling of them. After he tended to Bud, they made their way back to the tree that still held the Bambi.

It took awhile for Nat and Don to climb back up the tree. It was a considerable distance and it took awhile. The rest were combing the jungle floor for the things that were thrown out. Some of the things were still stuck in the tree.

Bud was sitting among the roots of a tree, leaning against it with his eyes closed, still shaking and wondering what to do next. He felt out of his depth and wished he could call his Dad.

He felt better after Dennis had set his arm and sewed the cuts that required stitches. Letty's case was well supplied with the necessary equipment he needed. There were some pain pills that had dulled the pain, but he still felt some discomfort.

Dennis was using Letty's emergency medical supplies from Uncle Albert's case to treat the scratches on Ginger, Ellen, Carla, Nora and Letty. Carla treated the scratches and cuts Dennis couldn't reach on himself. He had already tended to Nat and Don before they went up the tree. He also had to treat a few more scrapes they had acquired during the process.

Ellen was the one who found the medical kit. *Maybe this will make up for my ridiculous behavior in the helicopter,* she hoped. She was embarrassed that she lost her composure and even Ginger had not.

Nat and Don had retrieved the Bambi piece by piece. They had to disassemble it to bring it down carefully. It was made of a hard, but pliable plastic. They were able to recover eight triangular pieces, one a bit larger than the others were. Nat set them out on the damp jungle floor. As each of the bags were recovered he put them in a piece. When Ellen and Don's bags were found, he put them in the large piece. All the food and cooking utensils were put in another piece, as were the medical things in a separate place. Then he called everyone together.

Bud had fallen asleep, so they went a little bit away from him so they wouldn't disturb him.

"We are going to have to hike out of here," Nat began.

"Thanks to Letty we have two compasses. The one in the helicopter was smashed. Nights in the jungle can be cold and wet. The ground is always soggy and damp. Every kind of insect, snake and critter comes out at night to feed. You don't want to be on the menu. We will use our piece of Bambi for the floor of the tent. We will get a straight branch for the pole. We will use anything we can find for the covering. Did you bring any rain gear? Clothes, or we could use those soft-sided bags, or those fold over garment bags to cover it, even some of those large leaves. If you do use any of the leaves, be sure there are no insects on them. I have a large roll of duct tape, thank God. What would we do without duct tape? We can use the lines from the Bambi and tie the lines to the Bambi pieces and pull them like sleds along the damp ground. Don and Ellen, you will have the large piece and will sleep together. The rest of you will make your own tent. This smaller broken piece will be what we carry the rest of the equipment in. To keep the critters out of it we will have to make a binding for it. If we are unable to fit everything into it, we will parcel out things among you and you will be responsible for them. We will only take what we really need so it ought to be doable.

"Watch me while I assemble my tent, then you can start on yours. I will start on Bud's, but if you need help, just ask. If anyone has an idea we can use, speak up. I am new at this too and will welcome your suggestions."

They all watched attentively as Nat started to make a tent, too stunned to make any comment. It was like a small sailboat, with a branch for the mast and the enveloping material he had assembled from the things he could find, starting from the peak and tucked in all around. There was an overlapping slit for the opening and soft moss and leaves for the floor. At the wide end there was room for the luggage. Not too bad, only you had to be sure there was no wildlife in the stuff used for bedding. It was dusk before all tents were ready for occupancy. They had a cold supper of peanut butter and jelly sandwiches and a Coca-Cola.

Nat gave Bud some more painkillers and they fell into their tents. It was a tight fit for Ellen and Don, but they didn't mind at all.

The next day they loaded up and started out. Nat and Don led the way. Nat had a machete and Don had a compass. They did their best to make an easy path.

Nat didn't know what to do about the guns. He wanted one near in case some animal became a problem. He would like to shoot something to eat. The things they had were more like snacks, which were running scarce. The shotgun was in the way and unhandy to carry and make a path for everyone too. He ended up placing it in his pack. Don had the Taurus holstered at his waist. Nat knew Don was familiar with guns and was himself a hunter. He and his friends went duck and deer hunting in the White Mountains every winter. Nat and Don decided to keep an eye open for something to shoot for food. If they got nothing, they would stop early and go fishing.

They were following the river back in the direction of the base camp. The undergrowth was thick because the sun was able to get to it along the river. Nat and Don held back obstructing branches. Ellen came next, then Letty. Then Dennis would hold the branches and Don would go up and stand next to Nat. Nora and Ginger came next and Bud brought up the rear. Then Dennis would go forward and relieve Don and so on like that.

There was not much talking. It was too arduous and hot for that. They were all pretty miserable, but thankful to be alive. Letty's jacket was inside her tent and she was in her t-shirt and shorts like everyone else.

At noon they decided to rest. They had been dragging their packs behind them, bumping along, sliding along the jungle floor.

The monkeys were creating a din that followed them. When they left one bunch, another bunch started in. They even threw dead branches down on them. The birds were making noise too.

They were not welcome here.

They had only a little water, so they each had a warm soda as they rested, and some beef jerky to chew on. They were sitting on their packs and waving their hands to keep the little flying things away.

"Where are we headed?" Don asked, wiping his forehead with a grubby handkerchief.

"We are going in the direction of the base camp, but I don't exactly know how far away it is," Bud answered. Surprisingly, his arm wasn't bothering him near as much as the stitched cuts were because of the sweat getting into them and stinging. All of them were feeling the same stinging.

"Let me put some more antibiotic ointment on your cuts, that will keep them from stinging," said Dennis, alert to their problem. He was having the same problem with his scrapes.

When they were all treated and had finished their sodas, they moved on. This time Don wielded the machete and Nat did branch holding duty.

At about 5:30 they were exhausted and agreed to stop. A slight drizzle had started and they all wanted to get into their little shelters. Letty made some instant soup with the rest of the water. They each had a paper cup, from a rescued package. The soup was divided among them. There were crackers, chips, peanut butter and jerky to fill up on too.

They turned in as soon as they put all the food away to keep from drawing any critters to them.

"Good night all," Letty said, and this was followed by a chorus of good nights. One wag said, "Good night, John Boy." Letty wasn't sure, but she thought it was Don. They slept to the noises of the jungle at night.

In the morning they dragged their aching bodies out of their shelters. Nat had designated the boys' area and the girls' area and they took care of nature's call in the correct place. There was

Hunter's Amazon Adventure

water caught in various leaves and that helped them get clean. Nat was able to collect some of the water to fill two canteens and a half of another. He carefully flicked out any ants that had fallen in. He didn't think he needed to mention the ants. They ate the same thing for breakfast as they had for supper—snack food. Letty heated some of the water for tea over a Sterno can. And Nat went off to find some antless water to refill the canteens.

When they couldn't put it off any longer, they packed up and started on their way again. Their muscles were aching from the unaccustomed exercise that they had endured yesterday. Sleeping in the damp hadn't helped any either.

Letty was saying a "finger" rosary (using her fingers to count the prayers in place of the beads.) as they plodded on in the humid atmosphere. She was having a hard time of it, but wouldn't let on. She didn't want to be a bother and make an already bad situation worse. Her back was killing her. She thought, *If I don't complain the younger ones won't do it either. Too proud. Complaining won't help anyway, just a waste of breath.*

She was right, the other girls decided that if Letty could make it, they sure could. The men would have died before they complained in front of the girls.

Nat was watching carefully and called for frequent stops. He broke out a small carton of gum and gave each a pack to chew when they wanted to. This helped a lot.

203

Chapter Sixteen

Garson, Fenton and Orem were each in a boat with two natives paddling down the river. The day was fine, a bit warm, but there was a soft breeze on the river. They hadn't had any luck finding any native settlements yet and they were discouraged.

The native paddlers were getting tired and wanted to turn back. Fenton told them in no uncertain terms that they were not turning back.

"Quit your bellyaching and keep on paddling!" he yelled. They didn't really understand his words, but they got the idea and kept on paddling.

Garson was not feeling so well and often resorted to his nitroglycerine under the tongue to relieve his angina. Orem was staying out of all the arguments and just doing what he was told.

They rounded one of the many bends in the river and spotted a village. What's more, the villagers spotted them and angrily came charging after them in about ten boats.

By the time Garson, in the lead boat, decided to turn his boat around and try to flee, they had lost valuable time. The two other boats turned also and the chase was on. The villagers had the advantage, they were fresh and the three pursuing boats were larger and had more paddlers. Paddlers who had been working hard for half a day manned Garson, Fenton and Orem's boats. It was a lost cause. They put up a valiant effort, but they just couldn't get away. They soon were surrounded and roughly escorted back to the village.

In the melee, Garson had dropped his nitroglycerine in the water as they manhandled him ashore. Fenton fought them every inch of the way. Orem could speak their language and tried to calm them down.

"We are just out looking for plants to study," Orem lied.

They didn't believe him. The boats had many guns, and ammunition, and didn't look very peaceful.

They were thrown into a small pen and were left alone while their captors reported to Kanchinapio and Maeuma in the meeting hut along with the Elders.

"Now we have some 'Others'!" Wanapio exclaimed, glad that all threats against his son Kamamar'e was gone.

"The Spirit of the Great Knife can be satisfied!" Panteri shouted.

They were agitated and aggressive to a white-hot frenzy. They wanted to execute the three at once. They had run off the six paddlers, but kept their boats. They had disappeared into the jungle.

"We will prepare the worship ceremony for sunset tomorrow," Kanchinapio decreed.

The pen was now in the late afternoon sun. They were given nothing to eat or drink. It was hot and they were parched. Garson was in a bad way, in pain and gasping. Fenton and Orem fell back on the old trick of sucking on some pebbles they had found in the pen. This deterred much conversation. They both knew they were in a dire situation. The worst part of it was that they couldn't do anything about it.

Morning came. The natives gathered around the pen. Garson had died during the night, so they removed his body. Fenton and Orem never did learn what they did with his body.

The day was spent preparing for the sunset ceremony. The women spent the day preparing all the special dishes they prepared for feasts. They made sure that there were plenty of their favorite intoxicating drinks.

The men made a special altar, and just beyond it built a huge bonfire, ready for lighting the minute the sun was out of sight.

Orem was speaking to one of the children who was hanging around the pen. He emptied his pockets. All he had was some string, some keys and a pocketknife.

"Hey, Fenton, whatcha got in your pockets?" he whispered.

"Not much, a small compass, a dirty handkerchief, and lint, that's all."

"Give me your ring, I think I can get this kid to get us some water."

As Fenton handed him the ring, he said. "It ain't doing me any good, and I could sure use some water!"

Orem showed him Fenton's class ring with a blue stone in it. He told him the ring had lots of magic because of the blue stone. "Bring two jars of water, but don't let anyone see you," Orem told him. "You'll get the ring when you do."

The little boy, about six, ran off and filled two large terra cotta jars with water. He could only carry one at a time. When he had made the two trips, Orem gave him the ring. They each drank about half of the water and saved the rest for the afternoon when the sun hit the pen.

The adults were so busy getting ready for the feast that they didn't notice anything that went on back at the pen.

Fenton and Orem rationed their water and had some left at sunset. They each had about a fourth left in their jars at sunset when the ceremony began.

Kanchinapio ordered that Fenton be stripped and brought to the altar. The Elders had decided to keep Orem as a slave and not offer a brown man to be sacrificed. They didn't want the Spirit of the Great knife to get a taste for brown flesh.

"It looks like this is it, Orem. You have been a good friend, goodbye," Fenton said bravely as they pulled him out of the pen.

"Bye, boss, you have been a good friend to me too." He watched as they dragged him to the altar where Kanchinapio stood with Maeuma at his side.

They gave Fenton a drink of a powerful sedative. They didn't want him resisting the Spirit of the Great Knife. It didn't take long to work and he fell to the ground. He was placed on the altar. Flowers were placed around him. They started to dance around the altar. Their naked bodies shone in the firelight. Slowly at first, then faster and faster they danced, chanting softly at first, then a rising crescendo, till it was ended in one huge shout.

Uanica held the Great Knife with the enormous emerald in the tip of the handle over the unconscious Fenton's throat. Then, with one motion, sliced his throat. Blood spewed in a fountain-like shower all over Uanica. This had been expected and desired. The bloody garment would be holy and have much power from then on.

There was a great yell at that moment. Orem couldn't see it, but he knew what had happened.

There was dancing and drinking and fornicating the rest of the night.

Orem poured the rest of Fenton's water into his jar. He took Fenton's clothes and shoes and wrapped them in a bundle and tied them to his belt with the string. He took his pocketknife and sawed through the thong that held the door of the pen closed. He slipped down the path to the boats, picked the smallest and set his course upriver, paddling as fast as he could. The minute he rounded the river bend, he slacked off a bit, knowing that he had far to go and that he needed to pace himself. The party was in full swing and no one noticed his escape.

The next morning everyone had a hangover and they slept late. It was almost noon when Maeuma discovered that Orem was gone. No one was blamed because no one had been appointed to guard Orem.

Panteri was miffed because he had planned to use him as a slave. Maeuma was sad because he wanted to talk to him and asks he about the 'Others' world.

Uanica's job was not over. He severed Fenton's head from his body. He gave the body to some young men who put it in the part of the river where piranhas were known to be. It wasn't long until there were only bones left and they sank to the bottom of the river and were moved along in the river's current and disappeared.

Uanica's next task was the building of a tiny hut with an animal skin over it. It was placed over some embers left from the bonfire in the far end of the Elders' meeting hut. Fenton's head was suspended over the embers, enclosed in the tiny hut and the process of shrinking the head was started. Unanica had Kamanar'e stay by the fire and tend to it; not letting it flare up too high, nor let it die down too low. When enough days had passed so that the head was cured, it was to be decorated and placed in a place of honor in the Elders' meeting hut, just above and behind the stone throne alongside of a few others that were there.

One day soon after that Kamanar'e came running into the village as fast as his poor deformed foot would allow. Maeuma was playing a game with the children, very much like tag, only one had to throw a circle of woven leaves and flowers over the head of the one to be IT. Teptykti was playing the game too.

"Maeuma! Maeuma!" he rasped, breathless from running.

"Kamanar'e, why are you running so fast?"

"I was hunting far out in the jungle when I saw one of the strange big birds fall out of the sky," he panted.

Maeuma disentangled himself from the arms of a clinging child and stood. "Let's tell my father and the elders of this."

They went to where the old Chief and the Elders were gathered.

"Father, Kamanar'e has seen one of the strange birds fall out of the sky!"

They were all surprised. They had seen different planes in the sky from time to time, but not very often. They knew that they were controlled by the 'Others', but none had seen one on the ground.

"We will all go see this fallen bird," said Chief Kanchinapio.

They went to get the carrying platform for the Chief, as he was too old and arthritic to make the trip without it. Uanica went to his hut and put on the regalia that the occasion called for.

When they were ready to travel, they said farewell to the women and children and were on their way, following Kamanar'e.

While they traveled on their own paths in the jungle, they softly sang one of their traveling songs.

After some time they came to the end of their previously made path and had to use the machete to make progress. They could see where Kamanar'e had passed through, but they had to widen the way for the carrying platform. This slowed them down some. They were coming at an angle and would shortly intersect the path on which the Hunter group was struggling to make headway.

Kamanar'e and Maeuma were in the lead. Suddenly Maeuma stopped to listen and made motions for the others to be quiet. They could hear the noise of the chopping and the murmur of the people talking a bit ahead of them. Also the racket the monkeys and birds were making let them know something was just ahead of them.

They circled around the 'Other' group and gradually closed in on them.

Don jumped in surprise when he chopped down some foliage and facing him was Uanica, the shaman, or witch doctor, of the tribe, in all his finery, facing him.

"Uh, ah, hi," Don said feebly.

Nat greeted him in several native tongues. The rest of them were struck dumb, even Ellen. The other natives made themselves known, and in a threatening manner they herded them in the center. This frightened all of them. They were intimidated, waiting to see if Nat could make contact with them.

Finally, one of Nat's dialects made some sense to them. They told him to follow them and they nervously set off.

"Don't be afraid, this is the best thing that could have happened. We don't have near enough food or strength to make it back to camp by ourselves." Nat tried to subdue their fears.

"Maybe we can hire them to take us by boat to the base camp." Bud tried to reassure the frightened group, but he didn't even believe it himself.

Maeuma silenced them and motioned for them to follow along. They bumbled along, sliding their packs along behind them, scared and worried.

They caused quite a stir when they finally entered the village. The women and children danced along with them, taunting the prisoners and even throwing lumps of mud at them.

They were herded into the far end of a long hut. It was the Elders' meeting hut, the kind open at each end. The Chief and the Elders and Maeuma were at the other end. They sat on the ground in a circle around Kanchinapio, still on his carrying platform. It was on the ground. He was not on the raised throne-like large stone he usually sat on, with some shrunken heads raised above it.

In one corner of the hut another head was being shrunk. It was a slow process of smoking over a slow burning fire, a tanning-like process that took many days. So far it was unnoticed.

Kamanar'e and the other natives were assembled outside the hut, waiting to see what developed.

While the natives were deciding what to do with their captives, Bud and Nat were trying to calm down their charges.

"Quiet now," Bud said. "It is best not to show fear."

"Ha! That's a good one," Don said, his arm protectively around a shivering Ellen.

"I think I had better go over there and do a little palavering," said Nat. He started over to the other end of the hut, but was roughly pushed down by Uanica, the witch doctor, who was standing near.

"I guess not," Nat said, rising and brushing himself off.

"Let's get ourselves a drink of water and sit on our packs and try to look nonchalant," Bud suggested.

When they did as he suggested, the natives stopped talking and stared at them.

" These 'Others' should be put to death, the same way the other invader was," Panteri, the old Chief's cousin demanded. "Then we will have many heads to hang over the Chief's Great Stone throne."

Kanchinapio was wondering what to do with them himself, but he didn't want to seem to be following Panteri's suggestion.

"Bring over the dark man who spoke and we will see what he has to say," the old Chief said.

Maeuma rose and went to get Nat. He led him in front of Kanchinapio. In their language, Kanchinapio asked Nat his name.

"Nat," he answered.

"What are you doing with this group of 'Others'?"

"They are my friends. I am showing them the beauty of our jungle."

"Are they trying to take some of our land?" asked Panteri, boldly stepping forward in an aggressive manner.

Kanchinapio didn't like it that Panteri butted in, but he was curious as well. Giving Panteri an angry look that made him step back, he asked, "Could this be their purpose?"

"No! They are supposed to go home in a week, back to their own land."

"Are they friendly?" asked Bokra.

"Yes, they are good people," Nat assured them.

They sent him back to the others and sat around talking things over. They called Nat back and one by one they had him bring each one to be questioned, and interpret the answers.

Nat brought Bud over to them first. He introduced him as their chief, the one who had control of the strange bird. He wanted them to have respect for Bud. He could tell from their comments to one another that he had succeeded.

Dennis was brought before them next. Nat told them that he was a great doctor or shaman and had repaired all their injuries from their fall. He pointed out Bud's arm and the stitches still in his cuts. Unanica was very interested in this.

Don was next and he brought Ellen along with him. He had to; she wouldn't let go of his arm. This didn't go so well with the natives, but she let out such a yell when they tried to disengage her that they let her stay.

"'The wheel that squeaks gets attention even in this far off place," Letty whispered to Nora.

They examined them as they had Bud and Dennis. Nat told them that Don owned a big marketplace in his land.

Next they escorted Nora in front of Kanchinapio, who had moved to the Great Stone throne.

"Is she of any use?" Kanchinapio asked Nat.

"What shall I tell them about you, Miss Nora?"

Nora surprised them all by doing about five back flips across the width of the hut, landing in a split. The kind you see in a gymnastic presentation.

She landed with a big grin on her face. "How do you like 'them' apples?" she said.

Bud clapped, Don whistled and Dennis yelled, "Way to go Nora!"

The natives were stunned. Nat took this opportunity to call Carla and Letty to join them. Nat introduced Carla as Dr. Dennis' wife, then turned to Letty.

She seemed to be frozen to the spot. She was staring at a spot above them and let out an ungodly EEEEEeeeek! They all jumped, even the natives, who grabbed their spears, startled, and looked toward where she was pointing at the shrunken heads.

The heads were decorated with Macaw feathers in their hair, which looked down on them with closed eyes. Uanica explained to Nat that they belonged to past enemies. He pointed to the unnoticed fire in the corner. "This one new enemy."

"Fenton!" shouted Bud when he went over to have a look.

"God Almighty! It's Fenton's head," shuddered Nat.

This agitated and angered the natives because they thought they were of the same tribe as the invader that they had sacrificed.

Things were looking bad.

They took a closer look at Letty and a big hullabaloo set in. They all milled around her. Kanchinapio got out off his perch on the Great Stone and came close. He fingered the disk around her neck. She had great respect from them all, even Panteri.

"What is that medallion around your neck, Letty?" Nat asked. "It is causing a big commotion."

"I found it in Uncle Alfred's case. He had traveled throughout the jungles of Africa and South America. I didn't know where it came from, evidently it must have come from here."

Nat translated this for the natives.

"Describe your Uncle Alfred, Letty." Nat told her.

"Well," she took a deep shuddering breath; she was still upset from discovering the head and was trying not to look at it. "He would have been in his middle fifties in the late '70s when he was in South America. He was about six feet tall, gray at the temples with brown hair. He probably wore shorts and short sleeved shirts. He usually had a red bandanna around his neck. Let's see, oh, he might have worn a patch over his right eye for a time, a branch snapped back and hit him in the eye and he had a small cut on the side of his eyeball." She turned and said to Dennis, "Luckily he had some healing eye drops and he fashioned a bandage out of the red bandanna by tying it over the right eye and around his head till it was healed. I remember him telling us about that, but I don't know when that was."

Nat told the natives what Letty had said. They murmured among themselves awhile, and Wanapio was doing a lot of the talking. They became very excited when they heard him. Wanapio was opening his mouth and they all looked in and murmured some more. They were smiling and looking at Letty and nodding.

Nat returned to the group.

"It was the red bandanna that did it! Wanapio, that guy over there, remembered that Uncle Alfred came to his village and he had it around his head, covering his right eye. He also said at the time he had a terrible toothache, and Uncle Alfred pulled it out. I guess it must have been abscessed because he said it was hurting a lot. He did a lot of other things for the villagers, lancing boils and lots of other things. That is why when he left they presented him with the sacred medallion. It means quite a lot to them, it seems, and wasn't given away lightly."

The whole atmosphere was changed from one of aggressiveness and threatening to a smiling friendliness that manifested itself by much touching and patting, not entirely appreciated, but much better in the long run compared to their attitude at first. They had the freedom of the village, but they were followed around. They especially liked Bud and Ginger because of their red hair.

That night there was a party with dancing, chanting, eating and drinking. They were given shelter in some huts that were emptied for them. They doubled up, and Nora and Letty, Don and Ellen, and Dennis, Carla and Ginger each had a hut to themselves. Nat and Bud had a hut too.

Bud was exhausted. His arm was aching, so he turned in early while Nat talked to Kanchinapio and Maeuma. He was arranging for a two large boats and supplies so they could go by river back to the base camp. They even said a group of them would escort them part of the way. Kanchinapio extracted from Nat a promise not to tell anyone their whereabouts. Nat agreed.

Nat asked Maeuma why Fenton, whom he described as a neighbor, not of his tribe, was killed. Maeuma told him the whole story about his periodic illness and Panteri wanting to take over the tribe on Kanchinapio's death. The belief that the Spirit of the Great Knife needed to be appeased so he wouldn't send the breath-stealing devil to visit him, making him unfit to rule. He also told him that he wasn't a great hunter like his father had been and that was against his ascending the throne also.

When Nat relayed all this to the group, Dennis was interested. Nat brought Dennis over to Maeumaa. Kanchinapio came over to see what they were doing. Nat informed him that the Great High Doctor had magic medicine and might be able to use it to help Maeuma. Kanchinapio assented and Dennis gave Maeuma an examination.

He found that Maeuma was an asthmatic and was nearsighted, outside of that he was very strong and healthy. Bud had a good supply of Theopholine and his inhalers in Dennis' medical bag. He also had an extra pair of glasses in there too, his backup pair to wear if he lost his container of disposable contact lenses. Dennis told Maeuma how to use the inhalers and when to take the Theopholine and that he would be able to conquer the breath-stealing devil if ever he visited him again.

Maeuma put the glasses on and was startled at the result. He kept flipping them up and down to see the change. He was amazed and thrilled. Now he could be a Great Hunter and fit to rule. He was so happy he called for a big hunting party the next morning.

Bud was just about to fall asleep when he was startled to see two young, naked native women enter the hut.

"What? What are you doing here?" he sputtered.

They giggled and by then there was no doubt what they wanted by the suggestive motions they made and came closer to his bed.

"Get out of here!" he roared.

This angered them. They were insulted. They turned around and mooned him, one of them farted, and they left in a huff.

This made him laugh out loud. He had a difficult time falling asleep because every once in a while he would laugh to himself again. He could hardly wait to tell Nat.

———— •••◉••• ————

The next morning, early, the hunters set off. Dennis, Nat and Don joined them. Bud stayed and rested his arm.

Maeuma, with the glasses firmly in place, led them at a fast pace.

They had a good hunt. They had taken various birds and assorted game, including a capybara, the largest living rodent. It was about three and a half feet long with no tail.

Maeuma had shown that he was a good hunter and was very happy. They had even killed a large anaconda snake. They dressed the kill and meted it out among everyone to be carried back to the village. They were singing their hunting song on the way back. Kamanar'e was very tired and gradually fell to the rear of the group. A jaguar was lurking near them. He was old and not so agile anymore. He was hungry and his bones ached.

He was stalking Kamanar'e. He sensed that this one was slowing down. Maeuma missed seeing Kamanar'e near him, as he usually was, he stopped and turned around in time to see him stumble and fall over a large root. At the same time the jaguar saw his chance and started to run toward Kamanar'e. Maeuma drew his poison dart tube, took a deep breath, deeper than he had ever been able to before, and sent it flying into the heart of the jaguar just as it leaped. It fell a foot from Kamanar'e's head, not quite dead yet, but the other hunters soon remedied that. A perfect shot. Everyone ran to take Kamanar'e away from the dead animal. He was shaken, but all right. Maeuma was the hero of the day, the week, the month, the YEAR! His succession to the throne was secured. They would tell about this for many years at the feasts.

There was feasting in the village that night.

The next few days Dennis held a clinic and examined every one of the villagers. He treated all their ills and took notes about what medical supplies they needed. He was determined to send a medical drop to them periodically, especially the asthma medications for Maeuma.

The ladies, on Dennis' orders and accompanied by Nat and Don, Maeuma, Kanamar'e and Uanica went into the jungle and gathered medicinal herbs. Nat dictated to Nora what Uanica told him about their properties and use and she wrote it all in her notebook, with drawings of the plant. They took many samples and packed them to take them with them when they returned. The plan was to exchange them for the medications they would send to them in the future. It took some time to get all this finished.

They learned the fate of Ed Garson. He had died of natural causes and his body was treated in the same way that Fenton's was. They didn't know where the other one, the brown one was. He and a small boat were missing.

Maeuma had a talk with his father Kanchinapio one day.

"I am treated as a great hunter by the people now."

"Yes, that is true, you have much respect. Panteri has stopped his bad talk."

"When you join the spirits they will accept me as their Chief."

"Yes, that is so."

"We must have a feast before the 'Others' leave. We must have a great hunt for the feast."

"Yes, Maeuma, is there something else you aren't saying?"

"Yes, I want it to be a wedding feast. I want to be joined with Teptykti at the feast."

"Yes, that will be the perfect time for it! Tell Wanapio I wish to see him. I will tell him it is my wish."

"What if he says no?"

"He will not say no, now that he is sure that you will be Chief. Before he was not sure what your position in the tribe was to be. You cannot blame him for wanting a secure place for her. He has enough to worry about because of Kamanar'e and his deformity, he wanted a good strong man for her. Now, because of the 'Others,' that is what you shall be. Now go, send him to me."

Maeuma left in a hurry to get Wanapio. The next one he went to find was Teptykti. He had a lot to tell her.

Early the next day the hunters went to the jungle. Dennis and Don went with them.

The natives remaining prepared for the feast. Everyone was busy. The group had their chores too. Nat and Bud arranged with the Indians for two boats and as much food and water as they could carry. They packed their belongings in the boats. They had given so many of their things away there wasn't much left.

The hunters were very fortunate. They found a great hoard of fairly large turtles. They made a rack that extended above their head and went over the shoulders and down the back. They tied the turtles on the rack. One man could carry a lot of turtles. They put the turtle eggs in a woven basket that they brought along with them. These men were sent back to the village carrying the eggs. The hunt was over for them.

They used bows and arrows, and blowpipes to get small game. Lances were for the tapirs and the peccaries. They sent the catch back to the village as they caught it so it could be prepared.

Dennis was worn out, he decided to cool off in the river. He was wading to go deeper when he felt a sharp pain in his foot. He fell in the waist-deep water, going under. His foot was on fire! He couldn't get up; he was floundering around, trying to stand up. He was having a hard time doing it.

Am I going end up drowning in waist-deep water? was going through his mind when strong hands pulled him up. It was Maeuma! He helped get Dennis to the shore. Uanica looked at his foot. Don came running.

"What's up?" he cried.

"Something bit me on the foot and I have a gash on it. Look how it is swelling up! It hurts like it's on fire."

Maeuma, Uanica and Kamanar'e were in a huddle. Maeuma dashed off. Uanica was saying something neither Dennis nor Don could make head or tail of. Kamanae'e tried to make them understand making motions, motions pointing farther into the jungle, not in the direction of the village.

"What's he saying?" asked Don, "I never was good at charades."

"Beats me, something about going farther into the jungle, but that couldn't be it. OWWW, this thing really hurts, look, the redness is going up my leg. I know that isn't good."

Maeuma came running back, winded.

The three had a brief confab. Agreed about something, then started to pick up Dennis.

"Wait, ouch, where are we going?"

They put him down. Maeuma touched his leg. It was swollen and hot and very painful. Maeuma placed his hands on each side of his face, stared straight into his eyes, willing Dennis to understand.

"Whatever he wants you to do, you better do it, Dennis. This guy isn't kidding," Don said.

"Okay, let's roll!"

They made a stretcher of two stout branches and their t-shirts. The four of them went into the jungle, following Maeuma's directions. After awhile they came upon one of the giant anthills. They set him down and began to make a fire.

"Wait a minute, that will take you all day!" Don said. He got a book of matches from his pocket. It was from that hotel in Miami. He struck one and handed it to Uanica. This was a cause of amazement to the three natives. He used it to set fire to the anthill! The ants came scurrying out, running in all directions.

"What are you doing?" yelled Dennis when they picked him up and held his foot in the smoke.

Don was stunned, but he helped hold Dennis' foot in the smoke.

"I don't know, man, but they seem to think this is the thing to do. This is their gig, so just let it be, okay?"

Dennis quit struggling and let them have their way. He said, between grunts, "I guess some of the things I did to help them seemed just as outlandish."

Now that Dennis had quit struggling, Kamanar'e let him go and fought off the ants that came their way. Don helped him shoo them away.

Maeuma and Uanica turned his foot so it got the full effect of the smoke on the puncture area of the foot.

"Hey, this is getting hot, isn't this bar-b-que just about over?"

Maeuma and Uanica didn't have to understand the language to know what he was saying. When Uanica decided it had been long enough, they started back.

Dennis was very uncomfortable.

When he got back, he put some Neosporin on it. It was all he had.

It took awhile, but it healed and all was well again. *Imagine that*, Dennis thought. *You learn something new every day.*

———

They weren't ready for the wedding for two more days. The food and drinks had to be made ready and the people had to be made ready too.

It was structured. Everything had to be just right.

It was fascinating to watch. It was too bad that they were out of film and lost the camera, but Nora was taking copious notes. She filled the notebook. She was watching all the preparations so she could tell Lois when she returned, whenever that would be!

The wedding was so nice. The ritual, what they understood of it, was very solemn. Teptykti was lovely with flowers in her hair and around her neck, waist and ankles. By now, they hardly realized that the rest of her was bare. Maeuma had an impressive headdress of many colored feathers. His waist and ankles were adorned with many colored feathers too. Of course, he proudly wore his glasses.

When the ritual was over, the place started jumping, literally! The drums and some hollowed reeds set up a rhythm that started everyone dancing. Don was doing the twist with Ellen. Letty was laughing so hard at them she didn't notice the Chief standing by her side indicating that she was to be his partner. It was their turn to laugh at her. She just followed him and did what he did and that seemed to suffice.

Bud and Ginger danced too, but not so much jumping. He didn't want to start his arm hurting. It was three weeks since he broke it and it was doing fine now, if he didn't jog it too much.

Nat was dancing with Teptykti's mother. He didn't know her name, there didn't seem to be a father, but they were having a good time. Her nudity meant nothing to him—he was used to it. Dennis and Carla were clapping their hands to the "music."

It was a happy event and they all had a wonderful time.

It was time now to pack up and go home. The native people couldn't have been nicer. They helped them load up and said their goodbyes.

Nat told them that Dennis would get medicines and other things they need to them in exchange for more of the medicinal herbs. They would not let anyone know of the whereabouts if their village. They would be safe.

The happy group started the rigorous trip back to the base camp early one morning. They were well supplied. They were given two of the large boats. They lashed the Bambi pieces to the sides, and stowed the food and drink in the boats. Bud, Dennis, Carla, Nora and Ginger and a portion of the supplies were in one boat. The other held Nat, Don, Ellen and Letty and a greater portion of the supplies in the other.

Bud only had the use of one hand, so he manned the rudder. The rest took turns paddling. Dennis' foot was still a little tender, but paddling didn't hurt it. He had fashioned a cane that he used when he needed to.

They rotated the two paddles, two resting, two paddling. In the other boat, Letty was the designated rudder person at first, then she and the other three rotated, with Don and Nat doing most of the paddling. Then occasionally Ellen and Letty would take a turn, though they weren't very good at it, and they'd rather do it themselves. Nat and Don developed a rhythm that scooted them along. When Ellen or Letty tried to help, the rhythm was gone.

Each day about six, they would break camp and start out, by noon they were more than ready to stop. They would have a cold lunch and a nap. By three in the afternoon they were ready to move on. They would go on till just before sunset. Then they would pull over, start a fire, set up the Bambi shelters and cook a meal.

Sometimes there would be fresh fish that the non-paddlers caught. If not, there was smoked 'mystery meat' prepared by the native women. Just because it didn't have a name was no reason it didn't taste good.

Uanica had taught them what they could get from the jungle that was safe to eat, so sometimes they could find some of those plants to go along with the meat. Bud and Nat wouldn't let them venture very far into the jungle without them. The incident of the jaguar was fresh in their minds, and too there were other snakes and critters that were just as dangerous.

After eating Dennis would check them for any open sores. They would sit around the fire and talk about the things that happened during that day, animals and birds they came upon and other events. The blue butterflies were their favorites. They looked beautiful flitting through the trees.

They didn't stay up very late. They were so tired, they fell right to sleep. Bud kept the fire going through the night. He felt it was the least he could do since he was unable to paddle. This was the pattern of their days on the way back to the base camp.

———

One day they were making good headway. The trees were almost touching overhead—the shade made the journey easier. Some of the branches almost touched the water. Don was paddling. Ellen was sitting behind him, resting from her turn.

All of a sudden a snake dropped down on Don. He yelled and dropped the paddle. In a second, without thinking, Ellen grabbed the snake and threw it into the water. Everyone was in shock, including the snake! Dennis picked the paddle out of the water and returned it to the other boat. Don was comforting Ellen who was crying and shaking in reaction.

"Ellen! Good for you!" Bud shouted.

"Ellen of all people!" said Dennis.

"Way to go, Ellen!" Nora cheered.

"What a brave thing to do!" Carla smiled.

"This makes up for anytime you lost your cool," Ginger said. They all congratulated her for her bravery.

Letty was sitting by her, just patting her shoulder. Nat was busy getting the boat on the right course.

"It's early, but let's stop for lunch," said Nat. "We need to get over this scare and rest a bit."

No one complained.

Chapter Seventeen

The phone was ringing. Lois hurried to answer it. Gordy was napping after his lunch and she didn't want him awakened.

"Hello, Hunter's residence," she said.

"At last! I have been trying to locate you. No one ever answers the office telephone. Is Mr. Hunter there? Or if he is not, does anyone know where he can be located?"

Lois heard Gordy stirring around so she said, "Just a minute, please." She put the phone aside and went into the next room and picked up the bedside phone and handed it to Gordy.

"Hello," he answered.

"This is Tom Murphy in St. Louis, do you know where my wife Letty is?"

"Hi, Mr. Murphy. Tom isn't it? I didn't know how to reach you, you weren't home, were you?" stalled Gordy, trying to get up courage to tell him what he had to be told.

"No, is anything wrong?" he asked.

"We really don't know," Gordy said. "The group hasn't returned on schedule, but that doesn't necessarily mean anything bad has happened. Something could have happened that has delayed them a while."

"What! You don't know where they are?"

"No, we don't."

"Am I speaking to Mr. Gordon Hunter?"

"Yes."

"Then why the Hell aren't you with her? I thought you were head man in that outfit?"

"Well, I had an accident and my eyes are bandaged and I have some broken bones, so my son and my partner went with the group."

"How old is your son, and how capable is your partner?"

"He is twenty-two and Nat is a Peruvian guide, an expert."

"Oh, my God! She's off with a kid and a native," he wailed.

"Listen here, Bub." Gordy, who had been trying to keep cool, understanding the man's concern, lost it. "That's my son and my best friend out there somewhere, and I am just as worried as you are!"

"I'm sorry, don't get excited, it can't be good for you in your beat-up condition, but I am going to get down there as fast as I can. What is your address? I'll get a plane out as fast as I can."

Gordy handed the phone to Lois. His hand was shaking. "Tell this guy, Murphy, all he needs to know, will you Lois?" he said as he handed her the phone.

While Lois was doing that he lay back on the pillow. His mind raced, he felt so helpless. When they didn't return as scheduled, he had a friend fly to the base camp. He found out that not only Bud and his group hadn't returned, but Garson and his group didn't return either.

Here he was laid up. He couldn't even see! What could he do?

Lois hung up the phone and went over to Gordy. "Tom Murphy is flying down here. I know you are worried, I am too. You have notified the authorities, there is nothing else you can do. Something has happened and now you just have to trust in Nat and Bud to overcome whatever it is and get back here safe and sound."

"When is Tom Murphy arriving?"

"The day after tomorrow."

"We'll put him up here with us. Poor guy, he's got to be frantic. I am sorry I mouthed off at him. He has a legitimate beef."

"I know, honey. You have been so frustrated not being able to do anything. The doctor is coming tomorrow, maybe he'll have good news for you." She tried to get his mind off of Bud and Nat and all the rest, but it was hard.

Ryti came in with some iced tea and cookies for them. Her eyes were red from crying. She was so worried. She knew how dangerous the jungle was, and the many things that could go wrong. They had never reached their destination. She had been in contact with the people at the very small landing strip where they were to have landed. They promised that they would short wave at once if any word was heard about the missing plane.

They were flying around the area between there and the base camp. They made a grid and were combing the area methodically looking for them. It was very hard to see anything. The trees were so thick you couldn't see anything below them. The trees even hung over the river and its tributaries on both sides. Some of the narrower streams were completely covered over like long green tunnels. A boat couldn't be seen in one of those areas.

Later that afternoon one of the helicopters saw a boat with an unconscious man in it floating erratically downstream, though the bow was pointing upstream.

They lowered a man into the boat. The man was still alive! They brought him to the hospital in Manaus. Of course it was Orem. They notified Gordy.

———— ••◆••• ————

Lois left immediately for the hospital in Ryti's car. Orem's sister, Mikant'u, and her husband Anawani were in the waiting room. The nurse introduced them and left. Lois explained her interest in Orem.

"So you see, perhaps Orem can shed some light on their whereabouts. He might have seen them. They were working out of the same base camp."

An hour later the nurse told Mikant'u she could see Orem for a short while.

When she saw Orem, she was shocked to see how emaciated he looked, he was dehydrated, feverish, bug bites were all over him, and scratches from the jungle foliage had become infected. They were giving him antibiotics and fluids by IV and by mouth when they could get him to swallow them.

Mikant'u told Lois that the doctor told her that Orem probably wouldn't be able to talk to anyone until the next day. So Lois went back and reported that to Gordy.

Ryti fixed dinner for them and went to her room. She was so very sad.

"Delay and more delay," Gordy said. "Please come read to me awhile, will you, Lois? I want to get my mind off things I can't do anything about."

"Okay, let's do that." She got him settled for the night, brought her chair up beside him and began to read the current mystery they were halfway into. After about an hour she put the bookmarker in place and closed the book.

"My voice is getting tired, and you need your rest, so good night, my darling." She kissed him and turned out the light.

"Goodnight, dear Lois, thank you so much for being here."

The next day when the doctor came he took the bandage off Gordy's right eye. The left one had to stay covered up for awhile. The good news was his sight in the right eye was as good as it ever was.

He still had to have his leg in a cast, but a new walking cast was put on. The new arm cast was smaller too.

"It is so good to see you!" Gordy said as he gave Lois a hug and a kiss. "I missed seeing your sweet smile."

"Well, I wasn't smiling very often with you banged up so much. It is good to see you partly unveiled. It will be easier for you to get around."

"Would you like to go talk to Orem after lunch?"

"That is what I must do as soon as possible."

Ryti fixed them a toasted cheese sandwich and a small bowl of her special soup. When they finished, they each took a piece of fruit from the bowl used as a centerpiece and made their way to the car. Ryti went along too, and did the driving. She wanted to talk to Orem about Nat.

They had to wait a bit to get into Orem's room. His family was visiting.

"How is he today?" Ryti asked Mikant'u when they came out of Orem's room.

"He is much better. The fluids and the antibiotics have taken hold. The doctor said he could go home tomorrow."

Gordy heard her and replied, "I am glad to hear that, he has been through a terrible ordeal."

Anawani gathered up their three children and left with Mikant'u.

The nurse said, "You may go in now," and left them and walked into the room across the hall.

"Hello, Orem," Gordon said. Lois placed a chair near the bed for him, when he sat down she put his one-armed walker against the wall.

"Hello, Mr. Hunter," Orem answered weakly.

"I am sorry you are in such bad shape, Orem. I hear you are lucky to be alive. I'd sure like to hear all about it, but the main thing is, did you see Bud and his group?"

"Yes, I did. We were at the base camp at the same time. We left the morning after they arrived. He had time to talk with Mr.Garson. Fenton and I saw him, but didn't talk to him, just waved goodbye to him as we left."

"We haven't heard from him since he left base camp. They radioed as they were leaving to check in. Not a word since."

"Did you see Nat?" Ryti inquired anxiously.

"Yes, he was there when we shoved off."

"Do you know what happened to Mr. Garson and Fenton?" Gordy asked.

"Yes I do." Orem shuddered. "It was terrible!"

"What happened?" they all asked.

Then Orem described their tragic ordeal. "I escaped and started paddling upriver, the way we had come. The water ran out soon enough. I was able to stop and get some rainwater from the larger leaves. I dug some grubs and ate them. I haven't done that in a long time. I am used to civilized food.

"It was the insects! They just about drove me wild. I wet a handkerchief and put it on my head and that helped, but they zeroed on the scrapes on my legs and arms that I got running through the brush trying to get away. I had to paddle hard to get ahead of the current, and after awhile I must have just passed out. When they found me, I was drifting downstream." He shuddered again. "Right into the hands of those savages again!"

"Wow!"

"Horrible!"

"My goodness!"

"At least Mr. Garson died peacefully," Gordy said.

"Well, if you call tied up in a pen with no water peaceful," Orem remarked.

"I'm sorry, you are right, I wasn't thinking. I was comparing his death to Fenton's agony."

"Yeah, Fenton had a lot of faults, but he didn't deserve what he got...on the other hand, he might have had something to do with your son's accident."

"What do you mean?"

"We were loading the three boats. Fenton was late showing up and I was sort of mad that I had to do all my work and most of his to get us ready to leave."

"Where had he been?"

"I never did find out, but he came back with a mean look on his face. We were in different boats and when we stopped, our boat was a bit away from his. We were busy with our jobs and there was no occasion for us to have any personal conversation. The next time I had to talk to him, we were tied up in the pen together. We were very scared. I could tell Mr. Garson was bad off. He had been hitting those tiny pills of his pretty hard, and when they grabbed him, he dropped them in the river."

"You were lucky you got away," said Lois.

"It is a wonder you survived," said Ryti

"I wonder if Bud and the others suffered the same fate," Gordon said sadly.

"I don't think they did. I didn't see any trace of them, and from what the natives said, they didn't either. Unless, of course, they ran into them later,"

"You understood them?"

" Most of them. They are a mixed up group, one that formed from ones who were escaping other tribes, and the whites who wanted them as slaves to tend the rubber trees. They spoke a mixture of many tribal languages, forming their own. I couldn't understand every word, but I got the sense of what they were saying."

"Well, Orem," Gordy said as he arose and Lois handed him his one-handed walker and pulled the chair back. "I hope you get well soon. When we both get well, we will see if we can do business together."

"That would be fine with me, sir." He felt pretty guilty and saddened about the part he played in injuring this kind man by doing what that jerk Fenton talked him into.

I hope I can make it up to him, he thought as they left.

Later, after dinner, Lois said, "Let's sit out on the verandah. We can see the sunset and enjoy the evening before the bugs drive us in."

"I was always going to have it screened in, but I never did get around to it."

"It is a nice place to sit after dinner."

"Yes, I'll have Nat…oh, God, where are they?" He put his head down and rested it on his free hand.

"I wish I could help. Now we'll have Mr. Murphy to contend with tomorrow. His plane gets in around noon. I'll meet him at the airport and bring him here for lunch."

"See. You are helping. I couldn't have managed without you." He gave her a weak smile.

It was dark now and the bugs were out in force.

"Let's go in." Lois slapped at a flying something that landed on her arm.

"Right," Gordy said as he started in. "Maybe we can finish that who-done-it if your voice doesn't give out."

"Okay, you're on."

Lois was waiting at the small terminal as the plane taxied to the docking place. Tom was the only one who disembarked, so she had no trouble identifying him.

"Mr. Murphy." She extended her hand. "I'm Lois Wadleigh, I am here for Gordon Hunter. We have lunch ready for you at his house, and a room you can use while you are here."

"Well, that is very kind of him, considering he is recovering from an accident. Was it serious?"

As they drove to the house, she filled him in on the accident, what caused it, his injuries, and how he was today.

"And now this is added to his troubles," Tom said, sympathy showed in his eyes.

"I won't lie to you, Mr. Murphy, he is very upset."

"Please call me Tom, may I call you Lois?"

"I hope you will. All of us are on first name basis here."

"What is your connection? Do you work for the Hunters?"

"No, I am one of the contest winners."

"Well then, how come you aren't lost with them?"

"It's a complicated story. When Gordy had his accident, he needed someone to help him. He was so helpless, his eyes were bandaged, and he needed medication instilled into them frequently. He had a broken arm and leg. Ryti, she works for the Hunters, couldn't take care of everything.

"I wanted to catalog the pictures and the notes I took on the first part of the trip, so it was made easy for me to do my work here and take care of Gordy at the same time. Er, and in the process we have fallen in love."

"What a romantic story, Letty will love it!" He sobered suddenly.

"I think she might have figured it out already." Lois said. "We all love Letty. She is such a joy to be around."

"I know what you mean. We've just got to find her!" He turned and looked out the window, blinking back unshed tears, trying to swallow the lump in his throat.

They continued the drive in silence, each lost in their own thoughts.

As they drove up the hill to the house, Lois pointed out to Tom the scene of Gordy's accident.

"Wow, it is a wonder he made it!" Tom said. "Did they ever find the snake?"

"No, it got away."

Lois parked the car, locked it, as they always did now, and they went inside.

Ryti opened the door for them. When Lois handed her the key, she said, "Did you lock it?"

"Yes, just like locking the old barn door."

"I know, but it's all we can do now."

Gordy was sitting at the dining room table, his arm resting on it and his leg out at an angle.

"Howdy, Tom! Pardon me if I don't get up." He smiled and held out his free hand.

"I'm glad to meet you, uhh, Gordy?" He hesitated to use the pet name, but that is the only one Lois had used.

"I guess that is only Lois' name for me. I'd be happy if you would call me Gordon."

"Fine, Gordon it is," he said as he sat in the chair Ryti was holding for him.

Ryti began to serve them ham and cheese sandwiches with potato salad and fruit, with iced tea.

"I was on the radio today with the people in charge of the search. They haven't seen anything of them, but they did find the wreckage of the helicopter. There were no bodies. There was some sign of the foliage being disturbed and some marks on the floor of the jungle. It looked like they were dragging something. It was getting dark and they left. They had lowered a man where there was destruction of a tree. He said that their best bet was to concentrate on the river. They would have to reach it to make any headway at all. Unless…" Gordon choked up and had trouble talking.

Lois said, "Unless they had been captured by a local tribe, I think that is what he is trying to say."

"Oh, my God!" Tom croaked. He put his head in his hands. "Are they savage?" he asked

"They might be." Lois then told Tom the whole horrible story that Orem had related.

"Now you know as much as we know," Gordon said.

A silence came over them. None of them could think of anything to say. They quietly finished their meal.

"You must be exhausted, Tom," Lois said. "I'll show you to your room and you can settle in and have a nap if you'd care too."

"I just might do that. The time change isn't bad, but would you believe it? I had to fly to Miami, wait there about three hours then fly to Manaus."

"Lois always makes me take a nap after lunch, and I've gotten to like it," Gordon said.

Lois got them both settled down and went off to the darkroom to do some work on her own project. She was almost finished with the pictures and notes she had on hand. She wondered what Nora had collected for her. She sighed. *I wonder if I will ever know.*

————— •••◉••• —————

At that moment Nora was paddling with a steady stroke upriver. She was a good paddler and she just started her turn so she was even enjoying it, a little. If she just knew how this movie was going to turn out, she could think of it as a great adventure. More than they had bargained for, that's for sure. *Hunters Amazon Jungle Adventure*! They weren't kidding.

The boat came out into the sunshine, the river widened at this point and they came out of their green tunnel.

It was warm and oppressive even, in the shade, but now it was really hot in the sun. She paused to get her sunglasses out of her pocket and put them on. Dennis, who was the other paddler at the moment, was thrown off his rhythm when she stopped.

"Hey, what's going on?" He looked back at Nora.

"I had to put my sunglasses on, you'd better do it too."

"I have them here, honey," Carla said. She took them out of her bag and got up so she could hand them to Dennis, at the same time they zigzagged to avoid hitting a floating log, and overboard she went. SPLASH! The current took her. Without thinking Bud dived in after her, and Dennis started to do the same.

"Don't," yelled Nora, as she grabbed his shirt.

"Stop, Dad," Ginger cried, "Bud is an expert swimmer, he will get her."

By that time Bud had her in his arms and let the boat come to where he was. It took awhile to maneuver the boat near them. The current made it difficult. They all helped them back in the boat, which was no easy thing. Bud lost his sling and bumped his arm getting in the boat. It was hurting again.

"Well, that cooled me off, and I didn't even drop your glasses. Here they are, honey," and she gave them to him.

He held her tight. "Carla! Do you know how precious you are to me?"

"I think so." She smiled and kissed him.

By that time their boat had become even with the other boat.

"That was quite a show you all put on. Rescue at sea and a romantic ending," Don said.

"Well, Don, some people don't like to show their romantic feelings in public..." He laughed, and drew Carla closer and kissed her thoroughly. "Most of the time."

Bud waited until they stopped for the evening to tell Dennis about his arm. It was hurting more now.

"Why didn't you tell me right away, Bud?"

He examined his arm. It didn't seem to be out of alignment. There were some aspirin tablets left. The stronger painkillers were gone. He took Bud's t-shirt, made some strategic cuts and made a tight sling out of it. Nat fixed his tent and they gave him some supper then put him to bed.

Carla felt bad because it was all her fault.

Chapter Eighteen

It was getting to be late afternoon. It was very humid and hot. Clothes were damp and sticking because of the atmosphere and the perspiration that was trickling down their bodies beneath them. Everyone was miserable.

They must stop now, so they would have time to set up camp and fix something to eat before dark. They were all exhausted and when Bud told them to pull into land no one objected. They had the camp set-up down to a system by now. They each took their Bambi pack and set up their bed/tent. Nat was the quickest, so when he was finished he started the campfire.

They had some fish that Bud caught when they stopped for lunch that day, so Nat started to broil them on the piece of metal they salvaged from the plane for that very purpose.

Nora finished her sleeping arrangements next and went looking for something the forest might provide.

Bud was busy finding firewood to burn through the night to keep the night roaming animals away. He needed to find a large amount because they had to have fuel for breakfast too.

Don and Ellen took all of the containers to the river and filled them, brought them back to the fire and filled their one pot and started to boil the water a bit at a time and refilled the containers with boiled water. This was a tiresome and lengthily process. Especially since they had to wash out the containers with boiled water before they could fill them with boiled water. This was the first day they had to do that; they used up all the water purifying chemicals they had in their kit.

Don was resting while the containers filled with water boiled. He scratched an itch on his right calf. It hurt when he scratched it, so he looked at the back of his leg. There was a large reddened lump on it and it was MOVING! He gave a muted "Yelp" that caught Ellen's attention. He was ashen and clammy with a look of horror on his face.

"What is it, Don?"

He couldn't answer, he just pointed and shuddered.

"Oh! What is that?" She raised her voice, and added a scream for Dennis.

He came running, lugging his medical case. He could tell by her scream that he would probably need it. Nat came along too.

"It is the eggs of an insect hatching," Nat told the group that had assembled. "It will have to be lanced, that's all."

Dennis prepared the skin and did just that, removing the wriggling larvae.

It hurt, but Don didn't say a word. He was shuddering like Humphry Bogart in "The African Queen" when he had the leaches all over him.

"There, this will be okay. I have some antibiotic ointment left that we can put on it. It will be okay, Don."

He nodded. He was still shaken, but was on the way to recovery.

When everything was calmed down, they all went back to their own pursuits.

Letty helped fill the containers and then went to fix her tent.

Dennis made the importance of cleanliness very clear the first night they made camp. He wanted no digestive upsets or parasites to add to their difficulties. His duty was to treat any cuts, bites or other injuries that may have occurred during the day. He also checked to see that the food and water was fit to ingest and wouldn't cause any harm.

Carla and Ginger went into the forest to look for food. They met Nora returning from her search, so Ginger took the roots and berries that Nora had found and brought them to Nat.

Carla and Nora went back to find something they could eat for breakfast. They couldn't find anything suitable and it was getting dark, so they retraced their steps. Ginger had rejoined them. They didn't go very far when all of a sudden a flock of birds rose up from the vegetation they had just passed, startling them.

Carla and Ginger screamed. Even brave Nora let out a shout.

"Wow! That sure scared me," Ginger admitted.

"Scare is too tame a word." Carla murmured.

"Those were big birds. They were as big as a small chicken!"

"Where were they when we walked by here before?" Nora queried to no one in particular.

"Where there are chickens there has to be eggs!" Ginger said as she bent down and began pulling aside the greenery looking for eggs.

Soon the three of them went on an egg hunt, crawling around the floor of the forest, disturbing various insects and sending them scurrying. They did discover some nests with eggs in them.

Bud came lumbering into their area, stumbling over Carla and falling flat.

"What happened? I heard the screaming and came running," he said, rubbing his arm after sustaining yet another trauma to it.

"We were frightened when we flushed a flock of big birds," Nora told him. She went back to robbing a nest of its eggs.

"Look, four eggs!" Nora said.

"I have two," Ginger added.

"Here are two nests with four eggs in each." Carla laughed, calm again after her fright.

They all scrambled around the underbrush looking for eggs until it got too dark. They ended up with sixteen eggs— admittedly small, but a great haul!

When they returned to the camp area with the eggs, they were the champions of the day.

Before he had made his rescue attempt, Bud had captured a huge river turtle, which Nat had butchered and was even now grilling on the piece of helicopter. The fish were set to the side, keeping warm near the fire.

Ellen was boiling the roots that Nora had found. Nat assured them they were edible. She made a salad of some shoots and new leaves that met Nat's approval. She used a huge leaf to toss it in with the last of their mustard mixed with the juice of some unknown fruit that was a little tart.

Letty was so tired and sunburned too. After she unloaded the water for Don and Ellen to start the boiling process, she went to Dennis to have him treat the blisters on her hands that the paddling had caused. She made her bed, draped the material around it, tucking it in all around. She lay back on the bed after she had it all put together, thinking to rest just a minute.

The next thing she knew, Ginger was shaking her awake so she could come to eat. She was so embarrassed, she kept saying how sorry she was that she let them down.

"Letty, don't you feel bad, not many people your age could put in a day of paddling in this heat, much less doing any camping chores," Dan said.

She looked at the different kinds of food that was set out on leaves for each one of them. They were sitting around on the ground waiting for her. She sank to the ground, cross-legged, and said, "This feast requires a blessing."

"Go ahead, Letty, give us a good one," Bud said.

Letty made the sign of the cross, and began. "Dear Lord, thank you for bringing us all safely through so many different dangers. The crash, the meeting with the natives, the trip in the boats, all these things could have had tragic consequences. And now you have provided us with this sumptuous banquet, just when most of our food ran out.

"You are the Good Shepherd and have watched over us. I pray that you will continue to watch over us until we are safe at home with our loved ones. Glory be to you almighty God, as it was in the beginning, is now and ever shall be, world without end. Amen."

They all said their "Amens" and started eating. They put the leftover turtle meat in a plastic box they had salvaged and sunk it into the river inside a plastic bag they were hoarding. This kept it cool and safe to eat the next day.

Everyone was glad to get to their beds. Muscles were sore, bites itched, they were hot and sweaty and they were exhausted, and they fell asleep at once.

Letty was especially tired. Her nap only made her want more sleep. She shinnied into the place she made for her nap, fully clothed.

Unbeknownst to her the foot covering had become loose and was not tucked in as before. She fell asleep at once and didn't notice it. She awoke with her feet on fire! Something was stinging them and crawling up her legs.

She screamed and leapt out of her bed, upsetting it in the process. She ran toward the water, slapping at her legs as she went.

Her startled companions found her still slapping at her legs, then finally sitting in the water. It was the only place she could assuage the pain.

"Fire ants!" she sobbed.

Dennis went for his depleted first-aid kit. He did the best he could with what he had, then filled a large leaf with river mud and gave it to Letty.

"Daub this on when it hurts, Letty, and try to get some sleep."

While Dennis was treating Letty's bites, the rest of the disturbed slumberers shook out her bedding and made it up for her.

They all settled down again.

———— ··•◦•·· ————

Everyone slept late that morning and one by one came to the fire that Nat had refreshed.

While they broke camp and loaded the boats, Nat made an omelet with the eggs they had found and some of the vegetation that he had saved for that very reason from the things that made up the salad they had for their evening meal. He thought about adding some of the turtle meat, but decided against it, figuring that it would be better if he saved it for the lunch stop. They were out of salt now, and mustard too, but he did have a little black pepper and that helped.

"How are you, Letty?" Dennis asked.

"My feet and legs itch, and then hurt when I rub them," she moaned.

"Here, take this. I made up another leaf full of mud, did that help any?"

"Surprisingly, it does help some. I feel like such a nut allowing that to happen!"

"You weren't the first and won't be the last to get attacked by fire ants. They are everywhere and are very unforgiving."

"You can say that again." She grimaced.

When breakfast was over, they packed the rest of the things and started another day toward the base camp.

———— ··•◦•·· ————

Back in Manaus that same morning, Tom awoke. He could hear people talking. It took awhile before he realized where he was. Then, when he realized where he was, he dressed in a hurry and joined Gordon and Lois at the breakfast table.

"Good morning, Tom, did you sleep well?" Gordon asked.

"Sit down and have something to eat," Lois said as she saw Ryti enter with hot coffee, fruit and assorted breads.

"I slept very well, thanks, and I would love some of that coffee," he said, allowing Ryti to fill his cup. "Have you heard anything from the base camp yet?"

"No, I haven't. I am getting so tired of waiting for news, I am thinking of taking the other helicopter and going to the base camp to wait."

"Gordy, do you think that is wise? You only have one eye exposed and are still in a walking cast," Lois cautioned.

" Well, Hell, I can manage. I've been sitting on my duff long enough."

"You had better ask your doctor before you decide to take off," Tom said sensibly. "You don't want to become another problem."

"Tom is right, get the doctor's permission first."

"Okay, I'll call him right away." He got up, adjusted his walking device and went to the phone in the other room.

"I can understand how he wants some action," Tom said. "I do too. I hope the doctor will let him go. I want to go too. I wish I knew how to fly, then there would be no problem."

"If he does go, I am going too. I would rather be there where the action is than just sit here and wonder what is going on."

"Me too," Ryti added as she poured more coffee in Lois' cup. Gordon returned and announced that they had to get ready and go to the doctor's office. The doctor wouldn't give his permission over the phone. He insisted on examining him first.

When the doctor saw Gordon, he wasn't thrilled at the thought of his patient flying to the base camp, but knowing GWH, he would probably go anyway. He removed the casts, the arm was better. The leg was still weak, so he had him wear a light brace. He gave them strict instructions that must be carried out to the letter. Armed with eye medications and pain medications, and careful instructions as to when to take what and just how much and such, they left and headed back to the house to pack for the trip.

Gordon phoned Bep. "Hello Bep."

"Hallo, boss, How you feelin'?"

"Okay. Uh, Bep, I want you to have the helicopter readied for flight. Also, I want some first-aid supplies and plenty of food and water. Just prepare like we would for a jungle trip, okay?"

"Yes, sir, Sounds like you are all well! Shall I call you when I have things ready for us to go?"

"Hell no! I'll be there as soon as I can. You just get things together as fast as you can, but get someone readying the plane first. I'm not taking off until I know it is in tip-top shape. I want to go, but I want to get back too."

"Okay, boss, right away!"

"Let's roll," Gordon said as he hung up, glad to finally be able to do something.

Later, the helicopter was loaded and Lois, Ryti and Tom were in their seats. Bep was helping GWH into his seat. After a few bumps and grunts he was seated and ready to go. He found he was able to operate the controls satisfactorily and they were ready for takeoff. His arm was completely well.

"Oh, Bep, did you pick up the mail and some things for Father O'Toole?"

"Yeah, boss, it's right heah in de pouch."

"Okay! We are on our way," GWH said as the helicopter rose and sped off.

Awhile later, they hovered over the village where Father O'Toole lived and cared for the natives. They tossed the pouch of mail and goodies. Father O'Toole had kept abreast of the lost travelers by radio and knew just as much as GWH did about them, which wasn't much. He and his flock were praying for their safe return.

On their way again, the flight was uneventful and in due time they landed at the base camp. They were greeted by all the inhabitants running to meet them, led by Ke'era, the head of the village. They even deserted their favorite TV show to run out to see the newcomers. When they saw that it was GWH, they laughed and held their hands out for the candy he always brought to them.

When they were settled, they went to the combination office/lounge/dining room. GWH radioed the far camp to see what their daily flight discovered. Nothing new, was the report. He sighed and reported to the others.

After dinner and small talk over cool drinks, they retired to their cabins. None of them fell asleep right away.

GWH tossed and turned, his leg was paining him again. His eyes were okay. Lois had instilled the drops in them and that was an instant relief. He didn't want to bother getting up to get his pain pill, so he tried to ignore it.

I wonder what Bud is doing now? I should have canceled the trip. Why did I let him talk me into letting him take the group? If I had refused to let him take charge of the trip, he would have never forgiven me. He would have thought I didn't trust him. Just when our relationship was healing, it would have been the fatal blow. I really had to let him go. That is one of the hardest things a parent must do, trust them to know what to do in difficult situations. In other words, butt out! Ow! I'd better get up and get that pill. He took the pill and soon was fast asleep.

Lois was thinking of Nora. They had been friends for so long. Their lives were intertwined. Though not alike in personality, they complimented one another, each drawing something from the other that they themselves lacked. Lois was drawn out of her quietness by following along where Nora led. Nora was offered an appreciation of art, literature, and different cultures from joining Lois on her treks from museums to art galleries and by reading books that she praised and recommended.

Dear Nora, I hope she is safe, I hope she is having the great Amazon adventure we hoped for. Maybe someday we will look back on this time and laugh at our fears. I wonder if she had time to make notes for me, and if Don took any pictures. If they did, I wonder if I will ever see them.

Tom was restless also. It seemed like an age since he had last seen Letty. He relived in his mind their excitement in planning their trip. *Letty was so excited,* he remembered, *no wonder she decided to go on the trip anyway when the family was so scattered. I probably would have done the same thing. I wish I hadn't had to go to Pittstown. God, how I wish she had stayed home! Dear Lord, I can't lose her, please don't let me lose her! I pray that she will be returned to me unhurt.'* He fell asleep praying the Rosary on his fingers.

Ryti was lying in bed in a darkened room, crying. She was very upset and worried about Nat. He was always right in the front in any disturbance. He would be very protective of Bud. He would do anything for GWH and he knew that Bud was the person closest to his heart. No, Nat would never let anything happen to Bud, he would die first.

He doesn't even know about the child that I am carrying. I wasn't sure when he left, but I am sure now. She hugged her body across the abdomen, and smiled through her tears. He will be so happy when I tell him. A baby is all that we need to make our happiness complete. *If I get to tell him,* she agonized.

In time, all of them fell asleep. Since all had a restless night, they all slept late. There was nothing anyone had to get up early for. They all ate at the lounge whenever they wanted to. There was no special time that anyone had to be anywhere.

Gradually each of them came to the lounge, and it wasn't until 11:00 a.m. that they all were assembled. GWH was the first to arrive and had already contacted the far camp by the time the others made an appearance. No good news there, the first patrol was leaving on today's search, and they would call when they returned, unless they discovered something before, then, of course, they would call right away.

After breakfast Gordon and Lois walked a short way to a bench by the river. They were sitting and talking when Lois said suddenly,

"Look, Gordy, look at that fish, no, it might be two fish, they are leaping!"

"Those are Splash Tetra, they are really strange ones. To protect their eggs from prey they lay their eggs on leaves of trees. See that branch overhanging the river? It is a perfect place for them. They get close together, so close they look like one, then the female nudges the male and they leap together, and simultaneously, she expels her eggs and he fertilizes them and the eggs stick to the leaf."

"Oh my, that sure is chancy."

"That's not the end of it, it is then the male's duty to keep the eggs wet by splashing water on them until they hatch and drop into the water. It is a good thing it only takes about three days or he would never make it. As it is, he is pretty well done in by then."

While Gordon waited, Lois went to her cabin for sketching supplies, and when she returned, spent awhile drawing the scenes. One picture was of the pair leaping and one picture of the male splashing his heart out to protect his babies. Gordon was impressed with her skill and enjoyed watching her work.

Back at the lounge, Tom and Ryki, tired of watching reruns on the old TV with a scattering of natives and decided to take a walk in the jungle. They searched out Ke'era to be their guide. Neither of them wanted to venture on such a jaunt without one. As they wandered about, Ke'era pointed out interesting plants, insects and birds along the way. He didn't have to point out the monkeys. They followed them chattering, sometimes screaming, occasionally throwing sticks or small branches at them for daring to enter their private dominion.

"What on earth is that?" Tom cried, stepping back a bit.

Ryti and Ke'era laughed at his fright.

"That is only a sloth," Ryti said with a smile.

"They don't hurt," Ke'era assured him.

"I thought they lived high in the trees all the time," Tom said, calm again.

"They do, except for once a week when they descend to defecate and urinate. They don't soil their living area you understand," Ryti explained.

"Why is he crawling along the ground that funny way? Why doesn't he just get up and walk?"

"You see those long and curved claws?" Ryti explained. "They are of great use up in the trees. They help in climbing and help them hold on while they sleep." Ke'era pointed out.

"Look, there are a bunch of insects where he dumped!" Tom exclaimed.

"Those are special moths that can only lay their eggs there. They wait until he does this and then hurry, while it is fresh, to lay their eggs then. They usually infest the sloth's hair the rest of the time."

They watched while the sloth slowly and deliberately ascended by pulling himself from branch to branch.

"Well, that was sure something to see!" Tom said. "I didn't know there was a green-haired animal."

"The hair is really a light brown or tan. The green comes from an incrustation of algae that forms in the hair and grows in the dampness of the forest. It is a kind of camouflage against jaguars and other natural enemies. When they are coiled in a small ball amidst the green leaves they are very hard to see," Ryti explained.

"I think that sloth is a female. Notice the baby clinging to her abdomen?" Ke'era pointed out.

"I think you are right! See the little head peeking out over her shoulder?" Tom said.

"They are not very pretty animals, are they?" Ryti said.

"The female has one offspring yearly," Ke'era informed them. "They also give birth upside down high in the tree."

"What a strange animal," Tom said.

"There are a lot of strange animals around here," Ryti answered.

"We better return now and see if there is any news about the lost ones." Ke'era said, and they started back.

Chapter Nineteen

Ke'era's son ran to where GWH and Lois were sitting, watching the valiant Splash Tetra tirelessly leaping to keep the new eggs wet.

"Sir, sir, the radio wants you, right away," he panted in his language that GWH understood.

"Okay, thanks," he said in the same tongue. He then hurried, as fast as a person in a cast could, to the office where the radio was.

"Turn the volume down," Lois, who had followed, said as she went to the TV at the other end of the room and silenced the program with an irritating laugh track.

"Hunter here."

"We are sighting two boats coming upriver." There was the "whuft, whuft" sound of the rotors in the background of the voice shaking with the plane's vibration.

"Can you tell how many passengers there are?"

"Uh, let's see, four in one boat and five in the other. They all must be okay because they are waving like crazy!"

"Thank God! Lois, get Tom, they're found and they are okay!"

Lois sped off to the jungle path they took when they left.

"What happens now?"

"Well, since everyone seems healthy, we will drop some food, water and meds, and a radio. After we talk to them, take it from there."

"What is their frequency?"

"It isn't that strong a radio. It won't reach you, but I will relay."

"Keep your end open so we can hear the play by play. I'll put you on the speaker."

"Will do!"

Lois didn't have to go very far to find the others, and soon Tom, Ryki and Ke'era entered in a rush, followed by Lois, just in time to hear GWH's last instructions.

They sat breathless, clutching one another, waiting for the next transmission.

"Careful with that package! Drop it upstream and let it float down to them. That's the way, it is floating." There was a pause.

"Now he's got it. Wait till he gets it on board before dropping the other box."

Assorted noises, rotor noises, scraping noises and static, then they heard, "Okay! The boxes are away, let's go back, fuel is low now. Hunter! You still there?"

"Yeah, we heard it all," he choked with emotion. Tom and Lois along with Ryti had tears streaming from their eyes. Ke'era was hopping around shouting something in his language. The natives in the room joined him in his joy.

Down on the river they were delirious with joy! Bud and Nat each steered their boat to the shore and opened the boxes. Bud reached for the radio, Dennis rummaged through the first-aid package, and Nat gave everyone a protein bar to munch on while he prepared a meal.

"Hello, can anyone hear me?" Bud made contact with the helicopter as it sped off.

"Hi! Are you all okay?"

"We are now, thanks to you and your goodie boxes. I can't thank you enough! We were just about out of food and meds."

"Is anybody sick or hurt?"

"Not anything extremely serious—sunburn, insect bites, small infections, and my arm is bugging me some."

"We are on bingo fuel so we must leave now. Is this GWH's son?"

"Yeah, I'm Bud."

"Your dad is at the base camp and knows you have been found. He will be very glad to see you when you show up."

"He is? He must be a lot better then. How long do you think it will take us to reach the base camp?"

"Paddling will be too tiring in your weakened condition and take too long. Stay put and I will bring you two motors and enough fuel to make it in a day or two. You guys rest, eat and treat your wounds and I will be back tomorrow."

That is just what they did, after their usual routine of setting up their camp, of course.

Back at the base camp happiness reigned. Everyone was smiling.

"Ke'era, can you scare up an extra boat," Gordon asked. "I'd like to go meet them."

"Yas, I can do that, you want men to paddle for you?"

"Gordy, what are you thinking?" Lois interrupted.

"You aren't planning to go boating in your condition!" Tom said, shaking his head.

"Why not, I won't be paddling. Besides, I'll go nuts cooling my heels around here."

"Well, for one thing, what are you going to do when you meet them? Hop into their boat? Will they have room? Will you have room for them in your boat?" Lois queried. "You'll end up shouting at one another, delaying their trip back."

"They will be here in a day or so, why don't we concentrate on a huge welcome home party?" Tom suggested. "You need to rest so you can enjoy the party," Tom added.

"But…"

"No buts! If you won't take care of yourself, I will have to." Lois leaned over and kissed him, softening her words.

"Well, okay then." He smiled up at her. He was touched. He wasn't used to tender loving care.

"Well, let's start planning the party," Tom said. "They are going to be starved for something besides nuts and berries."

"Let's have a pig hunt!" Gordon shouted.

Ke'era went out to get the hunting party moving.

"We can have the men go out, you stay here. That would be worse than boating," Tom said. "You can make a big WELCOME HOME banner."

"That is kid stuff. Do you want me to make a paper chain too?" Gordon pouted.

"I know, you can be the chef and cook the pig when they get it," Tom said.

"Would you like to do that, darling?" Lois asked.

"Yeah, I could do that. I have a special sauce that everyone likes."

"That's it then, let's go to the lounge and assemble everything you will need," Tom chimed in.

"It is good to make the sauce the day before anyway," Gordon added. "It lets the spices blend together," Gordon said, warming up to the idea.

———————

"Oh, I ate too much!" Don said, patting his abdomen.

"Me too!" Dennis said.

"Nat is such a great cook!" Letty extolled. "It's no wonder we all ate too much, but I think our stomachs have shrunk because of our restricted diet."

"I think so too. I used to be able to eat much more than I did." Bud answered.

"There is a little more ice cream, we ought to finish it off before it melts completely," Ginger said as she slurped up a gob of the rapidly melting chocolate ice cream.

"I can't believe they dropped us ice cream! It's almost decadent, eating ice cream sitting on a log in the jungle while swatting insects," Nora said, walking over and scooping up some of the dripping confection.

"None for me, I've had enough," Carla said.

"Come on, Nat, let's finish this off," Ellen said, scraping half of the remainder onto a paper plate and handing it to Nat.

"Thank you very much," he said, "This was a great surprise. I think I can squeeze in a little more."

"It will be nice not to have to paddle anymore," Letty said, looking at the Band-Aids on her blistered hands. "Not that I was all that much help."

Bud was standing near her, so he put his arms around her, rubbed his bearded cheek to hers and said, "If it wasn't for you and your Uncle Alfred's medallion we would all be dead by now, and very gruesomely so too. I can just see all our tiny little heads all in a row."

"Ugh, don't even mention it," Ellen said. "I still have nightmares about it"

"She sure does, I've got the bruises to prove it," Don said.

"I try not to think about it," Carla said.

"Well, I have to think about it and remember every single thing, so I can write about it for Lois. I have some of it, but I ran out of room in my notebook. I'm lucky I still have the notebook," Nora said.

"I used the last of the film on the natives," Don said. "I put it all in that old coffee can and sealed it with duct tape, but I lost her camera. I will have to replace it. When I get home, I'll send her the finest camera we have in the store and a year's supply of film."

"Do you think she will stay here with GWH?"

"It is hard telling. It all depends on what happened while we were gone," Nora answered.

"Hey! Let's not speculate on what's going on with my Dad and Lois. What happens, happens, let's let it go at that." Bud was uncomfortable the way the conversation had turned.

"Yeah," Nat chimed in. "That is their own business, but it would be a good thing for GWH."

"For Lois too," Nora answered. "But I don't think it would be so great for me. My that sounds selfish of me when I say it out loud, but I have to admit I have been thinking about it."

"It's only natural to wonder how it might change your life," Letty said. "They seemed pretty close when we left."

The sound of a helicopter stopped all the speculation about GWH and Lois' love life. They all ran to the riverside and waved to the circling whirlybird. There was no place for it to land.

"Hello the plane," Bud radioed.

"Hey there, Bud," the pilot answered. "I've got a big delivery for you. We put two motors in a rubber boat. We are going to drop it upriver a bit. Get your boat out here and catch it as it floats down."

"Okay, will do," he said, and he handed the radio to Ginger. He and Nat both ran to one of the boats. Don wasn't very far behind. They launched it in record time. The rubber boat came floating toward them. Nat and Don grabbed it and held it alongside while Don crawled into it. He took the protective wrapping off one of the motors, filled the tank from one of the large gas cans tied to the side and then fastened the motor to the back. It started right up and headed toward the river bank.

Everyone lined up on the bank was either laughing or crying or both. Finally Nat took charge.

"Pack up what you want to take and just leave the rest, we are going home!"

"I think we ought to take back one of the Bambi tents so they can see how we did it," Nora said, clutching her notebook to her chest.

Letty took her beloved Uncle Alfred's box. The supplies were gone, but the tools were still intact.

Soon they were on their way again. Each rubber boat had a native boat trailing behind with their gear packed in it. They decided the boats were too good to abandon. The people at the base camp could use them. Bud, in the boat with Ginger and her parents, Dennis and Carla took the lead position. He had the radio tuned to news, then tiring of that he turned to a music station.

When a song came on that they knew they all joined in. That wasn't very often though, it was mostly Portuguese music that had no words, none that they knew anyway. And too, it was hard to hear the radio over the motor noise. Though the weather was still hot and steamy, the speed of the motors created a breeze that made it tolerable. And, anyway, they were on their way back at last. Bud reported their position periodically.

In the other boat, Nat was the captain. Letty, Nora, Don and Ellen made up his crew. They had no radio and the motor noise made conversation difficult. They sat back and enjoyed the breeze and the fact that none of them had to paddle. They didn't even have to stop for lunch. Each boat had food and drinks and they ate whenever they felt hungry.

Back at the base camp, they were busy getting ready for the feast. The male natives were returning from an early hunting trip. They brought a jaguar, a tapir, some birds and two peccarys back to the camp. They immediately began to prepare the meat for cooking.

The women had their own trip to the jungle and the nearby garden. They set to work making Kawi, a drink made from maize, peanuts or tapioca. They prepared sweet potatoes, the staple manioc, corn and pumpkin. There were displays of exotic fruits. Bananas, papaya, and pineapple, with sticks of sugar cane here and there.

Lois and Tom were readying the sleeping quarters for them. Tom swept the rooms, making sure there were no insects. Lois placed fresh flowers in all the rooms. Ryti made the beds with fresh linens that they brought with them.

Chapter Twenty

All was ready. The only thing needed was the missing adventurers. They all went down to the riverside and got comfortable in the shade drinking some mixture of fruit juices.

The radio came to life and GWH answered immediately. It was the helicopter pilot that was keeping track of the two boats making their way to the base camp.

Tom got up and was pacing anxiously as the pilot said, "The passengers of the two boats are just around the nearest bend to the camp and will be there in about five minutes or so. Everyone looks well and happy. They say 'Hi, see you soon.'"

GWH noticed Tom's anxiety and asked, "Joe, did you tell Letty that her husband is here?"

"No, I didn't even know it. Should I let her know?"

"No" Tom said, "let's surprise her!"

"No, we'll surprise her," GWH told the pilot. "Come on in, I know they will want to thank you, and I want to give you a check for all your good work."

When Bud negotiated the bend in the river and they came in sight all Hell broke loose. There was shouting, whistling, laughing and even a few tears, which increased in volume and intensity, if that's possible, when Nat's boat came in sight. They were understandably a motley crew, much the worse for wear; sunburned, bruised, insect bitten, and so very tired.

"TOM!" Letty had just spotted her husband. "DARLING!" They rushed toward one another and met in a close embrace. Letty began to cry and couldn't stop. A paracsism of sobs shook her emaciated body. She was at the absolute end of her endurance.

She had been such a trooper, going through all the things that happened with such vigor and not only without a complaint, but also by being a role model for the others. Since she pitched in without complaining, how could anyone else dare do otherwise? Tom took her to their hut and shut the door. They had a lot of things to catch up on.

When GWH saw how exhausted they were he decided that baths and naps were in order till the feast started at 7:00. There were no protests and soon the camp was quiet.

Bud was the first one to surface. It was all GWH and Lois could do to let him sleep. They were very curious and wanted to learn all that happened on that fateful trip.

Father and son sat in the air-conditioned office, with Lois by Gordy's side. Bud told them all that had happened. GWH and Lois were astounded as they learned about each thing that had occurred.

The part about their capture by the natives really upset them.

"Are you sure it was Fenton's head there?" GWH asked.

"Yes, Dad, there was no mistake, it was Fenton alright."

"Orem was found and nearly died from infected wounds and insect bites. He is back at his sister's house now recuperating."

"We were wondering if he got back okay. We knew he had escaped. The natives told us."

"Thank God for that thing around Letty's neck!"

"We'd be just as dead as Fenton with our heads on the shelf beside his if she hadn't had it on."

Lois shuddered, then put her arms around Bud and held him close, the tears sliding down her cheeks, as she asked,

"How did Letty stand the trip? She looked pretty beat up when she got here."

"Surpassingly well, she had a bout with fire ants and her hands were blistered from the oar, but she pulled her own weight. They all did, each had a job and did it. Doc was the organizer. Nat did some hunting, fishing and cooking. Don, Ellen and Letty did a lot of water boiling. Nora and Ginger, Don and Ellen and Letty all searched the forest for things to eat and wood to cook with. Doc was determined that we stay healthy. He treated all sores at the end of each day. It's good that we had Uncle's box with all the supplies in it. Doc set up the rules and we followed them. He is what brought us through, he and Letty's uncle's doodad that she had on."

"I don't suppose you had much to do, huh?"

"My big thing was getting them all on the ground safely while saving my own neck. Then I helped out wherever I could with my bum arm. Doc fixed it up pretty good, and there were pain pills in the box that helped to keep me going after the bone was set. It feels okay now, but I'd better have it looked at, it has had a few bumps along the way. Letty's jacket sleeves made a good sturdy sling, but I lost it when I dove in after Carla."

"What?" they chorused. He then had to explain that part of the adventure.

Lois arose. "I think I will go talk to Nora and hear her story. See you two later."

When Letty woke up in Tom's arms, she was smiling. All the crying was past. Now was the time to go back over the trouble she had telling him where she was. She told him of the crash, thrashing through the jungle, the capture by the natives, and the miracle of the necklace that turned enemies into benefactors.

She related the hardships of their boat trip, the fire ants and their joy when they saw the helicopter and knew they were safe.

Gradually everyone joined them and added their own input of their adventure.

"You sure named your tour right! HUNTER'S AMAZON JUNGLE ADVENTURE TOURS! It was a little more adventure than I wanted," Don said.

"Now that we are home safe and sound, I'm sure you won't stop telling your friends all about it," Ellen reminded him with a grin.

"You are right about that, hon, you will have to back me up or they won't believe me."

Nora and Lois were chattering away in a corner of the room. Nora had a pad and pencil and was jotting things down as she remembered them.

"These are things I remembered. I ran out of room in the notebook and then ink too. I jotted some things on my handkerchief, till it ran out."

Lois said, "The first thing Don did was give me the film he had taken. He kept it in that funny bed you all had. He was so sorry about losing my camera. As if I cared! It is a wonder you all made it back safely, much less hanging onto the notebook and the film. With that my book will be finished in no time. I have already made the deal with a publisher. The publicity of your return will increase the sales considerably. I will have to have an epilogue explaining your part in it."

"No need for that, but tell me about you and GWH."

"Well, I call him Gordy, that is what his mother called him. I guess everyone can tell that I love him. What's even better is that he loves me too."

"Has he asked you to marry him?"

"No, not in so many words, but he has said how much he loves me and thanks me for being there for him."

"Humfh! With that and a stamp you can mail a letter."

"Nora! Don't talk like that. He is a little shy, believe it or not. That big rough and tough Great White Hunter is very shy. I just have to wait till he gets up the nerve to ask me."

"Will you say yes?"

"Oh, yes."

"Will you stay here with him then?"

"Of course I will!"

"What about your house and your job?"

"So much has happened and so fast, I haven't even thought about it."

"Well, you'd better start thinking about it. If you are going to quit, you'd better let the school know soon, so they can fill your spot. I can take care of renting your apartment, furnished, I guess. Do you want me to take some personal things out before I rent it? I can empty your closets and pantry and store things for you in my basement storage area. I have room alongside my sports equipment and stuff. Do you have much in your storage area? Anything you want to keep or have sent here?"

"Great Heavens! I haven't thought anything about that. I guess I must plan to go home, no matter what happens. There is too much to tend to. How do I find out if I am staying or not! I can't ask Gordy what his intentions are."

"Er, have you, um a…"

"Of course not!"

"Well, has he said anything about the future?"

"Only in general, like what we will do when he gets well again, things around here to do and see. He wants to show me everything"

"I guess you'd better plan to return as planned, the rest has to be up to him."

"I guess so," Lois said sadly.

Nat and Ryti's reunion had been passionate. They'd clung to one another for a long time. Ryti was finally able to tell him her secret that she was with their first child. She had not told anyone. She wanted Nat to know first. Their joy was complete. When they were ready, they joined the natives that were preparing the feast. There was lots of joy and laughter as they all worked together.

Don and Ellen, after their refreshing bath and nap dressed and were ready to join the others. He was glad he had turned the film over to Lois, it was a load off his mind.

"What a story I have to tell the guys!"

"We'll have a big party, including the wives." She raised an eyebrow, forestalling a strictly stag bash at the nineteenth hole.

"Okay, we can do that," he said, not ruling out some big doings at the nineteenth hole.

In their cabin, while getting dressed to join the others, Dennis, Carla and Ginger were having a heavy discussion,

"No, you can't stay on here till school starts. What are you thinking about, Ginger?" Carla hissed, not wanting their conversation overheard in the next cabins.

"I don't see why not," Ginger whined. "You and Dad have to go back home, I know, but I don't have to go home yet. I know GWH would let me stay. Bud would want me to stay till then too. Then we could both leave for school at the same time and travel together." Seeing a big 'No' in Carla's eyes, she turned to Dennis, a piteous look on her face. "Can't I, Dad?"

He had been hoping to stay out of the discussion, but it wasn't to be. "For one thing, you haven't been asked. For another thing, it just isn't done. I wouldn't think very much of Bud if he asked you to do something which would tarnish your reputation."

"I can't help it if some people have dirty minds!" She tossed her curls in anger.

"Then don't do things that look bad," Carla hissed again, to remind them that their voices were rising.

"If you would ask GWH to let me stay, I know he would say yes," Ginger wheedled.

"I am not about to do that! Even if he asked me if it would be okay, I wouldn't let you stay. I don't want to hear another word about it." Dennis was losing his patience now. "Let's go join the others," he repeated. "I don't want to hear another word about it."

―――――――

When Lois left them Bud had a chance to talk to GWH alone.

"Dad, how are things going with you and Lois?"

"Fine, just fine, I don't know what I would have done without her. She helped me in so many ways. She taught me how to eat by myself by placing things on my plate in positions like the numbers on the face of a clock. When I needed pain medication, she was right there with it. She kept me clean too. Sometimes it was downright embarrassing, but she acted as if what she had to do was nothing at all, so it made it easier for me. She read to me till she got hoarse. She described things to me so clearly I could see it in my mind's eye. With it all she was so darned sweet. Well, I just love her, that's all." He reddened.

"Have you asked her to stay, to marry you?"

"I haven't gotten up the nerve."

"Well, don't you think you'd better? She'll be going back home now."

"I really want to. Do you think she'll just think I want her to take care of me?"

"Have you told her you love her?"

"Yes, and I thanked her for taking such good care of me."

"At the same time?"

"Yes."

"I think you'd better tell her how much you love her and ask her to marry you right away. Do you still have Grandma's ring?"

"Yes, it's back at the house."

"Well then, what's there to stop you?"

"Not a damn thing, not a damn thing!"

"Well then, let's join the party!"

"Wait a minute, Bud. You were pretty nosy about me and Lois, how about the low down about you and Ginger?"

"We were all so close together all the time, I wasn't alone with her long enough to make any kind of move. Her parents were always around. I do love her, but she is so young. I wouldn't be doing her any favors by rushing her off her feet. She needs to go to college, that will enable her to make a mature decision when she is out of school. I want my marriage to last, no divorces for me!"

"I guess you're right."

"I would like to go to grad school too. I want to learn about the flora and fauna of the Amazon area. I want to be a help to you in your business. We could expand and improve the tours. If I had a degree I could teach and lecture off-season."

"Don't you think you ought to at least mention your feelings to Ginger? Make arrangements to keep in touch?"

"With e-mail we can be in touch every day. Don't worry, I am going to do everything I can to make her love me and stay in love with me, like Grandma and Grandpa Hunter. Theirs was a great marriage. I really believe that 'Till death do us part.' stuff and I don't want to act too impulsively and ruin things."

"I do too, only things didn't work out that way with your mother and me. Let's not talk about me though. I think you ought to talk to Dennis and Carla about your plans. They must be afraid you are going to sweep their daughter off her feet, and I know they don't want any part of that. If you let them know of your sensible plan, they will feel much better. I know they like you, and would be happy for you and Ginger, but just not now."

"That's a good idea, Dad. I will do it right away, and you'd better do some wooing yourself."

The feast was a wonderful thing. The low table was full of exotic fruits and some nameless vegetables. The meats were succulent and tender. The natives were happy and sang as they put the finishing touches on the long low table erected just for the feast. Then everyone sat on mats except GWH. He had a hard time getting down that low, so they made him a small table and had him sit on a chair brought from the office. He was at the head of the table, looking down at them all.

"Look at GWH, master of all he surveys!" Don yelled out.

"Pipe down and eat!" he answered.

" First I think Letty should lead us in one of her prayers of thanksgiving as she did on the trip home," Nora suggested

There was a chorus of agreement, and Letty rose, with her hand on Tom's shoulder began, "Dear Lord, we thank you for this wonderful feast you have provided for us. We thank you for bringing us home safely. You have answered your people in their sufferings. We thank you for your kindness and ask you to free us from all evil that we may serve you in happiness all our days. We ask this in the name of Jesus Christ our Lord and Savior, now and forever and ever, Amen"

A solemn quietness came over them. The miracle of their safe return, or the return of their loved ones, through such a perilous time became entrenched in their minds and hearts. They were truly thankful.

"Okay, everyone, let's eat!" GWH announced.

They did.

When they finished, the natives did one of their dances. Before long all of them joined in, except GWH, of course, and he even kept time by patting his one good foot.

Bud asked Dennis and Carla to walk down to the beach with him. Ginger was busy dancing and didn't see them leave. They went down to the bench by the river and Bud began his pitch.

I guess you know that I love Ginger..."

"Bud..." began Dennis,

"I know just what you are going to say, and I agree with you."

This surprised both of them. They were all set to argue with him and say that it was impossible.

"I know Ginger must go to school and finish college, and I want her to do just that. I want to go to grad school and learn botany and biology, so I will know all I can about this area. There are plants here that haven't been discovered yet. I want to discover some of them. I want to find uses for them. I have taken Economics and I believe I can be a great help to Dad and even improve the business. This place is becoming a popular travel destination and I believe Hunters Amazon Jungle Adventures can become better and better. My Grad school will take about two years. By the time Ginger graduates I will have had two years of the tour business and should know my way around by then, with Dad's direction. Then I will ask Ginger to marry me. I plan to see her, I plan to show her that I love her. I also plan to hold her in an open palm. She will be free to date and go to proms with anyone she wants to. I will not tie her down to any promises that will hamper her school fun in any way. Well, what do you think? Do you think this is a good plan?"

"Oh, Bud, you are such a darling!" Carla said with tears in her eyes.

"I didn't think you had such an old head on your young shoulders!" Dennis said.

"Do you think Ginger will want me?"

"I am going to have a hard time getting her to wait. It is up to you to convince her," Carla told him, smiling.

"She has no idea what to study. You can suggest to her what would be useful to major in. Maybe you can help her plan a curriculum that will enable her to be a help to you," Dennis said.

"Well, I really wish you would let her learn how to fly. Another pilot would be a great asset to the business. In four years she could become a very good pilot. She would love it too."

This was something else again. Neither one of them ever dreamed of giving her flying lessons! Dancing lessons, skiing lessons, gymnastic lessons, music lessons, any of those and more, but flying?

"This is something we will have to discuss, Bud. I still remember the trauma of her getting her driving license. Flying...I don't know," Dennis said with a frown.

"I don't think I want her to do that, Bud," Carla rejoined.

"Is Ginger a good driver?"

"Yes, she is, she is an excellent driver, very capable," Dennis answered.

"Our neighbor lets her drive her children places when she babysits. She trusts her that much," Carla bragged.

"Is Ginger smart enough to learn?" Bud asked

"Of course!"

"Certainly!"

"Well then, what is the problem? Would you hold her back from her place in this modern space age? I am not asking that she go to the moon!"

He had won them over. Talking to them in his matter-of-fact manner they couldn't help but agree with all that he proposed. They left him wanting this wise, caring young man for their daughter. They marveled at how unusual he was and how sensible for his age.

"I guess he learned the hard way, living through his parents unhappy married life, and afterwards. It made him mature very early," said Carla.

"It certainly made him sure of what he wants and doesn't want in his life."

———

Lois came back to the table after her dance with the natives.

"Whew! That was fun, but tiring. I am sorry you couldn't dance too, honey."

"While I've got you alone, I want to talk to you," he told her.

"Okay, talk." She smiled and held his hand.

"I love you, Lois. I want you to stay here with me and marry me," he said in a rush, cheeks aflame. "Will you?"

He had such a strained look on his face, the one exposed eye so anxious, that she had to laugh, then she kissed him hard. "Yes, yes, yes, my darling. I will marry you whenever you are well enough. We will let the doctor set the date."

"I guess that will be okay. I'll go see him the minute we get back. I have a ring for you that was my mother's. It is beautiful, I know you will like it."

"It will be an honor to wear it. I know how much she meant to you." They kissed, and kissed again.

Bud, Dennis and Carla came back to the table in time to see them. Bud whistled in appreciation

"Way to go, Dad! Watch out for him, Lois!"

"I'm not running," she said as she gave him another quick peck.

"I have just asked this beautiful lady to be my wife, and what's more, she said yes!"

"Now we have more to celebrate," Carla cried

"Everybody! Hear this! Dad and Lois are engaged!" Bud announced in a loud voice, loud enough to be heard above all the noise.

Congratulations and toasting began. Everyone came over and wished them well. It was a wonderful way to end the celebration.

Bud took Ginger's hand and led her away from the rest. He embraced her, taking her breath away and weakening her knees. She had never ever felt such a wonderful, heart thumping, erotic feeling before in her whole life!

"Bud," she breathed, "oh, Bud, I love you with all my heart!"

"Ginger, my one true love!" They kissed again, deeply.

When they came up for air, Bud led her to the bench by the river.

"We have to talk, my darling."

"You don't have to ask," she cried impulsively. "I will marry you, I will stay with you always and never leave!"

"Ah, my dearest love, how I would love to have you do just that. But it won't do."

"Why not? Is it my parents?"

"Yes, it's them, but it is me too."

"You?"

"Yes, I love you too much to cheat you out of the next four years. Years to grow, to have fun, to learn."

"I will gladly give up those years of school. It would be no problem at all. I don't want to leave you."

" I want you to be able to join me in my life's work. How can you do that with no education? As much as I love you and want you so much, it would be doing you a disfavor, and you would end up realizing it in the end and not thanking me for it either."

"I don't care!"

"I do care! So do your parents. They would never let you marry me now. In time they will be happy to see us together, but not now. Waiting is the right thing to do."

"It isn't the right thing for me! I love you and want to marry you right away."

"Don't you think that is what I want? I need more education too if I want to teach in the off-season, I need to learn how to utilize new plant discoveries and how to discover new uses for ones we already know about. I need to be able to lecture and explain things to others. There is a lot for both of us to do together."

"Four years is so long!"

"The years will pass anyway, and we will be so much better off if we stick to this plan. Please, Ginger, please think about the long run, not just the heat of the moment. People prepare years for their professions—doesn't matrimony deserve the same preparation?"

"I guess, but I love you, Bud. I want to do what you want, but I don't want to wait either. We could both go to the same college, we can see each other every day, we can..."

"No, we can't. It would end up with our living together on campus. I've seen it happen. The girl gets pregnant and has to drop out of school, or mama takes care of the baby, or they decide on an abortion. I don't want to be part of any of those scenarios."

"I don't either. My parents would kill me, you too."

"They approve of this plan."

"You have discussed this with them!" she gasped, furious.

"I had to if I wanted to get their blessing."

"You had a lot of nerve!" Angry tears hanging on her lower lids.

"I had to have plenty to get them to agree. Can you imagine the uproar they would have caused if we asked them if we could get married now?"

Remembering the wall she faced when she asked to just stay till school started, she nodded, the tears sliding down her cheeks.

Bud couldn't resist and started kissing her again. Then he pushed her away saying, "Ginger, honey, this is not solving anything. Let's go talk this over with your parents. We will have to eventually anyway."

"I guess you are right," she sniffed.

"They already agreed to your taking flying lessons."

"Flying lessons! I don't believe it! How did you ever get them to agree to that?"

"I talked them into it, saying that my wife would have to be able to fly if she was to be part of the tour business. They need to get into the 21st century."

"Well, as far as medicine is concerned, Dad is there. He is all for trying new things in his area of practice. Mother, however, is the typical mother hen. How did you manage her?"

"I don't know what did it. Her own good sense, or your Dad's influence. She was against the flying lessons though."

"I'll bet!"

They arrived back at the party and sought out Dennis and Carla.

"Hi, you two," Dennis said. "You look like you've been up to something."

"We are engaged!" Ginger smiled

"We are engaged to be engaged," corrected Bud.

"That's better," Carla said, grudgingly.

"What is this about flying lessons for me?"

"Well, maybe after your first year of college, if your grades are good enough," Dennis said.

"Sir, I think we decided she should start right away, ground school anyway."

"I really would like to start right away, I am going have to learn a lot in four years."

Relieved not to have a big argument with the possibility of losing, Dennis saw the benefit of conceding this point. "I guess we might allow the ground school to start at once then." He took Carla's arm and pressed it to his side, seeing she was about to object.

Seeing that she was bested, Carla relented.

"It's getting late. We'd all better turn in, we have a lot to do tomorrow."

Everyone agreed and with a chorus of "Goodnights" they all went to their sleeping quarters. Ginger and Bud sharing a chaste kiss in front of the group.

Chapter Twenty-one

The next morning before breakfast, plans were made by Bud and GWH to return to Manaus. They only had the one helicopter, the old one. They would make it in two trips. It would be crowded, but by leaving all luggage it could be done. Deciding who would go, and when, was difficult. They finally decided that Bud would fly Nat, Ryti, Letty, Tom, Ellen and Don first. That way Nat could reopen the tour schedule by making reservations for flights and hotel rooms. Ryti could get things ready at the house and make an appointment for GWH at the doctor's.

The next day Bud was to return and get GWH, Lois, Nora, Dennis, Carla and Ginger. Nat would return the next day after that and bring all the luggage back. It took a lot to convince GWH that he should go on the second trip, but somehow Lois managed it. Ginger wasn't very happy either. Bud wanted to be able to talk to her alone when he returned and discuss their plans with her. They would talk about the particulars of the plans with her parents on the flight back to Manaus.

Breakfast was served. They all enjoyed the camaraderie of one last jungle meal together. When the meal was over, GWH tapped his cup on the table.

"I would like to make an announcement." He struggled to rise to his feet, leaning on his cane.

Everyone became silent, waiting to hear what he had to say.

"I have decided to go back to the U.S. with you. I don't want Lois to go back home, leaving me alone. I want her to go back home as my wife. I would like for all of you to stay in Manaus as my guests until the marriage can be arranged. That is if my darling Lois will agree." He turned to Lois, who was sitting by his side, stunned.

"Will you marry me then, Lois? We will have our honeymoon in the States. When we have taken care of your affairs there, we will travel a bit, then return here. Would that please you, my dear?"

Startled at the question so boldly put to her in front of everyone, she blushed, stammered a bit, then with a beautiful smile on her face, she raised her head and said, "I would be delighted to, Gordy." She rose and they kissed, and kissed again.

There was a great uproar of congratulations, laughter, and a loud wolf whistle from Bud.

———— ••••••••• ————

The helicopter was gassed up. Bud, Nat and GWH did a walk around together and pronounced it fit. Those that were to go on the first trip got aboard. With Bud at the controls, they took off, waving goodbye.

GWH met with the native staff of the camp and took care of the business that had been neglected while he was recuperating. He was quite proud of the way they carried on without direction, and told them so.

With nothing pressing to do, Lois and Nora discussed plans for the move and the management of her property.

Dennis, Carla, and Ginger explored the area with native guides. They came upon a beautiful waterfall and a deep cool pool.

"Oh, let's dive in and play in the waterfall," Ginger cried.

"Last one in is a rotten egg!" Dennis yelled as he dove in, clothes and all.

Carla and Ginger did the same. They played in the water. The guides joined them. They spent about an hour in the pleasant water.

When they got out and started back, Carla began to feel a strange feeling between her legs. It was becoming hard to walk.

"Dennis, something is wrong. I believe something has bitten me." She sat sideways on a log. She was in real pain now.

The oldest native, they didn't know his name, was trying to say something to Dennis, pointing to Carla's body. He was agitated and was trying to make himself understood.

"Ginger, take the other guide and run and get my medicine bag, and hurry!"

They sped away and Dennis took the older man by the hand and walked with him a short distance and had him sit down, to give them some privacy. He returned to Carla and examined her. He discovered a wormlike creature in her vagina. He tried to remove it, but Carla let out a loud yelp. It had fastened itself to the membranous lining and wasn't to be moved. It seemed like an eternity before Ginger returned with the bag. He flooded the area with an antiseptic liquid soap.

He had Ginger hold a flashlight so he could see. He tried to insert a speculum, but was unable to bypass the thing. He grabbed it with a forceps. It had inserted barbs into the area that were preventing its removal. He took another forceps and crushed each barb, and then he was able to remove the vile creature.

Carla was clenching her teeth, not wanting to frighten Ginger.

I am not going to scream, she kept repeating to herself. She was shaking. Dennis was working as fast as he could. He swabbed away the blood, applied antiseptic ointment and a wide piece of folded gauze.

He held her close as she sobbed against his shoulder.

"Hey, sweet girl, it's all over! You didn't utter a peep when it was really bad, now you are bawling like a baby when it is all over."

She gave a shuddery sigh, and raised her head for his kiss.

"Are you okay now?"

"Uh huh."

"Do you think you can stand up now?"

"Please, can I have my shorts back?"

"Yes, but I thought you might like to go native awhile, these guys won't think a thing of it."

"Oh, Mother! This thing is so gross!" Ginger had used a leaf to pick up the critter and was examining it.

"Ginger, put that down!" Carla shouted.

"No, we'll bring it back. I want to know what it is."

They took their time going back, not wanting to rush Carla. They went back to their cabin and Carla went to bed until time to get up for dinner.

Dennis and Ginger took the "critter" as they called it and showed it to Nat.

It turned out that it was a Candiru, a wormlike creature that enters the genitals of bathers. It holds itself by two barbs and feeds on the mucous membrane lining. It can cause a painful death if not cut out. It wasn't in Carla that long to cause much damage. Prompt treatment and preventing infection did the trick and she had very little problem with it.

Still, it was an awful experience that she had handled like a trooper.

That evening they dined on the huge amount of food left over from the feast. They amused Tom, Lois and GWH by telling them all about the events of their adventure with the natives in their village. Carla swore Dennis and Ginger to silence. She didn't want to tell anyone about her adventure of the day.

When they landed at Manaus, Nat saw that the helicopter was taken care of and made ready to take off again for the base camp the next day. Bud had two taxis come and take them to GWH's house. Ryti got them settled and then she and Nat fixed a meal and they all went to bed.

The next day Nat made arrangements for rooms at the same hotel the group had stayed in before. The luggage they left behind was in storage for them. When Nat got them sorted out, Don and Ellen, and Tom and Letty had their rooms and bags, and Nora had her things in her room. Nat left them to explore the town on their own. They had GWH's office number and home phone number if they had any questions. He went to the office to clear up some odds and ends before his trip to the base camp to get the luggage. When he finished, he decided to go to the bar and tell the regulars there about the wedding.

"Hi, Nat!" the bartender said. " I heard you and the rest of the group were found. You sure had us scared. You'll be able to dine out for a long time on the stories you can tell."

"I'll leave the story telling to someone else. It sure was exciting. I've got good news though, GWH is going to marry Miss Lois!"

"Is she the one who tended to him while you were away?"

"That's the one, and a great lady she is too."

"When is the big doin's"

"Very soon, as soon as we can get everyone back, and before everyone takes off for the States, including Dad and Lois."

"Them too, huh?"

"Yeah, just me and Bud left to handle things here. Ryti, too, of course."

"It was horrible what happened to Fenton and Mr. Garson."

"It sure was, even though Mr. Garson's death was of natural causes, the causes of the causes sure weren't natural. He probably had some years left if he had been left alone."

"He was a nice guy too."

"I hear Orem is out of the hospital."

"Yeah, he had a tough time of it. Being in the jungle without supplies is very dangerous. He barely made it out alive. He had to go back to the doctor to get some of those grubs removed from his legs. They hatched under the skin of his legs from the eggs of the Berni fly. Those guys found him just in time. He is a changed man. He seems kind of depressed too, he just mopes around."

"That's too bad, I'll look him up when I get a chance. Maybe we can do something for him."

———

Bud's first chore that morning was to make an appointment with the doctor for Gordon. When that was done, he went shopping for a new car. He found a small bus that would be just the thing for business use, as well as getting them around. He drove it back to the house.

Nat was just leaving with Don, Ellen and Nora when he drove up.

"Wow!" said Nat. "That is just what we need."

"That shade of blue is beautiful!" Ryti said.

"Yeah, I'm going to put a sign on the door in white saying, 'HUNTER'S AMAZON JUNGLE ADVENTURES.'"

"I don't know about that," Don rejoined. "When people find out about the last one, they might not want to come."

"Maybe we could name it, 'BRING 'EM BACK ALIVE TOURS'," Nora wisecracked.

They waved goodbye as they climbed into Nat's car and drove off.

Back in the house once more Bud looked in his address book for the phone number of the place where he had bought the helicopter that crashed.

"Hi, this is Bud Hunter in Manaus. Do you remember me? I bought one of your helicopters...yeah, that's me...it was running fine, till I had a little accident. No, only a broken arm and some scratches. I am just about healed now. No, it wasn't any fault of the helicopter. It was sabotaged, the gas was all fouled up somehow and I crashed. I was a bit shaken up. Bottom line is I need another one delivered to the same place, same price, okay? How soon? Okay then. No, I don't need a refresher course in Houston. Thanks, I'll pay you when it gets here." Thanks to his inheritance from his mother, he could do that.

Now, that's done. One more thing to do, he told himself. He went to the short-wave radio and got in touch with Father O'Toole. When his call was answered, Bud found out that Father was in the midst of performing a wedding, and would return the call

With time on his hands he went in his room and started rummaging in his closet. There was a jewelry box with assorted gems that his mother left him, many of them given to her by his father. He selected a set of pink pearls; a necklace, earrings and a ring in a delicate setting. They had been Bud's grandmother's, bought for her by his grandfather in Japan in 1945. Just the thing for an 'engaged to be engaged' present. Simple, yet elegant, suitable for daily wear or with a formal gown. Not really "pink" but a warm cream, they are just called pink by some imaginative Japanese.

He wrapped it in one of May's dainty linen handkerchiefs and tied it with a white satin ribbon. He was putting it in his pocket when the short-wave radio erupted into action.

"Hi, Father."

"Hi, Bud. You want to talk to me?"

"Yeah, can you get off a few days, Father? Dad is going to get married and if you could boat to the base camp Nat can pick you up and fly you to Manaus and we can have the wedding as soon as you get here."

"He is way ahead of you, Bud! He called me last night and told me all about it. I pushed up a wedding I had scheduled so I am free to come. I am just about to start packing the boat now. This is a joyous occasion, Bud. It is about time he has some happiness."

"That is great, leave it to Dad! Grass doesn't grow under his feet, even if one is in a brace."

"I am so glad you are back in one piece, you had us plenty worried. I had the whole village praying for all of you."

"I really appreciate it. I know someone had to be watching over us. We were in real danger quite a few times."

"It will be good to see you, then. God bless you, son."

"Thanks, Father. See you soon, bye."

It was time for him to go to the airport and get going to the base camp. He thought about Ginger, and felt the special present in his pocket. He grabbed his small bag and was on his way.

Chapter Twenty-two

It was a lazy day at base camp. It was hot so every once in a while they would take a dip in the river, dry off and go watch TV in the air-conditioned office. Then Letty and Nora started playing Bridge with Dennis and Carla. With time out for breakfast and lunch, that's about all that went on the whole day.

Ginger was the first one to hear the distinctive sound of the helicopter. She let out a yelp and went dashing off toward the landing area.

"Let's let the kids have a little time alone." GWH gave a "stay seated" motion to the Bridge players. He put down the book he was reading and went over to the door and looked out. Reading with one eye was tiring, so he only read in short snatches. He saw the natives hurrying to greet Bud. He went back to his book, knowing Bud would find him there when he got around to it.

After he turned the plane over to the natives, who tended to its needs, Bud turned to the waiting Ginger. They clung together in a close embrace. It was such a short time that they were separated this time. They realized the next time that they would be parted would be much longer.

"Oh, Bud, how will we ever be able to wait so long?"

"It will be hard, but it is the thing to do. I have lived with the results of a wild passionate flame that was extinguished by the pressures of the differences that were never even considered. Everyday life was too much for it and it went out leaving dead ashes. I was raised immersed in those ashes. I had parents that pulled me apart. I loved them both, but it was an awful life for a kid. I am determined that I will have only one marriage and I want that one to be the very best. If we prepare ourselves to be able to be good at our life's work, enter into our marriage with a mature outlook and a love that is true, and not just sexual madness, ours will be a love that will last forever. That is what I want, and I hope that is what you want too."

"Oh, I do, Bud, I really do."

"We will see each other on holidays and vacations. There is e-mail too. We can keep in touch every day. You'll see we will be together forever before you know it. Another thing, your parents will be on our side, we won't have to fight with them, they love you so much, and they only want the best for you. They would hate me if I took you away from them too soon. I like them. I don't want them to hate me."

"They do like you, Bud, they said so."

"I am glad of that and I want to keep it that way. Honey, I want us to raise our children by ourselves, no childcare nurseries, nannies or boarding schools. I had enough of that growing up. It really left a mark on me. We can't do that and get an education and start a business too."

"Will we never be able to go off by ourselves occasionally?"

"Of course we will be able to get babysitters for a night or weekend away, and don't you think Dennis and Carla would love to take care of a grandchild or two?"

They laughed and entered into an embrace that ended in a long slow kiss.

Bud took the jewelry box out of his pocket. "Ginger, I have an 'engaged to be engaged' present for you. It was my grandmother's, my mother's mother's. I hope you like it."

Her mouth made a silent "Oh," when she saw what the box contained.

She opened the box and was so pleased with the beauty of the pearls. The ring, one large pearl in a dainty setting of smaller pearls, the pearls in the necklace and earrings were a perfect match. They were beautiful and when Bud put them on her, she was speechless. Teary-eyed she threw her arms around him again.

They found the rest of the group and told them of their decision to have the long wait till they would marry.

"I am so glad you are going to do the right thing!" Dennis exhaled...

"Darlings, you are so smart." Carla smiled as she gave them each a kiss.

"You two are heading down the right path to a great future together," Letty said.

"That's right," Tom added.

All the others gathered around congratulating them.

GWH was quiet while all this was happening. He couldn't believe that they would, or could do it. He was remembering the impatient erotic love that rushed him and May into their disastrous, impetuous marriage. So wildly happy for so short a time. They were so different, so stubborn, and so young, each wanting the other to change, yet unwilling to change in return.

"You got yourself a darlin' girl, Bud. I hope all your plans work out well." He turned to Ginger, "And you, you redheaded imp, you see that he lives up to all those promises." He gave her a hug.

The trip back to Manaus was blessedly uneventful.

Everyone had much to do to prepare for the trip back to the U.S.A. and home.

They went shopping for wedding presents, they all had to pack to leave and catch the same plane for Be'lem, then Miami. Then they would transfer to a different flight to their own home.

The appointment with the doctor was early, before he had to go to the hospital and GWH and Lois were on time. The doctor was very pleased when he took the bandage off GWH's eye. GWH wasn't too surprised because he had taken the bandage off and peeked the day before.

"Well, you won't have to wear this anymore," Doc said as he discarded the bandage. "The brace is up to you to decide now. If you are just sitting around the house or office, you don't need it. If you are doing a lot of walking, you ought to put it on. I sure would take it along on any trips if I were you. You still must take it easy. No lifting with that arm, or long walks. Avoid stairs when you can. No overdoing, or you will be back in the cast. I mean this, Mr. Hunter. I am not kidding. If you do what I say there is no danger, if you don't mind what I say, you will suffer."

"That is what you told me before!"

"Right, and you did it and you healed very well, didn't you?"

"I will see that he does what you say, you can be sure of that," Lois assured him.

"I don't want to go through this again, Doc, I'll behave."

GWH and Lois had another important duty. When they left the doctor's office, they went to the local Catholic Church to make arrangements for the wedding. He had not been to church in a long time. His faith was still there, but the day to day living got in the way.

Most tours either were on the weekend, or encompassing a weekend. Some were longer than that. Anyway, he got out of the habit of going to church. He prayed. You didn't have to be in church to pray. He thought that ought to take care of it.

He had married May in the church and Bud had been baptized there. They went to church while they were married. May had taken instructions as required, but it didn't take, and when she divorced GWH and took Bud away, he didn't have any more contact with religion.

That's about the time GWH became a Christmas/Easter Catholic. He did make the Easter Duty yearly; his conscience made him do that.

Lois and her family weren't churchgoers. Ethics were important to them, and that seemed to be enough. Lois had taken World Religions in college and knew about the different theologies, but it was just a class and that was the end of that. Now she had to think about it. She read all the little books the local priest gave her that day and studied them well. She realized that she could really believe these articles of faith, she wanted to believe them. She had never been baptized and told the priest that she would like to be baptized on her wedding day

At first the priest wanted to postpone the whole thing. He visited them after dinner. He talked to each of them alone and together. He was amazed at Lois' grasp of the beliefs of the church.

GWH radioed Father O'Toole and gave that priest a chance to discuss them with Father O'Toole. Later, when he was back at the rectory, to be on the safe side, he made a call to the bishop, took a long time to explain the whole thing to him, but in the end it was all arranged. The wedding was to be the evening before their flight to Miami. The baptism to be that morning at Mass.

"I am sure glad that is settled!" GWH breathed a sigh of relief when they were told about it in a late evening phone call.

"Me too!" Lois said. "I want to read over all this information about the church and get ready for my baptism. Do you realize that you will be marrying a sinless bride? Since I will marry you the same day of the baptism, I will be in a sinless state! Isn't that wonderful?"

"You are wonderful. I will never be worthy of you, but I'll sure try," he said before he kissed her.

Nat flew in with Father O'Toole the day before the wedding. He stayed at the house with GWH. Lois stayed with Nora at the hotel. Their luggage was at the hotel, ready to go to the airport in the morning. It was nice to have one last evening together. They had been such good friends for so long. They would always be friends. Nora promised to visit often, but it would be different now.

Everybody was at the church for nine o'clock Mass. The baptism took place after the homily. After Mass they all went to the hotel for breakfast. Lois' hair dried and with her simple hairdo, it looked the same. They were all to meet at the church for the wedding at six. They were finished the breakfast about noon. It had turned into a wedding shower, because that was the one chance they had to give the couple their wedding gifts. What to do in the time between noon and six o'clock?

Bud solved that problem. He brought around the new bus. They all piled in and Bud took them to places they did not cover on their last tour of the town. They sang, they laughed, they bought native souvenirs that they would put in their carry-on luggage. Time passed quickly and soon it was time to dress for the wedding.

Lois had a beautiful shantung suit in a luscious lavender shade that she had packed "just in case." She had never worn it and she was hoping she would get the chance to wear it on the trip. That chance never arrived and now she was very glad it didn't. She also had a lovely sheer shawl, purple with velvet flowers in it. It looked well with the suit. The colors complimented one another. Now she had a veil.

Nora knew about the suit, and she and Ryti had fashioned a wedding bouquet of jungle orchids. They went with the outfit perfectly. A sheer white blouse, white sandals, and earrings and necklace of pearls made her a lovely bride. When she was shopping for clothes for the trip, she saw this suit in the store and she fell in love with it. It cost way more than she wanted to spend, but she wanted it so much that she threw caution to the wind and bought it. She told herself that she could wear it at some fancy occasion at the school sometime. She never imagined that she would be married in it! She was extremely happy.

It was time! GWH, Nat, Ryti, and of course Father O'Toole left for the church in Nat's car. Bud drove everyone from the hotel in the bus. It was a beautiful wedding. The dinner after it at the hotel was jolly. Delicious food and drink, of course, but so much joy and laughter made it special. What a perfect ending to an Amazon Adventure.

Epilogue

Four years later…

Letty came into the living room licking her fingers. She had just put a cherry pie in the oven and still had some of the cherry filling on them. Tom came in with a handful of mail. He had been cutting the grass when the mailman came by. They had a chat, and since the mower was turned off anyway, he decided to bring it in and get a much needed drink of pink lemonade that he knew that Letty had in the refrigerator.

"Hi, sweetie," she said when she saw him. "You must be hot. Shall I fix you a cold glass of lemonade?"

"You read my mind! Here's the mail." He fell into the lounger "Whew! I'm bushed. It is really hot out there."

"I don't see why don't you hire one of the neighborhood kids to do that," she said as she left the room. This wasn't the first time she had asked him that question.

"Well, I need the exercise for one thing."

"Yes, but you don't have to do it when it is eighty-five degrees and the humidity is so high! You stopped shoveling the snow in the cold, I think you should think about having the grass cut too. You can get your exercise on that machine taking up all the room in our bedroom. Do it in the air conditioning. You can put on a CD and go at it. That's what I do."

"I am inclined to agree with you at the moment. I would really like to cut the grass early in the morning, when it's cool, but it wakes the neighbors."

Letty had been looking through the mail, setting aside bills to pay, junk to throw away. Here was a large envelope, birthday card size, but they weren't having a birthday this month. Return address said Evans in Florida!

"Tom! Look at this, it's from Dennis and Carla. I'll bet it is a wedding invitation, or at least a graduation invitation."

"Well, open it and see."

"It is a wedding invitation for the third of July. Great! It is to Bud, of course. Good for them, they did what they said they would. Isn't that wonderful?"

"It sure is. Call Kathy Lemon and see what kind of airline deal she can make—hotel and rental car too."

"How long do you want to stay?"

"Make it a very long weekend. We can get there on the first." He was leafing through the desk calendar. "The fourth is on Sunday. Monday at the airport will be a zoo. Let's come home on Tuesday afternoon. We can get together with the gang and party on." He grinned.

"Okay, you party animal, you. I hope the rest of the gang will come."

"It would be great to see them all again."

"Well, at least Lois and Gordon will be there."

"Why don't you call Nora and I'll call Don?"

"Okay, I wonder if Nat and Ryti will be able to come."

"Naw, they probably have to mind the store."

Letty had their address book in hand and was paging through it in the esses. "There, Smythe." She started dialing. No answer...

"This is Nora, I'm not home now, leave a message at the beep."

"Hi Nora! This is Letty Murphy. We just received THE wedding invitation. I am sure you'll be going. Call us and we will make arrangements to stay at the same hotel. It is going to be so much fun! Bye"

She looked up the number of the Evans' in Maine and gave it to Tom.

Tom started dialing.

"Hi, you have reached the Masons. We are not here just now, leave your number and we will return your call." It was Don talking.

"Hello, Don, This is Tom Murphy from St. Louis. I know you have my number and my e-mail address. We just received Ginger and Bud's wedding invitation today. We will be there and hope you will come too. Put down that golf club for a while and come. Call me and we can make arrangements to stay at the same hotel. I'm going to rent a car so we can drive around the town together. I might even pick you up at the airport if you get there at a decent hour. Bye, call me."

While Tom was calling, Letty was writing their acceptance and inserting it into the enclosed return envelope.

"There! Now we are all set. I wonder where everyone is?"

"Not everyone is retired like we are, honey. We should have waited till later. I guess we jumped the gun."

"I guess so."

Tom drained his glass and got up out of the chair. "I guess I'd better finish cutting the grass. I think you are right, I'll have Eddie start cutting it next week. He is going to high school in the fall and will be glad to have the extra money."

"That's a good idea. Both of you will benefit by it." She reached for the phone again and sprawled in the lounger that Tom just left.

"Hi Carla! This is Letty. I just put the stamp on the RSVP and I am so excited about coming, I just had to call."

"Letty, it's so nice to hear from you. I am so glad you can come. How is Tom?

"He's fine, out cutting the grass."

"My, even Dennis doesn't do that and he is a bit younger. We have a service that takes care of the palm trees. They are such a mess. They are beautiful, but high maintenance. The grass cutting is part of the deal. They even treat the trees for a disease that the palm trees get. It must be done or the trees will die."

"Who would have thought that? How is Dennis?"

"He is busier than ever now. He has expanded to a study of native remedies and is just about to submit his study to the 'Powers That Be' to see if he and a new company he is in the midst of forming can start producing a medication he has been testing. He produced it from some of the plants he picked up in Amazonas."

"Does he get his supplies from GWH?"

"He e-mails Father O'Toole all the time and then Father makes the connection with Ke'era at the base camp village by radio. Maeuma comes to the base camp about once a month with the plants that Dennis needs. He leaves orders for any medicines that the tribe needs. Kamanar'e radios Father O'Toole. Father O'Toole orders what he needs too. This helps both his village and Maeuma's village. We still keep Maeuma's village location a secret. Nat picks up the plants from the base camp. He drops Father O'Toole's mail and medicines on his way. Maeuma comes to the village by boat, then takes the medicines back, leaving another boatload of medicinal plants.

"It sounds like they have quite a business going now. How are they doing at the village?"

"Uanica died last year, and since then Maeuma and Kamanar'e have been taking over his duties. They each have picked an apprentice so the knowledge will not die with them.

Dennis made sure they know the importance of this for the future of the tribe and, really, the future of the world.

"The old King, Kanchinapio, died the first part of this year and now Maeuma is King and Shaman. He is training Kamanar'e to take over that job. Dennis thinks he will be able to do it with his two helpers."

"It's sad about Uanica and Kanchinapio, but they were very old when we were there, and that was four years ago, I guess you have to expect it. I guess this keeps Dennis very busy."

"It sure does, He still sees patients at the hospital too. He has a group of doctors that work together in the same office, so he keeps his hand in treating patients. He hasn't gone entirely into research. We still have our family time, though it's getting hard to juggle the free time with Ginger and Dennis so busy. We are going to have an even harder time of it after Ginger and Bud are married."

"I am just about to make reservations at an hotel. Which one would you suggest?"

"Why don't you stay at the hotel where the reception will be held. The address is on the invitation."

"Of course, I probably would have come to that conclusion if I had waited before calling you. I wanted to call right away. We wondered if Nat and Ryti would be able to come."

"Oh, yes. Father O'Toole is coming and he is bringing them and their son with him. They are so excited, they can hardly stand it. We have already reserved two rooms for them. Let me make your reservations for you. We can get a special rate since the wedding reception is to be there."

"That will be great. I can hardly wait. Tell Ginger we love her and wish she and Bud much happiness."

"I will, and we will be so glad to see both of you. Bye now, see you soon."

"Bye bye."

She sat quietly for awhile thinking.

I've got to look at my wardrobe and figure out what to pack, she mused. She started for the stairs. *Florida in July! Oh my! That will be a challenge. It would be different if my upper arms were less wrinkled and I could wear sleeveless things like everyone else. Shorts and t-shirts are fine for daytime, but there will be the rehearsal dinner, the actual wedding, and evenings at dinner. I have to go shopping!*

Later Tom came in from the yard looking forward to a shower, then a cold beer and finishing the current novel he was reading.

"Hi, Tom, how do you feel about going out for dinner tonight?" Letty encountered him as he was coming upstairs.

"Right now I'm heading for the shower, hon. I guess it will be okay. Where do you want to go?"

"How about the food court at the mall?"

"What? You must have an ulterior motive. Are we going shopping for a new dress?"

"My, you are sharp! I could never fool you, could I?" She giggled and started to tickle him.

"Okay, okay, we'll go. I am going to need a new novel anyway. I'll be ready in a bit and we'll go. I'm all set, I don't need anything new."

"We'll see," she said to his retreating back. He didn't seem to hear.

They entered the mall and headed for the food court. Tom headed for the Mexican food and Letty was torn between the fish and the chicken. She was heading for the chicken when she passed the Oriental area. She turned back and ordered coconut shrimp and cashew chicken. They enjoyed their choices.

"That was good," Tom said as he gathered up the dirty dishes and put them on the tray.

"It sure was, I'll meet you at the bench by the bookstore, okay?"

"Okay," Tom said as he headed for the bookstore and Letty headed for Lord and Taylor.

Ellen arrived home around 4:30 p.m. Her arms were full of packages. She had to make two trips. She went into the kitchen and started opening everything. It was cooked food in oven-proof covered dishes. She put them in the oven. She looked at the clock—she had plenty of time. She went out to the mailbox and brought in a single letter. It was the wedding invitation. She smiled and put it on the bulletin board so it wouldn't get lost and started making two salads, then set the table. It didn't take long, even with a trip to the garden to get some cut flowers to pretty it up. She went out in the sunroom and picked up her embroidery and watched the news on TV while waiting for Don.

Don came home whistling. His golf game was pretty good. He did well in the card game afterward.

"Hi, Ellie, how did it go at work today?"

"The cooking school went very well. I have the leftovers in the oven. We can eat as soon as you want to. It is on hold."

"Let's eat right away. It smells so good, what is it?"

"Apricot glazed Cornish hen, fresh steamed green beans, tomatoes with basil and parmesan. There is some couscous and Bibb lettuce salad," she said as she placed the dishes on the table and they sat down.

"Sounds good. Since you started that cooking school in the kitchen department the menu around here sure is varied, and even exotic."

"Well, I can't teach just meat and potatoes, everybody can do that. I like to give the students new challenges, and yet keep it simple. For instance, wait till you see what we have for dessert."

"What's that?"

" It's chocolate stuffed steamed pears."

"That sounds hard to do."

"No, very easy, you just lop off the top of the pears, use a melon ball scoop to remove the core, place five chocolate chips in the hole, put the top back on, put it in a custard cup and set in a saucepan with one inch of water, cover and simmer for about twenty minutes and serve hot. We sell the melon ball scoops, custard cups, and of course the sauce pans. Most people have the saucepans, but I sold some custard cups and melon ball scoops. When they serve them at parties, their friends might ask for the recipe and maybe buy some too."

Don laughed. "You are really something! This is really good."

"We received a wedding invitation today."

"Who is getting married?"

"Bud and Ginger, July 3. I wish we could go."

"We ought to be able to make it."

"Oh, no, I must hold my cooking school. I plan to do a back yard cook out for the Fourth of July. Beef, peppers and mushroom kabob's and…"

"Ha! Do you remember the fit you threw four years ago when I didn't want to go on the cruise? Now who is wanting to pass up a good time?"

She stopped and thought for a minute. "Well, I guess you have something there. It would be fun seeing everyone again. Ginger and Bud make such a cute couple. I could do the back yard thing when we come back. You're right, we'll go."

"Fine, now how about those chocolate stuffed pears."

"Coming right up," she said with a smile. She served the pears and sat down.

"You know, I can understand how you can love what you are doing so much that it crowds out everything else. I am so glad you listened to my plan of expanding the housewares department and start the cooking school. I want to thank you, dear, for letting me try my hand at it."

"I've never been sorry, honey. You have really put that department on the map. It never has done so well, and it is all because of you."

"I've been meaning to talk to you, Don. I have a good idea for the fabric department."

"What's that?"

"I could do the same thing there with sewing lessons, especially for the high school age kids. Then they could have a style show and model what they made. We could even get the cosmetic department involved and give them lessons in applying makeup."

"My God, Ellen, I would never get to see you. That is too much for you to take on."

"I could hire a seamstress to do the sewing lessons and a cosmetician to teach make up, and even a cook to teach the cooking lessons. I could get there in the morning, meet with them, get their reports, tell them what I want them to do, and by noon I could join you at the club for lunch." Her eyes were twinkling as she smiled up at him.

"Wait a minute! Are you serious?"

"As serious as a heart attack. I've got the women coming for the cooking. The teenage girls would come for the sewing, style show and makeup, I know it. It would give them something to do for the summer months."

"I guess you are right. You sure improved the housewares department with the cooking lessons."

"Yes, and don't forget getting the different venders to send their people to demonstrate their products. I have something going on almost every day. They demonstrate juicers, different kinds of peelers, knives, and appliances. It doesn't cost us a penny and the sales go up."

"I have to admit it worked out like that in housewares, it was a winner."

"I have to think of something to do for the men and boys. We could do the same thing in the sports department and the hardware department. Do you want me to start working on that when I get the other things going?"

"Could you leave something for me to try, please? After all, this is my family's store, you know. I do know a little about running it." He was a bit miffed. It had been quite a while since he had been very interested in actually working at the store. He had been on "automatic" for so long because it didn't require any incentive to keep things going. Lately, seeing Ellen's enthusiasm, he missed the opportunity to launch forth a new project. Ellen had started him thinking of possibilities for the sports and hardware departments.

"I'm sorry, darling, you're right. I just got carried away with all the possibilities."

"When we come back from the wedding, we'll talk about it. Now, about that wedding. Where is it going to be?"

"The name of the hotel is on the invitation. That's where the reception is." He took it off the bulletin board and read it.

"How about calling Carla and tell her we are coming, and I will go on line and get our airline tickets."

"Okay." She went to the phone, secretly pleased that she saw his interest in some changes around the store.

Don went to his home office.

"Hello?"

"Hello, Ginger, this is Ellen. I received the happy news today. I am so happy for you, dear. I guess you and your mother are very busy these days getting ready for the big day."

"Oh, yes, but everything is going according to plan. Do you want to talk to Mother?"

"Yes, if she isn't too busy."

Ginger went to get Carla.

"Hi there, Ellen. I hope you are calling to say that you will be coming."

"Yes, Don is on line getting the tickets now."

"Would you like for me to reserve a room in the hotel where the reception is to be held? We can get a small discount for you."

"That would be great. I'll have to call back; I don't know which days we'll be there yet. Bye, I'll call you right back."

She went upstairs to talk to Don. He was at the computer tapping away.

"Honey, Carla said we could get reservations at the hotel where the reception is going to be, and she can make them for us. What days are we going to be there?"

"I'm just getting my confirmation number now. There, I just have to print this out and we're good to go. We get there the second of July and come back the sixth. We'll have a nice visit with the old gang."

"Yes, we leave cool New Hampshire and go to hot and steamy Florida and are looking forward to it! I'll call Carla and let her get us a reservation."

———

Nora was making lunch. Soup and sandwich was on the menu. Bacon, lettuce and tomato on whole wheat, with cream of mushroom soup, and iced tea to drink. There was a beautiful arrangement of flowers on the table set for two. Nora sniffed the flowers, smiled and went to the back door and called. "Martin, lunch is ready, come and get it."

"Coming."

He gave the weed he was working on an extra tug and out it came. He put it in the trash bag. On his way to the kitchen he tossed it in the trash can and went in the house. Nora was waiting for him with a big smile on her face. He entered and gave her a big kiss.

"Happy anniversary greetings, sweetheart, again," he said as he released her.

"Same to you, darling, though that first greeting this morning was quite spectacular." She gave him a quick peck on the nose.

"First anniversaries should be spectacular. You are spectacular!"

"Thank you, honey, now come and eat your lunch, before the soup gets cold."

"I'll just wash up at the sink." While he was at the sink he said, "I thank God for that blessed day that I came to you to rent that apartment."

"Me too," Nora answered, stirring sugar into the iced tea.

"Working together at the same school was Heaven-sent too." He dried his hands on a dishtowel.

"It took you long enough to ask me out." She made a moue at him, followed by a smile.

"I know, it wasn't your fault. I had my eye on you from the first. I've told you about Iris' long drawn out bout with cancer. It does something to you, something that isn't easy to shake."

"Yes, I know, even if you lose someone quickly, as I did, it isn't easy to overcome."

"Those walks to and from school did a lot to help us get acquainted."

"Then when we were assigned to be in charge of the senior prom we really got acquainted." Nora laughed, remembering how they first kissed in the storeroom getting the things they needed to decorate the gym.

"I hung around on Saturdays helping with the yard work just to be near you."

"Yes, you even started going back to church on Sundays, I knew you were getting serious then.

"Listening to you sing in the choir is a real pleasure." He gave her a little grin.

"You have made me so happy, Marty. This last year has been pure Heaven."

"For me too." He kissed her, hard. They went into the bedroom.

The soup cooled, the iced tea warmed and the sandwich dried up a little. They didn't mind when they returned. Nora and the microwave and some ice cubes took care of that.

Nora had Lois write down some of her favorite recipes before she left four years ago. She had lots of time to try them out. The TV dinners didn't satisfy any more since she had so much of Lois' home cooked meals and now knew how to fix them. It is a good thing too, now that she had Marty to cook for.

Later, Martin went outside to get the mail. He came back and tossed it on the table in the front hall.

"Any good mail?"

"There are a bunch of cards, probably congratulations from your brothers for our anniversary."

"I'll bet you're right." She started opening one of them. "Oh, not this one, it's an invitation to a wedding. I've told you about Ginger and Bud from the South American cruise. They are being married July 3. We've GOT to go to that!"

"Yes, that will give me a chance to meet all those people on the vacation from Hell."

"Parts of it were bad, I admit, but for pure adventure it can't be beat. Those people that took the trip were real troopers. Everyone pulled together and made it work. Including Lois, who stayed behind and took care of Gordon. You met them at our wedding, Bud too."

"It is too bad that I wasn't there too."

"Impossible, if Lois hadn't married Gordon and stayed in Manaus, then the apartment wouldn't have been empty and we wouldn't have met."

"I would have worked at the high school."

"That's true, but it would have taken much longer. What about those walks? That's when we really got to know one another."

"You're right, I owe a lot to that trip you took."

"I'll call them now. Lois told me on the phone the other day that this was coming. We are all to stay at the same hotel. You will really enjoy this, Martin. They will enjoy you too. Some of them don't even know you exist."

———— ···•●•·· ————

Nat hovered over Father O'Toole's village and tossed the mail pouch. It held a few letters and a box of medications. He waved and went on to the base camp. He landed there and was greeted by Ke'era and a group of natives. They all had shorts and t-shirts in various colors. Don Mason had donated cases of the garments to them. He donated some to Father O'Toole's village too. They loved them.

"Hi, Ke'era. How are you and your people?"

"All okay. No one sick or hurt, and we have medicine here if they do need it."

"Is Maeuma here yet?"

"No. Never know when he is coming. He just appears."

They went into the office to discuss business.

Later Maeuma paddled up to the dock in one boat and was followed by another paddled by Kamanar'e. Both boats were loaded with woven baskets full of the different plants Dennis had ordered.

Maeuma, with Kamanar'e now walking with a smooth gait beside him, went into the office. He was used to it now, well almost, but this was the first time for Kamanar'e to enter the base camp. Even though Maeuma had prepared him for it, he was astounded. The TV was exactly as Maeuma had described, but the reality of it awed him to silence. He seemed to be mesmerized.

"Maeuma!" Nat caught sight of him. "Hi!"

Maeuma had learned a little English, greetings and goodbyes and a few other words. He noticed Kamanar'e. He went over to him and placed his hand on his shoulder, shaking him out of his trance. Maeuma stood beside him and made him aware of Nat.

In a combination of sign language, and different native words and charades, they chatted. Greetings over with, they talked about the packages in the boats. They walked down to the boats and unloaded them and put them in the plane. Then they took the packages that Dennis sent for the village and put them in one of the boats and covered them up with a waterproof tarp and tied bungee cords around the whole thing. They used more cords to lash the whole package to the boat.

Maeuma had made the acquaintance of some of the natives and brought Kamanar'e around and visited them. They fed the two of them and showed them where they could sleep.

Nat had returned to the office. He was talking business with Ke'era when the wireless radio came alive. It was Father O'Toole.

"Hey, Nat, I got your message. I am glad you and Ryti are going with me to the wedding."

"Isn't it something? We were so surprised when GWH suggested it. We are even bringing the baby. Isn't that great?"

"Yes, it is. Have you all had your shots yet?"

"Oh yes, all of us."

"Nat, has Maeuma arrived yet?"

"Yes, he is visiting some friends he has made here. He brought his shaman, Kamanar'e, along. They brought two boats this time."

"That is great. I want to bring Maeuma with us as a surprise for the gang and as a treat for Maeuma. It will also get him a lot of brownie points with the folks at home."

"Wow! I don't know about that! That is a big deal."

"I will bring the serum for his booster shots with me. Dennis had me give all the people in my village injections for everything going. The base camp too. Maeuma was there at the time, so he got his shots about three years ago.

"Dennis insisted that all the natives be inoculated. I went to his village and took care of it. I don't know what he told them, but they all turned out. The shaman was dancing around rattling a skull on a stick. He had a big feather headdress and they lined up like soldiers. Not a peep out of them!"

"That is great."

"Believe it or not, I have a passport for Maeuma. I said he was the King of our village, stretching it only a little. What is the matter of a few miles down river?"

"What is he going to wear? I know the Florida beaches are a little bare, but he'd cause a sensation in the airport."

"Oh, I've got that all figured out. I have a suit he can wear with some of the t-shirts Don sent. A black suit with a colorful shirt is not unheard of, is it?"

"What about his tattoos and his hair?"

"We can get him a haircut and some dark cover-up make up in Manaus. Even if he won't go for that he won't look too much different from those punk people and their purple hair and everything pierced, will he?"

"I guess not, what about shoes and socks?"

"I have the socks and underwear, even a belt. We can get shoes in Manaus."

"Well, okay. It will be a surprise all right. Kamanar'e can take the boats back and tell the tribe. That will boost his stock for sure. By all means be sure to keep the location of his village secret."

"I have already put his name on the list of our natives. I put it on a few lists from the past too. That ought to hide him well enough."

"I will ask him today. You don't tell him to do anything now that he is King. He has seen cities on TV, so it shouldn't freak him out too much. The helicopter fascinates him too, I know, but he hasn't asked for a ride yet. I have been expecting it because he shows so much interest in it. This is going to be some experience for all of us!"

The next morning Nat motioned to Maeuma and Kamanar'e to follow him. He sat on the bench down by the river. He finally got them to understand that he wanted Maeuma to stay with him and that Kamanar'e was to take the boats back to the village alone. Then he brought them to the helicopter. He pointed to it. Then he pointed to Maeuma and presented the idea of him joining him on a ride.

Maeuma was quiet for a short while, then he had a conversation with Kamanar'e. Kamanar'e's face showed surprise and consternation. They conversed further. Then Maeuma and Nat talked awhile. The gist of it was that Maeuma wanted to go. He told Kamanar'e to tell the village he would be away about a week and that Panteri would be in charge while he was gone. He wasn't sure where they were going though.

Nat told him that Bud and Ginger were going to be married. He was very happy for them. He had the idea that the wedding was to be in Manaus. Nat tried hard and finally got him to understand where the wedding was to take place. This was something else again.

Maeuma became very serious. He wasn't too keen about going so far. When Kamanar'e found out about the plan, he became very agitated. He had just seen a John Wayne picture in the office. The effect it had him was traumatic. He didn't want to have Maeuma go there.

Nat talked a long time to both of them. He told them it was Ginger's home village, She wasn't afraid to be there. She would think he was not a brave man if he didn't come to her wedding.

"Didn't she attend the wedding of Maeuma and Teptykti while she was with them? And didn't she have fun? She had even danced in the circle of natives, Bud had joined in and they had a good time."

Maeuma decided he would go. It was the right thing to do. He told Kamanar'e to go home and explain what was going to happen and that it was a great honor to be invited and to ride in the great bird. Kamanar'e calmed down, still a bit worried, but in awe of what Maeuma was going to do.

They prepared the boats for the trip. Ke'era packed a food basket for him and containers of water. They waved as he left for the village, paddling the lead boat with the other one secured behind it.

Nat had given Maeuma three shorts and t-shirt outfits, a blue set, a white set and a red set. It didn't matter which he wore, they all went together. He put them in a sling he wore over one shoulder. Nat had to be very forceful to make him leave his knife, bow and blowpipe with Ke'era until he returned. He made him understand that it wasn't right to go so heavily armed to a friend's village.

The next day after refueling the plane, they took off. Maeuma was clutching the seatbelt and hanging on for dear life. When they arrived at Father O'Toole's village, they lowered onto an area that the natives had cleared at the end of their village.

When Maeuma saw how they were dressed he put on the blue shorts and shirt before he alighted from the plane. Father O'Toole was ready. Nat gave the treats he had for the natives to Maeuma to distribute. They had a good time and everyone was very happy and waving as the helicopter took off again.

Father and Maeuma had met once in the base camp village. They both happened to be there at the same time. Father was adept at communicating with natives and they were soon friends. Now they took up where they left off. He helped Maeuma relax and even enjoy the rest of the trip to Manaus.

The three of them had an odd sort of conversation. None of them were absolutely sure of what exactly was said all of the time, but they managed to get their meaning across after a few tries.

It was dark when they reached Manaus, though the airport was well lit. Ryti was there to meet them with the bus. She had her little son with her. Nat turned the helicopter over to the airport people to tend to and ran to them. After kissing, Ryti he picked up his son and hugged him tight.

Father John was coaxing Maeuma out of the plane. He reluctantly descended, bringing his sling with him.

He was very nervous and was clinging to Father John's hand and looking around frantically.

"Hello, Ryti, this is Maeuma, the king of the lost tribe. He is a bit upset at the moment, could you make him welcome?"

"Capitdo," she bowed. "Welcome."

Father John made sure that Maeuma knew that capitdo was the name for men of prestige used by the Tapirape' tribe. Maeuma knew that and it reminded him of his position and it gave him courage.

He used the Tapirape' word for thank you. There were several people from that tribe in his village and he could converse in that language. Nat, Ryti, Father John and GWH all could speak it and Bud knew some, enough to use the basic words and so did Ginger.

Nat ushered them all into the bus. Maeuma hesitated, then got in when he saw Ryti and the baby get in. He smiled at the baby and asked the baby's name. When Ryti realized what he was asking she answered, "Champukwi," and smiled.

" And wouldn't you know it, GWH calls him Champ all the time," Nat said to the world in general. "A perfectly good Indian name and he Americanizes it!"

When Champukwi heard his name, he laughed and pointed to himself. "Me," he said laughing.

"Ryti," she said pointing to herself. "Me."

"Father John," he said pointing to himself. "Me."

"Nat," he said pointing to himself. "Me."

They all looked toward Maeuma expectantly.

"Maeuma." He laughed and pointed to himself. "ME."

Nat started the motor and drove off. This frightened Maeuma and he clutched the seatbelt that Ryti had fastened around his waist as she did to Champukwi. He was trying to regain control of his emotions. He saw that no one else was concerned, even the baby.

He was very interested in all that was to be seen. The other cars, the buildings, the people in clothes, but especially the lights. They were beautiful.

It wasn't too long before they arrived at the Hunter house. Nat tooted the horn, again startling Maeuma. While they were getting out of the car, GWH, Bud and Lois came out of the house.

They were astounded when they saw the native in a black suit, barefooted, and wearing a red t-shirt.

"Maeuma!" Bud recognized his pal from the village. "How are you? Welcome to our house," he said in Tapirape'.

GWH and Lois realized who this was.

"Welcome, King of the lost people." GWH bowed his head, he spoke in his language.

Maeuma answered GWH. He was impressed by the respect he was given.

"Blessings on your house." He smiled at both of them.

Bud introduced them to Maeuma, saying that GWH, his father, was the Capitido here and Lois was his wife, but not Bud's mother, but a beloved stepmother.

"You did very well in his language, Bud. I am proud of you," His father said in an aside not meant for everyone to hear.

The rest of the group went into the house.

'Well, he became my friend while we were in their village. As far as we know we are both the same age, sons of important men, and afraid we will never measure up." He gave him a slight apologetic smile.

"We were teaching one another. I gave him my extra glasses, the ones he has on now, and Dr. Evans sends him an inhaler and pills for his asthma and he was able to win his father's and the rest of the members of the tribe's confidence. He was a better hunter and could compete with the rest of the young men in the tribe.

"They realized that he could handle the job of being king. And now he is."

They all went into the house.

Ryti and Lois had fixed a great dinner, bar-b-que, potato salad, slaw, tomatoes and coconut cake. It was a meal that could be put on hold until the guests arrived.

They went into the dining room. Bud took Maeuma in tow and was explaining everything to him. Maeuma was very puzzled and unsure of himself in this environment, but with Bud leading the way he was managing, and no one laughed when he did anything odd. He enjoyed the meal very much, especially the coconut cake.

When Ryti and Lois were clearing the table after the cake had disappeared, Ryti asked, "Now that you have a guest that you haven't planned for, what are you going to do with the King?" They both started to giggle.

"Do you think His Highness will mind sleeping on the sofa bed in the living room?"

"Well, it surely isn't done in European Royal circles, but it will be a step up for this King. He seems to be a sweet boy," Lois said. "Bud has certainly made a pal of him, and that's a good thing."

"Let's get these dishes done," Ryti said. Champ was hanging onto her leg and whining. He wanted to be picked up.

"We'll just soak them in the sink. Kamerti is coming early in the morning to fix breakfast and she can finish them. Let's join the fellows."

They joined the men in time to hear Bud telling of the travel arrangements to Florida.

"Tomorrow, July 1 at 3:00 p.m. we will all helicopter to Be'lem, stay there for dinner, then at 9:00p.m. we will get on another plane and head for Fort Myers International Airport. I have a limo on tap to take all of us to the Diamond Head on Estero Island. The next day, Friday, sleep as long as you want. We can do whatever we care to until 6:00 p.m. when we go to dinner in the hotel dining room for the rehearsal dinner. Feel free to make a toast." He smiled and took a drink of his wine.

GWH, his own rugged self again, with an intriguing, but not unattractive scar on his temple near his eye, was telling his guests of their latest trip.

"It was very successful and the clients had a pleasant trip. Some of them were talking about another trip with other friends in the future."

"That's the kind of talk we like to hear," Bud added.

"We were lucky and were able to photograph some rare species of flora and fawna," Nat mentioned.

"I was able to get copies for my new book from the gentleman who took the pictures," Lois joined in. "The first book was a beautiful coffee table edition that sold very well. Not only that, one college used it as a textbook in one of its Biology classes. The new book was to be about medicinal plants of the rainforest."

After dinner, Lois and Nat showed Maeuma the first book. He smiled as he recognized the different plants and animals and birds. When he got to the bird section he would point to a bird and imitated its song.

Nat and Ryti took a sleepy Champ home.

Lois saw Father John smother a yawn after awhile.

"It's getting time for bed. Father John, you have the other bedroom and I have a sofa bed for Maeuma." She started taking off the cushions and placed them on an arm chair. When she flipped the bed open, Maeuma jumped aside in amazement. He had been sitting on it before and he couldn't figure out how it happened.

He looked at Father John and said in his language, "How seat grow?"

GWH closed it then opened it again. Maeuma closed it and opened it again, enjoying the transformation. Lois put some of the pretty and colorful flowered sheets on it with two plump pillows in the same fabric. Lavender had been in the closet and had given the bedding a lovely aroma. They were the ones used in her former bedroom, the one now designated for Father John.

Maeuma picked up one of the pillows and buried his face in it, inhaling deeply. Of all the wonderful things he had been introduced to that day, the bed and pillows were the very best. He thought again and decided that maybe the coconut cake was the best.

Bud took him to the bathroom where he was in for another assault on his senses. The shower and the toilet boggled his mind. For nightwear Bud gave him the white shorts and t-shirt. He was right in the same nightwear style as GWH, Bud, and even Father John.

When they wanted Maeuma to get in bed, he didn't get it. He wanted to lie on the carpet near the bed. They finally convinced him what it was for and tucked him in.

Lois kept the bathroom light on and left the door ajar so it wasn't completely dark. She and Gordon retired to their room. Bud said a last good night to Father and tousled Maeuma's head as he went to his old room.

They were left to think their own thoughts before they nodded off

The next day was beautiful, very warm, but that was to be expected.

Father John and Bud took Maeuma shopping for shoes. He didn't like them at all. They finally settled on a pair of black loafers. Whenever he got a chance he slipped out of them and walked around in the socks. They valiantly tried to make Maeuma understand what was going on. He seemed quite lost, but very attentive. He was uncomfortable in the shoes and clothes and he longed to strip. They went back to the house for lunch. Lois made a point of admiring the new shoes.

Eating with silverware was another challenge. He watched and learned.

The trip to Be'lem was uneventful. The trip by boat takes six days, but by helicopter it is just a little over an hour. Maeuma was used to the helicopter now and took it in stride.

The airport in Fort Myers was something else again.

The steep escalator to the ground floor freaked him out. They sought out the elevator and that wasn't much better. The crowds of so many different types of people had him gawking while holding on to Father John's hand in a death grip.

Bud went to pick up the limo. They all piled in and off they went. The trip to Diamond Head was beautiful to Maeuma. Especially going over Matansas Pass on the big bridge. The plethora of neon lights were overwhelming to him. He excitedly pointed out to Father John that even the trunks of the palm trees were wrapped around with tiny white lights! They would never believe this back at the village!

They checked in and were very ready to go to bed. It had been a long day.

They took their time in the morning, sleeping in.

"Can't I call Bud now?" Ginger asked Dennis.

"It's only seven o'clock, Gingy honey. You ought to wait at least until eight."

They had rented a suite, also, so they could be near everyone and not have to go back and forth in their car. Carla was still in bed. Dennis had ordered breakfast and was enjoying his coffee and morning paper. He was used to rising early.

Ginger went out on the deck and watched the gulls and the pelicans swoop over the flashing waves. It was a lovely morning. There was a breeze from the ocean, so it wasn't too warm yet. She couldn't wait another minute!

"Dad, I am going to call Bud. It's seven forty-five. What difference does fifteen minutes make?"

"Oh, go ahead, give him a call."

She took the phone out on the deck and pulled the sliding door as closed as she could without damaging the cord.

Carla came out of the bedroom. She smelled of mouthwash when she kissed Dennis.

"What's Ginger doing up so early?"

"She is waking Bud up at this very minute."

"It's too early, she should have waited."

"She wanted to call him at seven, but I made her wait."

When Ginger came in off the deck, she was in a rush. "I'm going to meed Bud in the coffee shop for breakfast," she said as she flew into the bathroom to shower and dress. They didn't see her again until she rushed through the room and out the door.

"See ya," was all she managed in her haste.

Gradually they all assembled in the coffee shop. It was a great noisy reunion.

After breakfast, Nat, the Murphys, Masons, Marty and Dennis loaded up in the rented limo.

They had to wait until Father John and Maeuma showed up. Nat was to take the visitors on a sightseeing trip around the area. This gave those that were concerned with the wedding preparations time to do those last-minute chores that always need to be done.

When Nat got them all together, he took them for a sightseeing trip around the city. Nat described the points of interest to them. They went to Shell City and marveled over the variety and beauty of the shells and of the surprising things that were made with them. They watched the Dancing Waters fountain. Maeuma was fascinated by the various colors of the fountain and the patterns of the spray. They went through Edison's House and the Firestone house next door. This didn't interest Maeuma nearly as much.

Nora, Carla and Ginger joined Lois, Gordon and Bud. They were making sure all was set for the trip to the church that afternoon. It was just a matter of checking that things were all in place and there were no glitches to mar the evening. Clothes were the next concern and everything was checked and rechecked. Flowers were inspected, any wilted looking blossom was ruthlessly discarded and replaced by a fresh one. Nora, Lois, Carla and Ryti were the arrangers. GWH, Bud and Ginger and Father John took some of them to the hotel manager for the table decorations. Marty went along and enjoyed getting acquainted. He had met Gordon and Lois, but that's all.

Then on to the Church of the Ascension, just a little way from there, with the rest for the altar and along the aisle.

Bud introduced Father John to the pastor of Ascension Church, Father Gallagher. The two Irish priests became friends right away. They had a lot in common. They even knew some of the same clergy hierarchy. After arrangements were made for the services, the next day they became even more friendly over a few beers.

On the way back to the hotel Bud asked Father John, "I meant to ask you, How is Oram working out for you?"

"Just fine. He is a diligent worker, smart and the people really like him."

"Uh, is he honest? Are you ever missing anything?"

"No, never. His behavior is faultless."

"Does he fool around with the girls?"

"No, in fact they make advances to him and he rebuff's them."

"That doesn't sound like the Orem I know. I'm glad to hear he has turned himself around."

"I wasn't going to say this until things were more definite, but he has been hanging around the clerics. He has been talking to them about religion. I think he wants to be a cleric too. He hasn't said anything, but he shows all the signs."

"What does he do for you?"

"He does secretarial work and accounting too. It frees me to spend more time doing the parish work. Visiting the sick, teaching the children, coaching the teams, you know, stuff like that."

"I will tell Dad how much he has changed, he'll be glad to hear it."

Later when he saw GWH he mentioned what Father John said about Orem.

"I'm not surprised. After his accident he was a different person. It seemed to turn his life around. You remember we took him on some trips with us and he did well. I was the one that suggested Orem help Father John out when he asked us to find someone. He was always so eager to please that I thought he would be just the one for Father John."

"Why, what's up? Had he been misbehaving?"

"No, just the opposite, Father thinks he might be getting ready to ask to be able to become a cleric. He isn't sure, he just has a feeling about it."

"Wow, that really is a turn around. Good for him!"

Tom and Marty were shocked by Maeuma and didn't know how to act around him. Of course he couldn't understand them or be understood. That just left smiling a lot. Nat would interpret for all the visitors the little that the amazed Maeuma said.

When the tour was over it was about four in the afternoon and they retired to the hotel to rest and get dressed.

Father John was already there laying out the clothes they both were to wear. Maeuma enjoyed the shower too much, Father John had to come and get him out so he could get dressed.

The Diamond Head had gone all out for the dinner. The decorations were a tropical theme. It was in the manner of an Hawaiian feast. Leis for everyone. Soft island music was playing as they took their seats. There were toasts and laughter and eating and more jokes and laughter. Maeuma watched in wonder at "the native celebration" just as they had watched the wedding in the jungle.

They had fun reliving the events of the trip, including Maeuma as much as they could with the language restrictions.

After all the amusing toasts that he didn't understand, Maeuma rose and said, with Father John translating the Tapirape', "To the people who traveled to my land, and their friends." He raised his glass. He said and Father John translated, "Your land is BIG. Your land has many things to surprise the eye. You people are surprising. You go far when you do not have to. I am happy that you do. I am happy that I am here to see your land. I will be happy to return to my land where life is not so loud, not so busy every day. It is nice to be here at this time. I am glad to see all again. I didn't think I would ever do that. I will tell my people of your land, they may not believe me. Happiness and many children to Bud and Ginger!" He drank his drink as he had seen them do and sat down to loud applause. He stood up again. "I must honor Dennis. He sent a great shaman to cut Kamanaer'e's bad foot. By and by he can walk, he can run and has no hurt. I have not had a time to tell Dennis we thank him for that."

There was more applause. There was a translation for those who didn't understand him.

Dennis was overcome with emotion, he waved off the applause as he blinked tears away.

"I can't believe they got Maeuma to come!" Don said to Carla across the long table from him.

"It was a surprise to everyone." She smiled. "Father John just showed up with Maeuma in tow. Maeuma must be overwhelmed but he tries to hide his amazement."

"Gordon, how did he do in Manaus?"

"He was sort of stunned, but very curious and wanted to see everything. He has a new bearing, now that he is King. He is very aware of the dignity of his station, but once in a while the boy in him shows through."

"I am so glad to see him. I have heard so much about him from Bud," Lois joined in. "They have become good friends. When Bud knows Maeuma is going to deliver a load of plants he tries to be at the base camp."

"Have you gone on any of the tours, Lois?" Letty asked.

"Oh yes, I went on the very first one Gordy conducted after his recuperation. It was great, and not one accident. It was perfect. That is when I started collecting plants to use in the second book. We did get to meet Uanica at the base camp. He came with the young man with the bad foot with the plants one time. He was a great help. We went into the jungle with Nat and he showed me many plants and I wrote down their uses and took some seeds with me. The young man was learning too."

"We have your first book at home and showed it to our friends at every opportunity," Tom said.

"Thank you, Tom, but it wouldn't have been complete without the work Nora and Don did. Not to mention how much trouble it was to carry it with them on the grueling journey after the crash. I don't see how they did it!" Lois answered, then turned to Nora and Don. "I don't know how to thank you for caring for my information so well." She nodded to them.

"Well, I guess the nice tribute you gave to us in your book did that job very well," Don said.

"Yes, and the book itself is the perfect memento," Nora added.

"Nora, now that we have met Marty, tell us about how your marriage came about. I didn't even know you were married!" Ellen demanded with a smile.

Nora leaned over and clasped Marty's hand and smiled up into his face. He put his arm around her shoulder. "Well, we told Lois and Gordon, and they told Bud, and he told Ginger, and she told Carla and Dennis. I guessed it stopped there."

"Oh, no," Ryti said. "Bud told Nat and he told me,"

"How come you didn't tell us about the coming wedding or send an announcement?" Ellen asked.

" That is a long story," Marty said.

"Well, tell us how it came about, Marty," Don said.

"I was teaching English and Art in a high school in Colorado Springs and I heard of this opening in Boston at Lincoln High School for an English teacher and an Art teacher. I had never been East and wanted to move on. My wife had died after a long illness, and I just wanted to be in new surroundings. It seemed like a perfect opportunity. When I was hired, the principal told me about the apartment that Lois owns. It sounded very convenient, so I went over to see about it and SHE answered the door." He leaned over and gave her a peck on the cheek.

"There he was standing on the porch, surrounded by luggage that he had toted on the bus, and it was raining. He looked so bedraggled and tired I asked him in, when I found out who had sent him, of course. I made him some hot tea and I had some of those lemon squares you taught me to make, Lois."

"I think it was the cookies that did it, Lois." He smiled at her. "I knew I was home and I didn't ever want to leave, and I haven't."

"Oh, yes you did, our honeymoon, remember?"

"Yes, but that came three years later." He looked around at the others. "I am not a fast worker." He hunched his shoulders and grinned.

"Continue on now, what did you do in those three years?" asked Tom.

"We became acquainted."

"We went to the movies, we watched TV together, we went to school functions and faculty meetings. He even went to the girls' games and waited for me afterwards. When we won, he took the girls for ice cream with me," Nora enthused.

"She came to all our plays and art exhibits."

"When a new exhibit came to town, we were the first to see it."

"Then came the prom and we were put in charge of arranging it."

"I didn't have a clue about putting on a prom, I just did what she told me to do, and it turned out to be the best ever."

"Remember, Lois, when I sent you that SOS. I knew you would come up with some good ideas, and you did. The jungle theme had never been done. I wasn't going to do another '50s theme. That has been done to death, with the poodle skirts and all."

"I had the art class research and they came up with some fabulous decorations."

"And I remembered the real thing!" She smiled at Maeuma.

Bud imparted the idea of a party with decorations that Nora had remembered from his home. Maeuma seemed pleased.

"I remember Bud writing me an e-mail about that," Ginger exclaimed.

"Yes, Lois sent me some things to use as decorations. I had them stored in that closet off the gym. Remember, Lois?"

"Yes I remember all the volleyball stuff was in there."

"I will never forget that wonderful closet!" Marty said grinning at Nora.

"Nor will I. There is where he finally got up the nerve to kiss me!"

"I will never forget that wonderful kiss, it shook me to my toes!"

"Me too!"

"Then what?" Dennis asked.

"Yes, then what?" Letty chimed in.

"Well, we soon were engaged and started to plan the best honeymoon ever!"

There was a chorus of, "Where?"

"We decided to go on a trip around the world!" Nora announced triumphantly.

"Wow!" Father John said and chattered away with Maeuma, explaining it to him as best he could. He needed some help from Gordon and Nat. Ryti had excused herself to call the babysitter at the hotel to check on Champ. She had given up and now called him Champ too.

"We planned it meticulously. It was so much fun doing it together," Nora said.

"She thought of places I never would have thought of, and some of them were the most interesting, like Ankor Wat. That was really something."

"We hit every art museum in the WORLD too!"

"Yes, and I really appreciate your patience, darling."

"I got used to doing that when I traveled with Lois, and I enjoyed it too, really."

"The only trouble was one of Nora's bags was lost."

"I had my carry-on with my makeup and extra shoes and a change of clothes and my night things. All my nice things and other shorts and shirts, slacks, skirts and a few warm things were lost. I ended up wearing some of Marty's shirts and sweaters."

"Yes, then we did some serious shopping in London and I got some nice things."

"I had intended sending out announcements as we went along, but the address book and the cards were in the lost luggage. Some addresses I knew by heart, but the rest I had to miss. When we got home, it just didn't seem the thing to do. And then, I had to start a whole new address book."

"Outside of that it was perfect," Marty said. "I acquired a lot of new things for my classes too."

"And I acquired some new things for the house. We have been redecorating it."

"That sounds like you two have been enjoying life," said Ellen.

"Yes, we have." Nora smiled at Marty and squeezed his hand.

"What have you been doing the last four years, Ellen?"

"Ha! Just wait till you hear!" Don laughed.

"Tell us," Carla implored.

"Well, Don finally let me help out at the store," Ellen said modestly.

"She does more than help out. She completely reorganized the housewares department. We have 'show and tell' every day by some vender or another, and she has a cooking school making the whole place smell delicious every day. Then she brings the leftovers home and she has dinner all ready when I arrive. The housewares department has increased sales more than any other department."

"I thought you didn't want her to go to work?" Gordon said.

"I didn't, more the fool, me. Now she wants to take over the fabric department and have knitting and sewing classes. I just might let her do it."

"I am going to do it." She tossed her head, "I know just the women to hire as teachers. They are empty nesters looking for something to do. The students will buy their patterns and fabric from the store. When their friends hear about it, they will want to come too. I will aim for high school age kids, though anyone will be able to come. It ought to boost the sales in that department too. When I get that running smoothly, I'd like to tackle the sports department. I have a few ideas about it too."

"Wait up, I might take on that department myself." Don seemed to be catching her mood. He was much more "Hands

On" at the store now. They have a lot to talk about now that she knew the same people he knew.

"That's okay with me, but if you get stuck for ideas, I've got a million of them." She laughed.

"Bud, how have you and Ginger managed these four years?" Letty asked.

"Well, it wasn't easy. We got together here in Florida for holidays, Christmas and Spring Break. Then we would visit Dad and Lois in the summer. Once Ginger and Carla and I went to Manaus. Dennis couldn't get away. Carla and Lois would go around together. Ginger and I would study the Indian languages and I would give her some flying time and even gave her the basics in the helicopter. She soloed at the end of her second year in school."

Ginger heard him talking and came over near them

"I loved my lessons. My teacher was a vet from Vietnam, and he really knew his stuff. He wouldn't stand for anything that wasn't just right though. He kept me taking off and landing so much until I would do it just right. I got quite good at it."

"She is a great pilot. I would fly with her anywhere! She has even mastered the helicopter now, and has her license."

"Thank you, darling. I have worked very hard. Now that I can speak two Indian languages and can fly the helicopter, I will be able to help Bud and Gordon." In an aside she said, "He told me to call him that. I will be a good help when we go on the jungle trips."

"There were times though when e-mail just didn't cut it and we would get very lonesome," Bud remembered.

"Were you able to go to the school dances and other events?" Ellen inquired.

"Yes, I had a special friend. Er, he is a homosexual. A chaste one, if you can believe it. He majored in design and cinematography. He is very serious about it and worked hard. We met in the library and studied together a lot. He would walk me back to my dorm at night, so I never had to be afraid. We went to the dances together and had fun without the tension we would have had if he wasn't the way he is. He is a dear friend. I asked him to come for the wedding, but he has an appointment in Hollywood this week at a studio in their decorating department. I hope it goes well with him. That he will get his foot in the door. He is very talented."

"Yes," Bud said, "we will probably meet someday, I have a lot to thank him for. School got very tedious at times, but it was worth it, but it was a long four years."

"What have you and Tom been up to Letty?" Ginger asked.

"We have been enjoying our retirement. We do all those things we didn't have time for. We go to the movies, museums and things like that. We help out at 'Hope House.' That is a place run by eleven churches in the area, all denominations. There is a food pantry, used clothes and furniture, and the people in charge try to find jobs for the unemployed, dress them up for job interviews, pay some utility bills till they get on their feet. It is very satisfying to help out. Our different churches have fund raisers and a food donation week every so often, at different times to keep the food pantry going."

"We have a new grandchild too, and that keeps us running. We babysit once in awhile so the kids can go on a trip together. They fly in with them from California, drop the children off in St. Louis and fly off somewhere. Then we have a little visit when they return to pick them up. That is really fun," Tom said. "We haven't taken care of all three of them yet, only the two."

"Yes, Maureen and Jerry have three children now. The oldest is Emily, our cute curly head, who is seven, then there is Terry who is five. Oh, he would want me to say five and a half, and now a beautiful five months old, bald headed girl named Siobhan."

"What? I don't think I have ever heard that name," Dennis chimed in.

"It is Irish for Joan, and Jerry's mother's name is Joan. It is spelled funny too, you know, like Sean is spelled different than it sounds. Well, it is spelled S I O B H A N and pronounced Sha-vaun. Maureen got it from an Irish actress she once saw, and never forgot her beautiful name."

"She is going to have one heck of a time when she gets to school!" Dennis answered.

"Oh well, we will educate some people," Letty laughed.

"Are you doing anything in the business line, Tom?" Don asked. "I remember you were doing something that kept you from going on the trip."

"Occasionally, when the guy I sold my business to gets in a bind I help him out, but that doesn't happen very often. I am busy just following Letty around. She finds lots of things for us to do. She doesn't let any grass grow beneath our feet."

"Oh, and our son is engaged to a darling girl from Texas."

"How about you, Carla?" Ellen asked. "We know about Dennis and his herbal medicine studies and his successes with that. He must be kept so busy, how do you fill your time?"

"I have been alone a lot, with Ginger away at school and Dennis so busy. I was quite sorry for myself for a while there."

"Yes, one day I came home early for a change and found her weeping. I never wanted that to happen, but I would get so tied up at work, and it was so interesting that I had a hard time tearing myself away."

" What happened?" Marty asked

"I hired a young assistant to do some of the grunt work and took myself home at a decent hour."

"Yes and I have started writing a novel based on our jungle adventure and that has kept me very busy during the day. I still have my card parties and charity meetings. Dennis and I now have 'date night.' Every Thursday we have a date. His associate is on call every Thursday and we go out to dinner and a show, or a concert, or just stay home alone, whatever we want. It gives me something to look forward to and gives Dennis a break from his work. I manage to keep busy now. I realize that Dennis has an important job, I was just being silly."

"No, you weren't, darling. I needed that wake up call, and I'm glad I got it. Too many in my profession neglect their wives and it brings on trouble."

"Tell us what you have been doing." Don wanted to know.

"We have been trying to replicate the elements we produced from the plants we brought back and the ones we get from Maeuma and his tribe. We have had some success. Now we have to wait until we get permission to start producing a safe usable drug.

"I recently came in contact with the Amazon Conservation Team. It is headed by a Harvard man, Dr. Mark Plotkin. He has spent more than twenty years in the jungles of Suriname looking for plants that heal. We didn't go to that part of the jungle. He is trying to glean the knowledge that the shamans of the different tribes have handed down through the centuries. He is encouraging the young men of the tribes to keep the knowledge alive. When one of these shaman witch doctors dies, that mass of knowledge is gone forever.

"He is in a movie about them. The Miranda Productions Inc. made one called, 'The Shaman's Apprentice.' It tells of the fight to keep the knowledge of the Shamans alive. They are the most endangered species in all the Amazon. It is the story of Doctor Plotkin's quest to preserve the ancient wisdom of our species. It interweaves their knowledge with western science and the grim realities of extinction. I hope that we can find the intelligence and cooperation that is essential for saving one of the most glorious places on Earth."

The talk ended when the waiters in island garb brought trays of a flaming dessert to the table, and it was all Father John and Nat could do to keep a startled Maeuma in his seat.

The next day, the day of the wedding, was as beautiful as they get in Florida. Sunshine, a light breeze, lovely!

That was the theme of the whole day, lovely.

Everything went off just as planned. Not one glitch. No one was late. Everyone looked their best in their party clothes, even Maeuma. Ginger was gorgeous, Bud was handsome. The Mass was impressive. When the soprano sang "Ave Maria" eyes got misty. When Bud and Ginger kissed on the altar, it was just right, neither too short nor embarrassingly long. Then the pastor of Ascension Church, Father Gallagher, introduced them as Mr. and Mrs. Gordon Hunter, Jr. The organ swelled and they walked down the aisle. It was a happy joyous day. The wedding breakfast was delicious, the cake, outstanding. The toasts were amusing. The one Dennis gave was touching and there were tears being blinked away by Carla and Ginger.

There was a lot of catching up to do. There was dancing too. Letty took Maeuma in hand and showed him how to slow dance. That was a sight to behold! They did all the wedding events, the garter thing, and Ginger's fifteen-year-old cousin caught the bouquet.

Bud and Ginger went to one of the rooms in the hotel to change clothes. They returned to have a last dance. Bud danced with Carla and Ginger danced with Dennis. Then it was time for Nat to drive Bud and Ginger to the airport. They were going to on an art connoisseur's tour of Italy. There was a flurry of goodbyes and good wishes and they were gone.

"Let's go swimming!" Nora said. "Let's get out of these fancy duds and go out on the beach."

That is just what they did. Maeuma created quite a stir on the beach with his fancy tattoos. Gordon and Father John convinced him that he should wear his shorts in the water. He thought they were crazy.

Ryti and little Champ had great fun playing in the water and with the sand toys. No one has more fun than a toddler does at the beach.

Nora and Marty, and Carla and Dennis rented Wave Runners and were zipping around the area. But not before Dennis made the rounds with sunblock. He was still watching out for them. Letty decided she would like to parasail. She had always wanted to, but never did. So she and Tom went off to see about it.

Gordon, Lois, Father John and Maeuma were cavorting in the surf. Nat returned and joined the group in the beach fun. They all waved at Letty as she floated by. Tom declined the experience.

Don and Ellen were ecstatic. The water was warm, and the huge white sand beach was soft as powdered sugar. They were used to tiny Hampton Beach in New Hampshire, full of big rocks and ice cold, even in summer. They had a hard time getting Don and Ellen out of the water. Carla had tickets for the Barbara Mann Theater. "Chicago" was playing. They were to go to Snug Harbor for dinner before the show. They had to hurry and get ready. The girls had to dry their hair and primp a bit. The beach is so hard on a girl's looks.

Letty had a great time on the parasail and was raving about her ride on the way back to their room.

Nat and Ryti didn't go to the show, they were tired and Champ was a little sunburned and fussy. They didn't want to leave him with a sitter again.

The show was very good. Maeuma couldn't believe his eyes and ears. What a lot of tales he had to tell when he returned! People in the theater couldn't believe their eyes either when they saw Maeuma.

The next day Letty bought a bunch of post cards for Maeuma to take home to help him tell his friends about the wonders of the U.S.A. They went swimming again and stayed on the beach to watch the sun go down. They went to dinner at the "Reef" and had all the frog legs they could eat.

Maeuma was cautious because he used frog sweat to use as poison on his blow darts, not as dinner. They made it an early night because they had to pack and leave early in the morning to catch the various planes to their different destinations.

The next morning there was a hurried continental breakfast, promises to write and heartfelt goodbyes. Nat got the limo again and they headed for the airport. The traffic on the San Carlos Bridge was light at that hour, a large boat gave a loud blast as it went under the Bridge in Matansas Pass heading for Key West.

There were more goodbyes at the airport and they were on their way to St. Louis, Boston, Manchester, Manaus, and the native village, and at last the base camp where Maeuma shed his clothes and stepped into a small boat to go home. He had many souvenirs, t-shirts with FLORIDA on them, the suit and shoes he returned to Father John. He kept the sandals Don bought for him and a pair for Teptykti. He had a box of good things to eat, mostly candy. The chocolates were melting, but still good. He was bringing some pretzels and potato chips, trinkets made of shells for his people. He brought Teptykti a bikini swimming suit he thought she could wear to feasts, certainly not for swimming. He was humming "He Had it Coming" as he paddled home. Life was good.

After seeing Maeuma off, Father John and Nat left the base camp and headed for his village in the helicopter. The natives were wild with joy when they heard the whup, whup of the rotors. They knew he would have presents for them. They landed on the new helicopter pad to a great welcome.

The clerics reported to him the next morning. Everything had gone well while Father was gone, but they missed the ceremony of the Mass. These clerics had worked with Father John for five years. They had a good hold on the precepts of the church.

He had written to the Vatican a year ago and reported that he thought they were good candidates for the priesthood. In the mail that came while he was away there was a letter from Italy. It was an answer to his query. It outlined all the things that had to be done for this to happen. He had explained that he needed someone to carry on after his retirement.

Orem asked to see him, privately. Father John was intrigued and made some time for him right away.

"Father, I must confess something that happened before my trouble."

"Okay, give me a minute and I'll get in the place for confession."

Later in the confessional he told Father John all about his part in GWH's accident. He told him how sorry he was and that he had been trying to make up for it by trying to do good.

"I still feel bad about what I did to GWH. He has only done good things for me and I keep thinking about how bad I have been. I can't get it off my mind."

"There is only one thing you can do then."

"What is that?"

"You must ask him to forgive you."

"Oh, I can't do that, I can't. He will hate me."

"You have to take that chance. It is the only way. I will go with you to base camp the next time he goes there and you can tell him then."

⸻ ⬥ ⸻

The next day he told the clerics what the letter from the Vatican said. They were thrilled, but subdued. It was a serious thing and they didn't know if they were worthy. They had some training to do to finish all that was required. They worked hard and by Christmas they were ready.

Father invited all the Hunters and Maeuma and Teptykti and Nat, Ryti and Champ to come for the Christmas Mass and the Ordination.

The surprise was Maeuma and Teptykti' receiving the Sacraments of Baptism and Matrimony, and the Holy Euchrist.

Father John had been meeting them at the base camp and giving them instructions. Maeuma was struck by the ceremony at the Ascension Church and asked Father John about the Faith. They had serious discussions about the Sacred Knife, the breath-stealing Devil and many other things. Father gave Maeuma and the Elders a course on asthma, its symptoms and treatment. The Great Knife had nothing to do with it.

The visit to America showed him another way to look at things. Father John explaining that Asthma didn't have a thing to do with sacrificing anything with the knife, was hard to believe, but the treatment and its result was proof. They had long conversations and many of his questions were explained, more than once. He brought Teptykti with him many times when he was delivering the plants and picking up the medicine. It seemed very plain to her that the Holy Spirit was much better than the mean spirit of that old knife anyway.

It was decided the eldest cleric, now a priest, should return to the village with Maeuma and Teptykti and teach the rest of the tribe the principals of Christianity. They could keep the Great Knife as a relic of their history. They could keep the skull with the finger bones in it as a historical relic of their past, but without any power. The shrunken heads were to be given a burial and the process was never to be done again.

The new priest took the name of Father Peter, the Rock on which the church was built. The one that stayed with Father John was Father Paul. Their job now was to train two more clerics.

Now was the time to talk to Orem about telling GWH about what he did. He finally talked him into seeing GWH. He was due to be at base camp soon, so they met him there when they brought Father Peter to meet Maeuma and to go with him to his village.

When he finally met GWH, he was very anxious. Father had only told GWH that Orem had something to talk to him about.

"What's up, Orem? Father John told me you wanted to see me."

"I must tell you something. I don't want to, I am too ashamed. I have been so sorry for so long. I must ask your forgiveness now, or I will have no peace."

"What, did you steal something from me?"

"No, if only it were that, I could give it back."

"Well, what is it then? Get it over with and tell me what you want to tell me!"

"I am the one that put the snake in your car. I wish so much that I had said no to Fenton, but I agreed and I did it. Please forgive me, I am so sorry."

The shock of his confession stunned GWH to silence. Extreme anger was his first reaction. Orem looked so sorry and dejected. Father had told him how much he had changed.

If you can't forgive, how can you ever say the Our Father? Forgive as you want to be forgiven, GWH remembered his mother teaching him, long ago. *If Orem hadn't done what he did I would have gone on the trip with Ed. My head most probably would be there with Fenton's, or instead of Fenton's. I wouldn't have had that time with Lois. We might not have married. All in all I am better off, outside of some pain. I am better for it, even Orem is better for it.* He couldn't stay mad.

"Orem, I will forgive you. We will go on as before and stay friends."

Orem couldn't believe his ears. He took GWH's hand and kept shaking it. "I will be the best friend you will ever have, forever. Thank you, thank you." He went back to the village with Father John a happy man.

━━━ •••●••• ━━━

Maeuma took Father Peter to his village. He could understand and speak to the villagers. That helped him spread God's word. There was opposition though. Some still feared the spirit of the Great Knife. It would take a while to convince some of the Elders. Most of the young people followed Maeuma and Teptykti. Kamanar'e was the first to be baptized by the new priest.

They had a great feast when they had the ceremony of the burial of the heads. Most of the elders didn't want to miss that so they reported to Father Peter for instructions. He didn't go after any of them, he let them come to him. Panteri was the last one to ask for Instructions.

━━━ •••●••• ━━━

There was another mailing about eighteen months later:

Mr. and Mrs. Gordon William Hunter Jr.

Announce the birth of their Twins

Gordon William Hunter the Third, weight 5 pounds 4 oz.

January 15, 2005 —:10 a.m.

and

Denice Carla Hunter, weight 4 pounds 9 oz.

January 15, 2005 —:20 a.m.

Fort Myers Beach, Florida

Printed in the United States
47983LVS00003B/153